I0557943

DARK CARNIVAL

DARK CARNIVAL

KEITH FERRARIO

GABRIEL'S HORN PRESS

Copyright © 2023 by Keith Ferrario

All rights reserved.

No part of this book may be reproduced in any form or by any electronic or mechanical means, including information storage and retrieval systems, without written permission from the author, except for the use of brief quotations in a book review.

This book is a work of fiction. The names, characters, places, and incidents are products of the writer's imagination or have been used fictitiously and are not to be construed as real. Any resemblance to persons, living or dead, actual events, locale or organizations is entirely coincidental.

Second Print Edition: Gabriel's Horn Press, LLC.
Minneapolis, Minnesota
www.gabrielshornpress.com

ISBN: 979-8-88846-100-6

ACKNOWLEDGMENTS

I would like to thank the following people for their time and support: Susan Clark, Tracy Cummings, Sherri Lunsford, Deb and John Sheets, Tammy Wolfe. It is always difficult to know if a story can stand on its own and through the efforts of these people I believe this one can. Thanks all for your comments and honest criticism. Also, thanks to Marj Wyatt, who allowed me more time to write.

PROLOGUE

T he black Porsche roared down the secluded interstate. The beams from the headlights were the only other thing visible on that strip of road. Gregory DeMont, behind the wheel, glanced over at a bored Laura Royal, the wife of his former employer, his current lover, and partner in murder.

It had been six months, which seemed so long ago, but still the memories playing back in his mind had Gregory reliving the events each day. He remembered the orange glow of dusk and the long, soft shadows stretching out across the brick patio at the small open-air cafe. He and Laura were surrounded only by empty tables. It was the perfect setting for a couple in love.

Laura sipped her tea. "You have to kill him," she said, pausing for the waiter to pass on his way to a far table to collect his tips. "It's the only way." She smiled at Gregory. "The only way we can be together."

She tossed back her long blonde hair and pulled a broken strand from the shoulder of her tight black sweater. Around her neck hung a string of perfect pearls, which touched down to the edge of her breasts.

Gregory played with the small delicate handle of the porcelain teacup, rubbing the glazed material between his thumb and forefinger. He hated tea. Laura had ordered the foul tasting brew.

Reaching over, Laura brushed the outside of his thumb with her fingertips. He released the cup handle and reached out for her. She cradled Gregory's hand between hers and squeezed gently. His eyes met hers, but then fell back to the tabletop.

"You want that too," Laura whispered. "I know you do."

Gregory's free hand shook as he reached into his jacket pocket for his cigarettes.

"Do you have to smoke now?" Laura asked gently.

He dropped the pack to the table. "It's not as easy as you make it seem. I've been with him for years. Years before you." He met her gaze. "I curse the day he first saw you—the day *I* first saw you."

She laughed, but her expression quickly grew cold. "You chauffeur that old man, that's all. You're just an employee to him. Nothing more." A smile returned to her lips. "But to me you're so much more. You…we both deserve so much more. We can have it all. A life together. A perfect life together. With all his money we can do anything—have anything—go anywhere. The perfect life." She squeezed his hand again. "Do it—kill him—for me—for us. After, we can be together—forever."

He slowly nodded. "I do want you all to myself."

Laura's plan was a simple one. Owen, her wheelchair bound, sixty-two year old husband, could not keep away from the bottle and by late afternoon, as usual, was drunk asleep in his chair. After making sure he was seen driving Laura away from the house, Gregory snuck back, and slipped in through the back entrance. Once inside, it became a simple matter of going to Owen's room, finding him passed out, wheeling him to the edge of the staircase, and…and…Gregory couldn't finish the thought.

As Laura had assured him, the plan worked perfectly. The police reasoned Owen had drank too much and wheeled himself too close to the staircase. The whiskey bottle the old man had concealed between his right leg and the side of his wheelchair served to enforce the hasty conclusion. The bottle dropped out as the chair rolled end over end, shattering and spreading glass fragments all along the stairs. Gregory ended up digging a small piece out of the bottom of his shoe, afraid the police would suspect him. But with Laura playing the perfect grieving widow and vouching for his whereabouts, the precaution wasn't necessary.

The black Porsche jolted and slowed, bringing Gregory's thoughts back to the present. "Now what?" he said. He managed to pull the expensive car to the side of the secluded road before the engine died completely.

"Well, get out and see what's wrong," Laura ordered.

Gregory grumbled something, then complied. As he set the parking brake, he repeated his grumbling. He checked under the hood, and within seconds returned with his verdict. "It stopped," he said coldly.

"Do something," she snapped. "Fix it."

"It just stopped," he yelled back. "God only knows what's wrong. I'm not a mechanic!"

"Don't bitch at me. Remember who pays the bills?"

"Shut your yap. I earned it, remember!"

Laura threw her purse strap over her shoulder. "This isn't the time. We have to go for help."

"Where?"

"If you bothered to turn around, you'd see lights."

"Lights? What lights?" Gregory did turn and Laura was right. Off in the distance he saw lights. "They weren't there before."

Laura got out of the Porsche, slamming the door behind her. "Let's start walking."

Neither Gregory nor Laura noticed the large black shadow soaring high above their heads.

During the twenty-minute hike the two said nothing, and as they drew closer, the sounds of a carnival filled the silence. The carnival sat on a site that was normally a baseball field. The bleachers cornered several of the larger sideshow tents. The midway had various gaming booths and at the other end were towering amusement rides.

At the entrance was a bright red ticket booth. The light over the window gleamed off the glass. Gregory approached the booth—Laura stayed a step behind. Inside sat a thin man with a scruffy beard and mustache. He wore a fine suit, which included a top hat and black bowtie.

Gregory bent down to the small half-circle opening at the bottom of the window. "Is there a phone around here I can use?"

The thin man behind the glass gave Gregory a blank stare.

"Excuse me. Is there a phone?"

The man raised his hand and pointed to the far tent. "Around back by the seats." He didn't smile or frown. Gregory didn't see any hint of emotion on the man's face.

"Thanks," Gregory said, and walked back to Laura. "Wait here."

"Gregory—"

"You'll be fine." He started off, then stopped and turned back to her. "Don't get too close to him," he said, tilting his head toward the strange man in the booth. "He might bite." Gregory chuckled.

Laura let out a huff.

Gregory continued on to find the telephone, finally disappearing around the corner of a small brown tent.

Not a half-minute went by when Laura heard, "Many fine shows."

She turned to the booth. "Excuse me?"

"We have many fine shows," the man said, tipping his top hat back slightly.

"Is that a fact?"

"Only a dollar, worth every penny too."

Laura smiled at the scruffy man, then glanced over her shoulder toward the small tent.

"And we have games of all sorts."

"I can see that." Laura silently prayed for Gregory to hurry.

"And rides. How the children love the rides."

"We can't stay," Laura said. "We're a little rushed for time."

"There's always time," the man said, sliding something through the window opening. "Here, take these. No charge."

Laura stepped closer, seeing two red tickets with big black letters, which read: "Admit one." She reached out, but then stopped herself.

"Go ahead," he said. "They're good for any show—any show at all. I'm sure you'll choose a fine one. It is always your choice."

Laura finally took the red tickets. "We won't be here that long, but maybe I—" A hand touched her shoulder. She gasped.

"Why so jumpy?" Gregory asked.

"You just caught me off guard, that's all. Did you get hold of anyone?"

"Finally. I found an all-night towing service. It's dark behind that tent. Good thing I had a lighter. The one time when smoking paid off. But I almost started the phone book on fire a couple of times."

"When will they get here?" Laura said impatiently.

"Said about an hour. He had another call just before mine."

"An hour?"

"Relax, I was lucky to find him. He says he'll tow the car to a garage right next to a motel. Things will be fine." Gregory saw the tickets in Laura's hand. "You bought tickets?"

"They were free. That guy in the booth gave them to me."

Gregory looked back at the man. His blank stare had been replaced with a slim-lipped grin. "We might as well use them," Gregory told her. "No point waiting by the car doing nothing for an hour."

"Are you sure?" she whispered.

"We'll bum around for about forty minutes, then start back to the car. We'll be back in plenty of time."

"Guess anything's better than just standing here."

The couple entered through the main gate.

"I'm hungry," Gregory said. "Let's grab a couple of hot dogs."

Laura nodded.

"It's funny. The guy on the phone told me he didn't know there was a carnival out here. I had to tell him I was calling from the ball field. He must not get out this way too often."

In the red ticket booth the man with the top hat and black bowtie smiled and flicked off the overhead light.

～ ᐧ ⌒

After twenty minutes of games and rides, Laura remembered the tickets she had shoved in her pocket before their feast of hot dogs and soda.

"That strange man said they're good for any show."

"Pick one," Gregory said. "I'm game for anything you are."

Laura pointed to a tent marked with a sign reading "Hall of Destiny."

"I thought you'd pick the freak show or the mentalist or even the fortune-teller. But the Hall of Destiny? Do you even know what it is?"

"We'll see." Laura pulled at his arm. "Come on. You said you were game for anything."

Gregory agreed and followed her.

Outside the tent stood a woman wearing a long black robe. The fabric had fine gold embroidering along its edges. Her long black hair matched the robe exactly and from far away it appeared as if the woman were wearing a hood.

"The man in the booth by the entrance told us we could use these tickets for any show," Laura said to the woman.

"If you choose to. They are very special tickets."

Gregory had trouble taking his eyes off the woman. The fabric clung to her body, revealing all her curves. Her face was soft, a little pale, but very beautiful.

Laura handed the woman her ticket and waited for Gregory to hand over his. She elbowed him in the ribs when the action wasn't forthcoming.

"Sorry," Gregory said, "I was just thinking about the Porsche. I hope it's okay." He handed the raven-haired woman his ticket.

"Please enter," she told the couple. "I promise you'll find it interesting."

After they entered the tent, the curtain closed behind them. At first, there was only darkness.

"I don't like this Gregory," Laura said.

"Just wait. I'm sure it's all part of the show."

Moments later, overhead and running down both sides of the tent walls, small flame lamps brightened.

"See," Gregory assured her, "I told you. Let's keep going. It has to get better."

"I certainly hope so."

After two steps, a loud crunch came from under Gregory's foot.

"What was that?" Laura asked.

Gregory bent down and rubbed the bottom of his shoe. "Shit!" His middle finger stung. After pulling it back and examining his fingertip in the dim light, he saw a droplet of blood coming from a small nick. "I must have stepped on some glass." He groped along the floor.

"Be careful," Laura said. "Don't cut yourself again."

"I won't." He found something and picked it up. "Looks like a piece of a bottle. Damn thing to have laying where people walk. You'd think they would keep this place a little cleaner. Let's get out of here. No telling what else we'll step in." He gently sucked his fingertip.

"All right," Laura said. She turned and took a step, but didn't get very far as her face smacked into a hard wall.

Gregory snickered, but made sure Laura didn't see him. "The door's right...here." He pressed his hands on the panel. His palms moved across the hard surface five feet on both sides where he thought they had entered.

"Aren't we in a tent?" Laura said, watching him. "We're supposed to be in a tent."

"We are," Gregory said.

"Explain the walls then."

"It's some sort of trick. It has to be." He continued working his way down, banging his fist against the structure, but found nothing but a solid barrier. "I know it's a trick."

"Did you hear that?" Laura said.

"What?" Gregory stopped his pounding.

"Listen."

The couple didn't move or utter a sound.

"I don't—" Gregory started to say, then he heard it—a squeaking, which seemed to grow more distinct each second. He looked for the source of the high pitched whine, but it seemed to come from all directions. Then at the far end of the room he noticed an open passageway.

"Over there," he told Laura. "That opening."

"Opening? Where?" She grabbed Gregory's arm. "Something really weird is going on here. That wasn't there before."

"Sure it was. It had to be."

"Don't you think I would've noticed something as obvious as a doorway? It's not that dark in here, and I'm not blind."

"It's probably just a sliding panel or something. All part of the scare."

The squeaking became louder. It came down the corridor of darkness. The sound had a rhythm to it. Start, stop, start, stop, squeak—squeak—squeak. Each pause was followed by a more intense pitch of grinding metal. Then, finally, in the passageway, with the dim light reflecting off the chrome plating, an empty wheelchair stopped over the threshold.

"This is some kind of sick joke," Laura said.

The squeaking started again as the wheelchair crept forward. It rolled toward the couple and began to pick up speed. It rolled faster and faster, straight toward them. Laura screamed. The chair flipped on its side and skidded across the floor. Laura and Gregory barely managed to leap out of the way of the gleaming steel, which finally came to a halt three feet past where the man and woman had been standing.

"Let's get out of here," Gregory said. He grabbed Laura by the hand and led her to the passageway. Unlike the room, there were no lights, just a tunnel of black. "This must lead out." He squinted, trying to pierce the darkness.

"I'm not going down there."

"Doesn't seem we have another option." Gregory stepped through the entrance. He felt Laura's resistance. "It will be okay," he said, "I won't let go of you."

Gregory kept one hand on the smooth wall as he guided Laura. The two walked down the unlit corridor until they could go no further.

"Why'd you stop?" Laura asked. "Keep going."

"There's a door here."

"Open it! Let's get out."

"Shhh, listen."

"Do you have to smoke now?" a woman's voice said from the other side of the door.

"It must be the way out," Gregory said.

"Hurry, I can't stand being here another moment. I'm going to complain to the owners when we get out of this damn tent...building... whatever it is."

"Think it will do any good? It's just a two-bit traveling carnival. They get your money and that's all they care about."

"After the stink I'm going to make, we'll see about that. Just get that damn door open."

Gregory fumbled around for the handle. He found it and turned. The door creaked open. A heavy odor of tea filled the small passage.

"What in the hell is this?" Gregory said.

On the other side of the door, a man and woman sat at a small table. And nothing more. The surroundings were a seemingly endless white void. No walls, no ceiling, just white.

The man at the table spoke across to a woman wearing a tight black sweater and a string of pearls: "It's not as easy as you make it seem. I've been with him for years. Years before you."

"That's us," Laura said.

"It can't be."

Gregory and Laura entered and slowly approached their doubles. The seated couple paid no attention to them and continued talking across the table: "—have anything—go anywhere," Laura's double said. "The perfect life. Do it—kill him—for me—for us."

"Make them stop!" Laura cried out. "I can't listen to this."

"What can I do?"

"I don't care! Just stop them."

Laura's double continued speaking: "After, we can be together —forever."

On that final word, a bright glow silently exploded from the table, bathing Laura and Gregory in white light. Their eyes were forced away from the couple and they were thrown backward.

True to his word, Gregory did not release her hand. But then there was pain.

"My hand!" Laura yelled. "It feels on fire. Let go."

"I can't! I can't!"

Laura and Gregory screamed in painful harmony as the small muscles of their interlocked hands began to spasm. The outer flesh began to blister and tear. As the two watched in horror, their fingers melted and fused together like melting wax. Their hands lost all unique and separate form. The transformation progressed swiftly up their forearms, consuming their elbows, fusing their shoulders, forcing a merger of flesh, bone, and blood.

Their screams echoed in the white void.

"Lucas," the woman in the black robe said, "pass the word. We shall be leaving at first light."

"As you command, Lilith."

With her servant departing, Lilith stepped into the tent that housed the freak show and made her way up onto the small stage. "Ladies and gentlemen," she said, "welcome to my carnival. The first curiosity of nature presented this fine evening is Zamrah, half-man, half-woman."

The curtains parted. The group of spectators whispered as the hermaphrodite stepped into the spotlight. The left side of the creature was male with brown hair. His pectoral muscle had been bared to display that side's masculinity. The right side was unmistakably female with long blonde hair and a covered breast.

"Here in a single body we find both elements of male and female existing together. Never parting. Together—forever."

CHAPTER 1

The door of the Greyhound opened and a blast of hot, dry air hit Johnny square in the face. He had grown too accustomed to the air conditioning.

"Have a nice time," the driver said with a company smile.

"Right," Johnny replied, taking the last step. The steel and glass door closed behind him with a loud moan and hiss of air unique only to a bus. As the bus pulled away, kicking up a dust cloud, Johnny slung his canvas bag over his shoulder.

"You've really got yourself into it this time," he said aloud. Reaching into his pocket, Johnny pulled out a crumpled fifty-dollar bill—enough to get food and a clean room for the night. He entered the bus station and walked up to the ticket window.

"Where to?" the woman asked, before looking up from her magazine.

"Nowhere. I just got here."

"Then, may I help you?"

Johnny smiled, but not out of friendliness. Her transition amused him. "I need a motel."

She gave him a quick once-over. "The Spade Motel, about a quarter mile down the road. Can't miss it. Not too expensive. You should be able to afford it."

"Thanks," Johnny said as his smile disappeared. He knew he didn't appear the best, but when you have to steal the clothes you wear, you can't be choosy.

Johnny hiked down the road. The heat was unusual for late September even in Nevada with its dry climate. As the ticket lady promised, he couldn't have missed the motel. It seemed clean and in a way friendly. He entered the lobby and rang the small, shiny bell on the counter.

A girl stepped out of a back room. Its entrance was covered by a long red double curtain, which hung about two feet off the floor. "Yes, sir," she said, laying her paperback book next to the bell. She had short brown hair, a slim face, glowing green eyes that complimented her beaming smile. She couldn't have been more than nineteen, if that.

"I'd like a room," he said.

"You've come to the right place." She pulled a key from the mail slot. "Close to the pool or the diner?"

Her eyes. They look exactly like— Johnny quickly erased the thought. "Doesn't matter," he told the girl.

She put the key on the counter. "You'll be closer to the diner. You look like someone more interested in eating than swimming." She smiled. "That will be twenty-two dollars."

Johnny handed her the crumbled bill from his pocket.

"Out of fifty." The girl began hitting buttons on the cash register. "Please, sign our registration book."

Johnny picked up the black pen and held it for a moment, then scratched something out. Waiting for his change, he read the cover title of the book next to the room key: *Catcher in the Rye*. "Good book," he said, replacing the pen on the counter.

"It might be, if I didn't have to read it for English class." She handed him two tens, one five, and three one dollar bills. "That always spoils a book somehow."

"Always did for me too," Johnny agreed as he stuffed the bills in his front pocket. "It's a little early to be out of school for the day, isn't it?"

"I'm just helping out today over my lunch hour. My Uncle Gary owns this place. He and my Aunt Rachel are expecting their first child. She had an appointment with Doc Brown. So I do what I can." She shrugged. "My name's Amy—Amy Evans." She extended her hand. "Welcome to Arkham. A tiny little town in the middle of a big nothing."

"Hi Amy, I'm Johnny," he said, before realizing he was being too friendly. That could be dangerous. For now, he needed to keep a low profile. He took the room key and walked toward the door. He stopped and turned back. "Is there a carnival in town?" he asked.

She tilted her head slightly. "That's a strange question."

"I've got a thing for small town carnivals, that's all."

"Sorry, no. At least, I haven't heard of any."

Without another word he stepped outside.

"Have a nice stay," Amy said as the lobby door closed. She spun the registration book around to read the signature: "J. Solom." She leaned way over the counter and watched the man find his room. After he disappeared through the door, she picked her paperback up off the counter and fanned herself with it.

Johnny followed the sidewalk to room number three. He went in and dropped his bag on the floor. He moved across the room and flipped the on switch of the air-conditioner embedded in the wall. With a soft hum, cold air began pouring in.

Then Johnny walked over to the sink and turned on the light over the mirror. A face full of dark stubble greeted him. He had to be careful. All the photos of him were with a beard. Though two days' growth wasn't the same, it might be enough for someone to take a second closer look. He gently pulled at his brown hair. Besides dying it or cutting it all off, he didn't have any real options. He supposed it would be all right, since thousands of other guys shared the same shade. His six-foot-three, one-hundred and ninety-five pound frame made him stand out, and like his hair, there were no real options in that department either.

After a close shave, he flicked on the television set, hoping to catch the local news. Johnny backed up as the screen came to life.

"Now I wait." He sat on the edge of the bed and watched the glowing picture.

～へ＼ꞏ⁄↗～

Sheriff Jim McNee maneuvered his squad car down Oakdale Street. He was responding to a trespassing at JoLean Holt's. Margie Waite, his dispatcher, had radioed to his deputy, Nate White Moon, to respond to the call. But Jim intercepted the transmission, saying he was only a block away and he would handle it. One minute later, he pulled the cruiser up to the curb and quickly scanned the area for any unusual cars or trucks. One advantage of being a sheriff in a town the size of Arkham was he knew what cars belong where and to whom.

His eyes moved up and down the street. Everything seemed in order, but he had that feeling something was up. He used to get the same kind of tingling when he was a MP, stationed at Fort Dix, just before getting a call to break up another fight between two rival barracks.

Instead of pulling into the driveway, he parked the squad car on the street, and then he briskly made his way up the small cement path to JoLean's front door. Before he could ring the bell, the door opened.

"Hi, Jim, that was certainly quick," JoLean said, wearing only a bath robe with her wet dark hair tapered down to her shoulders. "I'm glad it's you responding. I look awful."

Not possible, Jim thought. "Special service for my favorite sister-in-law," he told her, removing his cap. "Margie said you heard someone banging around in your garage." He wondered, was this someone trying to get to him by terrorizing JoLean. The town did have its share of human garbage, but Jim never figured any were low enough or dumb enough to make it personal by bothering one of his family. Well, there was one, he could think of offhand.

"That's right," she responded. "I heard someone banging around out there. At first, I thought maybe Minky got out. You know how sneaky that cat can be. But when I came downstairs, she was eating from her dish." The woman glanced through the kitchen window. "I can't imagine how anyone could get back there, it's all fenced in. You have to go through the house." She turned back to Jim. "I suppose whoever it is could've climbed over. But with the woods and brush and stickers it doesn't seem a person would be that stupid to get himself all scratched up."

"There are a lot of stupid people out there, JoLean," he said. "You did the right thing calling the office. I'm glad you didn't try to confront them yourself."

"Dressed like this? Not likely."

Jim smiled. "I have to admit when your name came across the radio I figured for sure you'd be pullin' out that bat you keep in the closet."

"Well, if you're feeling old today, I can go get it."

Being ten years younger than Jim, JoLean was always kidding him about his age. Still, at thirty-nine, Jim McNee was the youngest sheriff in the history of Arkham, Nevada, but this job had a way of aging a man. He already had several strands of gray peppering his brown hair and each morning when he looked in the mirror he seemed to find another new line around his eyes. Jim received his appointment to Sheriff at the age of thirty when, his boss and mentor, Sheriff Lloyd Wary had been shot on duty out on Interstate 80. The man died in Jim's arms. After finishing out Lloyd's term, Jim considered not running for Sheriff—he wasn't a politician—but others, including JoLean, convinced him he was the best man for the job and that Arkham needed him. Jim McNee won both subsequent elections with over seventy percent of the vote.

Jim followed JoLean to the backdoor, but kept one eye on the garage in case the intruder tried to make a break for it. Outside, he could see the garage side door still ajar. He eased it open just enough to get a complete view inside. He smiled and waved to JoLean watching from the safety of the house. Jim entered the garage. After a few more bangs, out ran a large raccoon, immediately followed by the sheriff waving his arms up and down. The animal disappeared around the corner of the garage with Jim on its tail. After a minute Jim reappeared and returned to the house.

"It doesn't appear he caused any damage," Jim said, "but you might want to check. Probably looking for a place to sleep or something to eat."

"One of God's many creatures," JoLean said.

"You have a loose board on the fence. You can't see it from here, but I pinned it shut with a rock. It should deter the rascal for a time, while I grab a hammer and a few nails to fix it up."

"There you go again, Jim, being overly protective. I can fix it myself. It's nothing to pound in a couple of nails. You have more important things to do with your time."

"It's no trouble."

"Don't force me to use my bat." JoLean gently pulled the man by the arm.

On the way through the living room, Jim picked up a silver-framed photograph from the coffee table. It was an exact copy of the one he kept in his bedroom on the dresser. As he stared at the woman's face, he felt a sharp stab in his chest.

"I miss her too," JoLean said, taking his hand in hers. "I know how hard it's been on you and Allie since Katie's death, but you're strong. You're possibly the strongest man I've ever known."

"I should be getting back to the office," Jim said, feeling grateful and at the same time a little embarrassed.

"Thanks for taking care of my—trespasser."

At the front door, "Bring Allie over for supper," JoLean said, "I'll fix all your favorites and once again spare you and my niece from your cooking."

"You stay safe JoLean."

"And you, Sheriff. See you about six?"

Jim nodded and walked down to the cruiser. Again, his eyes moved up and down the street. It still didn't feel right. That tingling hadn't gone away.

"I hate English class," Nikki Bonn said, brushing her long blonde hair and admiring herself in the washroom's mirror. "It's so boring. Why do we have to read some lame book? *Catcher in the Rye*, what a stupid title. Who would give a damn about some guy named Holden Caulfield? It's a weird story. I don't get it."

"Hate it or not," Amy Evans said, "we have to go. Will you please hurry?" She stood with her arms folded across her chest, watching her best friend fussing and primping in her usual obsessive fashion. "And it's not a weird story. I re-read the first couple chapters. It's not bad."

"Please!" Nikki shrieked.

"A guy checked into the motel over lunch. He said it was a good book. So I gave it another try. You might want to—"

"Who? What guy?"

"Just some guy."

"He probably meant good and old. It had to be written in the seventies."

"Fifty-one."

"Fifty-one what?"

"*Catcher in the Rye* was written in nineteen-fifty-one."

"Only you would know something like that."

"And it wouldn't hurt you to remember it either. Mrs. Lacwent will have it on the test." Amy watched as her friend picked a small speck of mascara off her eyelid, then pull a lipstick from her tan leather purse. "Are you planning an entire make-over or what?"

"You know who could sure use a good make-over?" Nikki applied a fresh coat of scarlet red to her lips. "Old Mrs. Lacwent, that's who." The girl turned her face to the left, then to the right. Her eyes searched for any blemish or mar. Seemly satisfied with her face, she pulled at the side hem of her tight tee shirt, straightening out the fabric.

"Nikki, I'll go without you."

"Don't worry. Worrying only causes premature aging. You'll end up as wrinkled face as old stone-heart Lacwent at this rate."

"We have to go. Now!" Amy didn't wait for a response. She grabbed Nikki by the wrist and pulled her from the bathroom. Nikki barely had time to retrieve her leather bag from the counter top.

"Why do you always take so long?" Billy Clarksted said as Amy and Nikki emerged from the girls room. He had been waiting by the door, his arms full of books, which he quickly dumped into Amy's arms. His own books were neatly tucked away in the blue and gray backpack hanging from his shoulder.

"Don't blame me," Amy said, handing Nikki her two books. "Have a word with your girlfriend."

"Did you miss me?" Nikki said, slipping her free arm around Billy's waist. The top of her head came up only as far as his shoulders, and he stood six-feet, two-inches.

"Always," Billy replied and slipped his hand in her back pocket. He squeezed. Nikki gave out a tiny squeal.

"Save it for later you two," Amy said, rolling her eyes and shaking her head.

"You really need to relax more," Nikki said. "You need a boyfriend. Someone to help release all that tension." Nikki giggled and pulled Billy closer.

"We don't have time for this." Amy started down the hall.

"See what I mean," Nikki said, following right behind her. "You're so uptight. And you don't have to be. There's a lot of guys in this school who want to go out with you."

"Yeah, my bud Mark thinks you're a real babe," Billy told her, as if that would sway her.

"No thanks. Not interested. I'm sick of the guys in this school—in this town."

"Thanks a bunch," Billy said. "Makes a guy feel warm all over. So what is it? We're not good enough."

"It's nothing like that. I'm just not interested in dating anyone right now."

The two o'clock bell rang out.

"Great," Amy said.

The three teens ran the last fifteen feet down the hall. The door to the English classroom was closed.

"Terrific," Billy added.

All three stood staring at the door.

"Open it already," Nikki told him, breaking the silence.

He did.

As they entered the room: "Mr. Clarksted, Miss Bonn, Miss Evans," Dora Lacwent called out from behind the gray desk at the head of the class. "All three of you are tardy. I find behavior of this manner inexcusable." Her thin lips curved slightly downward.

This school year marked Dora's thirty-sixth. During those years she ran a strict routine in her classroom and even now nothing had changed, except, of course, the means. And those changes had been forced upon her. She often made clear her personal views on punishment in the classroom. "Back in my day, a teacher could discipline students—really discipline them. Not be expected to coddle and hold their hands. But nowadays," she would often complain, "if you even touch a student someone screams abuse." Her views disturbed some of the other teachers, especially those locals, born and raised in Arkham, who experienced Mrs. Lacwent's philosophy first hand. Several of the younger teachers would confess, as students in Dora Lacwent's English class, they were scared to death of her and to this day have as little contact as possible with the woman. One or two would even admit to receiving one of her paddlings and how hard it was to sit down afterwards. Others, however, couldn't help feeling pity for cold-hearted Dora. Thirty-six years of teaching the youth of this town and thirty-six years of being alone.

"Yes, ma'am," the three said in almost perfect harmony, which caused several of their classmates to snicker.

Mrs. Lacwent slammed her teacher's edition of the class textbook on her desktop with more force than one would think her frail arms could muster. "I'll have none of that." Her wrinkled eyes scanned the class. No lack of order would be tolerated. The students quickly stilled in their assigned seats. Mrs. Lacwent's punishments were still enough to keep strict order. "You three will stay after class," she said, returning her attention back to Amy, Nikki, and Billy. "I will see what I can find for you to do."

Nikki scowled.

"Or would you rather spend tomorrow in Saturday detention."

"For being late three sec—?" Nikki began to say.

"After class," Amy said, interrupting her friend, "will be fine, Mrs. Lacwent."

"Take your places," the teacher ordered.

CHAPTER 2

The carnival caravan had stopped for a late lunch. The trucks and trailers just about filled the parking area of the truck stop diner. It had been the only place to eat for miles. In fact, it had been the only thing on that stretch of Nevada highway for miles. Now, some of the carnies trickled out of the eatery, preparing to continue on with their journey.

Lilith watched from a distance as the men and women joked and laughed, dragging out the last few moments before having to hit the road again. "Lucas," she said, "hurry the workers along. We must make the next town by nightfall." Her dark eyes hid the anticipation those words brought: "next town."

"Yes, ma'am," the hulking man immediately responded, and without another word went off to carry out her orders.

Lilith started toward one of the trailers when she felt a hard piece of metal against her ribs.

"This here is a Bulldog .44 Special," a gruff, but female voice said, digging the gun barrel tighter into Lilith's flesh. "And unless you want a hole the size of an orange blown through your other side, I suggest you don't make any sudden moves."

Lilith's eyes moved, but not to the woman. Instead, she looked toward her workers still chatting as they walked to their trucks.

"Don't be expecting help from any of that crud," the woman said, her breath had the heavy smell of both cigarettes and alcohol. She had large, strong arms, and slicked back hair. Besides wearing worn cowboy boots and blue jeans, she had on a fairly new N.R.A. tee shirt. "They can't see the gun from this distance. Or you better pray they don't anyhow."

"What is it you want?" Lilith said, as if merely irritated.

"I want my family back."

"And?"

"And you took them." Again she jammed the gun barrel into Lilith's ribs. "Listen here, sister, I have nothing else to lose. You took my husband Luke and our boy Mathew. You gave them one of these." The woman threw a red ticket to the ground. "It's some kind of signal to your lackeys."

"It's a choice."

"What are you yammering about? A choice?"

"One must choose to use the ticket."

"Bullshit! You think you can fool me. I know who you are."

"Really?"

"Yeah, really. Carnival my eye. You're some covert government group. Hell, with all this fancy cover maybe even CIA. Leave it to the government to overdo it. To go to the extreme, like in Waco. Overkill, lady, that's how I figured it out—overkill."

Lilith laughed. "I have no concerns about the strife you have with your government."

"That's exactly what I expected you'd say. Another lie. Just like taking away our constitutional right to bear arms will protect us from crime. I never put it past the government to kidnap its own citizens, no better than those commies in China. Political prisoners, that's what my family are, political prisoners. Well, I'm going to get them back one way or another."

"And you thought you would handle such a task alone."

"I went to our so-called police. Of course, no one there believed me. They all acted like I was crazy. But I'm not as dumb as they think. They are all part of it. It's a conspiracy. We all know how the government works. They're always coming up with some elaborate plan and when they're found out they make people think you're crazy. But I'm not."

Lilith's eyes kept focusing on the group of workers getting into their vehicles, following the orders she gave Lucas. "Your plan seems to be lacking. Do we just stand here?"

"First smart thing out of your mouth." The woman nudged Lilith with the muzzle tip. "Get moving." She directed Lilith to the nearest trailer. The two women started walking around toward its blindside. With her back to her captor, Lilith let out a small sinister grin.

"I do remember them," Lilith said as they moved forward.

"What?"

"Your...family. I remember them."

"Good. Then you can tell me their exact whereabouts. See, I'm not crazy."

"No, not crazy. Paranoid. As your husband and son. You speak of conspiracy. You see the shadow of an intruding eye around every corner, watching your every move. You see the iron hand of a corrupt government closing down on you. And their spies are those who do not conform to your pitiful ideologies."

As the two women disappeared from view, the roar of powerful engines filled the air. The loud noise completely drowned out the short, smothered scream.

Lilith returned from behind the trailer, watching as the first truck started off. The caravan was once again on its way.

In Arkham, the sheriff's cruiser drove up and parked next to the curb. Jim McNee glanced at his watch. *Any time now.* He looked along the quiet street and knew the peace and serenity of the small town would be shattered at any moment.

Then it happened.

The signal.

The three o'clock bell dismissing school. Within seconds, mobs of children poured from the large wooden doors. Children of all ages and grades—Arkham had only the one school building.

As Jim watched for his daughter Allie, his radio crackled to life.

"Deputy to Sheriff," the voice said.

Even over the radio, the vocal qualities of his two deputies were sharp and distinct. Jim had no question of which man was making the call.

"Sheriff here, Nate. Whatcha' got?"

"Wanted to let you know I'll be cutting out early. Got a strange call from home, I thought I'd check it out."

"Any trouble?"

"Just a family matter."

"You do what you need to. Roger and I can handle things."

"Thanks, Sheriff. Deputy out."

Jim clipped the mike back to the dash in time to see Allie coming out of the green painted doors. Her walk was very authoritative for a third grader, after all she was the sheriff's daughter. Who else got to ride home in the sheriff's car.

As she approached, Jim saw her normal smile had been replaced with a pouting frown. He got out of the squad car to meet her. With each step a tear welled in her tiny eyes and her upper lip stiffened. It wasn't until he huggingly picked her off the sidewalk that the crying started.

"What's wrong, sweet one?" The sound of her crying always tore at him. "Did you hurt yourself?"

She shook her head and buried her face in the big man's shoulder.

"Can you tell me what's wrong?"

"Kenny West says you kill people," she mumbled through the cloth of his shirt.

A heavy thud hit Jim square in the chest. For a brief moment he was silenced. Then keeping his voice steady, he said, "I protect people, sweet one. I don't kill them. Remember the talk we had about my job."

She nodded and wiped the one blue eye that peeked out off her father's shoulder. Jim held his daughter close.

"Remember me telling you how important it is." He felt a second nod against his shoulder. "Next time you tell Kenny West that your father protects the whole town—including his family."

She lifted her head and met her father's gaze. "I knew he was lying. But he scared me." She wiped her other eye, then sniffled.

"Why would Kenny say such things?" Jim had his own ideas why an eight-year-old would spew such garbage. Gently, he brushed aside a lock of Allie's soft deep-brown hair that had clung to her tear soaked cheek.

"He said his uncle told him. He says you put people in jail for no reason. I told him he was stupid and I slugged him in the arm, but then he said that killing stuff. I wanted to cry, but I didn't."

Jim's instincts were right. "His uncle, huh. You tell Kenny that his uncle has spent plenty of time in jail, but not without a good reason. Okay?"

She smiled and hugged her father.

Jim held back his anger and returned his daughter's hug. He knew Dan West was a fine man, but his jail hound brother, Simon, was the town's biggest piece of living trash.

A mile or so outside the town limits of Arkham, Nate White Moon drove down a dirt road. The tires of the squad car caused a long trail of dust to follow him. As a child, he didn't mind living on the reservation, but as he grew he knew he couldn't stay. He never really fit in. He felt like an outcast among his own people. Though, the town's people of Arkham didn't exactly welcome him with open arms either. It was Jim McNee who gave him his job in the sheriff's office and eventually made him a deputy. Jim was the first non-Indian he could truly call friend. The sheriff saw personally to Nate's training, thinking with all the tribe's people coming into town, it might be prudent to have him as one of his deputies, making some potential hot situations easier to handle.

Nate turned onto a narrow side road. His eyes focused on an old beat-up truck parked in front of the small house he had once called home. A group of men stood to one side. Nate knew them all. He had grown up with each and every one. These were the type of men Jim McNee had in mind when making Nate a deputy, a go between— someone to smooth things over—a peace maker. That was the idea, which sometimes sounded better in principle than in practice.

Nate stopped the cruiser behind the pickup. Even before he got out, he felt eyes peering at him through the windshield. He took his hat from the seat and put it on. He stepped from the car. Nate wasn't particularly a large man, but he had a strong body. And Jim had taught him a few moves from his army training so he could better defend himself if it ever came to blows.

"Looky here, boys," Eugene Skyhawk said, leaning against his truck as Nate approached the house, "it's the law."

"Hello Eugene," Nate said cautiously, but without emotion. "Staying out of trouble?"

"Life is trouble." He looked at the others and grinned. "And I like life, and life likes me." He laughed. The others joined in.

"You can like life all you want, but not in town. Or I'll throw your ass behind bars—again." He walked toward the group, which split down the middle to let him pass.

"You're a traitor to your own people," Eugene yelled. The others became silent. "You wear that uniform, you bring shame to your family —shame to the whole tribe."

Nate paused a moment, then continued on his way up the old familiar stone walkway.

"Go back to your town, lawman. Go be with your own kind."

When Nate reached the small house, he didn't bother to knock. After entering, he closed the door, trying to leave his anger outside.

His little sister, Mandy, bolted down from upstairs. "Mom, Mom, Nate's home." At the bottom of the steps the young girl gave her brother a hug.

"How you doing, kid?" Nate asked, returning the embrace.

"Great. Are you staying for supper? Mom," Mandy called out again, "Nate's home."

"I heard you the first time," Faye White Moon replied coming down the short hall from the kitchen. When she reached her son she had him lean forward so she could kiss his cheek. "I expect you to stay for supper."

"Seems I have no choice. Why is Eugene here?"

Faye looked at her daughter. "Go outside. I need to speak with your brother." She waited for the door to close behind the child. "I hoped he'd be gone by the time you arrived. Did he say anything to you?"

"Only hello," Nate said. "What does he want?"

"Nothing. I asked him here…to find Samuel. I've been worried."

"Samuel? What's that old man up to now."

"Have more respect," the woman told her son, "he is your great uncle and a shaman. You must not refer to him in such a manner."

"Sorry," Nate said, "tell me what the problem is. Maybe I can help."

"It all began by him becoming very restless. When I spoke to him about it, he refused to explain. I worry he's not eating. No one can find him, not even Eugene."

"He's probably on a fast." Nate saw the worry on his mother's face. "When I was a kid, I remember him disappearing for weeks at a time."

"This is different," she replied. "I have never seen him act this way. Find him. You know his secret places. Bring him home. He'll talk to you. You were always special to him."

"Before, perhaps. I'm not too sure about now."

Nate left the house hoping to fulfill his mother's wishes. He hoped Eugene had the sense to leave, but deep down the deputy knew better. The group stood around the car whispering among themselves. A few, who had been friends with Nate years ago, couldn't look him in the eye as he approached. They didn't leave either. They wanted to see the show that would be coming.

"Leaving already, lawman?" Eugene asked.

"I'm going to find Samuel. Come with me, cousin. Let's show him we have ended our petty bickering."

"Leave my grandfather be. He has no time for you."

"He's my family too."

"Family? You call him family? You turned your back on him. He gave you a great honor and you threw it back at him."

"That's between me and Samuel. You hate me for something not of my doing. Look at yourself Eugene. We used to be like brothers."

"You speak of a dead past." Eugene stepped back as if to step away. Instead, he turned quickly and violently, his fist already in mid-flight toward Nate's jaw. Without a moment's thought Nate ducked. The savage blow missed him entirely. A second fist followed. As the first, the wild swing missed its target. Eugene being overextended was easily met with a blow from Nate. The one strike sent Eugene to the ground.

"Stay down, Eugene. Please, stay down."

The words only served to fuel Eugene's anger. He charged Nate. Nate performed a simple side step and threw up a knee, hitting his cousin square in the gut. Eugene, again, found himself face down in the dirt, this time gasping for air.

Assaulting an officer, Nate thought. He could so easily haul Eugene's butt to jail. His pals, of course, would try telling a different story of the event, but Sheriff McNee wouldn't buy it. Eugene could be spending a long time locked up. "I must be feeling generous today," Nate told his cousin. He walked away leaving Eugene sprawled out. Before starting the cruiser, Nate rolled down the window and said, "Your anger is the real reason Samuel chose me over you." He drove off.

After a short drive down an almost forgotten road, Nate got out and walked for five minutes. He had no doubt where his great-uncle Samuel would be and the sweet smelling smoke only confirmed it. Still a distance away, Nate saw the five stone monoliths, each over ten feet in height, forming a quarter circle. Each stone had its own unique symbol carved on its face. Samuel would sit with the stones to his back and a roaring fire facing him. "The stones watch over me—protect me," Nate remembered Samuel telling him, "And on very quiet nights, if I listen carefully, they speak to me."

Samuel had a very gentle nature, never holding his position out as one of power. And except for the amulet he wore around his neck, Samuel appeared as any other elder of the tribe. That was how Samuel always believed it should be. He wanted to serve his people, not be worshipped by them. Others, like Eugene, believed the shaman should exert control over the tribe and lead the council—a belief Samuel did not share.

Nate quietly approached the first monolith, not wanting to abruptly disturb the shaman's meditation. When Nate saw how thin Samuel had become, he understood his mother's concern. He opened his mouth to speak, but Samuel did so first.

"A storm is coming," were the words the old man spoke, not looking up. "It will be upon us by morning. I must prepare."

The skies were clear. The sun had barely started its descent.

"Please, ancient," Nate said, "come home. Your family worries."

The old man motioned for Nate to sit next to him.

Nate did.

"My place is here." For the first time the old man faced his nephew. "Soon I will rest," he said. "Still, I have one more task."

"Come home with me," Nate said again.

Samuel shook his head and cast his eyes to the sky. "I must wait." He threw a handful of dried herbs on the fire, which erupted, then returned to a small flame. A long heavy streamer of sweet smoke rose up into a pillar of white. "Do you remember the things I once taught you?"

Nate watched the smoke. For a brief moment it took on the shape of a cougar, then an eagle. He blinked and the shapes disappeared. "Some. Those times almost seem like another life," he said.

"For you, nephew, it was." Samuel stared deep into the fire. "You could always force me to return to the reservation."

Nate smiled a sad grin. "You know I won't do that. Besides, the moment I turn my back, you'd be right back out here with another fire."

Samuel returned the smile. "You were always the smart one."

"Smarts have nothing to do with it, old man. I know you." Nate stood up and began to walk away. He stopped, but didn't turn. He asked, "Uncle? I wish to know. Are you disappointed in me?"

"Disappointed? No. My one wish was for you to help our people. And you are. It doesn't matter the means. You are strong. And I am very proud of you."

"Thank you, uncle."

No more words were spoken as Nate made his way to his vehicle.

Samuel's words echoed in Nate's mind. They troubled him. It was as if his great uncle was saying goodbye. What could he tell his mother? Nate started the engine and headed back to town.

Evening came to Arkham, and like most Friday nights, the local hot spots were either one of the town's two bars. They were both always packed, but still no one considered opening a third. The crowd at the Lucky Seven Bar drank, laughed, and forgot about their daily grind. They came for a good time and to be among friends—most did anyway.

"You been watering down your whiskey again?" Simon West bellowed, holding his glass up to the light. Simon hated his name. His friends—and enemies—called him "Snake" after the large cobra he had tattooed on his right arm. His fist formed the serpent's head.

"You're crazy, Snake," Nadine Caster said from behind the bar. "That whiskey's straight from the bottle. Look here, I just broke the seal on this one. Your drink is just fine." Competing with Joe's Tavern, her only rival for the drinking dollar, Nadine had to put up with a lot of crap. For the most part her patrons were well behaved, except Snake West. She trembled each time he came through her door, though she never let him know it—nothing would stop him from trashing her place then.

"Fine? Fine? I've pissed out stronger stuff."

His lackeys laughed. Zeek Dyler, a thin scraggly man, slapped him on the back. "Good one, Snake," he said.

"Now how in tarnation do you know that?" Nadine asked. "Been drinkin' your own urine again?"

More laughs, but this time at Snake's expense.

"You think that's funny?" Snake said. He stared down the bar. A few of the other customers got up and found a table.

From behind Snake came: "I did. Thought it was real funny."

Snake turned. He knew that voice. "Shut that fuckin' mouth of yours."

"Sounds like you're the one with the mouth," Roddy Gills said, and took another sip of his beer. He set his glass back on the counter. "Must be all that piss you've been drinking. You should really cut down."

A few snickers came from a nearby table.

"I don't want any trouble here," Nadine said, her voice firm, hiding a tiny shake.

"Ain't no trouble," Snake said, glancing over at Zeek and two other men, all who nodded, got up, and left the bar. "No trouble to crush his skull. No trouble at all."

Snake moved in on Roddy, who swallowed the last of his beer. A baseball bat smashed down between the two men. Both simultaneously looked over the bar counter at Nadine standing there holding a Louisville Slugger.

"Take it outside, ladies," she said. "No fighting in here." She smiled. "It's too hard on my insurance rates."

Snake raised his hands. "That was always the plan."

"After you," Roddy said. The two men had always hated each other. This wasn't their first fight. Most of the town despised Snake West, so picking sides was never a problem.

The two goliaths lumbered toward the door. Snake stepped out first. The moment Roddy stepped out something hard hit him against the knee. The big man dropped to the ground. There was another blow to his back, sending waves of pain throughout his body. Roddy turned his head enough to see Zeek holding a four foot piece of two-by-four. The skinny man was laughing.

"He's mine now, boys," Snake said. He grinned and kicked Roddy in the ribs with the hard toe of his boot. He kicked again.

"Someone call the sheriff," a voice called out from the open door.

Zeek grabbed Snake by the arm. "We gotta go!"

"When I'm just starting to have fun?" With the edge of his boot, Snake kicked loose dirt into Roddy's face.

"They're calling McNee," Zeek said.

"We'll finish this another time, Roddy, old buddy."

Roddy's only response was the mixture of dirt and blood oozing from his mouth.

CHAPTER 3

ow what? Jim thought, when the wall phone began to ring for the third time within the last half hour at the McNee home. Not exactly the ideal Saturday morning. He stopped filling his daughter's dinosaur glass with orange juice and set the carton on the table. Nate White Moon had made the first call, telling the sheriff that even though Roddy Gills received three cracked ribs from last night's brawl, he didn't want to file a complaint against Snake West. The deputy couldn't reason why, until Jim made it clear that Roddy couldn't exact his pound of flesh if Snake was locked up. Jim feared another small war between Roddy Gills and Snake West. The second call came directly from Nadine Caster, complaining that nothing is ever done about Snake West and his buddies. She wanted action and she wanted it now! He told the irate woman he'd be more than delighted to throw Snake's ass in a cell, if she'd press charges. The phone went silent for a moment. Finally, she said she'd have to think about it and hung up. Case closed, Jim figured.

The phone rang out again.

"Coming, coming," he said to the noise.

Allie giggled.

"Finish your Cheerios," Jim told his daughter as he walked across the kitchen. He picked up the receiver, "Hello, Sheriff McNee speaking."

A gruff voice said, "This is Jasper Fallon."

The morning had now, unbelievably, taken a turn for the worse. "Hello Mayor," Jim said, forcing back the sudden flood of contempt those words brought. Jim couldn't fathom why the towns' people of Arkham voted the self-serving fat man into office for another four years.

"McNee," came pouring out of the earpiece, "there's some funny goin' ons out on Juncture Road, just outside town limits. Tents and wagons—things like that. Some kind of carnival or the like goin' up."

"And?"

The single-word question forced a brief pause from the mayor. Jim could almost hear the steam building over the phone.

"And I want you to check it out with me."

"But Mayor," Jim said, looking at Allie finishing off the last few spoonfuls of cereal, "can't Roger or Nate…?"

"A deputy won't cut it this time. I insist on the chief law officer to be with me, so those carny people know I'm serious. That I mean business."

Serious, Jim thought. *You're never serious about anything but money and how to get your cut.* "All right, Mayor. I'll need time to get ready."

"You've got thirty minutes, then meet me in front of the courthouse."

"I'll be—" Jim heard a click on the other end.

Jim didn't bother hanging up the phone. Instead, with the electric buzz filling his ear, he pushed out a familiar number. The line on the other end began to ring.

"Hello?"

"Hello, Barbara, this is Jim McNee. Is Amy home?"

"Hold the line please."

After a few seconds of silence. "Hi, Sheriff. This is Amy."

"Sorry to bother you, but something's come up. Do you think you could come and sit with Allie? For about an hour or so?"

Another brief pause. "Sure. Sure I can. I'd love to."

"Thanks, Amy. I really appreciate it. I have to be at the courthouse in a half an hour. Could you be over in twenty minutes?"

"No problem. See you then."

Jim put the receiver back on the hook. Having a next door neighbor like Amy Evans was sure a blessing. Now to tell Allie.

"See, Daddy, all done," his daughter said, displaying her empty cereal bowl.

"That's my girl. And you know what?" Jim forced enthusiasm into his voice.

Allie shook her head.

"I have a surprise for you. Finish your juice, and I'll tell you."

Allie took the glass in her small hands and gulped down the last two swallows. "All gone."

"How would you like to play with Amy this morning?"

Allie's eyes lit up. She loved Amy. "Yes, yes. Can we all have a picnic?"

"Well, maybe, but your dad has to run a couple of errands." Her expression changed before his eyes—her bright smile faded. "Amy will be here soon. You ask her."

Allie's smile returned.

Twenty minutes later, Jim came down the stairs in full uniform. He looked in on Allie watching TV. She was exactly where he had left her. He didn't really worry, Allie always minded him. She would stay in the living room, content in watching her favorite Saturday morning cartoons. Jim hated to use TV as a baby sitter, but he had to admit to himself that it did come in handy sometimes.

The doorbell rang.

"Allie, Amy's here."

The little girl jumped up from the floor and made a beeline to the front door. She turned the knob with both hands and pulled.

Amy crouched down to meet Allie face-to-face. "Hi, sweetie."

Allie wrapped both arms around Amy's neck and gave her a hug. "Hi, Amy. Can we do a picnic? My dad said to ask you."

"A picnic? Wow, that does sound fun...but I...." Amy saw Jim coming down the hall. He nodded. Amy took the cue. "Of course we can."

"But," Jim said, "you'll have to wait until I've finish my errand. Okay?"

"Okay, Daddy."

"That's settled then," Jim added. "You go back and watch your show while I talk with Amy a minute."

The child released her grip on the sitter and scampered back to the TV.

"I shouldn't be gone too long," Jim told Amy.

"Don't rush on my account. I love sitting with Allie."

As the words finished coming from her mouth a loud honk trumpeted from the street. Amy turned and saw Nikki waving at her to come to the car. "Hi, Sheriff," Billy Clarksted called out.

"Sorry about this," Amy said, "I tried to call Nikki, but she had already left."

"No, I'm sorry. I should've realized you would've already had plans."

"I don't. I mean, I didn't want to go with them anyway. They're just going to hang around by the shops until the movies open. The same old thing, not really my idea of fun. Spending the morning with Allie beats that any day."

"Are you sure? I could call—"

"I'm positive," Amy said.

There was another honk.

"I better talk with them," Amy said and started down to the street.

Jim watched as Nikki Bonn opened the door. Amy said a few words and closed it. After a brief discussion through the open car window, Amy's friends drove off. She walked back up to the house.

"I feel bad about this, Amy," Jim said. "It's no trouble for me to call Allie's Aunt JoLean."

"Please, don't. You're really doing me a favor."

Jim glanced at his watch. "I should get going. The mayor's probably counting each minute."

"What kind of sandwich do you want?" Amy asked.

"Excuse me."

"Sandwich—for the picnic."

Jim smiled. "There's some bologna in the fridge—that'll be fine. And speaking of bologna, I better not keep the mayor waiting. Be back in about an hour."

<hr />

The sheriff's car pulled up to what seemed the beginnings of a main gate. Jim McNee got out, followed by Jasper Fallon, a portly man, well dressed, who tugged at a gold chain, pulling a gold watch from its small pocket. He pushed the stem, and the faceplate popped open. Mayor Fallon grumbled something, snapped the watch shut, and shoved it back in his side vest pocket.

Sheriff McNee waited for the mayor to lead, which, without hesitation, he did. Jim hated the fact that this pompous ass was his boss. He had kept a private file on Jasper Fallon's questionable activities—all of which Jim knew to be true, but didn't have a shred of the proof he needed. The mayor was always very clever in covering his tracks. And on those very few times Jim McNee thought he had Jasper Fallon by the short hairs, the pudgy little man always slipped free somehow. One day,

Jim reckoned, the honorable Mayor Fallon would slip on his own crap, and he would be there with his shiny stainless steel handcuffs ready, willing, and able to slap them around those porky wrists.

"What's the smirk for?" Jasper Fallon asked.

"Just thinking about something I have to do."

"Keep your mind on your job."

"I am," Jim said.

The two men walked across the sparsely grassed, hard ground. The sound of men working was the first thing to greet them.

"Can you direct me to whoever's in charge here?" the mayor asked of a man, wearing torn jeans and a sweaty tee-shirt, who had just driven an iron spike halfway into the dry soil.

The worker said nothing, but pointed into the encampment with his thumb, then lifted a sledgehammer above his head. With one swing, he finished planting the metal bar with a loud clang.

Throughout the disassembled, disheveled carnival, the mayor asked several people directions to the boss. Jim stayed close behind, but didn't lend a hand. This was the mayor's show and that suited him fine.

Finally, they came to a large tent. As they approached, Jim could have sworn he heard groaning, but it stopped when they drew closer.

"Let's get this over with," Mayor Fallon said, and reached for the tent flap.

"May I help you?" a voice said from behind him. The mayor pulled back his hand and turned around to find a tall, slender woman with flowing black hair. Her eyes were so dark brown that you could barely see her pupils.

"May I help you?" she repeated.

"I'm Jasper Fallon, mayor of Arkham, and this is Sheriff McNee. We are looking for the owner of this—this carnival."

"You have succeeded. What can I do for you, Mayor?" Her voice was slightly raspy, but it suited her. She wore a long black coat, her boots peeking out from underneath.

"We seem to have a bit of a problem here," Mayor Fallon said, stepping closer to the woman.

It was obvious Jasper found the woman attractive. She was, but— Jim couldn't put his finger on it.

"Problem?" the woman said. "How so?"

"As it happens—Miss...?"

"Lilith. You may call me Lilith."

"Fine, well—Lilith, we were not aware your carnival was coming to our fair town."

"I'm not surprised. We didn't know either. We took a wrong road somewhere down the line. Instead of wandering around all night, I decided to setup here. How I love playing to small towns. The people are always so interesting. And kind."

"I'm afraid it's not that simple. There are permits to be applied for. A vote by the town council. You know, that sort of thing."

"Oh, I see. Maybe we can work something out. Come, let us discuss it in the comfort of my trailer."

"If you insist," Jasper said.

Both men started to follow Lilith, but the mayor signaled Jim to stop.

"I'll handle this, Sheriff—being town business and all. Wait for me by the car."

"Whatever. You're calling the shots here." *Snotty little man.* Jim headed back to the cruiser. His military training made following orders second nature, no matter what asshole was giving those orders. And God knows some of the officers he served under were brethren to Jasper Fallon, only in khaki.

Walking across the grounds, on his way out, Jim passed two men. The first had an unkept beard and mustache, the right strap of his overalls had been broken at the shoulder and hung loosely at his side. The second man was clean cut, and wore plain blue jeans and a light gray tee shirt. The sheriff wouldn't have noticed the men at all, except for the surprised, almost guilty, look the clean cut one gave Jim as he passed. He wasn't a local town's person, yet Jim had seen his face before—but from where?

<hr />

Inside the trailer, Lilith offered Jasper Fallon a chair. The furnishings were comfortable, but the whole place seemed sterile somehow.

"You got a beer or something?" Jasper asked. "I'm mighty thirsty." He looked around for a portable refrigerator or a cooler of some kind.

"I do not." Her dark eyes cut through the portly man. "You said something about permits?" A tiny smile formed on her lips as if she knew exactly what he was about to say.

"All business. I like that."

"Can we proceed then? I am very busy. I have my carnival to set up."

"That's the crux of the matter. You have to file for permits to set up any sort of carnival or fair. Then the city council votes for approval or disapproval."

"How long would that take?"

"Hard to say, it being the weekend. The council doesn't meet until Monday morning nine o'clock, and even then we have a whole lot of business that must come first." Jasper tried to get a read on this woman, but failed. "I presume you know how these things work."

"I've had some dealing in the past."

"You'll have to stop your work for now. I can use my influence to get the council to vote, possibly, early Tuesday afternoon."

"We can't delay for that long. We'll just pull up and move along."

"Such a pity," Jasper said. "All that work already done, not to mention the time wasted. Maybe we can work something out."

"I'm listening."

"For let's say, oh, thirty percent of your profits. I want to be fair about this."

"Twenty percent," she countered.

"Twenty-five."

Lilith nodded.

"I love to compromise."

"You love greed," she said, her impish smile returned.

"Greed? No, not greed, business. A man's got to make a buck when he can."

"And our *business* is over—for now," Lilith said, rising to her feet. The mayor followed her lead and stood up.

"It's been grand," he said, extending his hand. Lilith stood motionless, looking down at his pudgy fingers—she refused the gesture. Jasper's hand slowly dropped to his side. "I'll come back every other night to collect my share. Best not to be seen here too often. People might get the wrong idea."

"Oh, I doubt that," she said grinning.

"I can see myself out," Mayor Fallon told the dark woman.

As Jasper left the trailer, a sudden unexplainable eeriness crept over him. The man found himself trembling. He hurried on his way to the squad car, looking back over his shoulder the entire time. He saw no one, but had the bizarre feeling of eyes following him with each step. Then his shoulder hit something. Jasper turned. He was face-to-face with a grimy looking bearded man. "Pardon," is all Jasper said, and rushed on. He yanked open the car door and jumped in. "Let's go, McNee. Our business is finished here." He pulled out a handkerchief from the inside pocket of his coat and mopped the sweat from his forehead.

"What was all that about permits?" Jim asked. "There's no need for permits outside of town." He turned the ignition key. The engine roared.

"True, but I didn't want these slick carny people to think they can take advantage of our good citizens." Jasper stuffed the damp cloth back into his coat pocket. He felt himself ease some. "I just laid down the law and told them we'd overlook the paperwork if there are no shenanigans."

The squad car pulled out, kicking up dry dirt in its wake. Jasper Fallon gazed back at the carnival through the dust cloud. As his thoughts of money disappeared, he wondered if he had made a huge mistake by coming here.

～﹒～

Johnny Solom followed Calvin Tyler through the carnival grounds. Johnny casually glanced back, making sure the sheriff didn't turn around. After the trouble last night, he felt lucky to get out of that bar before the local law enforcement showed up.

It had taken most of the night for Johnny to start up a conversation with Calvin. He didn't seem the easiest man to approach. Calvin reminded him of some of the homeless people he had seen sleeping on the streets back home. His tangled beard and dirty pants would put most people off, but he was a means to an end. And once they started talking, his easy-going nature surprised Johnny. It was even Calvin who suggested he look for work at the carnival. Johnny couldn't believe his luck.

An overweight man rushed from a trailer. He pushed past them, almost knocking Calvin down.

"Pardon," the man said.

"Townies," Calvin replied.

Johnny was sure the man didn't hear Calvin at the rate he was moving. The man made a beeline for the sheriff's cruiser. Johnny would be more at ease with the car gone or himself out of sight. Both would serve equally as well.

Calvin made his way to the steps of the same trailer the portly man had come from. He wiped his feet on the small mat at the bottom stair and gestured for Johnny to do the same. He did. Reaching the top step the bearded man rapped lightly on the metal door, though his attempt to be quiet still produced a loud clatter.

"Enter," Johnny heard come from inside. He knew that voice.

"Now stay cool," Calvin told him, and gave the traditional thumbs up. Calvin turned the handle and stepped in.

Johnny followed close behind. His eyes needed a second to adjust to the dim lighting.

Lilith sat in her chair, looking up at the two men. She said nothing.

"Excuse us, ma'am, could we have a minute?"

"Yes, Calvin, a minute."

Johnny felt his heart pound. It was her.

"Ma'am, this is Johnny. He's looking for a job." Calvin took his newfound friend by the arm, pulling him forward a few feet.

"Is that right, Johnny?"

"Yes, ma'am, yes, it is."

"Lilith. If you wish, you may call me Lilith." Her dark eyes watched his every movement. "Is there something bothering you? You seem…nervous."

Relax, he thought to himself, *you've made it this far*. "It's just, well, I haven't had a steady job in quite a while and—"

"A steady job. Is that what you're looking for?"

Johnny nodded.

"Have you worked a carnival before?" She grinned.

"Once, a while back."

"I see." She knitted her fingers in front of her face. Her two index fingers touched her lips. "What are you running from?"

"Excuse me?"

"No one works carnivals unless they're a local looking to make a fast buck or they're someone on the run."

Johnny's heart pounded hard in his chest.

"You're not from around here," she continued, "so what are you running from?"

"Trouble back home." Johnny chose his words very carefully. "Trouble with a girl." He had to force control of his breathing. He now understood the chubby man's haste in leaving this trailer. Talking with the woman sent waves of fear through his body.

"Is that all? Girl troubles? Nothing more?"

"I can say that her father would like to find me." Johnny hoped his explanation was enough. It was the truth, though incomplete.

"That wasn't so hard after all, was it?" She stood up. "Calvin, he can work in the gaming booths with you. We'll see how he works out."

"Yes, ma'am," Calvin replied.

"Welcome to our little family," Lilith said, extending her long slender hand.

Without thinking, Johnny took it. Her flesh felt dry, almost scaly. The shock made him look down, but he saw only soft white skin, and its touch had changed in an instant to match the delicate fingers.

After the two men left her company, Lilith returned to her chair. "You heard?" she said to open air.

"Kill him," a voice responded. "He could bring others."

"Lucas, where is your sense of sport? Of the game?"

"My kind does not have such feelings."

"Simply killing one such as him," Lilith said, "would be a tremendous waste. No, he will join my carnival on a more permanent basis. He escaped me once, not again." Lilith paused for a moment, then added, "It is time we meet the fine people of Arkham. Such a lovely little town."

CHAPTER 4

It would be another forty-five minutes before the doors of the movie theater on Main Street opened. Most of the shops had opened hours earlier, so Nikki Bonn and the others were able to keep themselves slightly amused during the wait. After meeting up with Mark Boyd, they had all headed over to Gouward's Mini-Mart to grab a couple of quick sodas. Billy Clarksted bought two Snicker bars, saying he would sneak them into the show—no sense paying a buck per bar once inside.

The streets of Arkham were at their usual slow paced hustle-bustle. Harvey Nelson, driving the town's only street sweeper, made his weekly pass to clean out the gutters of dirt and trash. Chester Nich, the mail-man, dropped off his assorted variety of letters and packages to the shops and the few apartments situated above the stores. Ellen Houser hurried to finish sweeping off the sidewalk in front of her dress boutique before Harvey drove by.

Indeed, it was a typical Saturday in Arkham, like every other Saturday that had come and gone before it, but that would be changing. Something strange had come to town.

"Where to now?" Billy asked his friends. He made a jump shot, throwing his empty Coke can into the street garbage can. "Two points. I'm a star." He put his hands to his mouth and mimicked the sound of a crowd roaring their approval.

"Anywhere," Mark said, ignoring his buddy's ego. "Doesn't really matter to me. We have plenty of time. You call it."

"Don't let him decide," Nikki said. "You two will end up shooting baskets while I sit on my butt for the next half-hour watching you two having fun." She reached in her purse and pulled out a compact. She checked her face in the small round mirror.

"Speaking of fun," Mark said. "You told me Amy was going to come with us."

"We thought she was," Billy said. "Talk to her best friend here." Billy touched Nikki's arm.

"What about it Nikki? You said Amy liked me."

"Clean out your ears." She snapped shut her mirror and dropped it back in her purse. "I said, she needs a boyfriend."

"No you didn't. You said—"

"Doesn't make a rat's-ass difference now," Billy told Mark, "she's not here."

"Can you believe her," Nikki said. "Babysitting. What a waste of a good Saturday."

"Wow, look at that!" Mark pointed to a tall, raven-haired woman handing out fliers. "Such a babe!"

"You think everyone's a babe," Nikki said. "She's not so great. Is she Billy?"

Billy was as captivated with the woman as Mark.

"Billy!" Nikki said, pushing at his arm.

"She's no big deal," he said, winking at Mark.

"I wonder what she's handing out," Mark said.

"You should go ask her."

"Me? Why don't you?"

"God, grow up you two," Nikki said. "Why don't you argue a little louder? She's coming this way. She can see what a couple of idiots you both are."

The three teenagers watched as the woman continued passing out her leaflets while working her way up the street. "Tomorrow" was all Billy could hear her say, that is, until she came over to where they were standing.

"Such a lovely girl," Lilith said, which surprised the group. "Beauty is a gift my dear. You should appreciate it."

"Oh, she does," Billy said, "every time she sees her face in a mirror."

Mark snickered.

"Funny," Nikki said. "Maybe you'd rather not see it so often. That can be arranged you know." She took a step back.

Billy grabbed her arm. "I was only kidding," he said in his own defense.

"Come to my carnival," the woman said. "We open tomorrow." She handed a leaflet to Nikki and Billy.

"On a Sunday?" Mark asked. "You open your carnival on a Sunday?"

"And why not?" Lilith said, smiling at the boy.

"It seems odd. That's all. Same day as church."

"Ahhh, but Sunday is a day of rest. A day to relax. What could be more relaxing than a day of fun and adventure." She handed Mark a sheet along with a cold stare.

"It still seems odd to me," Mark said as he took the paper. It was mostly black print on white paper, except for the word "Lilith" in bright red lettering.

"Is that you?" Nikki asked, "Lilith?"

"It is. I hope to see you at my carnival, just outside your quaint little town. We'll be here for only five days. Come any time. We have fine shows and games. Rides to amuse and scare you. We have something for everyone." She smiled and started off.

They watched her work her way farther down the street, handing out more of her leaflets to all passersby.

When Mark was sure she was out of earshot, he said, "I still think it's kinda weird."

"Shut up, Mark," Nikki and Billy said in unison.

A few blocks down Main Street, other residents of Arkham had much different concerns, and how to spend a day of leisure was far from being one of them.

"And that loaf of wheat there," Dora Lacwent said to the baker, Tom Thatcher. "Not that one. The fat one on the left."

"They're all the same, Dora," he said, stretching his arm to its extreme.

"I thank you to let me pick my own loaf if you don't mind."

"Yes, Dora." Tom had owned the bakery for the past eleven years. In all that time he would have thought he'd have gotten used to Dora Lacwent's pickiness, but he hadn't. He wrapped the bread in plastic and handed her the loaf over the counter.

The small brass bell over the door signaled its opening, at the same time as Dora began eyeing the butter cookies.

"Be with you in a moment," Tom told the woman entering the bakery.

"I am not here to shop," Lilith explained. "I came in to ask if I could put a flier in your window." She handed one to Tom. He read it over. "Your shop seems busy," she continued, "it would make the ideal spot."

"A carnival, huh? Sure, why not?" He handed back the leaflet.

Dora Lacwent cleared her throat. "If you're finished? I'll have a dozen—" The small bell interrupted her again. "—butter cookies."

Dora left the bakery with her bread and cookies in a brown paper bag she held close to her body. She started to walk away when the red lettering caught her eye. She stopped to read the flier. "Carnivals—what foolishness."

"We all need a little foolishness," came from behind Dora. She let out a gasp at the sound and dropped her bag.

"My heavens, you could frighten a person to death…sneaking up on a body like that."

"Please forgive me," Lilith said. The dark woman bent down and retrieved Dora's bag. "It wasn't my intention." Then she held out the bag, returning it to Dora, who responded by snatching it back.

"If any of my cookies are broken—" she said, rifling through the sack of baked goods. Not one had so much as cracked. The teacher looked up. "What are you staring at?"

"Forgive me—again."

"I take it you are with this carnival group?" Dora asked.

"In a manner. It is my carnival. I am Lilith."

"Such nonsense." Dora started to walk away.

"Is it nonsense to enjoy life? To have fun? To crave adventure?"

Dora stopped, her back to Lilith. "Life is not supposed to be fun. It's hard work. Each one must find their own way or be pushed aside. It's people like you—" Dora turned to face Lilith. But Lilith was gone.

The door to the bakery opened. Tom stepped out. "Are you okay, Dora?"

"Never better. Why do you ask?"

"You were talking to yourself and—"

"Myself? Don't be idiotic. I was talking with that—that woman."

"I didn't see anyone."

"Are you calling me a liar?" Dora barked.

"No, I'm not."

"Then senile. That's it, you think I'm senile. I tell you she was here."

Tom looked both ways along the street.

"If you wore your glasses like you should—" Dora said, stomping off in a huff.

The single file line at the food table moved quickly. The chatter filling the air confirmed that this day's lunch was a very welcomed meal.

Several of the carnival booths stood as wood and steel skeletons waiting to be dressed in tarpaulins of canvas and plastic. Draping them would be the afternoon's task. Most of Johnny's morning was spent helping assemble the basketball shoot. Dean—Johnny was never told his last name—had been running the booth so far this season. A real moneymaker Calvin said, among the hours of useless information that spewed from his mouth. Dean, on the other hand, had said nothing except for the one time he grumbled for a wrench.

But it wasn't just Dean. Johnny couldn't help noticing that the other workers were also keeping to themselves. He would catch a few of them glaring at him, but turning away when he returned their stare.

And when he and Calvin stepped into the lunch line, the vocal camaraderie of the men ended. That eerie quiet lasted several minutes, and began again only as whispers, but finally returned to normal tones. Nevertheless, Johnny felt the uneasiness as he waited his turn for food.

"Great chow here," Calvin said, at the same time signaling the server to spoon on another mound of mashed potatoes. Pieces of roast beef already hung over the edge of his plate and he lost a few peas every other step.

Johnny had other things on his mind besides food, but he had to admit to himself he was hungry. He had saved his last couple of bucks by skipping breakfast. Still, hungry or not, he had questions he needed answers to and he had to be very careful, very subtle about asking. "You'd think there'd be more people here," Johnny remarked, taking a half-pint carton of milk from an ice filled tub.

Calvin glanced around. "Nope, this is most of them. Maybe just a couple missing." He grabbed another carton and placed it on Johnny's tray next to the first. "It's a long time 'til supper." He patted Johnny on the back.

"The whole carnival is run by these few people?" Johnny asked, fishing again. He took a shiny, plump apple off the table.

"Take two," Calvin said, "save one for later."

Johnny complied. After all, it wasn't a bad idea.

"Mostly these are the gaming people," Calvin said to Johnny's query. "The rest run the snack stands." Balancing his full tray, he pointed. "There's a free spot." They walked over to a half empty table. A chunky red-haired woman smiled at Johnny as he sat.

"Hi," Johnny said, being polite. The heat from the green enamel painted bench bit through his jeans as he adjusted to get comfortable. The field had no shade, so the table and bench absorbed the full energy of the day's sun. Calvin commented that it was one sure way to make certain nobody would be sitting too long. After other small talk and trivial matters, Johnny led his companion back around to the topic of the carnival. "What about the sideshows? Who runs those?"

"Full of questions, aren't you?"

"Just trying to learn the ropes," Johnny said, cutting his meat. "I figure sharing a booth with you is just temporary. And it couldn't hurt a guy to—"

"Listen to him," Calvin laughed. "Haven't even got our own booth up yet and he's already planning to ditch me."

The chunky redhead across the table smiled too. "Calvin, who's your friend?"

He swallowed the mouthful of roast beef before speaking, which impressed Johnny. "This here's Johnny Salem."

"Solom," Johnny said, correcting his partner.

Calvin nodded, still snickering, "Right."

"Nice to meet you sweetie. I'm Thelma Walker." She had a pleasant smile and seemed genuinely kind. "I do the cotton candy bit. Or mini doughnut sometimes. All depends on—"

Calvin interrupted the woman. "Boy, don't you know, it's like they say: you got to learn to walk before you can run." The bearded man shook his head as he chuckled.

"It's nothing like that," Johnny said, feeling a little exposed by Calvin's excessive bellowing.

"Forget the sideshows, kid. The sideshow performers stay on their side of the carnival. They don't eat or associate with us grunts, no way, no how. They have a pretty easy bit, if you ask me."

"Maybe they could use another barker."

"I said forget it. Lilith handles that department…personal like."

"By herself?"

"She has Lucas to help her with the freaks, but," he shoved a piece of bread in his mouth, "for the most part," the bread was a white gob between his teeth when he spoke, "she has the shows on a schedule. She must have it all pretty much timed out to the second, too, 'cause she never misses a show."

"Lucas?" Johnny asked. "Who's Lucas?" That was a new name. And the way Calvin's voice quivered, that might be something.

"Don't be in too big of a hurry to meet him, sweetie," Thelma told Johnny. She lowered her voice. "He's a real weird one, but I guess you'd have to be, workin' with those…those kind of people."

"Yeah," Calvin whispered back as if mocking Thelma, "but *those people* bring in the rubes."

"Must be pretty rough," Johnny said, "running all the shows."

Calvin shrugged. "What else does she have to do? It's us hired hands that do all the backbreaking work around here. But she pays well—and good chow." He shoved a forkful of mashed potatoes in his mouth.

"They got ya at a booth yet, honey?" Thelma asked.

"He's working the bottle ring toss with me," Calvin spoke out. "With his face we should really pull in the little townie girls. Huh, Johnny?" He laughed again and elbowed Johnny's arm.

Johnny wished Calvin wasn't such a big laugher. The potatoes sticking to Calvin's yellowed teeth made him lose his appetite.

CHAPTER 5

Nikki Bonn and Amy Evans had been friends since the third grade when Nikki's father got a job with the City Planner's Office. Not a great job, but one away from Los Angeles. Away from the traffic jams, crime, earthquakes, and the general stress that caused his second heart attack.

On the first day of school, Mrs. Logan made Nikki stand at the front of the room and tell something about herself. She told her new class about the other school she went to and how she missed her best friend MaryJo Cambell. The teacher told her what a fine job she had done, smiled, and sent the girl back to her seat.

During recess, Marty Crowley, already a bully at nine, told Nikki her old school sounded stupid and pulled the little girl's hair. He didn't let go until Amy slugged the boy-terror in the gut.

Nikki and Amy were close ever since. Over the years they had had their share of fights, some even ending with: "I never want to see you again," but they always made up. Last year Amy dated Billy Clarksted for about two weeks until she found out how much Nikki liked him. It was the real cause of Amy and Billy's split, but in Amy's mind it had been as good of a reason as any. Nikki told Amy, she wouldn't date Billy either, but Amy told her best friend that was stupid. If she wanted to date Billy she should. Nikki didn't require a lot of convincing.

"You want some more popcorn?" Amy asked, sitting on the floor, leaning against her bed. "I can throw another bag in the microwave."

"I'll finish this one," Nikki said.

"Finish what? There's nothing left but old maids."

"Old maids?"

"You know, the kernels at the bottom that didn't pop."

Nikki snickered. "Sounds funny—old maids."

"That's what my mom calls 'em. And it's not that funny." Amy grabbed a pillow off the bed and threw it at Nikki. The puffy bag hit her straight in the face, but that didn't stop her giggling.

Amy let out a laugh too. She hadn't had Nikki stay overnight in a while and had forgotten the fun they used to have. But now, instead of talking about horses and what kind of weddings they would have, their discussions turned mainly to harmless gossip about the other girls they knew, and when and who those girls would lose their virginity to. Amy was shocked when Nikki admitted that she lost hers to Billy last summer. Not shocked that they had sex, but shocked she waited so long to confess. Nikki smoothly shifted the conversation to the topic of Mark Boyd and his finest attribute. Nikki liked his butt.

"Too bad you couldn't come with us today," Nikki said.

"Why? I bet you just hung around on Main Street."

"Still, it had to be better than babysitting."

"I enjoy sitting with Allie. She's a sweet little girl. I don't get to do it that often. Usually the sheriff brings her to his sister-in-law. I sit for emergencies and only for an hour or two, like this morning. He must be working tonight. I saw him and Allie drive off. He seems lonely since his wife died. If it wasn't for Allie...." Amy smiled. "It was so cute. Today, somehow, she got her dad to promise to have a picnic. So I made sand-wiches, set out a blanket, the whole bit. It was fun."

"Sounds like it," Nikki said in a deadpan tone.

"It was."

"It must be a pain to live next door to the sheriff. You can't get away with anything."

"What's there to get away with?"

"Stuff. Just...stuff."

Amy heard a scratching at the door. Nothing loud, but a definite noise. She signaled to Nikki to keep talking. Nikki looked confused, but did what her friend requested.

"Ahmmm, we had a great time," Nikki said. Her mind raced for something to say as Amy quietly snuck across the bedroom. "There's a carnival in town. Some lady was handing out fliers. The guys were drooling over her—you know how they get."

Amy lifted her hand and slapped the door hard. There was a loud whack, then a scream on the other side.

Nikki jumped.

Amy started to yell. "Stay away from my door, you little creep. You eavesdrop again and I'll cut off your ears." Amy didn't even have to open her door to know it was her little brother Benny.

"Little shit," she said to Nikki. "You're lucky you don't have a brother."

"Easy for you to say. It would be sort of nice to have a brother or sister."

"Want mine?"

Nikki steered the discussion back to the subject of Mark Boyd. "I'm not kidding," she said. "You should give him a chance. He really likes you."

"He's not my type."

"Type...? Type...? He's perfect for you. Not your type?" Nikki glanced at the digital clock on the dresser. Its electric blue numbers shifted to 9:00. "You have to admit he's pretty cute," Nikki said.

Nikki thought half the boys at school were cute, but in this case, Amy had to admit to herself that her friend was right. But she didn't have to admit it to Nikki.

"If you like that kind of guy." Amy reached over, grabbed her can of Pepsi, and took a swallow. She needed something to hide her smile. One sip did the trick.

"That kind of guy?" Nikki said. "You don't like blonde hair, blue eyes, and great shoulders?" Her eyes staring wide at her best friend.

"All that's okay, I suppose." Amy shrugged.

"You suppose!" Nikki shrieked. "You're nuts!"

Amy couldn't hold back her laugh. "I'm just kidding. He's cute enough. But I don't know."

"What's there to know?"

"If you think he's so great, why are you dating Billy instead of him?"

"I have my reasons." Nikki grinned.

That grin intrigued Amy. "What reasons?" Her best friend was holding something back.

"I can't tell you. It's embarrassing." Nikki turned a light shade of red.

"Now you've got to tell me."

Nikki's blush deepened.

"Tell me!"

"His tongue. He has a great tongue."

"So he's a good French kisser. Big deal."

"I'm not talking about French kissing."

Amy was puzzled for a moment, then: "Nikki! Gross! I don't want to hear about that."

"You asked," Nikki giggled. "You practically begged me to tell you."

"I know, but I didn't think—can we just change the subject, please?"

"I'll make you a deal." Nikki glanced at the clock once more. "Next time Mark asks you out, you go. Then I'll stop bugging you."

"Promise?" Amy said.

"Promise."

Amy took another sip of her soda. "It doesn't matter. He's not going to ask me out again. He must be sick of my cold shoulder routine by now."

"You never can tell."

As if on cue the phone rang. It was Mark. Amy gave Nikki a dirty look. Nikki returned a "who? me?" face.

"Did you hear there's a carnival out on Juncture Road?" Mark asked.

"Nikki mentioned something."

"Ask her, already," Amy heard Billy whisper to Mark on the other end.

Amy looked over at Nikki and mouthed, "You did this."

Nikki shook her head and mouthed back, "Not me."

"I was wondering," Mark continued, "would you like to go— tomorrow—with me?"

"Sounds fun." She paused. "You know, it would be fun too if Nikki and Billy came with us. Maybe you could call Billy and see." Nikki threw a pillow at Amy. Amy ducked and it caromed off the side of the bed, landing next to her.

There was a muffling sound on the phone as Mark covered the mouthpiece with his hands. Amy could have sworn she heard Mark say "she knows."

Mark spoke up. "Shouldn't be a problem. I'll see you tomorrow then —around two?"

"Two sounds perfect. Bye."

Amy hung up the phone. "You set me up." She pulled the pillow from the floor and started hitting Nikki. Nikki grabbed her pillow and the pillow fight was on.

"Worked pretty good, didn't it?" Nikki admitted.

Roaring engines and tires tearing up the roadway suddenly shattered the quiet darkness out on Juncture Road. Side by side, the two muscle cars gained speed. One would manage an inch lead, only to lose it seconds later.

"That piece of shit can't beat me," Snake told Zeek as he shifted his '68 Mustang into second gear. The car's body, like its owner, displayed the marks of a hard life. The red paint had several deep scratches and the metal had many small dents.

"Eddie's been workin' on it. Put in a bigger engine."

"Not big enough." Snake shifted again. His Mustang started to pull forward slightly, but Eddie's Camaro easily closed the gap. The two cars kept pace for about a half a mile, neck and neck all the way. The engines screamed out, the exhaust bellowed, but neither car proved to be the better.

When it seemed the race would end in a dead heat, up ahead, an unsuspecting station wagon turned onto the road. The driver, with no way of knowing about the vehicles zooming toward him, was barely halfway to the posted speed.

"You better ease up," Zeek nervously said, though the second the words left his lips, he knew they were wasted on Snake.

"And let Eddie win. Not on your life. I can pass him."

Zeek stared out the windshield at the glowing red taillights of the puttering auto. "You're gonna have to slow down." His foot pushed against the empty floorboard as a reflex.

With Eddie's Camaro to his immediate left, the drainage ditch to his right, Snake West knew he was beat. "Damn." He slammed on the brakes.

Eddie honked his victory.

Angry, Snake pulled up as close as possible to the station wagon. He blasted his horn. The brake lights flashed once and their bumpers touched. In a vain attempt to escape the wrath of Snake West, the bulky vehicle picked up speed.

"Who is that?" Snake asked.

"I think it's Clyde Burns."

"Asshole cost me fifty bucks. I'm gonna make him pay." Snake backed off a second, then changed lanes. He drove up, positioning his Mustang alongside the wagon.

"Yep, that's Clyde, all right," Zeek said, evilly waving at Clyde Burns, an elderly man, who, like so many of the townspeople, knew the dangers of angering Snake West and his friends.

"Watch this," Snake said, and swerved sharply into Clyde's lane, then as quickly steered clear.

Clyde sounded his horn, which caused both Snake and Zeek to laugh and holler obscenities out the window.

Snake veered into the lane again. This time, either by accident or design, sparks flew as the fenders collided. Clyde turned sharply away, causing his station wagon to crash into the ditch. Snake, again, blasted his horn, but this time in cruel triumph, while Zeek hung out the window waving and laughing.

Down the road, Snake and Zeek saw Eddie waiting off to the side. He and Barry were leaning against the Camaro. Snake pulled over and got out with Zeek right on his heels.

"That will be a cool fifty," Eddie said, holding out his hands.

"You can't count that," Snake yelled. "Damn old man Burns and his rolling piece of shit got in my way."

"Don't matter," Barry said, shaking his head. "Bet's a bet. Pay the man."

Snake pulled the bill from his pocket and slapped it in Eddie's hand.

"Hello General Grant." Eddie kissed the bill and shoved it away in his front shirt pocket.

Zeek took a step back, figuring there was going to be a fight.

Instead, "What the hell is going on here?" Snake asked, looking at the tents and wagons, the booths and rides.

"Some carnival," Barry said.

Snake let out a large grin. "Let's go have us a good ol' time."

"Not open," Zeek said.

"We'll see about that."

As the four approached, a man wearing a plaid shirt standing guard stopped them before they could gain access to the grounds.

"We're looking for some fun," Snake told him.

"We're not open. Come back tomorrow."

"I told you so," Zeek said.

"Shut up," Snake replied. "You must not be hearing me," he said to the carny worker. "We're looking for fun." Snake moved up nose-to-nose with the man, grabbed him by the shirt, and cocked his fist back.

Stepping from the shadow of the first tent, Lilith said, "Can I help you?"

Snake turned to his men and smiled, then turned back to Lilith. "You sure can, sweetheart." He released his hold on the carny. "We want to see a show. You have any strip shows? Preferably with you doin' the strippin'."

"I'm sure you were informed, we are not ready for the public quite yet."

"I told them." The guard seemed scared, but not of Snake or the others. "I told them right away. I did."

"You may leave," Lilith said to her worker. "I will deal with them."

"Yes, ma'am," he said as he hurried off. The guard looked back once at Lilith, but not at the men.

"Well, ain't we the lucky ones," Snake smirked. "She's goin' to entertain us all by herself." His eyes ran along the curves of Lilith's body. "My, my, you're a pretty little thing. You want to dance for us?"

The others let out catcalls.

"You've been told, the carnival is not ready." She stepped closer. "Come back tomorrow."

Zeek inched toward Snake and said, "You want we should take her for a ride?"

"Would you like that?" Snake asked the woman.

Lilith said nothing. Her hand shot up in front of her face. The sudden action made Zeek jump back a foot. "I said, come back tomorrow." In her hand were four red tickets. "But, please, take these with my compliments. They are good for any show. We have some fine shows."

Zeek looked at Snake, then at the woman.

"Take them. They are—free," she told the scrawny man.

Zeek stepped forward and yanked the tickets from the woman's fingers, then dashed back behind Snake.

"Mighty kind of you," Snake said, "but I want a show."

"Tomorrow."

"Now." Snake stepped closer to Lilith, but a sudden flashing light and blast of siren stopped him cold.

The squad car drove across the hard dirt and pulled up alongside Snake. Sheriff McNee emerged from the cruiser. "You have a problem here?" he asked.

"No, Sheriff," Snake said, "just sightseeing."

"Shut up," Jim said. "Any trouble, ma'am?"

"No, Sheriff McNee," Lilith said. "These men were about to leave."

"Yeah," Zeek added, "we're leaving. Come on Snake."

Snake grinned at Lilith, then he, Zeek, Eddie, and Barry started back to their cars.

"I'm afraid it's not that simple—Simon," the sheriff called out.

The others snickered.

"Don't call me that." Snake stared at his cohorts. The snickering stopped.

"Seems there was some trouble down by the Bently road turnoff. Clyde Burns was run into the ditch. You know anything about that, Simon?"

"I said, don't call me that."

"The vehicle I'm looking for," Jim continued, ignoring Simon's request, "is a red '68 Mustang."

"Has to be a couple of that make around these parts—it's a classic—very popular."

"But the one I'm looking for is bound to have several fresh scratches." Sheriff McNee started moving toward Snake's car. With his index finger, he signaled Snake to follow. "Like these." Jim shined his flashlight on the front right fender.

"Hell," Snake said, "I've had those for a couple of days now. Ain't that true, Zeek?"

"Sounds ab-bout right," Zeek stuttered. "A couple of days."

"Get in the cruiser, Simon." The sheriff motioned the man to the squad car.

"You can't take me in. Can he boys? I didn't do nothing."

"I think different." Jim put his hand lightly on his holster. "We can make this real messy if you want." Jim made sure to keep Zeek and the others in clear view. "Keep your hands in sight and move alongside the squad car."

"Happy to cooperate, Sheriff," Snake said. "You know me."

"Damn straight I do. Keep your hands away from your body. Start walking."

"What about my car?"

"Evidence. I'll call for a tow truck to pick it up."

"And us, Sheriff?" Zeek asked.

"Get goin'. You're lucky I don't haul all your asses in."

Jim put handcuffs on Snake, while still keeping an eye on Zeek and the others, making sure they didn't double back. After securing Snake's arms behind him, Jim frisked his prisoner. "What do we have here?" Jim said, pulling a switchblade from Snake's front pants pocket.

"Just a big ol' toothpick," Snake smirked.

"Try using dental floss from now on."

Keeping the knife, the lawman opened the cruiser's back door for his prisoner. "Careful not to hit your head," Jim said. "Be a shame to cause you any undo suffering."

Snake leaned in the car, butt first—his feet still touching the ground.

Jim thought of Allie crying yesterday. One good slam of the car door right now would make him feel real good.

Snake pulled his feet in. Sheriff McNee shut the door.

Jim went around to the still open driver's side and got in.

"You're just wasting your time, Sheriff. You won't have any witnesses. Who's going to testify against me?"

"We'll see."

Jim picked up the radio microphone with one hand while securing the switchblade in the glove box with the other. "Dispatch," he said into the mike.

"Yes, we will," Snake snickered.

"I read you, Sheriff," the radio voice crackled.

"Margie, call Ben Clemens. Tell him there's a job out here on Juncture road. Simon West's Mustang needs a tow to impound."

"Ten-four, Sheriff."

"Out," Jim McNee said. He leaned back in his seat and shifted the cruiser into gear.

"You're just wasting your time, Sheriff. Just wasting your time."

Jim spotted Lilith watching them from the carnival entrance. "Maybe," he told Simon, "but I'm the one going home tonight."

As he drove off, Jim watched Lilith following the squad car with her eyes. Even as he turned the car around one hundred and eighty degrees, using his rear view mirror, he saw the dark woman still staring as if she had been deprived of a prize rightly hers.

CHAPTER 6

T he sun hadn't yet broken the crest of the horizon when Johnny crept out of the sleeping trailer he shared with Calvin and two other guys. Calvin, in the lower bunk, kept mumbling in his sleep about some girl named Lolita. He would snicker, then snort, then snicker again. The noise kept waking Johnny out of an already restless sleep, and to a certain extent, it amazed him that the others weren't up as well.

As he stood in the morning darkness pondering all the bits and pieces of information he had gathered his first day on the job, Johnny came to the sad realization he had learned very little, if anything. He only confirmed what he already knew—that this was the carnival he and Becka had gone to that last night together. He remembered Lilith's face, which had been burnt into his brain during each long minute he rotted in jail. During that time, all he could think about was the carnival and the woman in black. He ran it over and over again in his mind. All the things he and Becka did. What they saw. Who they saw. Down to the littlest detail, even as far as the fixin's on his hot dog. He recalled Becka's beaming smile as he won a stuffed elephant at the ring toss booth. Calvin's booth. Though now, without his beard and with all the people playing his game that night, Calvin had no way of knowing him or suspecting what he really wanted. It had been a grand time, which led to him being branded a killer.

A sharp and sudden moan froze Johnny's thoughts. His entire body dropped down several inches and his head snapped from side to side trying to locate the eerie sound. Listening closely, he realized it wasn't a single moan, but several blending together in a chorus of pain. Johnny began moving away from the trailer. He cautiously took a few steps, stopped, then started off again, letting the wailing be his guide.

Finally, Johnny detected motion by a far tent—the source of the moaning. He stopped and stood perfectly still. Several people were walking in the small clearing next to the large tent, though it was much too dark to see any faces, only shapes and forms. It wasn't an orderly march as each person seemed to be going in their own direction.

As he stared through the blackness, the shapes he could make out had unusual, strange outlines. They bent and curled, stumped and slouched. Some were too twisted to be real. At that moment it became clear that these pitiful creatures were the performers from the freak show. Probably leaving their tent under the cover of night was their only sliver of freedom from prying eyes of those who would gawk and laugh at them.

Johnny squatted down low and in an almost duck walk fashion, he moved closer to the wandering group. Voices became stronger with each step, but still not enough to hear clearly. He stopped. He listened again. They weren't words really, more like garbled nonsense. And for a moment, Johnny thought he heard the sound of crying. He pressed his body to the ground, having doubts about it being wise to move any closer.

The freaks began swirling around the tent. The moans were replaced with low shrills. Then Johnny heard a voice loud and clear.

"Back!" the voice yelled. "Back into the tent." A loud crack ripped through the air. "I said back into the tent, all of you!" A second crack shot out.

Johnny recognized the sound that time. The sound of a hand striking flesh had an unmistakable sharpness to it. He remembered, from lunch, Thelma telling him about someone called Lucas who handled the freaks. Now he understood why she whispered. Even in the dark, he could see Lucas flinging his arms wildly, pushing and shoving the misshapens back. Even though Johnny could see no other details, two things about Lucas were apparent. First, he was a large man. And second, he was brutal.

Johnny waited until the field was clear before starting back to the sleeping trailers. Was this another dead end? There had to be more going on here than simply rides and games. Johnny decided he had to take a more direct approach to find his proof.

He quickly moved through the twilight as the sun began peeking its rays over the horizon to destroy the night. Soon the crew would awaken and he would prefer not having to explain to Calvin and the others where he was if they found his bunk empty.

As he hurried away from the clearing, Johnny was unaware of the eyes peering out from the tent, following his rapid retreat with immense interest.

～ ı ～

Jim McNee entered the sheriff's office and the sight of him in his street clothes surprised Deputy Roger Anderson, who sat at the desk doing the morning paperwork. When the deputy heard the door open he looked up and there was Jim, wearing a pair of blue jeans and a short sleeved button up shirt. Still, no matter his attire, the sheriff looked like a man who demanded respect. And respect he got.

"Weren't you spending today with your little girl?" Roger asked, letting his black pen drop to the desktop, which came to rest on a pillow of papers spread out on top of an open manila folder.

"I am. JoLean took her for an ice cream. I just heard from Jake Cantell that he saw Simon West roaming the streets." He walked over to the door leading to the lock-up area. He found only empty cells. He hoped Jake had been wrong. The open cell door told him differently.

"Sorry to say, he probably did." Roger leaned back in the chair—it creaked as it moved. "Clyde Burns called. He says he doesn't know who ran him off the road last night. Says he got a good look at the driver and it wasn't Snake."

"Is that so," Jim said, putting his hand where his gun normally would be. The empty feel of the cloth of his jeans made him flinch. For that split second he forgot he was off duty. "How did he know we had Simon at all? I haven't talk to him yet. You or Nate say anything?"

"Not me, Sheriff. And Nate's probably in bed by now. I relieved him at eight." Roger glanced at his watch. "A good five hours ago. Unless Nate ran into Clyde on his way home, but I doubt it, being the time and all."

"I doubt it too," Jim said. His eyes told Roger he already had the answer. "You can bet Zeek Dyler had a hand in this. Must have threatened Clyde. With Eddie and Barry along, it wouldn't have been too difficult."

"Probably right. But what can we do? If Clyde Burns doesn't want to press charges—"

"Nothing. For now." Jim looked at the desk. "Is that the paperwork on Simon West?"

"Almost three pages worth...so far." Roger could almost see the wheels turning in Jim's head. His expression, the way he stood, the sheriff had something in mind.

"Write down every word Clyde said to you. And the time, to the minute, when you released our buddy Simon." Jim thought another moment. "And don't mark it closed just yet. I'll go have a word with Clyde Burns personally. Who knows, we might be getting a few charges against Zeek Dyler and the others while we're at it."

"I'm on it, Sheriff."

The door opened again.

"Daddy," Allie cheerfully shouted. "Look, a double scoop chocolate." The small girl had a smear of chocolate ice cream on her chin. Jim pulled a tissue from the box on the desk and wiped his daughter's face clean.

She giggled and took another bite from her cone. Another smudge appeared.

"It's a losing battle," JoLean said, standing in the open doorway, holding out several used napkins. "I figure if we wait until she's done we'll have a fighting chance."

"Hi, JoLean," Roger said, rising to his feet.

"Sit down. This isn't a formal event. We just came in to see what was taking my workaholic brother-in-law." With her chestnut hair flowing free to her shoulders, a tanned complexion, and hazel eyes, JoLean seemed to glide across the floor even as she dumped the chocolate spotted napkins in the trash can situated at the side of the desk.

"A twenty-four hour job," Jim said. "A sheriff's got to keep on top of every little thing."

"Yeah," Roger said, "like filling out paperwork—life savin' stuff like that."

Jim's smile curled down.

"Just kidding," Roger said. "I'm finishing it now."

"Let's let the deputy here do his job." Jim looked at Roger. "Every word. Don't leave out a single thing." He took his daughter's hand and started to the door. "And Roger—try to spell all the words right." He smiled.

"Yes, Sheriff." Roger smiled back.

"Excuse me, ma'am," Nate White Moon said, suddenly appearing in the doorway the very moment JoLean stepped out. The two bumped, but not enough to do any harm.

"It was my fault. I didn't see you coming."

"What are you doing back?" Jim asked.

"Figured I'd put in a little O.T.," Nate told his friend and boss, but his face hinted that something was wrong.

"As long as you're here," Roger said, about to stand. "I'll run down to the diner for some lunch."

"Stay put," Jim told Roger, then turned his attention back to Nate. "Go home. Get some rest. You look beat."

"I'm okay," Nate said with a forced smile. "A guy likes to feel useful."

"You're not listening. I said—" Jim felt a tug on his arm.

"Daddy," Allie said, tugging again.

"Honey," JoLean stopped the child, "your father is speaking."

"Please," Nate told them, "don't let me keep you."

Jim glanced down at his daughter. She hung onto his large hand with both of hers. "We'll talk later," he said, pointing his finger at Nate.

After the trio left and the door was tightly shut, Roger asked Nate, "Mind if I run and get some food?"

"Knock yourself out."

Roger left his chair, picking up his hat in the same motion. "I tell ya. If it was me, I'd sure find anything else to do besides comin' into work."

"That's you, not me."

Roger adjusted his hat, but was careful not to mess his wavy brown hair more than could be helped. "For instance, right now Lizzy Mason is on duty over at the diner. Unlike you," he said matter-of-factly, "I see this as an opportunity. Slowly but surely, I'm wearing her down. It's only a matter of when and where. I've been wanting to jump her bones for a long time."

"Sounds like the same old song to me."

"I know what I'm talking about. I have it all under control." Roger headed for the door. "You want something?" he asked, purely a second thought.

"No, thanks."

Roger shrugged. "Your loss."

Nate sat alone in the sheriff's office. There in the quiet, he pondered his Uncle Samuel's words. Things seemed calm enough, but Samuel was never wrong. And that scared Nate.

Outside town limits, on Juncture Road, Amy and Mark, Nikki and Billy drove to the carnival in Billy's beat-up Dodge. Its cracked muffler roared, making conversation almost impossible, which gave Amy an excuse not to speak. She had promised herself to try and make the best of the situation, but still felt somewhat awkward. She didn't exactly feel forced into this date, knowing she could have always said no. But she knew Mark had more interest in her than she had in him. When he smiled her way, she would force a smile back.

Amy faced forward when Billy stopped his Dodge. They had arrived. At least three dozen cars were parked neatly in the field next to the gate with the banner spelling out in giant red letters: Lilith's Carnival.

As soon as the four teens jumped out of the car, they were bombarded with the sights, sounds, and smells of the carnival. The fragrance of hot dogs and popcorn. The squeals of delight and mumbling of many voices melding together. The gleaming chrome and sparkling music of the rides.

They walked toward the main entrance, passing the ticket booth where a thin man wearing a top hat and black bowtie sat watching them.

"Such a fine group of young people," the man said. "All ready for fun and adventure." His eyes studied each of their faces, then his glance returned to Nikki. "Step up to my window and get your tickets here," he told her. "Tickets for all the shows. We have fine shows. Just pick one. The choice is yours. It is always your choice."

Something in the man's eyes frightened Amy. "Let's get them later," she said. His thin beard and mustache obscured what seemed a cruel smile. "I'm starving, let's get some food first," Amy added.

"I want to see some shows," Nikki said.

Amy tugged at Mark's arm, who was more than willing to follow her lead.

"Wait," Nikki called out.

Billy grabbed his girlfriend's hand. "There's lots of other things to see first," he said, pulling Nikki through the gate.

"Come back when you wish," the ticket man said waving. "I've no doubt there's something in our carnival that will suit you."

Mere moments later, the door at the back of the booth opened. Instead of a thin man in a top hat, out stepped a man with large arms and a completely bald head. He watched the four teens venture farther into the carnival. He began to laugh.

CHAPTER 7

"Three rings for a dollar," Calvin Tyler bellowed from behind the counter at the Coke bottle ring toss booth. "Win a prize—three rings for a dollar."

"I'm goin' to take a break," Johnny said, after picking up the last set of missed throws from between the coke bottles.

"Got it covered," Calvin said, then continued with his banter. "Three rings for a dollar. Hey, buddy," he shouted to a young couple, "win your girlfriend a teddy bear. Only a dollar. What da ya say?"

Johnny looked back at Calvin and wondered how someone could live this kind of life day in and day out. Moving from town to town. Hustling people with games they had a slim chance of winning. He'd be glad when this was over. And for him it would be over one way or another. It was the "another" part that scared him.

He needed more answers, but working the booth straight for the past seven hours didn't give him a whole lot of opportunities. And the other carny folk were still pretty tight lipped. He knew he could eventually work himself into their confidence, but that would take time, something too precious to him right now. Everyone he'd met so far, except for Calvin, acted like he had dog crap on his shoe.

Still, Johnny knew he couldn't take the chance on bleeding Calvin any longer. He could see the suspicion building in his partner's eyes. Then it hit him—maybe there was at least one other person he could talk to. He made his way to the cotton candy wagon.

"Hi, Thelma," he said through the window. "Busy?"

"Can't say I am," she said, pushing back a loose strand of red hair. "Kinda been a slow one." The white apron around her ample stomach had a streak of pink where her body leaned up against the shiny vat while she spun the sweet sticky webs of sugar. "How you doin'?"

"Pretty good. Calvin and I've been moving 'em through."

"No doubt," she said, smiling. "The ring toss is a real money grabber. I worked that last year. It looks so simple." She chuckled and shook her head, which caused the fat on her face to jiggle.

"I just came by to apologize for yesterday at lunch," Johnny told her. "I wasn't the friendliest. You know, being the new guy and all."

"Don't sweat it. It's the same way for everybody on their first day."

"So you've been with this carnival a long time?"

"Heck no," Thelma said. "Just signed on last month."

"But you said you worked the rings last year."

"Did. Not with this outfit though. I was with a carnival down south. It went bust. I was lucky to get a call from Lilith. Told me she had work. Packed my bags and here I am. Same with a lot of the other guys. Some from my old troupe, some not, but for most all the same story. You too?"

"Oh, sort of…not really…I…I needed a job."

"We all do, honey. Want a wad of candy? Have plenty."

"Not hungry, but thanks anyway. Do you like working here? Lilith—she seems a little cold."

"You ain't just whistlin' Dixie. She's not like any other boss I've ever worked for. Usually the bosses are one of us, carnies that is. And it's like a family. All lookin' out for one another. But Lilith doesn't get too chummy with her workers. She probably has her reasons."

"Reasons?"

"For one thing, the high turn around rate. Especially with all the stops we make. We never stay more than four or five days in any one town—no matter the size or the amount of cash we pull in."

"I came through Ely. The folks there said the show was in and out fast. Sounded pretty good to me. Figured there might be a job available."

"You were right, weren't ya." Thelma got a puzzled look. "You trailed us from Ely. We were there over three weeks and four towns ago. Mighty slow on job hunting."

"Had a few problems with the local authorities, but I worked them out. Then I followed the interstate and—" He shrugged. "—here I am."

"You a trouble maker?"

"No, just had a run of bad luck."

"Too bad. I like trouble makers." She snorted.

"Glad to be out of there. The whole town seemed on edge."

"Wouldn't know," Thelma said. "Didn't see a whole lot of it."

"Guess they had some people go missing. During my *stay*, the local police kept going on about maybe there was a connection with this carnival. Some big uproar about a girl. Her father was an important judge or something like that."

"Yeah, I remember that," Thelma said. "A whole set of State Troopers came in searching—goin' through all the wagons and tents. You should have seen this one cop's face after finding the freaks." She cackled. "It was between shows and he didn't know what tent he was goin' in. He came out running. We all about died laughing when we saw he peed his pants." She cackled again.

Johnny let out the best fake laugh he could muster. "It couldn't have been that bad," he said, hoping to sound convincing as the misshapen forms of the pre-dawn replayed in his mind.

"You haven't seen the freaks yet, have you?"

"I really haven't had the time."

"You can wait. Believe me, you can wait. It's a tad bit spooky just being so close." She pointed with her eyes.

Johnny turned his head in response. "It's only a tent."

"It's not the tent—" Her words broke off. "See him," Thelma whispered.

From out a back canvas flap came a giant of a man. His overly wide shoulders, barrel chest, and huge arms were disproportionate to the rest of his body. And terminating his thick limbs were hands so large they looked as though they could crush stone with ease. His head was completely bald and seemed dwarfed being attached to such an immense upper body. But with each step he moved with a smooth, strangely flowing grace.

"Who is he?"

"Lucas. Lilith put him in charge of the freaks. You can see why."

Lucas suddenly turned his head toward the cotton candy wagon. Thelma let out a gasp, terror clearly showing on her face. Even from this distance, Johnny could see the cruel little smile on Lucas's lips as he disappeared back into the tent.

"That wasn't at all weird," Johnny said sarcastically. He remembered the hulking form herding the misshapes in the predawn darkness. And that voice. Only that bellowing chest could produce a voice like the one he heard thundering through the morning air. Without a doubt, this man Lucas controlled the freaks.

"He gives me the creeps," Thelma said. "Just that—the creeps."

Johnny feared his best lead was slipping away. He had to get her talking again. "So what happened with the police? Must have been pretty weird. They never found the girl, did they?"

"Not that I heard. But the day we moved on, it was all over the radio that the police arrested her boyfriend on suspicion of murder. And even then they still couldn't find a body. Don't know how it all turned out though." Thelma cocked her head to one side. "Why so interested?"

"Just wanna know what kind of place I signed up with."

"Is that all?" she questioned. "Nothin' more to it?"

"It's fair to say I can do without any unexpected visits from the law." That much was true enough, Johnny reasoned.

"You're not alone there, hun—half the guys here...."

Johnny, trying not to look too anxious, nodded and smiled.

"Listen," the woman said, "maybe after your shift, maybe we can—"

I asked for this, Johnny thought.

"—we can get together. You know, see if any sparks fly." Thelma laughed.

Johnny half wished she'd go back to being scared. "I'm working a double to closing—midnight."

"Don't it figure? I'm off in an hour. I got lucky and pulled only the early schedule."

"Maybe next time," Johnny said.

"Lookin' forward to it, hun." She winked at him.

"I should be heading back. Calvin's gonna be pissed at me."

"Calvin's really a pussycat. He gives you any trouble, you send him my way. I'll straighten him out."

Johnny faked a grin and started on his way. Not a total waste of time, but not what he was looking for either. The real answers had to be here somewhere. They had to be. It's his life on the line. He couldn't keep running. One of these days he was bound to make a wrong move.

So caught up in his thoughts, he didn't see the girl walk in front of him. They collided, spilling her soda over his right pants leg. The cold liquid penetrated the cotton fabric, causing him to jump back.

"Oh, God, I'm so sorry," a feminine voice cried out.

Johnny brushed off the small pieces of ice, along with the cold, sticky wet that couldn't soak into his already-saturated jeans. "No worries." He looked up and saw a girl holding another, but unspilled, soda, and a boy with two wrapped hot dogs in each hand. Johnny recognized her, but the boy—not a clue.

"Well, hello again," the girl said. "I bet you don't remember me. I checked you in at the motel. Seems you were right about there being a carnival in town."

Johnny smiled. "It's Amy, isn't it? Do you always pour your drink on a guy to get his attention?"

"I'm so sorry," she repeated.

"If you looked where you're going," Mark snapped.

"Mark!" Amy said. "It was an accident."

"No, he's right. I wasn't paying attention. Let me pay for your drink." Johnny reached in his pocket for a dollar.

"Please don't bother," Amy told him.

Johnny froze for a moment. Those green eyes. "I insist," he said, pulling out a bill. "I really want to."

Amy gently pushed back his hand, refusing to take the money.

After a brief pause. "All right then."

"What about your pants?"

"What about 'em?"

"You're soaked."

"He'll be fine, Amy," Mark told her. "Let's go."

"Yes, I'll be fine." Johnny parroted the words.

"You sure?" Amy asked.

"Not a problem."

"Let's go already," Mark said, taking Amy by the arm.

Amy looked over to Johnny. "Bye," she said.

"Have fun. Maybe I'll see you around. It's a small carnival."

Amy smiled and left with Mark. Johnny didn't miss her glancing back once as they walked away.

⤙ ⚬ ⤚

Fifteen minutes after Amy and Mark had returned to their friends with the food, Billy took charge and decided it was time for rides.

Loud screams came from the Tilt-A-Whirl. The lights blinked on and off as the base of the large machine spun clockwise and its small dome chairs spun faster and faster counter-clockwise. The force pushed the passengers tight against the padded backrests.

"Let's get in line," Billy said, grabbing Nikki's hand.

"We just ate," Nikki said.

"So?"

"If I throw up...."

"Just aim away from me," Billy laughed.

"We don't have to go on this," Mark told Amy, "if you don't want to."

"It looks fun. Let's go." The two got behind Nikki and Billy in line for the Tilt-A-Whirl.

As Amy sat down on the padded seat, she was high enough to see the ring toss booth again. She had a clear view of Johnny giving change to a very tall man, then handing him three brown wooden rings.

"You okay?" Mark asked.

"Me? I'm swell. Why?"

"You look a mile away. It's not too late to change your mind."

"Can we play some games after this?" Amy asked him.

"Sounds good to me." Mark shouted the question to Billy and Nikki in the next domed chair. Billy shouted back their agreement.

The motors under the ride began to hum and the backdrop of people began to move. After the first slow go-around, Amy saw the tall man leaving the booth and Johnny handing three rings to a woman with a little boy. Soon the vision of the carnival was a spinning blur. The chair spun faster and Amy felt herself being pushed back. Mark's shoulders pressed against hers. He said something, but Amy couldn't make it out as the air whizzed by her ear.

After the spinning slowed and finally stopped, Amy stood up. Her legs felt shaky and Mark was right there with a supporting hand, which she rejected. Instead, Amy took hold of the handrail that led to the promise of stable ground.

"That was fantastic," Billy said, coming off the small set of stairs, followed closely behind by Nikki. Even through her makeup, the girl's face looked drained.

"No, it wasn't," Nikki snapped, only now the color returning to her cheeks. "I need to sit down."

"You *were* sitting down," Billy said.

Nikki gave him a cold stare.

"How about those games now?" Amy asked.

"Anything but another ride," Nikki said, fanning her face in hopes to get more fresh air.

"I need another hot dog," Billy said. Nikki hit him in the arm. "Hey!? Oh, sorry."

"Can we just walk down the midway," Amy said, "and see what we can find?"

"Works for me," Mark said.

Nikki nodded and continued to fan her face.

Billy was still rubbing his arm. "That hurt."

All four strolled down the center of the carnival past the rides. Along both sides were a variety of games: basketball and hoops, darts and balloons, even one game where the object was to lift up a small plastic duck and read the number on the bottom. "Everyone's a winner," the barker cried out as a tiny girl pulled up a pink duck. And with the cheap prizes, it was no wonder.

"I'm still hungry," Billy said, this time moving faster than Nikki.

"Your stomach can wait," Amy said. "Let's play that one."

"Which one?"

Amy pointed to the ring toss.

"Too lame," Billy said. "You guys can play that one if you want. I saw a game of hoops. I can't lose." Billy sunk an air ball.

"Basketball, please," Nikki said. "Can we try something different?"

"After," Billy said, taking her hand.

Nikki pulled back. "Let's not split up," she said.

"Who's splitting up? We'll meet back here in fifteen minutes."

"Sounds like a plan to me," Mark said, grabbing his chance to be alone with Amy. "See you in fifteen."

Billy and Nikki walked away as Mark and Amy watched them go. They couldn't make out what Mark said, but Nikki punched him in the arm again.

"Feeling lucky?" Mark asked Amy.

"Don't know—yet."

"Well, I do. I'll win you a stuffed animal." As they approached the booth, Mark recognized Johnny. "Hey, isn't that the guy—"

"Oh. Yeah. I think it is."

Amy took a step ahead of Mark. She smiled at Johnny.

"Told you it's a small carnival," Johnny said.

"You were right, again," Amy replied.

"Six rings," Mark said coldly.

"Two bucks." Johnny handed him the small wooden hoops.

Mark handed two bills to Johnny, who slipped them into the pouch around his waist.

Mark threw the first ring, bouncing it off an empty Coke bottle six rows back.

"Your pants dry?" Amy asked.

"They're getting there."

Mark threw the second ring, producing a loud clank as it hit a glass neck, then ricocheted hard off a second bottle, and flew into the canvas wall of the booth.

"I'm so sorry," Amy said to Johnny, not paying attention to Mark's failed efforts.

"It's not like you did it on purpose."

Amy watched Mark throw the final four rings with the same accuracy of the first two.

"Darts are more my thing," Mark said, and took Amy by the arm.

"Bye," Amy said to Johnny as Mark hurried her away.

"Where you goin' champ?"

"I'm done."

"You don't want your prize?"

"What prize?"

"There's your ring." Johnny pointed to an edge row bottle.

"Not mine. I missed."

"Must have bounced on," Johnny told him. "I always clear the bottles before each player. It wasn't there before you started, so it has to be yours." Johnny turned to Amy and said, "Pick a prize."

"The teddy bear—the one with the cowboy hat."

"Excellent choice." Johnny took the bear off the shelf. "Good work, champ."

Amy smiled. She knew what Johnny had done.

The two teens walked away from the booth, but neither spoke. Then Billy's voice made them both turn.

"He cheated. He switched balls on me. I don't know when or how, but he did."

"Can't you just leave it be?" Nikki said.

"No. I won't. We're goin' back. I want to try again. And this time I'm goin' to watch that creep a lot more carefully."

"Troubles?" Amy asked, holding her prize.

"Billy's just mad because he lost."

"The guy cheated!"

"Nice bear," Nikki told Amy.

"I won it," Mark boasted.

"I'm goin' back," Billy said. "You coming?"

"I don't feel so good," Nikki said. "You better take me home."

"But—"

"Please, Billy." Nikki coughed.

"Okay, but we *are* coming back. And I'll show you he cheated."

"All right already," she said, "we'll come back, we'll come back, but please take me home now."

"You guys can stay, if you want," Billy said. "I can pick you up later."

"Nah, let's go," Amy said. "It wouldn't be as much fun without you two." She hoped she didn't hurt Mark's feelings, but agreeing to stay without Billy and Nikki would only send the wrong message. Besides, any attraction or ride she had missed could wait until next time. She glanced over to the ring toss booth. She would most definitely be coming back.

CHAPTER 8

On the far side of the carnival where the tents for the sideshows had been setup, Snake West and his cohorts pushed through the crowd. People who saw them coming moved out of the way. Others who did not were shoved aside.

"You got those tickets, Zeek," Snake ordered more than questioned.

"Right here." Zeek pulled the red slips from his shirt pocket. Snake grabbed one, followed by Barry, then Eddie.

"Let's see what we can find," Eddie said. "Maybe they really do have a strip show."

A line had formed in front of a red canvas tent. The sign overhead read: *The Great Tanin—Mentalist Extraordinaire: Knows all, tells all. The truth revealed to all who enter.*

"Let's go in here, Snake," Zeek said.

Snake scratched his unshaven face. "Sure, why not?"

The four men cut to the head of the line. No one offered a word of complaint or resistance. Snake handed the man at the rope gate his ticket, Zeek and the others trailed right behind him. "This better be good," Snake told Zeek.

"It will, it will. I saw one of these guys on TV. They know all kinds of things."

"It's all a trick," Barry said, slapping Zeek on the side of his head.

Zeek pushed Barry back.

"Please move along," the ticket man said. "Only a few minutes 'til the show starts."

"We're movin', we're movin'," Zeek said.

Inside the tent there were a dozen long benches. A skinny man directed the incoming crowd, making sure there would be enough seating for everyone. Snake plopped down dead center of the third row. When the thin man signaled to Snake to slide to the end, Snake returned a signal of his own. He held up his middle finger. Barry, Eddie, and Zeek all snickered then sat.

The tent filled quickly. A woman with two boys took the spot next to Snake. She looked at Snake, then put the smallest boy on her lap and slid over, leaving a gap between herself and the brutish man.

After the last patron sat, the tent lights dimmed. A female voice came over the two speakers on the sides of the canvas structure.

"Welcome," she said. "May we have total silence as the Great Tanin comes on stage."

"You sure can," Zeek yelled out, causing the people in front of him to jump in their seats. That caused Snake and Barry to bust out laughing— no one else in the crowd laughed.

"Silence please."

The curtain opened to darkness and to a shapeless figure. Then a spotlight shot a beam on stage. A man stood there in a pure white suit and white shoes. The shirt was buttonless, but the seam stayed closed. He wore a small turban on his head. Around his eyes was a pitch-black blindfold. The only item of color other than white.

"Nice hat," Eddie whispered to Zeek.

"Must use it as a towel after his show," Zeek said. The two snickered.

"Can I have silence please," the Great Tanin demanded.

Zeek and Eddie hushed.

"I feel the presence of a woman," Tanin started, "a woman who has heavy guilt—guilt over a child who has run away from home."

The crowd mumbled—heads turned back and forth across the rows.

"You wish to know if she is safe."

"Yes," a voice shouted. A frail woman with wild hair stood up. "Please tell me—do you know what has happened to my Cindy?"

"I do."

There was a long pause.

"Tell me, please."

"Can you face the truth?"

"Yes, I can." The woman's voice sounded unsure. "Please, tell me."

"Your Cindy is alive," Tanin said.

The woman's face eased.

"After a long, hard struggle, she has found happiness with a man she now calls husband. She has a child, a little girl. Her life is joyful. She is content."

"When will I see her again?" the woman asked.

"You can expect to see your daughter—never. It was your cruelty and neglect which caused her to leave you. You will never share in her happiness."

On the verge of tears, the woman sat down.

The room was silent except for Snake's snickers.

Other people had questions for Tanin. And for the most part, they were answers they didn't want to hear.

"Truth," Tanin said, "is a hard thing to bear. But it cannot be changed. You all live with the truth you yourself create and the consequences that follow."

"A pile of shit, if you ask me," Snake said. "You're a fake." He turned to the crowd. "I've seen his trick before. The blindfold's a fake. He can see us all just fine. He's watching you to see if he is guessing things right. He can tell by your expression if he's getting anywhere."

"You tell 'em, Snake," Zeek slapped his hands together in applause.

"Yep, I've seen it all before."

"Stand up, sir," Tanin said, almost in the tone of a dare. And Snake never turned down a dare. He stood.

"I have seen many men like you before," Tanin said.

"Oh, what kind is that?" Snake laughed, and bumped Zeek on the shoulder. "He's got me all figured out," he told Barry and Eddie.

"Now isn't that just amazing," Eddie said. "No wonder they call him 'Great.'" All four roared.

"You are a man who demands loyalty and admiration from others," Tanin said, "but truly never earns or deserves either. In your own mind you are a courageous man, but you hide behind others who do your bidding. You are a true coward."

The crowd gasped. Fearing Snake West's temper, which almost always turned to violence, some of the women, and a few men stood up and quickly exited the tent. Others, braver souls, sat back and enjoyed the events now unfolding.

Tanin moved across the stage to its very edge. "You bully to get what you want. And if faced with a true challenge you collapse under its weight. Shall I continue?"

Snickers erupted from those people who had stuck around. Many had been on the receiving side of Snake's bullying. They were loving the show.

"I'll give you a challenge," Snake shouted, with fists clenched tight at his side.

"Will you have your friends there help you? As you did two nights ago outside the local bar."

"Fuck you." Snake rushed forward. He knocked people out of his way and hurtled over the bench that stood between him and the stage. With one powerful leap he stood almost nose-to-nose with the blind-folded man.

Snake yanked the black sash off Tanin's face. He gasped. There were no eyes under the mask, just blank patches of flesh.

"You see, my friend, the truth is hard to bare. I was once like you—a coward, a liar."

"What kind of freak are you?" Snake said.

"One who doesn't need eyes to see the realities of life."

The crowd watched Snake step away from the man. They started laughing. Snake glanced over at Zeek and the others as they signaled him to hit the blind man. He did. Tanin toppled to the stage floor.

"The truth hurts sometimes, don't it?" Snake said.

"Stop," a voice yelled out.

"You again," Snake said. "We just keep runnin' into each other, don't we, pretty lady?" He jumped off the stage and stood only inches from Lilith. He gave her a hungry grin as he stared at her breasts.

The ticket man ran from the tent.

"You have quite a show here," Snake said, "but it would be a whole lot better if I fling that luscious body of yours up on stage and you do a strip tease for me and my boys."

Behind him, Zeek snorted out a laugh.

"Leave now and feel fortunate," Lilith said, glancing around at the crowd. "Feel very fortunate."

The ticket man returned with five other large men.

"Snake," Barry said.

"Shut up. Can't you see I'm talking to a lady."

Two more men entered the tent.

"We better do as she says, Snake."

"I say what we do." He turned and found himself surrounded.

"Come on, Snake," Zeek said. "There's too many."

Out matched in sheer numbers, Snake pushed Zeek away and stomped out of the tent. Zeek, Barry, and Eddie followed close behind.

"Make sure they find their way off the grounds," Lilith ordered.

The biggest man nodded then signaled for the others to follow as he trailed Snake West and his cronies out of the tent.

"Enjoy the rest of your evening," Lilith said to the few remaining onlookers. She made her way to the tent flap. Her men were doing as she directed though the expression on her face was almost one of anger and disappointment.

Snake shouted back to her. "This ain't over."

"I'm counting on it," she whispered. "I'm counting on it."

⌒⌒

With the end of a long day, night brought peace and quiet to Lilith's Carnival. Except for the wandering guard, the camp was still. Two hours earlier, the lights had been turned off, the rides shutdown, the food stored away. The workers had retreated to their trailers off in the field adjacent to the show tents, surrounded by no wind and a clear half-moon sky.

Broken whispers and scampering feet spoiled the silence, but not enough to call attention to the four men. Snake, Zeek, Barry, and Eddie had crept in from the road. All, except Snake, carried red metal gas cans filled to the cap. The plan was a simple one. To slip onto the carnival grounds and start three different fires. A single fire would be an easy matter to extinguish, so might two, but three fires at different locations, burning at the same time, would be next to impossible. Snake signaled to Barry to take the west side, Eddie the east, he and Zeek would take the tent of *The Great Tanin*. Snake thought that only fitting.

Barry Russell watched the others split-up. He hesitated for a moment, but his fear of Snake West and the reprisals for chickening out got his feet moving. Staying to the shadows, Barry kept a sharp ear open. He hadn't gone twenty feet when he heard footsteps. He froze, then ducked down against the back of the hot dog wagon.

A stout man holding a flashlight came up and shook the handle of the wagon, making sure it had been locked, after which he stood still for a moment.

Barry didn't dare breathe—didn't dare move. But his hand twitched slightly, shaking the gas can. It rumbled as the liquid sloshed inside. As gently as he could, Barry set the container on the hard ground and released his grip. Crouching halfway, while peering through the gaps between the boards that hid the wagon's wheel, he saw the security guard's shoe. A shot of adrenaline rushed through his body as Barry dropped to the ground, landing flat on his stomach—a beam of light came inches from his face. With his heart pounding, his lungs pressing hard against his rib cage, Barry had already resigned himself to the idea of bolting if found. Suddenly, the guard retrieved a half-filled popcorn bag from the ground and mumbled something about pigs. Barry gently exhaled as the man threw the trash in a nearby steel barrel.

When the light began drifting away, Barry retrieved the gasoline and decided it would be best to go in the exact opposite direction. The splashing of pouring liquid could give away his position and he didn't think he could stand another close call.

Barry hurried along until he reached the last gaming booth—a gun shoot with small painted animals that rotated on spinning wheels. He stepped into the narrow walk space between it and the next booth over, the milk bottle throw. Feeling secure from prying eyes, Barry twisted the cap off the gas can.

Vapors rose up, filling the air with a pungent, almost sweet, odor. He began pouring the gasoline onto the canvas walls of the two gaming booths, being careful not to get any on his pants or shoes. He continued stepping backward, drenching the cloth and wood frames, all the while making sure the path out was clear.

Coming out behind the gaming booths, Barry tossed the empty can aside before pulling a road flare from his back pocket. He peeled off the igniting cap and struck the white tip, which burst into a blinding red-orange light—the hard smell of burning sulfur caused his head to kick to one side. Barry took three steps back, making sure he was on dry ground and out of the way of the soon-to-be fireball—the second the flare hit the fuel, flames would explode upward and outward from the narrow passage.

Barry was about to lob the flare when something large and fast swooped down. Its giant wings beat against the night air. It grabbed his forearm with sharp dagger-like talons, easily penetrating flesh and muscle. Barry heard a loud crack. The pain shot up his arm to his shoulder—it was so intense it was numbing. Shock stopped him from crying out until he saw his hand, still grasping the flare, bloody and detached, laying on the ground.

His screams were cut short as more dagger talons buried themselves into his skull—effortlessly crushing bone and brain. What was left of Barry Russell fell to the ground.

The creature flew off and disappeared within the black sky.

"Shouldn't we have heard something by now, Snake?" Zeek whispered, his voice cracking. "Maybe they got caught. Let's get out of here."

"Shut up," Snake replied in the same hushed tone, "they didn't get caught. If anything, they probably ran off. And that's something we're not gonna do." Snake grabbed the gas can from Zeek and twisted off the cap.

"Wait." Zeek grabbed Snake's arm. The one with the namesake tattoo.

"What now, damn it?"

"I hear something," Zeek said, squinting his eyes trying to pierce the darkness.

"You didn't hear shit. You—"

"Look." Zeek pointed to the large tent.

"Well, I'll be damned." Snake saw Lilith push the flap of the tent aside and walk in. "This is gonna be even better than I reckoned." Snake recapped the gas can. "Come on," he told Zeek, "this is goin' to be sweet."

"Let's go home, Snake! It's not worth it."

"Maybe before," Snake snarled, "but it sure as hell is now." He looked at Zeek. "You can go, if you want, I'll just find you later. And we can talk over the whole thing. You and me, one-on-one like."

Zeek understood. "I'll stay with ya, Snake. I'm with ya all the way. I—"

"Shut up and get movin'." Snake started off toward the tent.

Zeek nodded and followed behind, looking once over his shoulder.

The two men kept to the side of the midway, blending in with the darkness. Snake made sure not to bang the can on anything and Zeek kept glancing back to make sure they weren't spotted. At the tent opening Snake put down the gasoline.

"You want me to dump it?" Zeek asked, and reached for the can.

Snake stopped him. "Not yet. We're going to have us some fun first."

Oh God, Zeek thought. "Whatever you say, Snake."

"Our lovely hostess is all alone. Right?"

"Suppose so." Zeek didn't like standing out in the open. Some of the sleeping trailers were in sight. If he could see them, they could see him.

"A pretty lady should have some male companionship."

"Not that Snake. Let's just burn a few tents and wagons. Like we planned."

"We will," Snake said with a sneer, "but pleasure before business."

"But what if—"

Snake grabbed him by the shirt. Zeek felt the pain of several chest hairs being yanked from his flesh in Snake's grip.

"I told you, you can leave," Snake said, "any time you want." The hot breath poured out on Zeek's face.

"No, Snake, I'm with you—really."

Snake released the scrawny man. "Good. Come on." He pushed the tent flap open and walked in.

As always, Zeek followed—being more afraid of Snake than anything that could be within. He took one more look back—all was clear. The closing flap hit him as he entered.

Inside Zeek found only a tar black void. If it weren't for the feeling of the hard dry ground below his feet, Zeek would have sworn he was floating in outer space.

"Snake? I can't see a thing. Where are you?"

"Are you stupid? I'm right in front of you. You almost knocked me down."

"Not me." Zeek felt a slight breeze hit his face. "Snake…? Snake…? That you?" He tried groping his way through the darkness. Something brushed past him. Something big. He spun around, then to the left, then right—only blackness surrounded him. Zeek stopped and stood perfectly still. His head bobbed from side-to-side. "Snake?" he whispered. "I can't see you." He waited for an answer. "Stop kidding around," Zeek pleaded, "this isn't funny. I can't see a damn thing. Where are you?"

Again a breeze rose up and with it, a foul smell. His fear of that place just became stronger than his fear of Snake West. Zeek took a step forward, his arms extended out as far as possible. He had only one plan, to walk until he found the wall of the tent. He would then feel his way along the canvas until he reached the opening. Not an ingenious plan, but for him it was good enough.

Zeek hadn't gone very far when a sharp edge scratched his left arm. "Damn you, Snake!" Grabbing his forearm, it felt wet and sticky. He was about to run when another pain struck him—a pain like four daggers ripping down the right side of his body. Before he could scream out, large, powerful hands held him on both sides of his rib cage and squeezed as if he were in a giant vise. His body convulsed as every rib snapped and a stream of blood poured from his mouth. In the darkness, Zeek Dyler dropped to the cold, hard ground.

"Where in the hell is that asshole?" Snake West said to himself. His eyes still unaccustomed to the darkness. "Chicken-ass Zeek." His leg smashed up against a metal railing. "Goddamn it," he said, rubbing the sore spot. Taking hold of the bar, he used it as a guide. After several minutes of roaming blind, he had almost forgotten why he had entered the tent. And his thoughts at this particular moment were keenly focused on how to get out.

A spotlight snapped on, drenching his body with a white beam. It stung his eyes, forcing them closed. "Who's that?" Snake shouted. He opened his eyes a crack, but had to shield them with his hand. A second spotlight came on. But this time lighting up the stage.

"Don't you know? You saw me enter the tent, Mr. West," a woman's voice said. "No, that's not right. Not West. You are called 'Snake.'"

"Yeah, so what." He managed to open his eyes a bit more and saw Lilith appear on the lit stage. Snake stumbled forward, but the burning light followed. With each step Snake took, the hot beam stayed on him.

"If your desire is to see a performance," Lilith continued, "I'm sorry, we're closed for the evening."

"You have it all wrong," he said. "There's gonna be a performance. You and me."

She laughed. "Just you? What about the others? Your friends?"

Snake realized for the first time he didn't have his usual backup.

"Tanin was right. You can't face a challenge by yourself."

"Turn down the fuckin' lights." Snake kicked over a bench, before running into a second. "I'll show you who's right." With one hand shielding his eyes and the other swinging in front of his body, Snake made his way close to the stage—and Lilith.

"Show me? No need. Tanin is always right—now." She moved across the stage. The spotlight followed her.

"I said, kill these fuckin' lights." Snake knocked over another bench.

Without as much as a whisper or a single movement from Lilith, the lights dimmed.

Snake lowered his hand from in front of his face.

"Is that better?" Lilith asked.

"It's just you and me now, lady."

"Come now, don't be silly. We are not alone." She pulled back the curtain.

Snake screamed.

Barry, Eddie, and Zeek hung against the wall behind the curtain. Snake recognized Eddie only by his clothes. His head had been completely twisted off. Barry wasn't much better—the top of his head was flattened, but his face was still recognizable. Zeek's chest was crushed with several blood covered ribs protruding out from his slashed shirt.

"Such worthless creatures," Lilith said, letting the curtain drop from her grasp. "Not worth my attention really. You on the other hand, you will fit my needs very well indeed."

Snake turned and ran—the light following him to the tent wall. He grabbed at the canvas, searching for the entrance. He found none. Snake tried to pull up on the heavy cloth, hoping to make his escape underneath, but it seemed bolted to the ground.

"You wanted to be with me," Lilith said, standing directly behind him. "Now here you are. And here you will stay."

"We'll see about that," Snake said, raising his fist. Before he could strike, a loud hiss came from his hand. His snake tattoo moved then rose up off his arm. The snake hissed again and wrapped itself around the man's forearm—squeezing tight with each coil.

It bit.

A burning pain flowed up to Simon West's shoulders. He dropped to one knee. The pain swiftly moved through his body, then down through his legs. His hands and fingers began to throb.

"I can't move my arms," Snake cried out.

"Arms?" Lilith said, her voice was cold and sharp.

Snake's flesh crackled and dried. His arms thinned and withered as if being sucked dry. He managed only a long shallow gasp as they finally crumbled to dust.

"What ar-r-e you doing to meee?" The words slurred as his tongue took on its new fork-like shape. Large scales formed on his face and his nose flattened to nothing. His body twisted and convulsed as it became a limbless, tapering, mound of flesh.

"Why...ssss...sssss?" was the last human word he spoke. His new tail whipped and slashed back and forth, hitting the canvas with loud slaps.

"They call you 'Snake', don't they?"

Lilith walked over and stroked her newest troupe member as he coiled up in the corner of the tent. A superb addition to the freak show. It had been a good first day. Lilith wondered how many more would be joining her carnival. After all, it's their choice. It is always their choice.

CHAPTER 9

"Was Billy mad that we had to leave so early?" Amy asked Nikki as they left their eight o'clock Biology class.

"I didn't ask," Nikki said. "It was his fault I got sick." She popped open her tan purse. "Hold this for me," Nikki told Amy in the same moment she handed off her textbook.

Amy wasn't ready and had to make a grabbing catch. "You were the most amazing shade of green," she said, cradling both hers and Nikki's book in her arms.

"When I got home I puked," Nikki said. "After that I didn't feel too bad." She pulled a compact from the leather bag. "So did Mark kiss you?"

"Nikki!" Amy almost dropped the books. She had to apologize to the boy she bumped into while regaining her composure.

"I wasn't asking if you two had sex," Nikki said, taking the small brush and applying pink rouge to her cheeks as they walked. "Just if he tried to kiss you. Simple question." Nikki snapped the compact case shut and tossed it back in her purse.

"Simple answer—no," Amy said. "And if he tried, I wouldn't have let him. He must of known that, and that's why he didn't bother." She handed Nicky back her textbook. "You said you'd drop the subject of Mark if I went out with him. I did, so drop it. He's not my type."

"I still don't get what you have against him. He's a nice guy."

"He *is* a nice guy and it's nothing against him personally. It's just the same old thing. I want something different."

"Good luck with that," Nikki told her. "There's nothing different in this school. Look around. All the guys dress the same, act the same, and do pretty much the same things. What can you do? It's a small town. There's nothing different to find."

"Maybe—maybe not." Amy smiled. She felt herself starting to blush and had to turn away from her friend. Her face grew warmer, which embarrassed her more, which turned her face still redder.

"What are you not telling me?" Nikki stopped and stepped in front of Amy waiting for an answer.

"How about outside of town?" Amy smirked. Her grin would tear her flesh if it stretched any farther.

"Huh? I don't—" Nikki's face and voice almost exploded with glee. She grabbed Amy by the arm and dragged her to the edge of the hall next to the wall, out of the way of school traffic. "You met someone at the carnival, didn't you!" Nikki glanced around, making sure she wouldn't be overheard. She acted as if it was big news—too big to share.

"Sort of...not really. Mark and I bumped into him. Well, I bumped into him. Literally. Dumped my coke on him."

"On purpose? Interesting way to meet a guy."

"No. That's more your style."

"Oh, really?" Nikki said. "Okay. Maybe. But I wouldn't put it past you."

"It was an accident," Amy insisted. "I was so embarrassed. And Mark seemed angry about the whole thing."

"Why didn't you tell me about this before now?"

"I have my reasons."

"Reasons? Don't hold back now. What's his name? Where's he from? Is he cute?"

"One, Johnny—Solom, I think. Two, I didn't ask. He's the guy who checked into the motel last Friday afternoon. And three, very cute."

"Let's go back there tonight. Maybe he'll be back too."

"Oh, he'll be there," Amy said with a most assured tone.

"Did you talk to him? Make plans? In front of Mark?"

"I talked to him, but it's not what you're thinking. He works there."

Nikki's eyes shot open. "You're not serious—he works at the carnival?"

"At the ring toss. Mark played while I talked."

"My God, Amy, the guys who work there are so gross!"

Amy quickly looked over her shoulder at the group of classmates only ten feet away. Luckily, none of them gave any indication of hearing Nikki's words. Amy took her friend and moved farther down the hall. "Keep it down," she whispered. "This is exactly why I didn't tell you. I knew you'd freak out."

"Are you crazy?" Nikki asked, still rather overcome by Amy's revelation. "He could be dangerous."

"Not him, he's different. He doesn't seem to fit in with the others. There's something about him. Something sort of sad."

"You should stay away from carny workers. All they want is money—or whatever else they can get."

"You're starting to sound like my mother," Amy said.

"You told her?" Nikki screeched as if she had just been told the world was about to end.

"And end up spending the rest of the week chained to my bed? Not likely."

Nikki gave out a small sigh. "You scared me with all that *mother* talk."

"And I mean it. You sound just like her."

"Now you're being mean. I will never sound like a mother—even when I am a mother. Mine's always on my back. I'm just concerned for you. Some of those carny workers look awful scary."

"Scary is definitely not a word to describe Johnny. And he doesn't act like a regular carny guy. You should have seen it. Mark lost the game, but Johnny told him he had won anyway. I saw him slip a ring on one of the bottles. He told Mark to pick a prize. You saw the teddy bear—Johnny handed it to me."

"I've got to see this guy for myself," Nikki said. "Let's go back tonight."

"Should we tell Billy?" Amy said.

"Tell me what?" Billy asked, coming up from behind. His words made both girls jump.

Nikki moved closer to her boyfriend. Touching his arm and batting her eyes, she said, "Amy and I want to go back to the carnival tonight."

"We can't. You forget? It's my pop's birthday. You know, the party. Remember the tool set I had to hide at your house?"

"Not a problem," Nikki said. "We can go after the party."

"It could go to ten, maybe even eleven," Billy said. "How about tomorrow instead?"

Nikki looked over at Amy, who nodded. "We'll go tomorrow then," Nikki said with a hint of disappointment.

"Great! I'll get another shot at the basketball shoot. This time I'll catch that cheating bastard."

"And we're going to see a sideshow too," Nikki said.

"If that's all settled…." Amy said.

Amy, Nikki, and Billy went off to their next class, confident in the plans they had just made, not knowing what evil hid in the tents and wagons of Lilith's carnival—an evil waiting for them.

~·~

Dora Lacwent tugged open the small refrigerator kept in the back corner of the teacher's lounge, and removed her brown bag lunch. She always looked forward to the quietness and solitude of the noontime hour. Dora never ate with the other teachers, preferring her own company.

"We went last night," Pamela Larson, the third grade teacher, told Principal Wright Dalson, both sitting at the table closest to the refrigerator. "My husband and I had a wonderful time. I haven't been to a real carnival in years. I'm thinking of bringing my third graders out for an afternoon. If that's allowable."

"It's a wonderful idea," Wright said, taking a bite of his sandwich. He swallowed. "You'll need to get the parental consent for each child."

"That shouldn't be a problem. What do you think, Dora?"

Dora stood up. With both hands, she held her bag tight in front of her body like a shield. She turned to her colleague and said: "I wish not to be included in such inconsequential matters. But let me tell you this —this school is an institution of learning, not of frolicking and carrying on."

Principal Dalson laughed. "You must see the benefit in some harmless fun for the students, Dora. We must encourage growth in the spirit of life as well as in knowledge for the mind."

"Fun in its proper time and place is one thing, Mr. Dalson. Serious studies have their place as well and it is here where those studies are to be given their full attention. Good afternoon." She took her lunch out the door and back to her classroom.

"She hasn't thawed in all these years," Wright remarked, and started to peel his banana.

Back in the isolation of her classroom, Dora took her seat behind her heavy gray steel desk and unloaded the contents of her bag, putting each item in what she saw as their proper place. Ham on wheat bread in front, orange up to the left, small carton of milk to the right. For an extra treat today she included three Oreo cookies tightly wrapped in cellophane—she put them next to the milk. After taking a small bite from her sandwich, Dora peered inside her bag for a napkin only to discover it was the one thing she had forgotten. And it was after opening her second drawer for a tissue, an ample substitute, she noticed the red ticket and note lying on the upper left corner of the desktop. She thought it was strange that she had missed seeing both items before sitting down.

Dora wiped her mouth with the tissue, then her fingertips. She moved the ticket aside and picked up the folded note. Reading it, it simply said: "Ticket good for any show."

She handled the red ticket with only thumb and forefinger—staring at the black print: "Admit one."

"Foolishness," Dora said, throwing both the note and ticket into the trashcan at the side of her desk, then she continued to nibble at her ham on wheat.

The children of Mrs. Larson's third grade class hurried back into the classroom. With one minute left before the lunch period ended, classes would resume for the day. Allie McNee brought her Bugs Bunny lunch box back to the cloakroom and placed it beneath her coat. As she came out, she heard: "Did your creepy dad shoot anybody today?"

"You shut up, Kenny West!" she immediately responded. "My dad's the best sheriff in the whole world."

"My Uncle Simon says he's a shithead," Kenny said from behind blond bangs and freckles, causing the other students to gasp, except for Kenny's best friend Brad Fisher—he laughed.

"I'm telling Mrs. Larson," little Mary Taylor said, her eyes almost bulging behind her thick plastic framed glasses.

"Be a tattletale," Kenny sneered. "I don't care."

"You're in trouble—you're in trouble," Mary sang out.

Allie tried to get back to her seat, but was stopped by Kenny.

"I bet your dad will try to put me in his stupid old jail."

"Don't be dumb, Kenny," she said, facing him. "He doesn't care if you say bad words."

"Doesn't matter. My uncle says he puts people in jail for spitting on the sidewalk."

Allie shook her head.

"Then he beats 'em with a nightstick," the boy added.

"He doesn't!"

"Your dad is a shithead," Kenny said. Brad laughed again.

"You stop saying that!"

"Shithead! Shithead!" Kenny pushed Allie, knocking her down. "Shithead, shithead."

Allie rose up, curled her soft delicate fingers into a tight little ball and slugged Kenny West hard in the stomach. The boy dropped to his knees. Now it was the other children who laughed. Though Allie didn't. She felt bad about what she had just done.

"Take your seats children," Mrs. Larson's voice boomed over the class. She stood in the doorway, holding a small stack of papers. The group broke up and she saw Kenny down on the floor. "Kenneth West, get to your feet."

"Allie hit me," he said.

Mrs. Larson's eyes almost doubled in size. "Who hit you?"

"Allie did," the boy said, pointing to his attacker.

"Is that true, Allie?" Mrs. Larson asked in a strangely quiet tone. "Did you hit Kenny?"

"Kenny started it," one child blurted out.

"He called Allie's father a bad thing," another added.

"Kenny said naughty words too," Mary Taylor tattled.

Kenny scowled at the girl.

"He said the poopy word," she added and stuck out her tongue at the boy.

"I see. Kenny take your seat."

Kenny got up, not hurt, and made his way to his desk. A couple of the children snickered as he passed them.

"Kenny got beaten up by a gir-r-rl," one boy squealed. "Kenny got beaten up by a gir-r-rl."

"Shut up," Kenny said, pushing at the boy's shoulder.

"That will be enough from all of you," Mrs. Larson said to regain order. "I had some good news for the class, but now I'm not sure if you deserve it. I talked to Principal Dalson." She walked to her desk and put down the papers. "As you all must have heard, our little town has been visited by a carnival. And I've asked Principal Dalson if we could go Friday afternoon as a treat."

All faces lit up, including both Kenny West and Allie McNee.

"But now, I may have to change my mind."

"Please, please," came from a few students.

"We'll be good," came from others.

"If you all promise to work hard the rest of the week—"

Some of the students seemed to be holding their breaths.

"—we can go."

"Yes, yes," the children called out.

Mrs. Larson smiled, taking up the stack of papers. "I need you to bring these permission slips home tonight." She gave a few to the first person of each row with instructions on passing them back. "Have your mother or father sign it. The trip is for Friday so this form has to be back on Thursday." She gave the last row the remainder of the stack. "If you don't return one, you can't go. Do you all understand?" She scanned the room. All children nodded.

⌁

At the carnival, Johnny had cleared the rings from the bottle platform. There hadn't been a winner all day. It amused Johnny somewhat to see how some people refused to give up—until they blew ten bucks or more. It all seemed so different from this side of the counter. He had played this game himself, lots of times, and thinking back he didn't fare much better than today's losers. It looks so easy. It was easy—for the carnival. People literally threw their money away. What did Thelma call it, "a real money grabber"? More like a real money stealer.

Johnny gave out a tiny chuckle, but stopped himself. He realized he was getting way too caught up in all of this. He had to keep a tighter focus, if he ever wanted his life back. He had to continue his search. And there couldn't be a better time. With the other workers trying to milk a buck and the sideshows doing a good business, Johnny was certain his next target would be empty.

"I'll be right back," he told Calvin. "Gonna get myself a hot dog or something."

"Maybe some cotton candy?" Calvin snickered.

"Not today." Johnny grinned. "Be back in ten. That a problem?"

"Nope." Calvin shrugged. "I can handle it."

After taking off his money apron, Johnny left the booth, and quickly got out of Calvin's sight. Then he slipped behind the dart throw. To his relief, the path was clear. No one should spot him moving behind the tents. He'd be out of view from anyone who could give him away.

The sun beat down on the back of Johnny's neck, but a chill ran through his body. His hand shook. Each quick step brought him closer to his objective. He wanted answers and had a pretty good idea where to look—Lilith's trailer.

Glancing back over his shoulder, Johnny almost tripped over a tent rope spiked to the ground. Pulling himself back at the last second, he let out a breath seeing the rope still taunt and motionless. He had to be very careful not to hit a support line. Any motion on the cords would send ripples through the canvas structure telegraphing his presence. At this point, he didn't need someone coming back to investigate.

Reaching the last tent, Johnny peeked around the corner.

The silver trailer stood alone, far away from the workers' accommodations. Johnny dashed the twenty feet using the trailer itself to hide his actions. He stopped under a back window, which was just out of reach for his height. A nearby log gave him the extra stature he needed to prop himself up and spy through the glass. To his disappointment, Johnny found the curtain drawn and he saw nothing except a swatch of white cloth.

Johnny returned the log to the same spot he found it and brushed away the indent in the dirt under the window making the area look undisturbed.

With only one alternative to see inside, Johnny went around front. Casually he took the two steps up and knocked on the door. No answer —he knocked again. A quick glance confirmed he was still unobserved. Johnny tried the handle. It turned easily and the door opened. After holding the door for a second and taking one more glance around, Johnny went in. He swiftly but gently pulled the door closed behind him.

The inside of the trailer was spotless, not a thing out of place. It took him only a moment to realize that there was nothing of personal value. A strange thing for a person who lived from town to town for what could be months at a time. There were no books, no plants, no pictures, nothing to show the personality of the owner. In fact there wasn't even a single piece of garbage, not as much as an empty bottle or can.

The bed was a mattress covered by only a spread, no sheets or pillow cases. The closet was also empty—lacking even a single scrap of clothing. At first Johnny thought in his hurry, he had entered the wrong trailer. That maybe he got himself turned around. But a peek out the window told him he was in the right place.

The only thing that seemed of use was the large chair he saw the woman sitting in during his first meeting with her. The whole trailer appeared to be a facade. A shield to cover the abnormal with the appearance of normalcy. Nothing here could help him.

Johnny cracked the door open enough to see out. The coast was clear. He slipped out as quickly as he could and started back the way he came.

He had just turned the corner of the trailer when he heard: "Hey, you."

Johnny's instincts kicked into high gear—he ran.

"Come back here," the voice yelled.

Johnny covered the distance with long, quick strides, then ducked along the side of the nearest tent. He waited a moment, then stepped into view of his pursuer. Timing it perfectly he was almost run over by the large roustabout.

"Look out!" the man said.

"What's going on?" Johnny asked innocently.

"Caught someone snooping around the boss's trailer. Didn't get a good look. You see anyone?"

"Yeah, I saw someone—a kid."

The roustabout scanned Johnny up and down. "What are you doing back here?"

"Just gonna take a whiz. That's all."

"If you see that kid again, give me a holler."

"You'll be the first person I tell." Johnny watched the big man move on before stepping out between the tents into the main walkway. He felt as if he was still being watched. It wasn't the roustabout—he would be halfway to the other side of the carnival by now. Then movement caught Johnny's eye. By the freak tent, someone or something in white disappeared behind the large flap.

CHAPTER 10

The bell rang, ending the school day. In almost perfect unison, the students pushed their chairs away from their desk. Screams and moans of metal legs against the wood floor drowned out the ringing. Not one student had finished Mrs. Lacwent's test early. No one ever did.

"Bring your papers up as you leave," the teacher said from behind her steel desk. "Make a neat pile. You will receive your grades tomorrow. I hope some of you fare far better than you did on your last examination."

Grumbles accompanied the students as they ushered themselves out of the classroom. A lone girl, however, was still at her desk, scrambling to finish one more question.

"Test time is over Miss Anderson. Please bring your paper up."

The girl signaled for a second more, but to no avail."

"Now, Miss Anderson."

Debbie rose from her desk and put the paper on top of the pile, but she did not let go. "Mrs. Lacwent, I know I didn't do very well." The girl kept the paper tight in her grip as if releasing it to the pile meant certain doom. "My father's been really sick and I'm the only one who can take care of him."

"That is no concern of mine."

"Since he's been ill, I haven't had a lot of time to study and—"

Dora glared at the girl. Her wrinkled eyes narrowed at what she heard as contempt. "Miss Anderson, my responsibility is to grade you on your work. Nothing else. You will receive the grade you deserve."

"Yes, but maybe I could have a make-up test or possibly some extra credit work. Anything, anything at all."

"Would that be fair to the others? The ones who didn't frolicked their time away."

"I wasn't frolicking. I told you—my father. I had to—"

"And I told you," Mrs. Lacwent snapped back, "that is none of my concern. Now if you don't mind." The elderly woman began to straighten the test papers, making sure none were placed upside-down.

On the edge of tears, Debbie ran from the room.

Dora didn't bother to look up as she straightened up the bundle. She pulled a fat rubber band from her top drawer. As she wrapped the band around the stack, it snapped, flying back toward her.

"For Heaven's sake!" The band landed in her lap. Dora took the useless rubber strip and reached over to her waste basket. There she saw the red ticket sitting on top of her discarded lunch bag. "Foolishness," she said, at the very idea of a carnival. "And a waste of time. That's all. A waste of precious time."

She stared at the ticket for over a minute before reaching down and retrieving the red slip from the trash. Good for any show, she remembered the note saying. She studied the ticket, studied the black printing: "Admit one." The paper felt strange in her hand and it provoked old memories of her childhood. Images she thought had died off decades ago. A time when she would laugh and play—before life became work—when she could still smile.

Dora was about to return the ticket to the rubbish pile, but instead she glanced up at the door, making sure she was unobserved. She took her purse from its usual spot in the bottom drawer of her desk. Snapping open the clasp, Dora threw the ticket inside.

～ ı ～

Mrs. Larson's third grade class hurried to put their books, paper, and pencils away before final bell. They left the room with cheerful chatter. Talk of going to the carnival was on all the children's lips.

Allie McNee started out the door, when her teacher's voice stopped her.

"Allie," Mrs. Larson said as she wiped the day's math problems from the black board, "can you stay for a moment."

"My father will be waiting for me," the little girl said, standing near the door with her head slumped downward.

"This will only take a minute. I'm sure he won't mind waiting a few moments more."

Mrs. Larson put the chalk soaked eraser on the thin metal ledge that ran across the bottom of the slate then faced one of her favorite students. The room had completely cleared out except for the single child and teacher. "You know it's wrong to hit others," Mrs. Larson told Allie as she took a step toward the girl.

"Yes, ma'am." Allie looked up at the teacher with slightly welled eyes.

Kneeling down, Mrs. Larson met Allie at her own level. She smiled. "Why did you hit Kenny?"

"I don't know." Allie stared down at the floor again.

"Did he say bad things to you? Is that why you hit him?"

Tears formed on the rim of Allie's eyes. "Yes," she squeaked out. A tear ran down her face. "He said mean lies about my daddy."

"It's okay, honey." Mrs. Larson gave the small girl a hug, then she met her gaze. "I just want you to understand that we don't hit people for the things they say."

"Even Kenny?"

"Even Kenny. You're a little lady. You just ignore him next time and then tell me. I'll make sure he stops."

Allie nodded.

Mrs. Larson reached in her dress pocket and pulled out an unused handkerchief. She wiped away the child's tears.

"Is everything all right?" a strong voice said from the open doorway.

Mrs. Larson stood up. "Oh, hello, Sheriff."

"When Allie didn't come out with the other kids, I worried something was wrong."

Standing there in full uniform with this particular look on his face, Pamela Larson understood, if only for a brief moment, what it must be like to face Jim McNee as a lawbreaker. The word "formidable" was not even close to the right word to describe Jim at that precise moment. "It's really nothing," the teacher said.

The big man stepped farther into the room. "Nothing? My girl doesn't cry for nothing. Do you, angel?" Jim stroked his daughter's hair.

"Allie could you please wait in the hall while I speak with your father?"

The little girl glanced up at him with sad eyes.

"We won't be long," Mrs. Larson said as Allie closed the door behind her.

"Now," Jim said, "explain to me why my daughter was crying."

"It seems she's having troubles with one of the other students."

"Kenny West?"

"You know?"

"Allie told me about him."

"I see."

"It's that uncle of his. Simon West. He's been feeding his anger of me to Kenny—"

"And," Mrs. Larson said, cutting him off, "Kenny's been directing it back to Allie."

"It's an easy bet."

"I plan to call Kenny's father about this situation tonight. Kenny has been getting in more trouble lately. And with what you've told me, the cause seems clear."

"There is no 'seems' about it. You call Dan West. He can straighten his boy out. But Simon West—he's mine."

The tone in the man's voice surprised the teacher. "I sympathize with your anger, but…. Sheriff, Simon West is not worth—"

"Don't you worry. I won't do anything outside the law. In a way, that might be exactly what Simon wants. He'd love me to lose my cool. But I'm not stupid."

Mrs. Larson grinned. "No, Sheriff, you're not."

Jim tipped his hat back a bit. He didn't really smile, but the expression on his face eased some. "I'd like to thank you for taking care of my daughter." He extended his hand.

"It's my job. And Allie's a special child. I only wish I could have done something before it came to blows."

Jim's jaw tightened. "Kenny hit my daughter!"

No," she grinned again. "She hit him. And from what I could see, she knocked him on his butt."

Jim's face turned red, but only with embarrassment. "Oh," was the only word he could find at that moment. The big man walked to the door and opened it. His daughter stood on the other side staring at the hall floor. "Thanks again," Jim said to Mrs. Larson. "You ready to go home?" he asked Allie.

"Yes, daddy," she whispered.

"Goodnight, Allie," Mrs. Larson called out from the classroom.

"Goodnight," the small girl said in return.

"Don't forget about your permission slip," the teacher added.

The walk to the car was a silent one. But before Jim opened the door to the squad car, he spoke. "Your teacher told me what happened."

"Am I going to be punished?" Her voice just above a breath.

"It all depends. Do you think you did something wrong?"

"I punched Kenny."

Jim wanted to break out laughing, but it would give his daughter the wrong message.

"If you truly understand what you did was wrong, young lady, I can't see how punishing you will make any difference." *And how could I punish her for defending her father?*

"I understand. I won't hit Kenny no more. I'll do what Mrs. Larson said to do. I'll ignore him."

"That's my girl." He opened the door for his daughter. She jumped in and for the first time since Jim saw her in the classroom, she smiled. He hurried around to the driver's side and got in. "What's this about a permission slip?"

Allie pulled the folded paper from her pocket. "The whole class gets to go to the carnival this Friday—the whole class. Can I go? Can I go?"

"Let me read your paper first, but it should be fine."

"Thank you, daddy." She wrapped her tiny arms around the big man's chest as best she could and hugged.

He brushed her hair with his empty palm. "You're very welcome, angel."

Jim made sure he spoke in only calm, gentle tones on the drive home. He didn't want Allie to think his anger was directed at her. He had never lied to his daughter and wouldn't now, but not wanting Allie to know the rage he harbored, he told her only that he had a quick errand to run. He let Allie decide who she would rather stay with while he was gone, her Aunt JoLean or Amy Evans. After a few moments Allie picked Amy. Jim hoped she would be available, not only because Allie picked her, but because being Monday JoLean worked till six at the bank. Jim couldn't wait that long—he had waited too long already.

The sheriff pulled the squad car into the Evan's driveway. Allie had the car open and was halfway to the front door before Jim stepped out his side. Amy was waiting on the stoop as if she had read Jim's mind on the drive over. After a minute of conversation, it was all settled.

Ten minutes later, Jim drove the cruiser to a second driveway. Fortunately, his two best bets for finding Snake West were in the same area. Being the closest, Dan West's home became the first stop. Snake's Mustang wasn't there, but maybe he could still get information to his last known whereabouts. Jim hustled up to the front door and rang the buzzer.

Dan West answered. "Hello Jim," he said. Except for his mustache, the family resemblance was striking. Seeing a likeness of Snake brought out Jim's anger all the more.

"Evening Dan. Can I have a word with you a moment?"

"Please," the man said, holding the door open. "Come on in."

"I'm not sure I have the time. What I have to say won't take too long."

"Jim, I heard what happened," Dan said, apparently knowing what was on the sheriff's mind. "Pamela Larson called me. I'm truly sorry."

"It's not you who needs to be sorry, Dan."

"Kenny's my boy. I have to take responsibility for the way he behaves."

"My trouble is with your brother. His car's gone. I'll take that to mean he's not here."

"He didn't bother coming home last night, but that's really nothing new. And I can tell you this, when he finally does show up, he'll be packing his bags. I'm sick of all his crap. He's been telling Kenny all that garbage behind my back." Dan shook his head.

Jim stood with a dead stare.

"He lost his job," Dan added, "which didn't surprise anyone, so I let him stay here 'til he got back on his feet. He's family, Jim. I used to trust him."

"I appreciate that, Dan. And I hold nothing against you, but I still want to have a few words with him myself. Do you know where he might be?"

"With his buddies, somewhere. You could try the Lucky Seven. God knows he always finds the money to get drunk."

"That's my next stop. I'll be seeing you Dan." Jim tipped his hat.

"Jim," Dan said, "You should know that I take this very seriously. Kenny will not act that way again. For starters, I'm not letting him go to the carnival with his class. Allie must've told you about the class trip."

"She did." The memory of his daughter's smile eased his rage somewhat. She had always had that effect on him, no matter how bad he felt.

"I've arranged with his teacher," Dan said, "to have Kenny spend the time in Wright Dalson's office copying out of the dictionary. When I was a kid, spending time in the Principal's office was always the worst punishment." He extended his hand to the sheriff. "If Kenny does anything like this again, please call me. And be assured, he will be dealt with."

Jim nodded once and shook the man's hand. "Evening," he said and returned to the cruiser, not as angry, but Simon wouldn't get off that easy.

On the drive over to the Lucky Seven Bar, Jim kept a sharp ear on the radio, not wanting to miss any calls that might be tied to Simon "Snake" West. It would be his greatest pleasure to lock him up. Jim fought back that thought. As sheriff, he represented the law and he couldn't use his position for his own ends. He only wanted to have a *friendly* chat with Simon. To set things right—so to speak—once and for all.

Jim pulled into the tavern's parking lot and scanned the dozen or so vehicles already there. In a rusted Pontiac Firebird on the farthest side he saw a topless woman grabbing for her shirt. A pair of male hands reached up and yanked her down out of sight.

Despite the distraction, Jim drove the squad car into the space in front of the main entrance—yellow diagonal lines crossed the blacktop. He knew he had to act quickly. Snake's Mustang could be in the back and Jim didn't want anyone to tip him off. It would only take one person looking out a window to warn his quarry.

The voices of the bar deadened as Sheriff McNee entered. A few heads turned his way, but then as quickly the patrons went back to their drinks and the voices started up again. He walked over to the bar. Nadine Caster had just finished pouring a draft beer and slid it across the counter to a man who changed seats when Jim came up behind him.

"I'm looking for Simon West," Jim told the bar owner.

"Haven't seen him at all today, Sheriff. Thank God." She grabbed a damp cloth and began wiping down the counter. "But then again," she added, "I started at two o'clock. He could have been here earlier." Nadine called to one of her waitresses and asked about Snake. She hadn't seen Snake West that day either.

"When's the last time you saw him?" Jim asked.

"Couple nights ago. Though, I wasn't working last night. One of the perks of being the boss." The woman chuckled, which quickly ended when she saw Jim did not share her amusement. "Justin was working last night. You want me to call him and ask about Snake?"

"No, don't trouble yourself."

"Sheriff?" Lloyd Benter said from farther down the bar. He had to stretch his neck over the counter top to be seen. "I saw Snake last night. He was at the carnival. Him and Zeek, Barry and Eddie. He broke up one of the shows."

Jim listened to the man's tale and in his mind predicted the outcome.

"It looked like he was going to kill the guy on stage. Then this lady showed up...."

"Tall, black hair?" the sheriff asked.

"That's her. A real looker too. She told him to leave. But you know Snake—I mean Simon. She had a few of her strong men throw them all out."

"Nadine, I changed my mind. Call Justin. Ask him if Simon and his buddies came back here. More importantly what time they left—the exact time if he knows it."

"Whatever you need, Sheriff."

"And ask what kind of mood Simon was in." Though Jim had a pretty good guess by what he had already heard.

"Think there's something wrong, Sheriff?" Lloyd asked.

"Not sure."

Nadine was gone almost three minutes. When she returned, she said: "Yep, Simon West was here all right. And in a real foul mood according to Justin. He was sweeping up glass for a half-hour after closing."

"When did Simon leave?"

"According to Justin, a little after one in the A.M."

"Thank you, Nadine. You've been a help."

"You want me to tell Snake you're looking for him?"

Jim glanced around the bar. "Don't bother. He'll hear it from someone before he's in next."

As Jim walked through the door a couple came in. He recognized the female as the topless woman in the Firebird. He smiled and tipped his hat. "Ma'am," he said.

She blushed, then slugged the guy standing next to her.

Sitting in the cruiser, Jim took off his hat and scratched his head. He picked up the radio mic. He held it for a minute before speaking. Something didn't quite add up.

"Sheriff to base." Jim released the button and his hand cramped up. It wasn't until then he realized how hard he had been squeezing.

"This is base," the woman's voice crackled.

"Margy, have there been any calls on Simon West within the past twenty-four hours?" He scratched his head again.

"Hold on, Sheriff, I'll check the radio logs."

After a minute of silence: "Nothing listed for Simon West."

"Anything on Zeek Dyler, Barry Russell, or Eddie Pratt?"

"Hold please—"

Jim straightened his mirror while he waited. He saw Dwayne Dunham come from the bar and stagger to his Chevy truck. Dwayne dropped his keys and bent down to retrieve them.

"Nothing there either, Sheriff. Nothing at all. Anything wrong?"

"Don't know—yet. Margy, we got an empty cell?"

"Got two, Sheriff."

The drunk managed to get into his vehicle and start the engine.

"I'll be bringing Dwayne Dunham in."

"10-4, Sheriff."

"Out," Jim said, as the pickup pulled forward and past the front of the cruiser.

Immediately, the sheriff started his own engine and turned on the roof flashers, stopping Dwayne twenty feet out of the driveway. Jim approached the truck with caution even though Dwayne had a rep of being a happy drunk.

"Hell, Sheriff, I thought you were inside," Dwayne said, rolling down his window.

"Was, but now I'm here. You should know better, Dwayne."

"I just meant to have one," he replied, then held out his hands for the cuffs.

Jim put Dwayne in the rear seat of the cruiser, then went over and locked up the man's Chevy and pocketed the keys. "I'll be seeing you soon enough, Snake," Jim said to himself, walking back to the squad car.

CHAPTER 11

Dora Lacwent stood at the main gate of Lilith's Carnival gawking at all the people and deciding if she should return home. She rarely left the borders of Arkham—though the carnival was only a short jaunt outside of town—it still was *outside* of town. As she tried to fathom what possessed her to come to this place, a group of teens passed her. She recognized one girl as the younger sister of Jeremy Fringmen, a student in her third hour. They both had the same bright red hair—the dim lighting overhead did nothing to reduce the color—and the same streak of laziness, Dora ventured a guess. The group laughed loudly. Dora couldn't escape overhearing them speak.

"It was fake," the girl said, holding a large stuffed Pink Panther under her arm. "It had to be."

"Looked pretty real to me," a boy said.

"God, you're so stupid! It had to be a mask or something."

"How about the body? All scaly and that tail. It sure seemed real enough when it moved."

The girl laughed. "You see things like that in the movies all the time. It's fake. There's no such thing as a snake-man." She laughed again and playfully hit the boy with the Pink Panther.

"Explain how…." The teens words faded the farther they walked away.

"Snake-man—poppycock." Dora was about to walk back to her car when—

"We have some fine shows," a small man in the ticket booth said. "Fine shows indeed."

"Excuse me," Dora said, looking down over her nose at the man. "Were you speaking to me?"

"All are shows are an adventure. Would you like a ticket?" He gave her a gentle grin.

Dora had her red ticket clutched in her hand. "I already have one." She held it out for the little man to see. "It's good here I believe."

The man gazed at the red slip of paper, then at Dora. He grinned again. "My, aren't you special. That ticket is good for any show—any show at all. Simply choose one. We have some fine shows."

"You already said that." She pulled the ticket back, holding it close to her body.

"And you must be a special person to receive such a ticket." He gazed at it a second time.

"This is all foolishness," Dora said.

"Then why come? You could have stayed in your quiet home —alone."

"That's most certainly none of your concern."

"You are right, madam. I'm but a humble ticket man. It is not my place. Please, please go in and—enjoy yourself. You will find something that will suit you. The choice is yours. It is always your choice."

Dora didn't respond. She stiffly marched through the entrance the same way she marched into her classroom each and every day. Many of the people she saw she knew—students from the many long years past. There were families and couples and groups of teens. No one spoke to her, but several gave her a glance of recognition.

She stayed on the main footpath, but stuck to one side. After walking up and down the midway, still tightly clinching the red ticket, she came upon a small tent with a simple white sign that read: "Stone Works." She entered. A tall, dark woman took Dora's ticket and said the show would be starting in a few minutes and instructed her to follow the narrow passage made by the curtains hanging from the ceiling. Dora walked briskly, she didn't like being there alone. Her nerves were eased somewhat when she heard the whispers of others up ahead. Turning a third corner, she felt as if she had walked quite a distance, but the tent didn't look very large from the outside. A carnival trick, she told herself.

The whispers stopped.

Passing through a final set of black satin curtains, the corridor opened to a display area. At first, Dora thought there were several people waiting, but as she approached, she saw that they were carved stone statues. Each in perfect detail, from the curl of hair to the teeth of their twisted grins.

"Welcome," a voice called out.

"Who's there?" Dora said in a very demanding tone. "Come out where I can see you!"

Lilith stepped from behind a curtain. "I did not mean to startle you, Dora Lacwent."

"How do you know my name?"

The raven-haired woman smiled. "There are no secrets here. I am Lilith. This is my carnival."

"A trick—like the whispers. A carnival trick. I'm not some silly adolescent."

"Shall we begin?" Lilith said, stepping up to the first statue.

Dora's eyes moved around the tent. "We're alone here. Shouldn't we wait for others?"

Lilith signaled for Dora to step closer. "Please, consider it a special showing for a special person."

"No sense wasting time, I suppose," Dora said, moving forward.

Lilith ran her finger down the stone cheek of the first statue. It was of a tall, handsome man. The details were exquisite, his suit, his watch, the pager attached to the stone belt. The work of a master craftsman. Lilith spoke: "This one depicts a man who was a doctor. A man promised in the care of others. A man promised to heal the sick. Instead, he cheated them, leached off their fears. Cut into their bodies for money." Lilith moved to the second statue. It appeared to be a large woman. "And this one, she abused all those under her care—the old and infirm. She would lock them in their rooms at night, leaving them to rot in their own filth. Again for the love of money."

"Only a sick mind would—" Dora began to say.

"It is *their* sickness," Lilith interjected, "portrayed here in stone." She moved to the third statue.

"Surely," Dora said, "you don't expect me to hear about all these sculptures. There are dozens."

Lilith ignored the teacher's words. "This man beat and tormented his own children. The figure next to him...his wife who knew of his abuse, but did nothing except turn a blind eye."

Dora was appalled but couldn't resist asking about the next piece, a statue of a small boy. The figure seemed to be pushing something away. His face frozen in a scream.

Lilith smiled. "This one is my favorite. The innocence of a child corrupted. He derived pleasure out of the torture of others. Small animals at first, a bird he would trap, poisoning a friend's cat, finally trapping a small neighbor girl down a well and returning several times to see if she had died. A process that took four days."

"I do not wish to continue," Dora snapped. "In fact, I wish to leave. Please show me the exit." Dora turned. "This show of yours sickens me."

"As your husband did. You were forced into a marriage you did not want. Forced into by your cherished father and mother. He was an older man, was he not? A much older man. A very rich man. You begged and pleaded with your parents, only to be answered by your father's backhand. He cursed at you for your disobedience."

"That's a lie. My parents loved me."

"As your mother said, as she helped you off the floor. Were you convinced by your mother's promises of riches after your betrothed's death, or convinced by your father's willingness to strike you again?"

"I won't listen anymore," Dora shouted, turning away. She moved to where she thought she had entered and pulled at the closed satin curtain.

"You need not answer," Lilith continued. "It does not matter. You married and each night your new husband would touch you in ways that repulsed you. Each night he would spill his seed within you. And each night you would pray he would die. No riches could be worth what you had to endure."

Dora had to fight back a scream. "How could you know...?" she said through a shudder. Her mouth became dry and with each word her tongue had to fight against the thick paste forming on the roof of her mouth. "Open this curtain! I demand to leave!" Her fingers clamped hard against her handbag and she felt the small muscles of her right hand cramping.

"Torturous months passed before you saw your mother's promises start to bear fruit. Your husband took sick. You watched him grow weaker...sicker. Each day his body seemed to be more and more eaten away. You rejoiced in the fact he was no longer able to come to your bed. The sickness lingered and you acted as a wife should, to care for him, to feed him, while each moment you wished he would hurry to his death.

Until finally, you heard him crying out to you. The end of your suffering was at hand. He called to you, but instead of going to him, you left the house—leaving him to die alone."

"It's not true." Again, Dora tugged at the black fabric. Its strength seemed unreal. "That's not what happened."

"You would be rich," Lilith said, smirking at Dora. "Or would you? On the day his will was read, you found he had left everything to your parents as per their agreement. That was the price for which they had sold their only daughter. It was on that day that all feelings, any feelings, you had died. The smallest trace of kindness or compassion snuffed out. You cared for nothing—your heart became as stone. As all the others here in my gallery."

The whispers started again.

"Foolishness," Dora gasped, having trouble catching her breath. "Nothing but foolishness."

"You hear the whispers of the past—the whispers of denied absolution—the whispers of redemption not given."

"It's a trick. You're using hidden speakers. You should be ashamed, trying to scare a person." Dora backed up into a statue. It hadn't been there before.

"Not a trick, Dora Lacwent, but a reward—your reward for a dead, unfeeling heart. Of feelings and emotions long extinguished."

"I'm going to report you to our sheriff. He'll close you down."

"Look closely at their faces—their pain-twisted faces. Faces of those who care for nothing but their own petty needs and lustful wants."

The whispers increased. The words blended and fused into a quagmire of sound.

"Look at the faces. See your own torment in them. But yours will be greater—for you care not even for yourself. Look at the faces," Lilith commanded.

Dora couldn't stop herself. Her gaze fell upon rows of silent shrieking mouths—of eyes squinting in anguish. Those eyes—they opened.

Dora screamed and backed away. Another statue at her back reached out for her, clutching her arm. She tried to run, fighting against the stone grip, but a sudden cramp stopped her—she couldn't bend her knee. Dora stared down as gray rock encrusted her legs and the pain rushed up to her arms—the weight of her hardened limbs hunched her forward. The agony continued throughout her body as her blood and flesh, bone and hair crackled. Her screaming stopped as her stilled tongue hung out past her frozen lips.

Outside the tent, a man and woman read the simple white sign: "Stone Works."

"How about this one?" the woman asked her husband.

"Honestly? It doesn't look very interesting. Besides, we should find the kids."

"It's an adventure, George. That's what's wrong with you, you never crave adventure."

"But the kids."

"Damn brats. All I want is a little excitement. Is that too much to ask? You go find them if you want. I'm going in."

"Ticket, please," Lilith said, reaching out for the woman's red ticket which read: "Admit one."

CHAPTER 12

L
ast call for breakfast had been made. Though most of the crew had eaten, the announcement gave the stragglers one final chance to eat. Johnny sprinted across the grounds from the sleeping trailer, while at the same time tucking in his shirt and latching up his belt. At the serving table, he was greeted by a single hard-boiled egg, two pieces of cold buttered toast, and a carton of milk floating in a steel tub of ice water.

Plunging his hand into the cold water helped to wipe away the final few cobwebs from his brain. It had taken him most of the night to fall asleep. Between his own restless thoughts and Calvin's babbling, it felt like the morning would never come.

Gathering up the final morsels of food and with tray in hand, Johnny set out for the closest table. Some were already being folded on steel hinges to be rolled aside. As he sat, he scanned the grounds, wondering where Calvin was. Getting the prize shelves restocked, Johnny figured. Yesterday, a couple of the other carnies complained that in the bigger carnivals they had a night crew to do that job. *It's better than being in jail*, Johnny almost said to his coworkers and was glad when he didn't.

Johnny tapped the egg against the tabletop and gently peeled back the shell. As he reached for the small containers of salt and pepper, a strange feeling made him glance up. Off to the side of one of the tents something didn't appear quite right. A piece of the canvas had torn free, but the colors were mismatched—white against olive-drab. After a short stare, he recognized the form as a body—a body wrapped from head to toe in a white shroud. The shape being half concealed by the tent and at that distance, it took Johnny a moment to realize he was being watched.

"You almost done?" a voice said sharply.

The abrupt words startled Johnny enough to shake him in his seat. "What?" he said, twisting his head to find Calvin slouching against the table. Johnny almost threw his lowly egg at the grungy man, but his hunger beat out the temptation.

"You almost done eating? There's work to do."

"Just started." Johnny took a bite from his egg, but barely chewed before swallowing. When the hot dog wagon opens he'd make sure to get himself a foot long.

"If you got out of the sack on time—"

Johnny wanted to tear into Calvin right then and there. *If you didn't keep me up half the night with your goddamn mumbling*, he wanted to say, but instead simply asked, "Calvin, who's that?"

"Who's what?"

Johnny's head spun back toward the tent. "Over there." Whoever it was in the white shroud had disappeared. "There was...I saw.... Skip it."

"Already have," Calvin said, scratching his head. "When you're done filling your pie hole, meet me down by the dart throw. I told those guys we'd give them a hand re-anchoring the support ropes."

"I shouldn't be too long," Johnny said before taking another bite of his egg—this time breaking into the yoke, which was still a touch warm.

As Calvin started off he told Johnny, "Watch out for Thelma. She's got the hots for you."

Once more Johnny turned his focus to the tent. Being somewhat tired, he wondered if he had just imagined the thing in white after all.

After eating, Johnny joined Calvin and the others. No one, not even Calvin, made any comment about his late arrival. Instead, someone threw a piece of rope in his hand and told him to attach one end to the main support pole, then tie off the other to the steel spike ten feet in front of the booth. Easy enough, Johnny supposed, only a real idiot could mess this up.

"Make sure them back ropes are secure," a husky bearded man yelled out, wiping his hands against an already stained tee shirt. "I don't need this damn roof crashing down on me." He glared at Calvin. "Like the last time."

"It was bad dirt," Calvin responded. "Too much sand. Stakes couldn't get enough hold."

The bearded man grumbled and stroked his chin before walking away.

"Man, that was a-half-dozen towns ago. I'll never hear the end of it. You finish here. I'm gonna check on the other side." Even as Calvin turned the corner of the booth, Johnny still heard him whining.

Then it happened again—that feeling. If asked he had no clue how, but he knew he was being watched. The only difference this time, he swore he heard his name being whispered.

He turned.

There, as before, all in white, a figure, half hid, stood watching him.

"Hello," Johnny called out, making sure not to sound too anxious. "I'd like to talk with you."

Before Johnny spoke another word, whoever—whatever—ducked into the closest tent.

Johnny quickly tied off the knot and rushed toward the canvas flap. It didn't cross his mind that he may be getting into something he'd surely regret. His mind blocked any thought of reason. Something instinctual drove him to follow, almost sensing answers would be found inside.

Without pausing, Johnny entered the tent—the grayness inside a sharp contrast to the bright sunny morning. For the first time he hesitated, but only to let his eyes become accustomed to the gloom. He listened for footsteps, for breathing, any sign to guide him, while he stood in the grayish void.

"Hello," he said. "Please. I won't hurt you." An eerie feeling draped over Johnny—the space within this tent seemed endless. He found he needed to summon his courage. "I only want to talk," he added with a cool voice.

"You sure?" a little man said, while striking a match.

The blast of light surprised Johnny and he stumbled back a single step. As he regained his balance, Johnny saw the little man lighting a cigar. The oversized stogy gave an almost comical appearance to the man's small stature.

"You sure you want to talk—talk here." The little man blew his smoke toward Johnny.

Johnny nodded. "I saw someone come in here." The smell of the cigar, more than the actual smoke, made Johnny cough.

"Then they probably belong here. Unlike you, pal." The small man tapped the ash off his cigar, at the same time putting his pack of matches back in his pocket, at the same time handing Johnny an unlit cigar. "Smoke?" he asked.

Johnny blinked hard as he spotted the third arm. The cigar smoke must be blurring his vision.

"You just don't belong here," the man said, scratching his head with a hand resting at the end of yet another limb.

Johnny held back his gasp as he realized that he had rushed headlong into the freak tent. Thelma's story of the cops back in Ely automatically replayed in his head, followed by the sound of her sharp cackle.

"You deaf, boy?" Hands three and four disappeared into the man's jacket pockets, while hand number two placed the cigar back between his lips. He sucked in, then released a white bellow of smoke. "Pop them eyes back in and start talking."

"I can hear just fine, sir," Johnny said.

"What's this 'sir' bullshit. The name's Rex. Not that that should really mean anything. It's just what they call me—now."

"I'm looking for someone," Johnny blurted out, his voice stronger than his stomach.

"No one here for you. Leave now—for your own good."

"Somebody's been spying on me all morning. And whoever it was ran in here. I want to know why."

"Why they're spying or why they're running? Make up your mind. Which is it?"

Before he could respond, something large caught the corner of Johnny's eye. He turned his head, and had to force himself to keep his mouth from dropping open.

"I see a pretty boy," a grossly obese woman said. She grinned and the rolls of her cheeks quivered with her giggle. Her arms were as wide and round as telephone poles. It didn't seem possible that her legs could support the weight and Johnny was shocked when she took a step toward him. "A very pretty boy."

"He would never satisfy your vast appetites, my dear Lulu," a skeleton thin man said through dried lips that stretched tight against his teeth. His dull eyes set deep in their sockets and at times, the openings appeared void of any tissue in the dim light.

"Can't a girl enjoy a snack now and then?" Lulu laughed, which sent ripples across the exterior of her body. Rex and the skeleton man joined in her amusement with guffaws of their own.

Johnny's eyes moved quickly around the tent as other voices added to the chorus of laughter. The twisted shadows he saw at early dawn were barely an indication of the misshapens that now surrounded him.

But not all the freaks were laughing. "Fools, all of you," a reptilian skinned man said through a long extended jaw and sharp crocodile teeth, "he's a spy for Lilith or Lucas." The freak looked up and down, examining Johnny with a close eye and shook a clawed hand. "Hell, he could *be* Lucas."

"Shut your mouth," Rex commanded through a puff of cigar smoke. "He's a normal. Plain and simple."

"How can you be so sure?" another freak said through boarlike tusks. "He sneaks in here and starts snooping around. If not a spy, then a thief."

"I'm not a thief," Johnny objected. "Or a spy. I told you—"

"Yeah, yeah," the scaled man said. "We all heard. You're looking for someone—blah, blah, blah."

"I won't say this again," Johnny yelled. "Someone was watching me." He moved forward while holding his courage, but froze when something wrapped around his arm. At first Johnny thought it was some kind of snake until he heard another man say, "Calm down." Where the cigar smoking little man had extra arms, this man's limbs barely fit the term. His arms tapered to long curving tentacles and the boneless flesh effortlessly wrapped around Johnny's elbow with a gentle strength that didn't seem possible.

"Calm down, friend." The tentacle gracefully slipped free. "Calm down all of you. He has done us no harm."

"He's here," the living skeleton said. "Isn't that enough? We should deal with him ourselves."

"Now who's the fool?" Rex asked. "You know the rules about normals. It is not for us to decide."

"Decide?" Johnny said. "Decide what?"

"Let him leave then," the hermaphrodite Zamrah said with a strange tone, as if two separate voices blended together. "Who knows. Maybe one day...." Its words died off with a strange smile.

"Leave this place," the tentacled man whispered to Johnny. "Today. Leave this place."

Rex tapped out his half-smoked cigar, then said, "If you don't mind the pun, I could use a hand up."

Gently wrapping his tapered arms around Rex's waist and shoulders, the man picked Rex off his stool. It wasn't until then that Johnny realized that Rex had no legs and what height he appeared to have, came from his perch. Both men, followed by the rest of the freaks, disappeared through the curtain that hid an inner chamber.

With no one remaining and his questions still unanswered, Johnny left the tent only to find himself greeted outside by a dozen or so of the other carnival workers. Their faces revealed both surprise and bewilderment that Johnny didn't come running out screaming at the top of his lungs. The grumblings of disappointment were surpassed by Calvin yelling, "Pay up! Pay up!"

Several of the workers cursed Calvin's luck as they slapped the bills in the scruffy man's dirt covered hand.

"Taking candy from a baby," Calvin said. "From a baby." He laughed, counting his money on his way over to Johnny. "Here you go, kid." He shoved two twenties in Johnny's shirt pocket and kept the rest for himself.

"What's that for?" Johnny asked.

"You did good—real good." Calvin spat on the ground. "I knew you had balls—real balls." He wiped the remaining spittle from his lips with his sleeve. "Those others said you'd be dropping shit bricks as you ran. But I knew better—I knew better."

"I didn't mean for anything like this to happen."

"Of course you didn't. Dean saw you mosey into the freak tent and I saw a way to make a fast couple of bucks."

"You bet on me?"

"For sure. Other guys have accidentally wandered into that particular tent and in less than a minute ran out screaming." Calvin laughed. "Dean took even less time." He put his arm on Johnny's shoulder. "When I heard you went in I had a hunch. A good hunch." Calvin displayed the fistful of bills. "And it paid off big."

"Great," Johnny said, knocking Calvin's hand off. "That's all I need. Those guys are going to hate me now for making them lose their money. They weren't exactly that fond of me to start with."

"Relax. Think of it as a rite of passage. They'll respect you now. Don't worry about it." Calvin chuckled. "Let's get back to work."

As Johnny made his way to the other side of the tent, a couple of the workers patted him on the back and commented what good sport it all had been. It seemed Calvin was right after all.

"You're a brave one," a woman said. Her words ironically startled Johnny.

"Not at the moment," he admitted. The woman had short brown hair cropped below her ears, brown eyes, smooth skin, and a tiny button nose. Johnny had never seen her before—he would have remembered. "You work here?"

"A fair assumption, I suppose," she said with an impish smile.

"We haven't met. I'm Johnny Solom." His manners kicking in on cue. He had always found it easy to be polite to pretty women.

"You're right. We haven't met, but I've seen you around." She looked him over from head to toe. "And stop being so modest. Not too many people can meet those freaks on their terms."

Johnny didn't like the tone her voice had just taken. "Just got my tents mixed up, that's all."

"You don't look like a man who is easily confused."

"Looks can be deceiving."

"Yes, they can," she said. Her smile all but disappeared. "What did you want in the freak tent?"

"I told you, just got my tents mixed up. Who are you?"

"An admirer," the woman said. "See you around." She swayed off, not once looking back.

"Why don't you just paint a bullseye on your back," Johnny said to himself. He knew by sundown the entire carnival would hear about his little adventure with the freak tent. Up to now he had been careful to keep a low profile—hopefully he could repair the damage. By what Calvin said, several others had done the exact same thing—sort of a club of fools—so maybe it wasn't really that bad.

After one of the straggling carnies laughed and slapped Johnny on the back, Johnny returned to his work helping out at the dart throw.

Back around another tent, out of sight, the pretty woman stopped. She stood motionless for a moment, then on silent command her delicate features began to twitch and contort. The brown hair pulled itself back on her head until nothing remained but bald skin. Her skull plates expanded, stretching the smooth flesh that hardened as it rested on the new frame. Her arms and hands, legs and feet almost doubled in size. The woman's tapered ribs and narrow waist also increased several inches in all directions, forming a huge barrel chest. The transformation was completed with a deep laugh. "See you around, Johnny," Lucas said.

CHAPTER 13

Deputy Roger Anderson, having placed a freshly poured cup of coffee on the desktop, took his seat behind a small stack of incident calls and began thumbing through them, some of which he had responded to personally.

By the lack of complaints, last night ended up to be a quiet one. The weekend would always produce calls in the double digits, but Monday nights usually had their share as well, making the small number of disturbances a pleasant surprise.

Now he had the boring, but necessary, task of filling out and filing the paperwork. He had two on-sight domestic calls, one broken window, one smashed mailbox. That was all. It almost didn't seem worth the time or the paper. But Roger knew the sheriff would think differently.

As the deputy dug through the desk drawers for a blank report form, the telephone rang. He hoped it would be Lizzy Mason calling from the diner, but glancing at his watch, he realized it was the start of the lunch hour and Harry, her boss, wouldn't give her a free moment to use the phone.

Roger took a quick sip from his cup before grabbing the handset as the phone rang a second time. "Sheriff's office, Deputy Anderson speaking." He leaned back in the chair, pinning the receiver between his ear and shoulder. "How may I assist you?"

"Hi, Roger. Wright Dalson calling."

"What can I do for you? Problems at the school?" Vandals jumped to Roger's mind, but that happened more in the springtime when some of the senior class got edgy on their final days. Leaving their mark on the back walls of the building was almost a tradition, which frequently ended with a bucket, soap, and a good stiff scrub brush.

"Not the school exactly." An uneasiness filled the man's voice. "It's one of our teachers, Dora Lacwent. She didn't show up for her classes today. I can't say I'm just a little concerned by her absence. It's not like her to miss a day of school."

"I remember," Roger said, "she didn't miss a day when I had her." *Though, I always wished she had.* Roger grinned.

"Every morning since I've been principal, each and every morning, Dora would come into the teacher's lounge. Like clockwork. 8:30. She'd put her lunch in the fridge and take a cup of coffee, then straight to her desk. Always the same. For the past thirteen years."

"But not today?" Roger asked.

"Not today," Wright confirmed. "We've tried to call her at home but got no answer." He paused. "She's not the easiest person to get along with, yet I can't help worrying. Would you mind sending someone out to her place?"

"Has anyone else tried going over. Maybe she's just not answering the phone."

"I sent one of our student teachers and she's here in my office right now. She said the house was dark. That's why I'm calling. We can't go barging into the woman's home. I don't have the authority, but perhaps—"

"Maybe she just left town and forgot to tell someone."

"Dora wouldn't be so irresponsible to do something like that. I'm afraid this is more serious than a simple excursion."

"All right," Roger said. As cold as Dora Lacwent could be, no one could ever call her irresponsible. "I'll send someone over to her place for a look-see."

"Thanks, Deputy. You can reach me here at school or at home later, if you need my help."

Roger heard the phone click on the other end. *A lot of trouble for one crotchety old woman,* he thought. He was about to stand, but instead picked up his coffee, finding it still hot enough for his liking. Roger imagined himself knocking at Dora Lacwent's door, her answering, and him getting chewed out for his trouble. He called out to Margy and told her to raise Nate on the radio.

Nate dropped his guard for a single moment and the kick landed square on his chest. The blow sent him flying backwards onto the mat.

"That's three," Jim said, extending his foam-padded hand to his friend and deputy, helping him to his feet. Jim wondered how many times he was going to have to knock Nate on his ass before the deputy would reveal what's been eating at him. "Try again," Jim added, adjusting his bright red foot gear. "And keep your elbows in more."

This time Jim threw a jab, reverse-punch, round-kick combination, one of the first combos Nate learned to block and counter during his Tae-Kwon-Do training with Jim. Not this time, however. As Nate picked himself off the mat again, Jim shook his head. "You're not concentrating."

"You got lucky, that's all."

Nate had a lot of pride. Pride that sometimes came at great cost—usually in flesh and blood—his own. During his initial patrol, with Jim showing him the ropes, a call came across the radio about a brawl at the Lucky Seven. The fights broke up about a second after Jim stepped through the front door, except for two bruisers in a back corner too busy with themselves to notice. When Nate stepped between them, the biggest one commenced by calling Nate "Red Man" followed by other colorful adjectives, and ended up taking a poke at the deputy. Being Nate's first night, Jim thought it best to step in. And it was at that point in time Nate White Moon's pride first revealed itself with the words: "I can handle this."

The guy outweighed Nate by an easy fifty pounds, but even after a bloody nose, bruised cheek, and cut lip, Nate managed to handcuff, then haul that bad boy to the squad car. "See I told you I could handle it," Jim remembered Nate saying as he wiped his blood on the sleeve of his torn jacket. Right then and there, Jim knew the raw material he had to work with.

In all the years of their friendship Jim had never seen Nate so distracted. However, the last couple of days Jim sensed something wrong and he wasn't buying the same tired excuses any longer.

"Let's have it," Jim said.

"Have what?" Nate replied, lifting his hands off his knees as he straightened-up.

"Fine, if you want me to kick your butt all over the mat, that's one thing. I'd be more than happy to oblige." Jim took no pleasure in speaking this way to Nate—he was a good deputy—possibly his best. "But, damn it, if you don't let out what's eating you, I'm gonna be forced to give you a week off."

"Suspend me?"

"In words of one syllable, yes. You're no good to me the way you are. And don't give me the 'what-way' crap." Jim put his hand on Nate's shoulder. "I'm your friend—talk to me."

"It's stupid," Nate reluctantly admitted.

"Stupid enough to let me bounce you up and down this room? Spit it out."

"I can't really explain. It's Samuel."

"He's sick?"

"Nothing like that. It's—" Nate's words died off.

"What then? Don't hold back now. Remember, a week off," Jim said, repeating his threat.

"He's acting strange. And before you say it, stranger than usual. He's been out in the desert for God knows how long. Not eating, probably not sleeping, he just sits in front of his fire."

"If you know all that, then you must have seen him—talked with him. Did he give you any reason?"

"You're kidding, right? My uncle, the tribe shaman, give a reason for anything? Sorry, not his way."

"Samuel does have a habit of tending toward the mysterious, but by the way you've been acting he must have said something."

"It's not what he said, more like how he said it. He spoke as if he expected to be dead soon."

Things were starting to become clear for Jim. After Nate's father died, Samuel practically raised him through his teenage years. Jim remembered Nate once saying that he had let Samuel down, though never volunteered any details, except for his greatest wish being to make it up to the old man. That was a few years back and he never made it his business to find out anything more. Nate had a right to his privacy, only now the strain appeared to engulf the man. "I'm sure Samuel will be around for many more years to come," Jim said. "But he's getting up there, you know how some people get when they think their end is drawing near. The idea affects them funny. They regret the time lost, of things they would change if they could do them all over again."

"Not Samuel. I've never seen or heard anything even slightly resembling self-pity. There's something else going on. I can feel it. And Jim, I'm scared."

Jim had his own doubts and worries about Allie so he could easily feel for Nate. Still, he never let his uncertainties overwhelm him enough to interfere with his responsibilities as the sheriff of Arkham. Though he would have to admit that each day, as of late, his uneasiness had grown in strength. However, that was something he would have to work out another time. His concern at this moment focused on his deputy, not himself.

"Family," Jim said, "is a blessing and also a burden. It's hard to detach yourself, but you can't let it interfere with your job. When you're out on patrol, you have to have all your wits about you. You can't afford to slip. The cost is just too high—your life."

"You're right. I know you're right. But I just...I just can't ignore Samuel, whatever the problem may be."

"I didn't say anything about ignoring your family or not having emotions. I only meant don't let your feelings consume you to the point where they affect your other duties."

Nate nodded and threw a punch at Jim, which he easily blocked. The two men continued their workout for the next thirty minutes, neither knowing of the evil that would soon challenge them both.

CHAPTER 14

"Finally," Nikki Bonn exclaimed, "here he comes." For the past twenty minutes the girls had been standing, waiting for Billy, next to Amy's car in the makeshift parking area in front of Lilith's Carnival. About ten minutes into the delay, Nikki told Amy to go in by herself. As excited as she was, Amy declined her friend's suggestion, saying she'd wait until Billy showed up.

"Sorry," Billy said, pushing down the lock and slamming the door. "I tried to get here as fast as possible. I had to convince my mother why I couldn't bring my little brother with me. I ended up bribing the little shit."

Amy thought of Benny—her own little bundle of sibling terror. "No problem," she said. "I get it."

The forced calmness on Amy's face made Nikki remark, "She won't admit it, but Amy's a little nervous. She's hoping to meet up with her dream man."

"Nikki!" Amy said, her eyes widening. "He's not my dream man."

"Who?" Billy asked. "You meeting Mark? You're too embarrassed to tell me I was right about him after all."

"It's not Mark," Nikki said.

"Who then?"

"You don't know him." Nikki pushed Billy along. "If we don't see you later," Nikki told Amy—then winked, "we'll understand."

"Always scheming, you two," Billy said, catching the not-so-discreet gesture.

"Never mind," Nikki replied, grabbing him by the arm and leading him away. Glancing back at Amy, Nikki smiled and said, "Good luck."

"Thanks," Amy said. "I'll need it," she added under her breath, suddenly becoming aware of the tight knot in her stomach.

"We're gonna see some shows this time," Amy heard Nikki tell Billy as they walked away. "And no rides—I mean it."

"Okay, okay, but after I play that cheater."

Amy let out a small chuckle and shook her head. "What a pair," she said aloud. Then it dawned on her—this was it—time to act. The knot in her stomach doubled in size as she made her way to the heart of the carnival. A couple of carnies called out to her to play their games—"a winner every time." One rude worker made a comment about her jeans. She didn't think they were that tight.

Unsure of the best approach, Amy watched Johnny working the Coke bottle ring toss booth for nearly fifteen minutes racking her brain for an opening line. She must have repeated the words "Hi," "Hello," and various other greetings fifty times all in different tones and inflections. And all a dismal failure. In what she deemed a bold move, Amy strolled by the booth, but ended up being too tense to look up long enough to know if Johnny had even seen her. After that botched attempt she considered getting right back in her car to go home and tomorrow simply tell Nikki that things didn't work out. In a roundabout way, that would be the truth.

Sure, go home. To what? The TV? A book? The prospects or lack of them gave Amy a renewed determination. Though she knew if she was going to meet up with Johnny, she had better do it before she completely and thoroughly surrendered to her loss of nerve. "I'll walk by one more time," Amy whispered to herself. "If he looks at me I'll go talk to him— if not I'll just leave—this is it." She took a deep breath. Her heart pounded. If this is what it's like for guys to ask a girl out then Amy understood why they sometimes went to outlandish lengths to get her attention instead of just asking.

After taking about ten steps, Amy casually turned toward the booth.

Johnny was gone.

A scruffy bearded man stood in his place collecting money from a small boy before handing back three rings, while the boy's mother gave the excited child words of encouragement. Amy's heart sank. She had blown her chance. She had waited too long. Amy walked across to the hot dog wagon, turned its corner, then stopped. She peeked back at the ring toss booth, hoping Johnny would reappear. Maybe he was out of sight, clearing the bottles or something.

"Hi," Amy heard come from behind her. She swallowed, recognizing the deep voice. Turning around, Amy saw Johnny standing barely three feet away.

"Enjoying yourself?" he asked.

"Yeah, sure…I was…about to get a hot dog." Amy could feel herself starting to blush and mentally told herself to stay calm.

"Me too. Let me get you one."

"No…I…."

Before Amy could finish her objections, Johnny put his face up to the small window. "Two, Burt," he said.

The potbellied man inside gave a thumbs up.

"Ketchup?" Johnny asked Amy.

"Hmmm?"

"Do you want ketchup on your hot dog?"

"Please."

"Add ketchup to both of those, will ya, Burt. Extra on mine."

"Coming up," came from the wagon.

Burt handed the hot dogs out the small window. Johnny took them and said his thanks. He handed one to Amy along with a couple of napkins.

"Let me pay you for this," she said.

"It's on me. One of the fringes of working for a carnival. Free food." Johnny took a bite. The meat was a tad on the salty side. "We're going to need something to drink to go along with these things. Burt, could we have a couple of cokes?"

Amy smiled and nodded her agreement.

"Size?" Burt asked.

"Let's splurge—large."

"It's your bladder," Burt said, and grabbed two large paper cups.

Johnny took another bite, chewed, swallowed, then said: "Well, you can't beat the price."

After getting their cokes, the two decided to find a bench to sit down. Amy hoped she wasn't getting in over her head, but told herself that things were going well. He seemed like a real nice guy. And his smile melted her insides. "Do you have to get back to work soon?" she asked.

"My shift's over. I've been working doubles for the past couple days."

He finished his hot dog and threw the wrapper into one of the large blue painted steel drums the carnival used for garbage cans.

"Sounds like you're getting a nice break," Amy said. "What do you do with your free time?" She fought back a cringe. *Why did I have to ask that?*

"Nothing too exciting," Johnny told her. "People watch mostly—or sleep. Really not much else to do."

"Not much to do?" Amy's voice revealed her surprise.

"It's like working in a candy store and you can eat as much as you want. After the first couple nights, it all gets rather boring."

"You haven't been here that long. This must not be your first carnival."

"My first—and hopefully my last."

"If you feel that way, why in Heaven did you join up?"

Amy caught a sudden change in Johnny's face. For a moment his smile disappeared and a hint of sadness rose in his eyes.

But as quickly as it came, it went. He smiled again, then said, "I had a bad case of wanderlust."

"You don't look old enough to get wanderlust."

"Twenty-three's plenty old. The call of the road knows no age." He added a dramatic flair to his voice.

"Well, it's just…."

"How old are you?" Johnny asked.

"Eighteen. That too old or too young?" Amy let out a tiny laugh. "Sorry, I couldn't help myself."

Johnny's laugh returned as well. "Something you want to see?" he asked.

"I've seen it." Amy didn't like the way that came out. "I mean, I've seen the carnival before."

"I remember." He tipped his now empty cup over.

She couldn't stop the blush this time.

"I got an idea," Amy said. "Have you been to town yet?"

"Not exactly, but maybe that's not such a good idea."

"Scared I'll try to take advantage of you?"

"No…I…."

"Besides, I should be the one who's scared. I've heard stories about carnival workers. Preying on young, sweet, innocent girls."

"I'm not really—I'm not your average carny worker."

"I know silly." She touched his hand, realized what she had done, then pulled away. It seemed so natural to be with him. "You don't seem like you belong here," she added.

"Where do I belong then?"

"I'm not sure, but not here." She tilted her head as their eyes locked.

"Come on, you're thinking of something."

"I see you going to college—maybe in art—or writing. You know, something creative. Something that takes imagination."

"You can tell all that about me by just looking?"

"It's more by the way you carry yourself." *And your sexy smile*, she said inside her head. She felt her heart almost skip a beat.

"Carry myself? What's that supposed to mean?"

"The way you move—that tone in your voice—it's hard to say exactly —there's just something. So how about it? Go into town? My car's parked by the main gate."

"Are you sure?"

"I am." She touched his hand again, but this time she didn't pull back. "It's a small place, but it will be a change of scenery for you."

"You're right, but I have seen some of it already."

"Which parts?"

"The bus station and the motel, of course, not to mention the strip of road between here and there."

"Oh, then you've already seen half," Amy said smiling. She stood up but didn't release his hand. For a moment she thought that Johnny wanted to let go. She loosened her grip, and their hands did slip slightly, but he tightened his hold.

As they walked to her car they continued to talk. She really felt comfortable with Johnny, but she detected a sadness in his voice. Most of the time it was well hidden, but on certain words, at certain times, it slipped out.

A mile or so down Juncture Road, Amy's car stalled. She managed to pull over to the side where she hit her hands on the top edge of the steering wheel.

"Great! Now what?" she said. "Always at the worst time."

"Relax," Johnny said, "I'll give it a look." He undid his seatbelt.

"I'm so embarrassed. I really need a new car."

"This one seems fine. Body's in good shape. The interior looks great."

"It just died. You must've noticed."

"I did. I figured that out when we stopped moving. Pop the hood and wait here."

She pulled the black handle lower left of the steering wheel. A large clang came as the hood released, popping up about an inch. "Don't worry. I won't move a muscle."

"You don't have to go to those extremes. Just turn 'er over when I give you the signal."

Johnny jumped out of the car, walked around front, and raised the hood. After a few minutes, Amy saw his hand, and only his hand, waving at her. Then she heard: "Try now."

She turned the key. The engine showed a spark of life, then died.

"Once more," Johnny called out, waving again.

She turned the key a second time. The engine finally started and remained running. Johnny slammed the hood. He raised his hands in victory and returned to the car.

"You got a rag or something?" he asked.

"Maybe behind my seat." Amy reached down and pulled back a torn old gray sweatshirt. "Here." She handed it to Johnny and watched as he wiped the black smudges from his fingertips.

"Your carburetor's dirty. You should look into having it cleaned. I managed to scrape off some of the gunk. It will last you for a while. You should also get your distributor cap checked. I saw a small crack. Plugs could be changed. When's the last time you had a tune-up?"

"I knew you weren't a carny worker. You know too much about cars."

"I bet half the guys at the carnival have fixed a car or two."

"But that quick?"

"You caught me. I used to be a mechanic—a while ago. Had to give it up though—doctor's orders."

"Funny man. Thanks all the same." She shifted into drive, but then back into park.

"Are we going to go, or stay here all night?" Johnny asked.

She looked at him. "Do you want to kiss me?"

"Excuse me?"

"I said, do you want to kiss me?"

"I...."

"If you don't want to—" She faced forward and was about to shift the car in gear again.

"No."

"No?" she responded.

"I mean, no I want to…I mean yes I want to." He leaned toward Amy, who, in turn, leaned toward him. They kissed.

"You still hungry? Or did that one hot dog fill you up?" she asked.

"Famished." He kissed her again.

"I mean for food."

"I understood the question."

"I know a great place to eat."

"Not that diner by the motel—I'd rather have another of Burt's hot dogs."

"Not the diner. My house."

"This sounds like a trap."

"A trap?"

"You tell me. I meet this very pretty girl. She asks me if I want to kiss her. Then asks me to go home with her." He smiled.

"The kiss was for fixing my car, and my parents are home." She raised her right hand. "No traps, promise."

The two drove off.

"Just one thing," Amy said. "You can't tell my parents you work at the carnival."

"With Arkham being so small, won't they wonder who I am?"

"I'll tell them you're one of Nikki's cousins visiting from out of town."

"At least the 'out of town' part is true."

"You were just kidding about thinking it was a trap, right?"

"Were you kidding about the kiss being for fixing your car?"

"I guess we both won't know for sure," Amy said.

"Guess not."

As they continued down the road, Johnny started questioning his decision. He wondered if getting involved with this girl was using his best judgment. He glanced over at Amy—she reminded him so much of Becka. He knew one slip up could lead to disaster. Before he could give it another thought the car stopped.

"Here we are," Amy said, shifting into park.

"Nice place," Johnny said. Seeing the rambler made him long for a return to a normal life. It called back all the dreams and plans he and Becka had together, the split level house including the standard white picket fence, two children—one boy, one girl, even one golden retriever, all of it so perfect and now all of it gone. He promised himself he would find out why and most importantly who—who did this to him—who destroyed his life.

"Amy," Allie shouted with glee as she dashed across the yard after seeing her friend step out of the car. The little girl didn't notice the guy on the other side.

"Hi, Allie," Amy responded, kneeling down. The child jumped in Amy's arms and gave her a hug. "Whatcha been doing?" Amy asked.

"Me and dad just came back from Aunt JoLean's." As Amy stood up, Allie took her by the hand and tugged. "Come over and play with me."

"I'm sorry, Allie. I can't today. I have a guest." Amy smiled at Johnny.

Allie finally noticed the strange man. She took a step back.

"Say hello to my friend Johnny," Amy told her.

"Hello," Allie whispered.

"Maybe, I'll come over tomorrow. Okay?"

Allie nodded.

"There you are," Jim McNee called out. The large man followed the same route his daughter took. "Are you bothering Amy, young lady?"

"Of course not," Amy insisted. "I love seeing her every chance I get."

Unlike his daughter, Jim noticed Johnny right away.

"Taking a day off, Sheriff?" Amy asked.

Sheriff! Johnny felt the blood drain from his face. The urge to run swept over him, but at this point that would definitely be the wrong move. He forced himself to remain calm. Even the slightest twitch of nervousness could do him in.

"Only the afternoon. Picked Allie up from school and the rest of the day was ours."

Johnny saw the sheriff's car in the driveway. How could he have been so stupid?

Amy glanced over at Johnny. "Oh, I'm sorry. This is Sheriff McNee," she said, then waved Johnny to her side. "This is Johnny Solom."

The two men shook hands.

"You look familiar," Jim said. "Have we met before?"

"Doubtful. Haven't been in town that long."

"At the carnival. Mayor Fallon and I were out there day before last."

Amy glanced at the front door. Luckily, this small group of people hadn't attracted her parents—yet.

"Oh, yeah. I remember," Johnny said through a fake smile. "You looked a lot different in your sheriff's suit."

"You been with the carnival long?" Jim asked. It wasn't just the day before last. He had seen this man's face before, but where?

"For a while now. It's my second season. Would that be considered long?"

"Maybe for some." Jim looked down at his daughter. "We should be going now Angel."

"Can they come over to our house?" Allie asked with a tremendous smile.

"I'm sure these two have other plans."

"I'll see you tomorrow instead," Amy said.

Allie nodded once more.

"Bye, Sheriff," Amy said.

"You two have a pleasant evening," Jim responded.

"We'll try," Johnny returned.

Jim and Allie walked back to their front door. Before Jim entered the house, he gave Johnny one more glance.

Amy, mistaking the sheriff's interest, waved. "We can count that as practice," she said.

"Practice? For what?"

"For my parents. Remember what I told you—you're Nikki's cousin."

"How well is that going to hold up if your parents caught any of what just happened?"

"We're safe enough. If they heard anything they would've been out here by now."

⌒◝ ι ◜⌒

Guarded by the stone monoliths, Samuel Skyhawk had not moved from his seated position on the hard desert floor for the past few hours. That is, his body hadn't moved—his mind soared free. The sun finished its daily descent and the hot desert air pushed gently against the old Indian's face. A small fire made mostly of wood embers and covered with slow burning herbs produced a heavy, sweet smoke. Released from the confines of his mortal body, Samuel walked in another world.

In the far corners of this astral plane, with his spirit cougar at his side, Samuel heard the faint echo of tormented screams. High above, an eagle circled before landing on his outstretched arm. The bird let out a single caw and returned to its flight. The large cat ran ahead. Samuel followed the animals and with each mental step, the shrieks cut deeper into his soul with their power. He approached a large stone wall, and as he stared at the source of the wailing, faces of agony emerged from the hard, flat surface, crying out for help. But all he had to give was his pity.

With great speed and out of nowhere came a bolt of darkness, striking the shaman. He fell to his knees. Shaking off the pain, he called out for his attacker to face him, not to hide in the shadows. There was an evil laugh and a large winged beast swooped down on the old man. The faces of the rock wall screamed and retreated, leaving only an empty bluff.

The creature bared down once more. Samuel rose to his feet as the laughter continued with each heavy beat of wing. Standing, as if to meet his final destiny, he waited. The darkness covered the old man, but this time there was a blinding white flash and Samuel found himself back on the desert floor. The vision had ended.

CHAPTER 15

Back at the carnival, after leaving Amy, Billy and Nikki strolled hand-in-hand. Nikki hoped her friend would be happy, but she still worried. She knew Amy was a good judge of character—still Johnny was a roustabout. During their wait she made Amy promise to give her a full report tomorrow before class. Now, however, it was a time to spend with Billy. She gently squeezed his fingers.

"We're gonna see some shows this time," Nikki told Billy as they walked down the midway. "And no rides—I mean it." The thought of the Tilt-A-Whirl made Nikki's stomach flip-flop.

"Okay, okay, but after I play that cheater."

"Can't you just drop it?"

"I can't and I won't," Billy insisted. "He laughed in my face—'better luck next time sonny boy,' he said. I'll show him better luck."

The couple walked to the end of the midway—to the second booth from the end, between the dart throw and the squirt gun races—the basketball shoot.

"Let's get this over with," Nikki conceded.

"Not yet," Billy said, seeing the man behind the counter. "It's not the guy. It has to be the same guy."

"What's the difference?"

"The difference is, it's not him—he's not the one who cheated—I want to play the same guy who cheated me."

"Fine," Nikki snapped, "now what? We stand around waiting?"

"We'll come back later. Let's go to one of those sideshows you been aching to see. Anyone you want. Just name it."

Nikki looked around at the tents, at the colored posters and signs. Then she pointed. "That one," she said, her anger gone.

"You sure? The freak show?"

"Yep, that one."

"You know, you have a real twisted side."

Nikki giggled.

At the ticket booth, Billy happened to mention the pushy old man at the main gate. The woman behind the glass stared at him in confusion. She didn't know anything about an old man. He gave a brief description, but the woman still shook her head.

Billy bought the tickets for the freak show and figured it would take about thirty minutes to see the attraction and grab some food. Thirty minutes would be long enough to wait before checking back for his *friend* at the basketball shoot. He handed Nikki one ticket. "Lead the way," he told her.

"Ticket, please," the man at the rope gate said to the first person in line. "Thank you. Enjoy the show." He handed back the stub. It was the same for the ten people waiting in front of Billy and Nikki, except for a mother with her small boy.

"Sorry, madam. The law prohibits anyone under seventeen from going inside."

The lady had to pull the child away kicking and screaming.

"Like an R-rated movie, huh?" Billy said, handing the man his ticket.

"No. It's worse." He took the ticket and handed Billy back one half. "Enjoy the show."

Inside, the crowd settled along wooden benches. The flaps of the tent were closed, and a beam shot down from a spot light mounted on the center support pole. A raven-haired woman stood on the stage in front of a drab red curtain. Billy's eyes widened. She was the one handing out the flyers. He grinned only moments before feeling the sharp pain of Nikki slugging him in the arm.

"I know what you're thinking. Knock it off."

"You can read minds now?" Billy asked.

"Not your mind…the stupid expression on your face."

Billy rubbed his arm. "Do you have to hit so hard?"

The woman on stage began to speak. "I am Lilith. Welcome to my carnival." She wore a long black robe that matched the blackness of her hair. The fabric shimmered in the spotlight and the border had strands of gold embroidered trim. "It is here and only here where you will see true abnormalities of man and nature."

The crowd murmured.

Billy fought back a chuckle, but a squeak slipped out. Nikki gave him an elbow to the ribs.

"Be assured," Lilith continued, "the aberrations you are about to see have not been fabricated or counterfeited in anyway. These—creatures—are real."

At this point the spotlight moved off the woman and onto the curtain. "Behold Zamrah, half male—half female. Both elements together in a single body—forever." Lilith's voice continued speaking, but it seemed to come from all around.

"Nice sound system," Billy commented.

The curtain opened. A being stood in a tattered white cotton shirt and a pair of baggy pants. Its hair had been grown out long blonde on one half of its head, the other side short brown. "In this being is the essence of both sexes." The shirt of the person on stage slipped down to its waist, revealing on the right side a hair covered male pectoral muscle and on the left a large firm female breast. An old man next to Billy gasped at the sight. The curtain closed. From his front row seat, Billy got a good look at the hermaphrodite's face. He could have sworn it had one brown eye and one green eye.

"Next," Lilith's voice echoed, "we have Rex, the handy man." The curtain opened. A small man sat on a wooden stool. Sitting with no legs. He did have four limbs, but all arms. The dirty yellow tank top he wore displayed that indeed all the limbs were sprouted out of his torso—two on each side. The top hands reaching across to the lower hands in a firm self-handshake. The curtain closed. The audience made absolutely no sound.

"Let me introduce you to," Lilith said, "Carmus, the living incarnate of famine." The curtains opened once more and out came a man wearing nothing but a loincloth. His feet slid across the stage top. There was barely enough muscle on his leg to allow him to stand. The dry flesh was pulled tight against his body, revealing every bone, down to the bumpy knuckles of his hand. The skin was so tight on his hairless head his face was fixed in a perpetual toothy smile. One woman, two rows back, fainted. The curtain closed.

Billy whispered to Nikki that Lilith or someone must be keeping an eye on the audience, because the curtain didn't open again until the fallen woman was helped away.

When it was all clear the curtain opened for the fourth time.

"Told ya," Billy said.

"And here we have our newest attraction. The snake-man." The spotlight shined down on a glass tank being pushed by a man wearing all white including his cap. The creature inside coiled in one corner. The man used some kind of stick to prod the creature. It jumped forward. Several of the crowd screamed and jumped back, including Nikki.

"I've seen enough," she said.

"Hey, you picked it," Billy replied.

"Let's go."

"Just wait a minute."

The voice reverberated through the tent. "For those who doubt the validity of my pet. Please keep your eyes on my assistant."

The man held out a small wooden box, displaying it to the crowd. Finally pulling off the cover, he reached inside with a gloved hand and pulled out a rat—a large brown and black slum rat—about eight inches in length. He held it by the tail. The animal squealed in a high painful pitch. The woman next to Billy covered her ears, complaining that it was all so revolting. Billy wanted to ask her why she bothered coming in, if all she was going to do was whine, instead he held his tongue.

On stage, the rat arched its back, trying to bite the gloved hand holding it captive. The man in white held the squirming creature over the glass tank. The snake-man's long thin red tongue darted in and out, in and out for several seconds. Then the man dropped the rodent. With one swift upward lunge the snake-man caught the rat in its mouth before it could hit bottom. Two swallows and the rat was gone, except for the large lump slipping slowly down the snake-man's throat. It too disappeared a moment later.

"Let's go, Billy. Now!" Nikki bolted up from her seat and rushed to the tent exit.

"You picked it," Billy said, following behind.

Outside, Nikki stopped alongside a bench, which she leaned against for support. "That was the most disgusting thing I've ever seen." It wasn't a ride, but Nikki's face had almost the same sickly color she received from the Tilt-A-Whirl.

Billy laughed. "It was all fake."

"How can you say that?" Nikki said, sitting down to help regain her composure. "You saw it yourself. It was real."

"You bet! They have a real snake-man."

Hearing more screams from the freak tent, Nikki stood and began walking away. She had had enough of that place.

Billy followed, but not before glancing back at the tent and wondering what cool thing was causing such a stir inside. As he caught up with his girlfriend, he said, "Don't get mad at me but...."

"What now? And you better not say 'I picked it' again."

"Nothing like that. But you have to promise me you won't hit me."

"What?"

"Promise."

"Okay, I promise."

"I'm hungry. Want to get something to eat?"

Her eyes shot open and she slugged him hard in the arm.

"Ouch! You promised."

With all his coaxing, Billy couldn't persuade Nikki to let him buy her a hot dog, especially one of Billy's everything-including-the-kitchen-sink style. She flatly refused any offer of food, but did agree to a small Sprite, hoping it would help settle her stomach.

Nikki felt her inners kick when the hot dog man poured the thick chili and cheese-like sauce on top of the water-soaked, wrinkled tube of mystery meat. Billy continually rubbed his hands together in anticipation and enjoyed giving Nikki a little tease, when he commented about "going to need another" as he took that first bite.

Nikki threw the soda in the trash after only two small sips. "How can you possibly eat after seeing that thing swallowing a rat?" She grabbed a napkin and wiped off her still clean hands.

Billy looked thoughtfully at his food. "You know the government does allow a certain percentage of rat turds in each and every hot dog. So I guess it's sort of the same thing." He grinned and took another big bite.

"You're sick." She moved away.

"Where are you going?" he asked through a mouthful of meat and bun.

"To the bathroom. I need to check my makeup among other things. Do you mind?"

"Not at all."

"Good," she said snootily.

"Oh, Nikki," Billy called out in a gentle tone.

She stopped and turned. "Now what?"

"Watch out for rats!" He laughed. A tiny bit of bun flew from his mouth.

She stuck up her middle finger.

"Later, honey."

"Don't count on it," she yelled back.

Billy was still snickering when he saw the skinny guy who had cheated him walk by, heading in the direction of the basketball booth.

"Gotcha," Billy said aloud.

He took a long sip of his coke then began chomping down on the last of his hot dog. He wanted to finish his food before Nikki got back. For the last two days he thought about how he had been made a fool and how he would catch that creep at his own game. Billy could imagine the expression on the man's face when the bastard gets tripped up this time instead of the other way around like the first night.

Billy crushed his empty cup and hot dog wrapper into a tight ball and tossed it into a steel drum ten feet away. "This is going to be sweet."

Then Billy looked over to the brown plastic porta-potties. Nikki was in the third from the farthest end. It had been about three minutes. She got in right away, but now there was a line forming.

"She is the slowest," Billy muttered.

Another minute passed when the door finally opened and Nikki stepped out.

"About time."

A fat woman rushed past Nikki, almost knocking her down to get into the empty stall.

As Nikki approached Billy, she said, "Did you see that? You could get killed coming out of one of those things. Some people are so impatient."

"Maybe if you didn't take so long."

"It was pretty dim in there. I had to use the little flashlight on my key chain."

"To pee?" Billy said, sounding amazed at her statement.

"To fix my makeup, silly. I had some worn spots."

"Lucky that woman didn't explode waiting for you."

"I wasn't in there that long."

"Tell her that."

Nikki started to pout.

"Hey, I was joking. Let's go. I just spotted that cheat heading to his booth. Now's my chance."

"I have an idea," Nikki said, gently taking Billy's hand, "let's pretend it never happened and find someplace cozy."

"When Satan has to ice skate to work," Billy replied. "I'm going to bust that asshole and show him we're not a bunch of small town bumpkins."

The couple made their way through the carnival. At the booth, Dean was doing his usual calls to passersby. Emphasizing the ease of his game and the great prizes to be won.

"Told you. There he is." Billy could not mistake that rail thin body, greasy hair, and sharp pointed chin.

"Great," Nikki said, her voice dripping with insincerity. "I'm very happy for you both."

"Come on." Billy pulled Nikki by the hand, but didn't head directly for the booth. He felt a ruse on his part would do handily for his purpose. He and Nikki walked in front of the booth, but not at too quick a pace. Billy wanted to dangle the bait, so to speak.

"How about it, buddy?" Dean barked. "Win your pretty little girl-friend a prize. Only a buck. You look like a natural born athlete to me."

Right on cue, Billy thought. It was even the same spiel as before. Billy wondered how many times he used that line and how many people were suckered by it. He sure was. The feelings of being duped from two nights previous returned, as did the anger. Billy was going to make up for all that—even the score with this creep.

"Looks pretty simple," Billy said. He pulled his wallet from his back pocket. Removing a crisp dollar bill, he handed it to his adversary. Billy placed the billfold on the counter, letting the corners of several bills stick out, before choosing a basketball. Billy bounced the ball once. It felt all right this time. He bounced it again, purposely hitting his wallet, knocking it to the ground. While he bent down to retrieve his money, he quickly licked his finger, getting it good and wet. Then he rubbed his spit-covered digit in the dirt, making a gob of mud. He stood up. "Wouldn't want to lose this," he said, shoving the wallet in his back pocket, but being careful not to wipe his finger clean. He retook the ball and smudged it with the dark mixture of dirt and spit. Finally, he took his shot. The basketball hit the backboard and fell through the net.

"Good throw," Dean said with a large grin. "Two more and you win a prize. Simple, just like you said." He retrieved the ball from the bin under the hoop.

"Yeah, real simple." Billy took the ball. He spun it around to get the feel of it and to find the dirt mark. There it was. He shot. The sphere glided off his fingertips. He could have made these shots in his sleep—another easy basket.

"One more," the skinny man said, and after retrieving a basketball, "get ready to pick your prize young lady. Looks like we have a winner here."

Again Billy spun the ball in his hands. No mark. He double checked. The dirt mark was nowhere to be seen. Billy had him. He placed the switched ball on the countertop.

"Go on," Dean said. "Shoot. You only have to make this one basket. Pretty exciting, isn't it?"

"Can I have the other ball I was using before?"

The carny grinned. "That's it right there. Now shoot."

"This one's been over-inflated, the other one wasn't."

The toothy smirk quickly disappeared. "It's the same ball, Mac. Shoot already or get lost."

"It's the same ball, huh, just like two nights ago. You pulled the same shit then." Billy took the basketball, raised it in the air, and let it drop from two feet above the counter. It bounced wildly. He reacted quickly to grab the ball before it bounced out of his reach. He would not lose his one piece of evidence. Though he wasn't exactly sure what he would do with it.

"I make the first two shots, then you slip me an over-inflated ball. If it even touches the rim it will bounce the other way."

"You're delusional—get lost. I got other people waiting. Come on up folks. This guy's finished."

Nobody stepped forward. Most of them knew Billy personally, and the others who didn't had seen him play basketball for the school. They silently stared at the man in the booth.

"I marked the ball with dirt." Billy spun it around. "Do you see any dirt?" He practically shoved the brown sphere in the man's face. He looked over to the metal hoop. "I betcha the first ball is still in that bin under the net."

"I'm telling you, get lost."

A man behind Billy said, "Let's see what's in the bin."

An elderly woman voiced her agreement, "Show us what you're hiding."

"I ain't tellin' you again, chum." Dean reached out and grabbed Billy by the shirt. "Get lost!"

Billy grabbed the man's hand, pulling it free. "Not until I see the other ball."

"There ain't no other ball."

"Prove it."

"I warned you," Dean said, pulling a baseball bat from under the counter. He struck the tip of his weapon down with a loud smack. "Am I making myself clear?" he told the teen.

"Let's go, Billy," Nikki said. "It's not worth getting hurt over."

The crowd backed up a step.

"Best listen to the girl, sport. Makes a lot of sense to me."

Billy took the basketball, still in his hands, and shot it at the thin man, hitting him square in the nose.

Dean flew backward several feet. Using the bat, he took a groggy swing at Billy, but missed by a foot. He managed to jump over the counter with the weapon held high. He took another ineffective swing.

Several of the other carnies saw the commotion. Some left their own booths to help their carny brother, others stayed put but watched, cheering on the armed roustabout. It seemed like some great spectator sport.

"You're dead, boy," Dean yelled, winding up again.

"Is there a problem here!" a woman said in a harsh tone, which stopped Dean before he took another swing. He dropped the bat to his side. The workers who were on their way to help, quickly did an about-face.

Billy looked toward the voice. It was the woman Lilith from the freak show, still dressed in the same strange black robe. Seeing her alarmed Nikki, who half hid behind Billy.

"Just a smart-ass trouble maker, ma'am," Dean said. "Nothing I can't handle."

"Apparently—not," she said.

"I'm not causing trouble," Billy said. "That asshole's been cheating me. He's been switching balls when anyone gets close to winning. Did the same thing the other night except I couldn't prove it then, but I sure can now."

"He's full of shit," the skinny man said.

"Right," Billy said. "And you smell good too."

The crowd behind Billy and Nikki laughed.

"I marked the ball with dirt," the boy continued. "When I got it back, the mark was gone."

"Please, please," Lilith told the crowd, "return to your enjoyment of my carnival. I will deal with the situation. Please be assured it will all be taken care of in a fair and just manner."

The crowd broke up.

"Shut down your booth," Lilith ordered.

"But," Dean replied.

"Do you understand me?"

The man looked down at the ground. "Yes, ma'am."

"We will speak more on this matter. Come to my trailer in the morning."

The man nodded. Then started to pull down the large wooden shutter of his booth. He gave Billy a deadly stare. Billy ignored him, but couldn't help thinking, *gotcha.*

"You may have cost me—customers," Lilith said to Billy.

"Hey, I wasn't the one ripping people off."

Nikki pulled on Billy's arm. "Let's go. I broke a fingernail somehow."

Lilith smiled at the girl, then returned her gaze to Billy. "True, you were not the guilty one. Take these as a small compensation," she said, holding out two red tickets "They're good for any show. We have many fine shows."

"We'll pass," Nikki said. "We've already seen your freak show. It was disgusting."

"Freaks, as you call them, have a place in this world too. They serve to remind us that we should never take our lives for granted."

"Seriously?" Billy snickered. "You mean 'there for the grace of God go I.' Pretty hokey."

"Believe when I say *God* has nothing to do with it."

"Come on, Billy," Nikki urged.

"If you don't wish to see a show, you can redeem your tickets at any other attraction or ride. Whatever you wish. The choice is yours. It is always your choice. Please, take them."

Billy reached out to take the tickets from Lilith's hand. Once he had the red slips in his grasp, Nikki pulled him by the arm, wanting to put some distance between them and the woman.

"Enjoy the rest of the night," Lilith said, retreating into a nearby tent.

"She's really spooky," Nikki said, taking Billy's hand. After a few steps, she added, "I could use something to eat."

"Didn't you tell me you couldn't eat after seeing—"

"Don't remind me," she said, covering his mouth with her hand. "I'm hungry now."

"How about mini doughnuts?" Billy asked. "I saw a stand a ways down."

"Okay, but the ones sprinkled with cinnamon."

"You want cinnamon? You get cinnamon."

The lights of the carnival came on as night crept in over the next hour. Billy and Nikki were enjoying themselves. Nikki even persuaded Billy to try another game. He knocked over metal milk bottles with a softball. It seemed he couldn't miss.

"See, not all the games are rigged." Nikki said, holding a stuffed toy tiger as they rested on a plastic bench.

"News travels fast. They wouldn't dare try any funny stuff around me."

Nikki could tell he was joking. "Big shot," she giggled. "Feeling all vindicated now?" She hugged her tiger.

"You bet I do."

"I hope you know it didn't matter to me if you won or not."

"Sure, I know. It mattered to me."

"Now what do we do?" she asked.

"Weren't you the one who wanted to leave earlier?"

Nikki put her head on Billy's shoulder, keeping the tiger in her lap. "I was just a smidge wound up. I'm fine now."

"Maybe we should get going. Your dad will kill me if I keep you out past eleven with school tomorrow. Remember the last time."

"I'll handle my father. The carnival will be closing in a half-hour. We'll stay till then. Besides, we haven't even used those free tickets yet."

"I didn't think you wanted to."

"Why not?"

"Just the look you gave me when I took them from that Lilith woman."

"Think about what we had just gone through. Weren't you a little shook up too?"

"Who me? No way." Billy cocked his head and tucked his thumbs in his belt loops. "I had everything under control."

"Yeah, right." Nikki stood up, then pulled Billy by the arm. "Let's find something."

"A bathroom would be good."

"You couldn't have gone earlier? They're way down at the other end. There's nothing down here but gaming booths. Can you hold it."

"I'll try," Billy said, getting to his feet, but he doubted his own words and figured his bladder would have the final say.

After going about ten yards, Nikki spotted something of interest.

"Look, the Hall of Mirrors."

"Figures," Billy said. "If there's a mirror around—any mirror—you'd find it."

"Come on." She tugged him one way, nature-calling started pulling him the other.

"I really have to piss," he said. "You go in. I'll find a bathroom."

"It'll be no fun by myself. Just cross your legs."

"Cross my legs and keep walking. Good trick."

"Billy—"

"I mean it. Go in. You'll be done by the time I get back. I'll meet you outside."

She looked at the glass structure. "We can skip it."

"Will you go already? You'll love it." He kissed her. "See you in a bit."

"All right. Wait until I'm inside." She handed him the toy tiger.

"Just hurry." Billy bounced on his heels.

She went up the metal steps.

Hurry, please hurry, Billy thought.

She gave her ticket to the man on the top of the stairs, then waved to Billy.

He waved back.

Nikki disappeared threw the glass revolving door and Billy dashed down the midway.

Reaching his destination, Billy found a line of three people waiting to use the portable lavatory.

"Great," he said, giving the tiger a squeeze.

∽⌇↶

The glass door of the Hall of Mirrors swooshed as it turned behind Nikki. She stepped into a glass corridor with small white glowing bulbs resembling Christmas lights at the top and foot of each mirror. They were all normal reflecting mirrors so Nikki stopped out of sheer habit to check her makeup. No repairs needed. Though she did have a speck of mascara on her cheek that bothered her some. She had bought the no-flake kind. "It shouldn't do that," she told herself, scraping off the black spot with her fingernail.

With each step the wood planks underfoot squeaked. The place could use a good sweeping. Besides the dirt there were a few used napkins scattered about.

"People can be such pigs," she said aloud, her words slightly echoing. Nikki kept walking straight until she hit a mirror face first. Too late to do any good, her hands shot up against the glass. Her fingertips pressed along the cool surface until she found the path forward. After five feet, this time with her hands extended and at a slower pace, she hit another mirror.

She took a left, then a right, feeling her way through, being very careful not to crash into any more glass. Nikki decided that she didn't enjoy this as much as she thought she would. After two more rights, and a left, she became very frustrated and decided to turn back. Billy would get a real laugh when he saw she couldn't make it through to the end. She retraced her steps, made a right turn, then two left turns. Getting back out would be a lot simpler. She wouldn't hit any mirrors.

Suddenly she hit more glass. "That's not right," she said. She groped for another path, but found no other way but back. Nicky retraced her steps thinking she must have miss counted the number of turns. She took several more corners, but what bothered her most was the number of mirrors she kept crashing into. And that she should have seen the entrance's revolving door by now. She stopped.

"Hello, is anybody there?" she shouted in desperation, "I can't find my way out." There was only the sound of her voice. "Hello! Can anybody hear me?"

Nothing.

Nikki started off again. *Billy must be wondering where I am*. She walked along several straight corridors and made many more turns. Then it struck her. She must be going in circles. The distance she had walked had been more than the size of the attraction. It couldn't be bigger inside than outside—could it?

"Nikki?" someone whispered from up ahead.

"I'm here," she yelled. "Billy?"

The voice repeated her name, "Nikki—"

"Not funny, Billy. Help me get out of here."

"This way...Nikki...this way," the whisper continued.

Nikki ran down a corridor until a sharp pain drilled through her head as she ran hard into another mirror. She fell back and landed on her ass.

"Billy, stop playing games." Her voice echoed off the glass walls. "Please...please, help me."

She got up and felt her head spin as she did so. She reached out with both hands. After going ten feet she found another wall in front of her. She reached for the side, still glass, the other side glass—a dead end. She turned around to go back the way she came. She saw her reflection staring back at her. She spun around, feeling for an opening.

"Please...please!!" she cried. Nikki kept spinning in circles and circles while groping for the passage out. Her heart pounded wildly. Her hands hit upon one glass pane after another. Then without warning, she fell forward, landing with a hard thud. She reached up, her hands stretched as far as possible, fumbling in front of her. No glass. She crawled along the floorboards like some trapped animal. When the top of her head collided into more glass, like a pinball against bumpers, she turned and took a new direction. She couldn't think any longer, she could only react. In her terror, Nikki didn't realize that each choice made seemed to be the right one. On all fours, she scampered to her freedom.

At last, she came to an opening that led to a small room with white painted walls. But more importantly, over a door at the far end a sign displayed a red glowing "EXIT." No more mirror walls, only four framed full-length mirrors spaced a foot apart from each other—the final amusement. She started to laugh, which switched between a giggle and a cry. She stood up and walked toward the exit door.

The oak frames of each mirror were carved with small faces, all twisted and distorted with tongues sticking out of screaming mouths below bulging and extended eyes. Each different and in perfect detail— each line of agony etched deep into the wood.

Nikki looked in the first mirror. It made her head appear bloated, though still clear enough for her to rub the streaks of liner from under her eyes. She reached for her purse, only to find she had lost it some- where back in the maze. She wouldn't be going back after it. Nikki made her way past the second mirror and couldn't help looking. With all the energy spent on trying to get out of this hellish place, the mirrors drew her in. The distortions made her body look very tall and thin. The third mirror made her feet very large, her head very small.

In the fourth and final mirror her skin looked stretched out, her lips were pulled back, her nose pig-like. The angles made it appear as if she had very little hair and her eyes seemed to be popping out. A truly hideous form.

"It is said—" a voice came from behind.

Nikki turned around quickly.

"—that mirrors reveal our true self." It was Lilith speaking. "Is what you see disturbing?"

Nikki's gaze returned to the mirror. She nodded. Then Nikki's eyes widened as she saw Lilith's reflection. The woman's appearance remained unchanged, but the mirror had distorted her own image. She tried to speak, but only garbled noise came from her mouth. Nikki raised her hands to her face and felt her long stretched lips. Her nose had become round and flat.

Nikki's scream became a weird high-pitched screech. Saliva trickled down the girl's chin.

"See how ugly vanity can be," Lilith remarked.

Out of nowhere came the sounds of laughter, soft at first, but swiftly increasing in volume. Then the laughing turned to words. "Nikki—Nikki—Nikki." Many voices blended in an evil harmony. Nikki remembered the whispers that had called out to her, that led her to this room. Her eyes returned to the mirror. All the twisted faces around the glass were calling her name—their tongues lashing in and out of carved mouths.

"Nikki—Nikki—Nikki." She tried to block the sound out by covering her ears, but the voices seemed to cut through her skull and enter her brain directly. Nothing could stop the wicked chant.

To Nikki's amazement and horror, the smooth surface of the mirror began to ripple and warp. It pulsated and bent with the beat of the voices in her head. Then several glass arms burst forward as if out of a pool of clear water. The wooden, twisted faces continued to echo her name, "Nikki—Nikki—Nikki."

The many hands grabbed her, some tearing Nikki's shirt while pulling her toward the mirror, others holding her from getting away. Nikki tried to yank free, but as she broke the glassy grips of one hand two others would spring up and grab hold—the sharp fingers cutting her soft skin. All the hands pulled at her, forcing her ever closer to the mirror. Nikki could not fight any longer and was dragged into the silver pool.

The water-like ripples stopped and the glass was once again still. But in the right top corner of the mirror's frame a new face formed—Nikki's face. "Billy," came from the wooden lips, "Billy...."

CHAPTER 16

Billy Clarksted hurried back to the Hall of Mirrors, still carrying the stuffed tiger he had won for Nikki. He felt ridiculous holding the toy while waiting in line for the toilet. A little girl in front of him kept eyeing it. He briefly considered giving her the stupid thing, but Nikki would kill him—she really seemed to love the fuzzy prize.

He expected Nikki to be outside the attraction by now and not in the best of moods having to wait for him. She'd never believe how slow the line had moved. His only other option would have been to whizz behind one of the tents. Though getting caught would most likely have gotten him thrown off the carnival grounds. No big deal really since the carnival was closing down for the night, but he didn't want to have to explain why he didn't meet her back as planned.

Billy picked up his pace as he passed the vacant gaming booths—all the lights were going out and all the shutters secured. The rides had already been shut down and the food wagons locked up.

"We're closing now," a security guard told Billy as he walked by. Billy responded by saying he was just on his way to meet up with his girlfriend.

"Make it quick," the guard said.

In front of the Hall of Mirrors, Billy looked for Nikki—she wasn't there. He knew she wouldn't leave without him, so that left only one possibility. He spotted a heavyset man walking down to the bottom of the small ramp where he had last seen her. He watched as the worker put a chain with a closed sign between the railings.

"Mister," Billy called out, "my girlfriend's still inside."

"No way, sonny. I checked it over—same as every other night at close. It's empty."

"I'm telling you, she must be inside."

"I'm not going to argue with you," the man said, unlatching the chain. "Go through yourself. Wait 'til I turn the lights back on. Just don't bump your head. Want me to hold your tiger for you?"

Hearing the smirk in the man's voice, Billy responded, "He doesn't like strangers." He went up the ramp and through the revolving door. It was pitch black inside. Then the lights snapped on. Billy walked through the glass maze. A left turn, a right turn, another right, one more left. His foot hit something. Billy picked up Nikki's leather bag.

One more left and he found the exit sign. He pushed the door open and stood there with the purse and toy tiger. His eyes had grown accustomed to the bright lights inside, but he made out a dark shape waiting at the bottom of the exit stairs.

"Nikki? I found your purse."

"I told you, sonny," the heavy man said, "there ain't anybody inside."

As Billy's eyes adjusted to his surroundings, he came down the steps. "But I found her purse." Billy showed the man the tan leather bag.

"So? Keep it. I don't give a rip."

"She'd never have left it."

"What can I tell you, boy? I got to finish locking up. It's been a god-awful long day." The man waved his arm, summoning the security guard.

"Didn't I tell you, you have to leave," the guard said, recognizing Billy.

"I have to find my girlfriend."

"You already told me that one. I'm not buying it this time." The guard shined his light in the boy's face.

"I'd appreciate it if you stopped trying to blind me," Billy said, shielding his eyes.

"Aren't you the kid who caused all that trouble earlier tonight?"

"I wasn't the *one* causing the trouble."

"It's him all right," the heavy man said. "I knew I've seen that stinkin' face before."

"Let's go." The guard took Billy's arm.

Billy pulled away. "Not without Nikki."

"The carnival's closing," the guard said, "She's probably waiting for you out by the front gate. Let's not make things worse." The man rested his hand on the baton hanging from his belt.

Billy got the message. "Fine," he said, stomping between both men, pushing them aside.

"You little shit," the carny said, taking a step toward Billy.

"Leave him be," the guard said. "He's going. But in case he gets any dumb ideas." The guard followed Billy to the gate. "I hope you had a fun time anyway," he said as the boy exited.

"Just swell." *And as soon as you're gone, asshole,* Billy thought, *I'll sneak back and find Nikki—I know she's in there.* He walked to his Dodge and got in, tossing Nikki's purse and toy tiger to the passenger side. Glancing in the rear-view mirror, he saw the guard still staring his way. Billy started the engine and pulled away. The guard watched him drive down the road until a grove of Cottonwoods blocked the view.

Hidden by the trees, Billy steered to the side of the road, cut the engine, and waited.

After a time, he turned on the small ceiling light and looked at his watch. He had been sitting for about thirty minutes, enough time for things to cool down. Billy left the Dodge and made his way through the trees to the border of the carnival grounds. Except for a few workers picking up trash, the coast was clear. He darted down into the tall grass when he saw one of the workers look his way. The man started walking toward his position. Billy crouched low, bracing his body on bent arms, ready to run.

The worker stopped. He picked up what appeared to be a half-empty beer bottle. After dumping out the remaining liquid, he dropped it into his bag and moved onto the next piece of trash.

Billy let out a sigh of relief as the cleanup crew worked their way further down the midway. He eased himself up, but not enough to be seen. Stooping as he ran, he made it behind one of the tents. Staying in the shadows, the boy scooted low to the canvas.

He peeked around the corner of the tent, then back over his shoulder, all the while trying to hold back his labored breath. The workers were far down the midway, but Billy still heard their voices. He stood up only half his height, then dashed across the road, stopping to hide next to a handy hot dog wagon. He checked for the workers again before continuing on, careful to keep an eye out for anyone else cleaning up around the grounds as he returned to the Hall of Mirrors.

Safely out of view, Billy found the maintenance hatch on the back of the attraction—a large padlock kept the small door closed. He gave the lock a pull, but without the key or a good strong crowbar, it was staying put. After moving around the side to the main entrance, he waited a moment, trying to figure out a way to get up the ramp without being seen. An almost impossible task.

When the shuffle of footsteps came out of nowhere, Billy dove to the ground, lying as low as possible, hoping it would be enough to keep his presence hidden. His eyes widened as form followed sound. It was that strange woman again, Lilith. She was alone and passed no more than five feet from him. Billy couldn't help staring. Her robe clang tight against her body, revealing every curve. He felt himself giving into his lust and edged up to get a better view, then realized the danger and dropped back to the ground. If she had seen him, Billy reasoned, he would simply run. There was no way she could catch him herself. All she could do was to cry out for her workers and by the time they arrived he'd be long gone.

Billy kept an eye on the woman until she disappeared into a large tent. If anyone knew Nikki's whereabouts, surely she would. Again, he made sure the coast was clear before following the carnival owner. He had come too far to get careless now.

Inside the tent, it was dark except for a small flame in an urn dangling by a chain attached to a long pole. Lilith, seemingly motionless, gazed into the orange glow. Her back was to him, yet Billy saw she had already untied the sash that held her robe closed. Then the robe slipped down past her shoulders and landed in a heap at her feet. Lilith stood naked. For a moment Billy forgot why he was there and found himself wishing the raven-haired beauty would turn around to his full view.

Nikki's face popping into his head broke the enchantment—he took another step forward, entering the tent. Naked or not he would speak with this woman and demand to know what happened to Nikki. But before Billy even opened his mouth, Lilith began to utter words in a strange language. Within seconds, the flames were blocked out by a huge winged form.

Billy ran from the tent with a speed he had never managed before. Not watching his way, he tripped on a support rope and hit the ground hard. Without a second of thought, he pushed himself up, and continued his flight of terror. He headed for the Cottonwood grove that hid his car, not caring if he should be seen—by human eyes. The brittle sticks that littered the ground crackled and snapped under his feet. The night air rushed in and out of his burning lungs, spit grew thick in his mouth.

Up ahead he saw a white glow. He had accidentally left the ceiling light on in his car. It led his way like a beacon, but it also would lead the thing following him. He cleared the trees, and scurried up the road. He jumped in his Dodge, slammed the door, locked it, and started the engine. One turn was all it took. He threw the car in gear and floored it, kicking up half the road with his back tires. He looked back only to see the cloud of dust. Billy kept his headlights off, not wanting to advertise his whereabouts to the winged creature.

More than a mile down the road, Billy's breathing eased slightly and his mind cleared. While turning his car onto Route Twenty-five, he realized he had to get help. Sheriff McNee—he had to find Sheriff McNee. What he had seen seemed impossible, he almost had trouble believing it himself—how could he possibly convince others? Billy shook his head. No, he couldn't give into doubt. He would make them believe for Nikki's sake.

Without warning, a loud thud came from the roof of his car. The shock wave caused him to veer across the median line. After another loud thud, Billy rocked the steering wheel back and forth several times, hoping to deter the thing trying to stop him. After a minute of silence Billy relaxed some, but kept his foot hard on the gas pedal.

Then from over the top edge of the windshield the thing's face peered down at him. Its red eyes burned with anger. Billy screamed and slammed on the brakes—Nikki's purse and toy tiger flew off the seat. Without thinking, Billy sharply turned the steering wheel, forcing his Dodge to swerve violently. The creature's fist, if that was the right term, crashed down on the glass. The blow produced a web-like pattern, but the fragments held fast.

Unable to regain control, Billy ran his car off the road. It flew through a shallow ditch, and continued down into the nearby field. The car bounced several times while negotiating the hill, fracturing the rear shocks. The tires on the right side lifted high off the ground, but the Dodge did not tip. With a final jolt, it came to a halt in a growth of bushes and small trees. Both back tires were suspended midair over a deep rut. The rear bumper held in place on the other side by a mound of soft dirt.

Billy jammed the accelerator to the floorboard. The engine roared, the tires spun, but with no rear traction, he was trapped in the middle of a heavy thicket. Knowing he had no chance of defending himself empty handed Billy searched for anything that could be used as a weapon. On the floor behind the passenger's seat he found a rust spotted tire iron. After silently thanking God that he had been too lazy to return the tool to his trunk last week, he grabbed the metal bar. The weight in his hand wasn't as reassuring as he hoped. Taking a deep breath and counting to three, Billy threw open the door, forcing back a patch of leafy brush. He leaped out, and in almost the same motion, slammed the iron on the roof. The impact was great enough to shatter the rest of his window. The blanket of broken glass fell inside the car, draping over the steering wheel.

The blow, however, had been wasted effort. Even in the darkness, he could see he managed only to put a large dent in the sheet metal. The creature was no longer on the roof. Suddenly something blocked out what little moon light there was. A gigantic shadow swooped down on Billy. Like a sword he employed his weapon, slashing the flying thing on what must have been a foot. It screeched and flew off.

Billy ran.

The dark shadow doubled back, following the boy, who swung his weapon wildly in the night air while at the same time dashing across the field. From that distance there was no chance of hitting anything, but Billy prayed the action would be enough to keep the monster away. He saw the thing circling him from above, hovering just out of reach. It would fly up, then angled back down, ultimately pulling away at the last second—the thing was toying with him.

Billy's eyes had grown accustom to the darkness, but he knew it didn't make much difference, except for a few thin, scraggly, Bristlecone pine trees, a couple of anthills, and a dozen or so squirrels, there was nothing out there. Nowhere to hide. No cover.

The giant wings cutting through the air sounded somewhat like a steam locomotive starting on its slow descent, an easy, effortless stride that pulled with unmeasurable power. The thing hovered over Billy once more. He had no other option but to make his stand on that very spot. He held the tire iron high and shouted, "You ugly bastard. I'm gonna shove this piece of steel up your ass."

As if answering Billy's challenge, the thing soared down.

With every ounce of power, Billy swung.

But a great force stopped his arm in mid-swing. Billy cried out as a viselike grip crushed his wrist. Still in flight the other talon embedded itself in Billy's chest with a dull thud and lifted the teen off the ground. Billy's body twitched once before dropping, landing in a lifeless heap.

With its prey dead and the sport over, powerful wings carried the creature back to the dark carnival.

CHAPTER 17

Amy Evans stood impatiently at the usual spot in front of the girls' second floor washroom. The clock above the hall drinking fountain displayed a minute before first hour. Able to wait no longer for Nikki and Billy, Amy started off to class. She supposed Billy must have had some kind of car trouble on the way in. He was always fixing one thing or another on that junk pile. It wouldn't surprise her if the engine had blown altogether.

Hearing what sounded like Nikki's voice, Amy stopped and looked over her shoulder. Instead of her best friend, two other girls rushed past her also trying to beat the bell. Too bad—Amy continued her way down the hall—she had a lot to tell Nikki about the night before. How she ended up running into Johnny at the hot dog wagon. And how she took him home to get some real food. And the luck of an empty house.

Amy knew what devious thoughts would fill Nikki's head finding out that her parents had taken Benny to the movies and she had been alone in the house with Johnny. She could almost see the look of disbelief on her best friend's face when being told Johnny had been a perfect gentleman the whole time they were together and nothing happened. Well, if a kiss or two counted as nothing. Amy wasn't sure if she wanted anything more, but the main point was that Johnny didn't push himself on her. She really wanted to tell Nikki everything, but obviously that would have to wait until later.

The bell rang at the exact moment Amy stepped into the classroom.

"Take your seat," Mrs. Singer told her, while standing at the black-board writing out a three term algebra problem.

Amy walked to her assigned spot in the second row, third chair back. The seat next to hers, Nikki's, and the one behind it, Billy's, were both empty. A strange dread suddenly poured over the teen. For no reason that she could comprehend, seeing the vacant chairs conjured up all sorts of terrible images. Nikki had been her best friend too long not to be worried, but her imagination seemed out of control. She dismissed her fear and told herself that her friends would be racing through the door any moment—late again.

And the morbid thoughts came to full rest when the door finally did open.

"I knew it," Amy whispered to herself and smiled.

But instead of Nikki or Billy, it was another student who handed Mrs. Singer a folded note and then immediately retreated from the room.

The teacher read the paper, before calling out: "Amy Evans."

"Yes, Mrs. S-Singer?" Amy had to catch her breath.

"Principal Dalson would like to see you in his office. Here is your hall pass." The woman held out the note from her seated position.

Amy picked up her books and moved to the front of the room. On the way some of the other students made slight cat calls and you're-in-trouble-now noises. She took the slip of paper from the teacher's grasp and exited through the door she had entered only a minute earlier.

Why would Principal Dalson want to see me, Amy thought while walking down the hall, the sound of her echoing steps her only company. She tried hard to think of anything she had done to get herself in such trouble. Last year she and Nikki were caught peeking into the boys' locker room. That's when Nikki saw Mark Boyd's butt. For Nikki, the two Saturday's they had to spend in detention were well worth it. But for Amy, it wasn't. All she saw was Coach Spencer's hands grabbing them both by the shoulder. He held them like that all the way to Dalson's office.

Racking her brain, Amy couldn't come up with a single reason why the Principal would want to see her this time. For a long moment, Amy stood outside the doors to the main office going over the last few days in her head. After taking a deep breath, she finally stepped inside.

"Principal Dalson wants to see me," Amy said, handing his secretary the note.

"They're all waiting for you."

All? What did I do?

Amy knocked on the closed door.

"Come," the unmistakable voice of Principal Wright Dalson called out.

Even while turning the knob, Amy scrambled for an explanation to why she had been summoned. Knowing the answer she could come up with some sort of defense. Still, nothing came to mind. She felt her mouth drying and a strong pounding in her chest. The doorknob felt clammy against her palm.

When the door opened Amy saw the principal talking with two people seated in brown padded chairs in front of his desk. They turned to face Amy as she entered—the woman first.

Amy knew her—and the man. "Mrs. Bonn?" Amy said, seeing the deep redness in her eyes. The woman's usual perfectly styled blonde hair appeared limp and undone. That strange dread Amy felt earlier while waiting for her friend returned. "Has something happened to Nikki?" she blurted out before any of the adults uttered a single word.

"We were hoping you'd be able to tell us," Mr. Bonn said. The stocky man reached over and gently touched his wife's shoulder. His dark hair contained several strands of silver.

"That's why I called you here, Amy," Principal Dalson said. "The Bonn's are very concerned. Nikki didn't come home last night."

"Her bed hadn't been slept in," Mrs. Bonn said, on the verge of crying.

"We called the Clarksteds'," Mr. Bonn volunteered. "Billy didn't come home either. By the time we tried to call your house, you had already left for school."

"Wednesdays I have a yearbook committee meeting before classes start," Amy said, her thought processes put on automatic with the news of her missing friends. "I'm sorry."

"There's nothing to be sorry about, Amy," Principal Dalson said. "We just want to find out if you know anything that could possibly help us." The Principal leaned back in his chair. "How were Nikki and Billy acting the last time you saw them? Did they ever mention anything about running away?"

"My daughter wouldn't run away," Mrs. Bonn yelled, "she's a very happy child. We have a happy family. There would be no reason for her to run away from home."

"It had to be asked, Corin," Mr. Bonn said.

"Please forgive me," Dalson told the woman, "but we must cover every likelihood."

The adults stared at Amy, awaiting her answer. "Mrs. Bonn is right," she finally said. "Nikki loves her parents. She wouldn't run away."

"When exactly," Dalson asked, "did you see Nikki and Billy?"

"Last night. We all, her, me, and Billy were at the carnival."

"Did you three go anywhere afterwards?"

"I—I didn't leave with them. I went home early."

"By yourself?" Mrs. Bonn asked, a surprised tone in her voice.

"I didn't leave with Nikki or Billy, if that's what you mean." It was the truth, Amy reasoned. Johnny was none of their business.

"There is one possibility to consider," Dalson said.

Both parents stared at the Principal.

"Your daughter," he continued, "has turned eighteen?"

"Last month," Mr. Bonn confirmed.

"It's not uncommon for young people who think they're in love to secretly leave town to get married. Vegas is only a three hour drive."

"Elope?" Mrs. Bonn said. "She wouldn't—couldn't." The woman began to sob.

Mr. Bonn took his wife's hand, then looked at Amy. "Is that possible? Was there talk of marriage between the two of them?"

"Nikki sometimes says things. Only fantasies on her part, but nothing ever about eloping. She wouldn't have kept that from me. I'm her best friend, if she got married, she would want me to be there."

"It could have been a spur-of-the-moment thing," Principal Dalson said.

"No," Amy told them, "Nikki would've come and got me."

"This puts us nowhere closer to an answer than we were before," Mr. Bonn said.

"Thank you, Amy," Dalson told her, "you can go back to class. My secretary will write you another hall pass."

Amy turned and left the room. Before completely shutting the door, she heard Principal Dalson ask the Bonns, "Did you contact the sheriff's office?" Amy didn't wait for their answer.

⌒⌒⌒

"Good morning!" Johnny said, going up to the supply truck to get his load of prizes to restock the shelves of the Coke bottle ring toss booth. The man throwing out the boxes grumbled something about having to get up at five o'clock. Johnny smiled and stacked up three boxes, one on top of the other. Last night's sleep had been the best he remembered having in quite a long time and he actually felt refreshed. He picked up his load. It was a little awkward, but light enough to manage.

When Johnny got back to the booth, he saw Calvin had brought back two packs, but barely touched either of them. In Johnny's frame of mind, not even Calvin's laziness could get him down.

"I saw you with that pretty little thing last night," Calvin said with a smirk.

"Just a friend," Johnny said, setting the first carton on the counter, ignoring the innuendo. He pulled off the strip of packing tape and popped it open. It took him only moments to empty the container of stuffed animals.

"Oh, I'm sure of that, Johnny—sure of that." He snickered.

"She's a nice girl. Lay off," Johnny snapped, throwing the cardboard box to the ground. The switch in emotions stunned Johnny. Calvin was only being his usual crude self—no reason to chew his head off.

"Okay, Johnny. No need to get huffy. I didn't mean anything by it."

"Sorry, pal. Guess I didn't get enough sleep last night." A lie and Johnny knew it. It seemed his feelings for Amy were stronger than he realized. And that didn't please him.

"Where'd you take her? If you don't mind me asking, that is."

"More like where she took me. We went into town—to her house. She cooked and—"

"Keep your voice down!" Calvin said, glancing to see if his partner had been overheard. "The owner doesn't like her lackeys going into town. Doesn't like it one bit."

"What harm could it do?"

"I don't make the rules." Calvin pulled a fuzzy tiger from what was still his first box.

"You mean you've never snuck out of camp?"

Finally pulling the last toy from its container, then sliding the second box toward himself, a wide grin beamed across Calvin's face. "Now, I didn't say that, did I? All I'm sayin' is keep it to yourself—and don't get caught."

"Solom," someone yelled. "You, Johnny Solom."

"Sounds like you're being paged," Calvin said.

"Huh?" Johnny looked up from his work. The head carny worker, Lucas, came up to the booth. His barrel chest, wide shoulders, and huge arms blocked out the morning sun, casting a cold shadow on Johnny, who had to fight back a shiver.

"Solom," the bald man said in a deep gravelly voice, "you'll be working the basketball shoot for the rest of the week. If it pans out—it's yours as long as you—stay with us." He smirked.

"What happened to…?"

Lucas didn't wait for Johnny to finish his question. The strange man simply did an about-face and marched off.

"That one makes my skin crawl," Calvin said. "He never eats with us. Doesn't sleep in any of the other trailers. A few of us figured he was shacking-up with the boss lady. But look at him, and you've seen her. Can you imagine the two of them together?"

"Doesn't seem likely, but you never know."

"Suppose so, but one thing's for sure. He follows her orders to the letter. It must have been her who decided to give you your own booth— for good or bad."

"Pretty weird, isn't it?" Johnny asked. "Me getting a booth so soon?"

"Let's get rid of these boxes," was all Calvin said.

"What happened to Dean? Why did they give me his booth?" He spotted the sudden uneasiness in Calvin's eyes. He was afraid that the scruffy man would be as secretive as Lucas and not tell him. Or at least, not tell him the truth. To his surprise, the words that came from Calvin's mouth sounded honest enough.

"The story I hear is that he tried to cheat a townie."

"I see," Johnny said casually, breaking up the cardboard, shoving it into the last empty box.

"What do you mean, 'I see'? I thought you said you worked carnival booths before."

"Yeah, so?"

"This is the first carnival I've worked that didn't want to make the odds more favorable for the house, so to speak. And I've never heard of anyone getting canned from his booth for trying to pull in extra dough."

Johnny had to think fast. Calvin sometimes showed signs of being sharper than he let on—this slip could cost him if he wasn't careful about his next answer. "They're not all like that," Johnny declared firmly. "I've worked in fair carnivals. The games were hard enough to play without rigging them." He picked up the junk filled box, hoping he sounded convincing. "I didn't need to cheat people."

"Where you from? Mars?"

"I'm just saying there are fair carnivals out there. That's all. I need to bring this stuff to the dumpster."

"They may be fair, but I bet they're hurting for bucks."

"They do well enough."

"If you say so. All that really matters now is that you got your own booth." Calvin placed the torn packing tape strips with the rest of the garbage. "Don't be a stranger," he joked, "it was fun sharing the time with ya." Then he whispered. "Remember what I said about getting caught leaving the grounds. You don't want to mess up now."

As Johnny walked with his arms full of trash, Calvin's words rattled around in his brain: "—mess up now." Was that just an idle comment or was his ex-partner trying to tell him something?

After licking the tips of his fingers and slicking down a few loose strands of hair, Dean stepped up to the aluminum trailer door and knocked once. He found himself trembling a bit while he kept telling himself that cheating a townie rube wasn't any big deal. That the boss lady only said what she did to convince the local stooges that she ran clean games. She probably called him to her quarters to give him a lecture on not getting caught next time. Besides, he wouldn't be going in totally unarmed. If she truly intended to sack him, Dean had a bargaining chip. He was one to always keep an open eye.

He knocked again.

"Enter," Lilith said from inside.

Dean turned the small 'L'-shaped handle and pulled the door open. He didn't go right in. "You wanted to see me this morning, ma'am," he said from the stoop.

"Come, all the way," she ordered.

The interior of the trailer was dark and Dean barely made out Lilith sitting in her large chair. "Sure thing, ma'am," he said, taking that final step inside. Getting out of the sunlight his eyes quickly adjusted to the dim lighting.

"Close the door," Lilith said, not moving a muscle. Dean couldn't even see her mouth move as she spoke.

He did what she demanded. With his back to the woman, he took a deep breath. As the door moved into its frame, again Dean whispered to himself that he held the ace.

"You have something to say?" Lilith said from her chair.

Dean turned. "Just clearing my throat."

"You brought us unnecessary attention," the raven-haired woman said, jumping straight to the matter at hand. "Negative attention. The kind that has us looked at in an…unfavorable light."

"I'm sorry, ma'am. I just thought."

"Your problem is you *don't* think," she said with a steeping anger. "I doubt you are capable. You are incompetent and a simpleton."

"There's no call for you to say that. Who cares if I stiff a few marks. That kid last night deserved it—all cocky and such. I'm a good carny man. I rake in the rubes."

"Indeed, you do. But inciting a crowd of angry townies to gather around one of my booths—that is unacceptable. That kid, as you call him, came back last night snooping around. I cannot allow that. Nor can I allow any worker to act in such a way that may cause the situation to occur."

"So that's it, huh? I get your meaning. And I'm not as stupid as you think I am." Sweat began to form on Dean's forehead as he played his hole card. "You don't want anyone to know what else goes on here, do you? I know plenty. Plenty, I tell you."

"What do you know about my carnival?" Lilith said smiling.

The look terrified Dean, but he figured he had her. If he handled the situation right, it may be worth something to Lilith for him to simply keep his mouth shut. "I have eyes. I've been watching. Ever since that little visit we got from the police back in Ely. I've been watching."

"Watching what?" That smirk again.

"Just strange happenin's. People comin' in, but not leaving."

"I see. Who else have you told about your suspicions?" Lilith's palms came off the handles of her chair, she folded her fingers, and put her clasped hands snug in her lap.

A sudden shudder ran through Dean's body. "A couple of the other workers…they know."

"Who?"

"My friends would prefer to remain…anonymous. But me being their spokesman, you understand, the two of us can come to some kind of agreement."

"Tell me their names!" Lilith commanded, her eyes glowing with an orange flame. "Tell me," she repeated.

"I...no one...else...I...no one else knows." The words were ripped from his throat. Try as he may Dean couldn't stop the flow of his confession. "I've told no one—no one."

"So, you are a liar as well as a cheat. I will find you a more permanent place in my carnival. A place where you will be properly suited."

Outside, Mayor Jasper Fallon strolled through Lilith's Carnival. He had been stopped once, but after explaining who he was and whom he was going to see the unshaven, rather large man allowed him to pass unheeded. A few of the booth's shutters had been drawn up and the workers were busy getting ready for the day's business. It brought a twisted smile to the mayor's pudgy lips thinking that the more money they made the larger his cut would be. A very pleasing situation indeed.

Not all the men were setting up, however. Off to the side by the sleeping trailers, Jasper saw a couple of carnies still eating breakfast. The pleasant aroma of cooked bacon tickled his nose. He inhaled deeply and felt his stomach rumble. But ignoring his sudden hunger, Jasper continued on his way down to the end of the midway, stopping at Lilith's trailer. He climbed the stairs, helping himself up by the railing. Standing at the door's edge, he heard voices coming from inside. He put his ear to the frame—maybe he could learn something useful, something worth a few bucks. The more pocket padding, the better.

Abruptly the voices stopped.

He leaned closer but heard nothing more. Realizing how it must appear with his ear pressed against the aluminum door, he quickly straightened up, checking the collar of his coat and adjusting his tie. He scanned the area to make sure he had not been seen eavesdropping. Convincing himself his actions had gone unnoticed, Jasper knocked. The thought of money outweighed the sense of fear he experienced on his last visit.

"Come in, Mayor Fallon," Lilith said from the other side of the closed door.

Pulling the metal handle and entering, Mayor Jasper Fallon began by saying: "Sorry to disturb you, but—" He surveyed the enclosed area.

There was no one there except Lilith sitting in her high-backed chair. "I heard voices when I came up the stairs," the man admitted.

"Voices? Really? As you can see for yourself, I am quite alone."

She was right. The trailer was too small to hide anyone. "My mistake," Jasper said, fighting back his doubts. "Shall we proceed with our business? I've come—"

"For your...money." She pointed to the small table next to her, on top of which sat three banded packets.

Jasper hadn't noticed the stacked bills when he first entered the trailer. The voices must have thrown him, he figured. When it came to his business ventures, Jasper Fallon kept his eye, literally and figuratively, on everything, especially piles of green, crisp cash.

"Your twenty-five percent, per our agreement."

He picked up the middle packet and bounced it twice in his hand. The weight seemed right. He flipped through the bills, allowing the odor to reach his nose. "You do a fine business here," he said, enjoying the inky bouquet as it entered his nostrils.

"I do well," the woman said with a half-smile. "And I get what I need. Your town is a haven for the wealth I require."

"Wealth? Here? If it wasn't for my other enterprises I'd starve."

"Come now, Mayor. Starve?"

"A figure of speech."

Lilith smiled. "Can I interest you in a free show?" She held out a single red ticket. "We have some fine shows. Something for everyone."

"I'm much too busy," he said, taking the other stacks of money off the table. He stuffed them in his jacket pocket. "Maybe next time."

"Of course...next time."

"I understand Friday is your last day," Mayor Fallon said, adjusting the new bulges in his coat, making sure the money was well concealed.

"Yes—yes it is," Lilith said.

"Then I'll be back Friday afternoon for the last installment of funds. That way there will be no misunderstandings before you leave the area."

"I won't have the day's final total by then. It will be difficult to figure your percentage—your cut."

"Estimate. I trust you." Jasper grinned. "Besides, I imagine the amount shouldn't be less than today's—should it?" He tapped his right pocket, feeling the lump of money.

"If you say so," Lilith said, not moving from her chair.

"I do."

"Then Friday it is. May the rest of the week be as prosperous for me as its beginning. And Jasper Fallon, Mayor of Arkham, may you get what you desire."

With their business complete, the portly man left Lilith's trailer. As the door closed behind him, Lilith repeated her last words: "All that you deserve."

CHAPTER 18

Of all the things to do, Randy Porter's favorite was to take his air-pressure, pump action, Daisy BB-gun and his black Labrador retriever, Baron, out after school to hunt for squirrels. The boy was already a pretty good shot at the tender age of fourteen. He usually bagged two grays per outing, sometimes three, depending on how much time he had and how cooperating the tiny critters would be. On the best days, when the squirrels were in abundance, Randy would wait for the fatter ones to show themselves, though holding Baron back from chasing the scrawny ones sometimes proved to be too difficult a task. But whatever he managed to shoot, he always brought his kill to his grandfather, who would clean and throw the prized morsels into the freezer until he had enough to make a stew.

For Randy, his reward was the long, gray, furry tails. He kept the best one for himself and gave the others to his friends, which made him popular among the other boys his age. They all had squirrel tails hanging from their bike handlebars.

As Randy hiked through the field, he kept one eye on Baron and the other eye out for his prey. He carried his trusty gun with the barrel pointed down toward the ground for safety, exactly how his father had shown him. The one condition his parents put on him for owning a BB-gun was that he would never shoot it around houses or people. So Randy would go to the fields a quarter mile from home, the best hunting spot around. Baron would follow his master every step of the way.

The day couldn't be any better. With plenty of sunlight, and supper not until five-thirty, Randy had a good two hours for his hunt. The field had few trees, but lots of squirrels, rabbits, and even a few grouse. He always left the grouse and rabbits alone. The grouse were much too fast, the rabbits way too cute, which left his prized target. Besides, the squirrels were a easier to spot. His best chance of success came when the squirrels settled down in the trees—either holding on to the bark or sitting on a low branch. When they were on the ground they were hard to see in the sprigs of tall grass—same with the higher branches. Once he tried setting out food as bait in a clearing, but that was too easy. It took away from the challenge.

"Come on, Baron," Randy called to his dog. Baron had fallen behind while sniffing trees. "You smell 'em, boy? Are they here?"

Either because of the excitement in the boy's voice or at some level Baron really did understand the question, the dog barked.

"Good boy. Where are they?"

Baron barked again.

"Show me, boy. Show me." Randy motioned for his dog to chase out the small animals.

Baron tilted his head to the side, then shook. His long black ears flapped side to side with a sharp fluttering sound.

"Go get 'em, boy."

Baron darted off.

"Good boy. Let's get 'em."

Randy followed Baron as best he could, keeping an eye on his faithful dog at all times. When he caught up with the lab, Baron was nuzzling his nose against a short bush. He barked once.

"Is he in there?"

Baron lifted his head, barking again. He used his powerful front legs and paws to dig out some of the dirt from around the base of the shrub.

Crouching down, Randy peered between the leaves. "I don't see anything, Baron." With the tip of his gun, he probed the underbrush. "You're wrong this time, buddy."

The boy walked around to the other side of the thicket. "You can't win them all," he told his dog, while poking the gun barrel in the bush once more. Baron continued to yelp wildly.

Then a big gray squirrel ran out and over Randy's shoe.

Randy shouted in both surprise and glee. Baron raced around the bush after the big gray. "You were right. Good boy. Get him." Randy quickly followed his dog. The squirrel climbed up the first available tree. Baron jumped up, missing the critter's tail by inches with his snapping jaws.

Coming up fast and breathing hard, Randy patted Baron's head. "Good boy. I should never have doubted you." Both boy and dog watched the squirrel gracefully maneuver up the tree, then with a leap, soar to a branch on the next tree. The squirrel stopped and stared down at them as if to mock his pursuers.

Randy lifted his gun and took careful aim.

Baron barked.

"Hush now boy—I got this one." He gently squeezed down on the trigger, producing a loud hiss from air under pressure. But the squirrel didn't budge, it simply licked one paw clean. "Rats," Randy said, expecting the animal to be long gone by the time he could re-pump his gun.

Baron started to move toward the tree before Randy realized the squirrel hadn't scampered off for cover. "Stay," Randy commanded. The big dog halted and sat.

The young hunter hurried to pump up his Daisy BB-gun. He would've liked to have charged his weapon with more pressure, but he couldn't take the chance that his prey would become bored with its grooming and take refuge on a higher, more leafy, branch. He took aim again, held his breath, and squeezed the trigger.

This time, following the deadly hiss, the gray squirrel fell lifeless to the ground. Its small body making a tremendous rustle as it plunged into the bushes surrounding the tree.

"Right on the money," Randy shouted. Baron barked his approval.

"Fetch," the boy ordered, and immediately the black lab bounded off toward the fallen squirrel. "Bring him back, boy. Bring him back."

Obeying, Baron disappeared behind the bush. Randy waited for his dog to come running back with his quarry neatly mouthed. Instead, out of the boy's view, Baron began to bark wildly. "Come on Baron, bring him here," Randy called out.

But Baron kept barking. Randy started after his dog, thinking he must have only wounded the squirrel and that Baron must have it cornered.

Randy dashed around the bush to find Baron was not barking at a squirrel. The boy grabbed his dog by the collar and pulled him away from the bloodied human corpse.

Jim McNee stood solemnly staring out the patio window as his daughter frolicked in the backyard of his sister-in-law's home. Allie loved to play with JoLean's big Siamese cat Minky. The little girl had a toy mouse on the end of a long string, which she pulled around the yard. Minky would pounce on the yellow stuff toy, paw it back and forth, then wait for Allie to pull it again.

He watched in slight wonder the game the two played. Minky didn't like anyone except JoLean and Allie. The cat always ran from him and hid under the couch, or bed, or whatever handy coverage could be found. Unfortunately, this also included the squad car. Last April Jim got a good scratching, trying to pull the feline from under the cruiser before he drove off. Minky never scratched Allie. To look at the two enjoying each other, you would think Allie owned the beast, or the other way around.

"I'm not sure if I'm doing the right thing where Allie's concerned," Jim said with his back to JoLean—his hands tightly clasped together.

"You're wrong, Jim," she told him from her seated position on the plush sofa, "that girl adores you. You're her father."

"Every time I look at Allie I see her mother's face. I worry I'm not giving her the life she deserves."

"I see. You think love, food, clothes, a roof overhead, that's not enough. Tell me what you're leaving out, would you please."

"How about a real father?" Jim said, turning to face the woman. "How about a future?" He felt the anger building up again. What had he told Nate just yesterday about not getting consumed by his emotions? A sudden wave of hypocrisy washed over him.

"Now you're being ridiculous," JoLean said. "You are a terrific father."

"Sure, having to run off all the time. Having to leave my daughter with a neighbor girl or leave her with you. Any trouble at all and off I go."

"Damn it, Jim. That's your job. You're the finest sheriff this town has seen in a long time. And as for letting me sit for you, well, you'll never make that an argument with me. I'm family. Family helps family.

Besides, if you didn't drop her by, I'd twist your arm off. I love that little girl. When I look at Allie I see my sister too. But I also see a lot of you. Your strengths, your brains, and even a little of that pigheadedness of yours. You and Katie did a wondrous thing by bringing that sweet child into this world. I will always thank you for letting me help you raise her."

Jim couldn't meet her gaze. His head told him she was right, but his heart, that was something else.

"As for Amy Evans sitting with Allie," JoLean continued, "you show me one family in this whole town with small children who doesn't use a baby-sitter. Especially, the single parent families. That's all part of the game, you big lug."

"Nice words, but they don't change the facts."

"And which facts are those, Sheriff?"

Jim knew that tone of voice. Katie had used it many times during their precious years together, starting the first day they met. He thought that particular inflection must run in the female genes of his deceased wife's family. That don't-be-so-sure-of-yourself tone. Ignoring the memories, Jim said, "You just hit on it. I'm the sheriff of this little stinking town."

"We've already settled that one."

"We barely touched the subject. You say, I'm a 'fine sheriff'—well I got that way by throwing the troublemakers and rowdies in jail when they get out of hand. They all know—mess up and into the slammer they go."

"Your point being?"

"You don't make many friend's that way. But a lot of enemies."

"Friends? You have plenty of friends. You—" JoLean paused, her eyes shot wide open. "Is that what this is all about? The Simon West thing?"

"What do you know about it?"

"I keep my ears open, especially when it concerns my family. I'm a snoop. Sue me."

"I neither want nor need to talk about Simon West," Jim told his sister-in-law.

"Don't you?" she replied. "Could have fooled me. Be honest. That's what's really been eating at you. People like Simon West have to spend their hate where they can. It's sad, but it's probably all he's got. Without his bullying and intimidations Simon West is nothing."

"You don't know everything. Simon West is a worm. Something that crawls up in the rain, then slithers back into the mud when it stops. But it's not just him. It's all of it." He looked back outside at his daughter, laughing and running. "My little girl shouldn't be exposed to all the crap I'm subjected to. I try to shield her, when I can, but when she's at school or at the park, people talk. And what about the future, one of these days someone like Simon West could take me out. Where would that leave Allie?"

"So what's the solution? Quit your job—give it up?" JoLean stared at him.

"Maybe I should. I'd leave this tiny town, take Allie somewhere she can make something of herself. Get a good education."

"That's your decision. But you wouldn't—couldn't. This town needs you and you know I'm right. You wouldn't run out on all the people who depend on you. It's not in your nature. But one thing you must always remember—if anything does, God forbid, happen to you, I'll be here for Allie. That's in *my* nature." JoLean got up from the couch. "Call your daughter in. Supper's almost ready. Made your favorite, roast beef in mushroom gravy."

Jim slid open the glass door. He had to only call out once to bring Allie in and send Minky running. JoLean brought out a plate of wonderful smelling food from the kitchen. Allie jumped in her chair. Jim followed close behind.

Before JoLean had a chance to sit herself, the telephone rang.

"Who would...?" JoLean said, and returned to the living room. Moments later she called out, "Jim, it's for you."

He rose from his chair and passed by JoLean coming back to the table. He gave his sister-in-law a quick glance.

"I don't want to hear it," she said.

Jim picked up the receiver. "McNee here."

"Sheriff? It's Margy. We got a call from Ellen Porter. It seems her son, Randy, found a body in the field off Route Twenty-five. Roger's on his way to the scene."

"We got any ID?" Jim asked, turning his head so his voice wouldn't carry into the dining area.

"Ellen said Randy was too frightened to look at the face."

"Get Roger on the radio. Tell him, I'm on my way."

"Right, Sheriff."

Jim hung up the phone and walked back to the table.

"What's wrong, Daddy?" Allie asked through a fresh milk mustache.

"Nothing, Angel. Just daddy's job." He looked at JoLean. "Again." He smiled at his daughter, wiped off her lip, and kissed her forehead. "I have to go out for a bit. Will you be a good girl for Aunt JoLean while I'm gone?"

"Of course she will," JoLean said. "She's always a good girl." JoLean got to her feet. "Eat your supper, Allie, while I talk to your father." The little girl complied as JoLean walked with Jim to the front door.

"I'm not sure when I'll be back," he said. "I'm sorry."

"Don't worry. I'll warm up some food when you get back. It will taste just as good."

Jim stomped out of the house.

"And don't worry about Allie," JoLean called out from the threshold. "She understands."

Jim turned enough to give JoLean a half-grinned and a nod, but silently he asked himself: how could an eight-year-old really understand her father running off all the time?

The sheriff opened the squad car door, then remembered he was wearing his street clothes—he hated going to a crime scene wearing civvies. Jim hurried over and popped the trunk. Inside he found his lightweight sheriff jacket. "It'll have to do," he said, and put it on. Luckily, his hat was still on the front seat from the day before. With these two items he wouldn't feel so out of uniform. After starting the engine, Jim saw JoLean and Allie watching from the open door. The two waved at him. He waved back, then drove off.

"She deserves better," Jim said out loud, turning the first corner.

~·~

Lucas stopped at the tent entrance. Not often did he succumb to fear. The feeling disgusted him, deepening his shame. His hand gripped the edge of the flap and he stepped inside. Lilith stood alone looking down at the creature who was once Simon West, his scaled body resting along the bottom of a large glass case. With no hesitation, Lilith put her right hand next to the creature's head. Its fork tongue probed the woman's long fingers. As Lucas drew closer, the snake-man hissed loudly and thrashed back and forth before retreating to the corner of his prison where he quickly coiled up for protection.

"Mistress," Lucas said, ignoring the creature and falling to one knee, bowing his head, his eyes staring down and away.

"I am not pleased," Lilith said, before he could speak another word. "And your groveling offends me, only adding to my anger. Stand and face me."

Lucas stood and held tight his fear. Lilith's eyes burned hot red, her black hair twisting like living serpents. A moment later her appearance was normal, but Lucas knew that changed nothing.

"I sent you to retrieve the body," Lilith said, "not these trinkets." The woman threw down a tan leather purse and stuffed toy tiger. "A simple task—one suited to your many talents."

"People, many people, were around the boy. Swarming like the insects they are. I could not get to his body. I tried but as I drew closer one of the foul humans commanded me away. He wore a badge. I managed to escape before he became suspicious of me."

"You stupid fool," Lilith screamed striking Lucas hard across the face. "I do not want excuses."

Lucas fell hard to the tent floor, but he did not object or react in any way. As he rose to his feet, several thick silver droplets seeped from the small gash on his cheek. But a second later, the droplets retreated back into the gash where the flesh sealed itself.

"Feel fortunate you have served me so well for so long," Lilith said, the anger in her voice diminished some. "And I still have need for your special abilities."

"My race was created to be servants. My failure has brought disgrace to the few remaining of my kind. I beg your forgiveness."

"I have no forgiveness to bestow." Lilith turned away from her servant. She petted the snake-man on his scaly head. "I want the boy. I want to make him part of my carnival. He had such a strong life force, such a lovely anger." She walked across the tent. "This town is full of darkness. Still, I sense something else, something secret, something trying to keep itself hidden from me. Nevertheless, I will have my fill of this town Arkham."

"And I…I have failed you in your quest."

"You have, but that need not prevent me from my prize. I can use other means to gain what I desire. Return to your other duties."

Lucas did not move. He stood as if afraid to speak.

"Is there something else?" Lilith asked.

"The human—the one who calls himself Johnny Solom."

"What of him?"

"He continues to ask many questions—dangerous questions."

Lilith laughed. "Dangerous…? What did you call them? Insects? An appropriate term. He is nothing, but we shall deal with him in due time. Be assured of that. Now leave me."

"Yes, my Mistress."

CHAPTER 19

Out on Route Twenty-five, four empty automobiles of different makes and models, were parked nose to tail on the dirt zone just off the blacktop. A hundred yards farther up the road, a squad car and ambulance, both with flashing lights, stood outside a long strip of yellow police barrier tape that ran across and down the hill, squaring off a large chunk of land. Within the artificial boundaries several men performed a grim task.

"Easy now," Roger Anderson told the men as they picked up the covered stretcher and started up the incline. "Keep it in a straight line boys," the deputy added, closing off the inner circle he had made with more of the same yellow police tape that garnished the hilltop, marking the exact spot where the body had been found. Carefully, they made their way up to the road and the ambulance, which in Arkham, Nevada doubled as the coroner's wagon. And that seemed fitting since Doc Brown doubled as the town's coroner.

When the group reached the top of the hill, another man, wearing a white uniform, pulled back a piece of the yellow tape so the bearers could get through. The back doors of the emergency vehicle were wide open, waiting to receive its lifeless cargo. As Roger helped load the body for transport, the sheriff's cruiser pulled up with full lights and siren. Jim McNee got out, immediately putting on his sheriff's hat and buttoning up his jacket.

"Sorry for pulling you away from your dinner," Roger said, walking to meet his boss halfway, "but it couldn't be helped." The deputy didn't wait for Jim to ask the question. "It's the Clarksted boy, all right."

Jim stepped over to the taped-off edge of the hill. He pushed up on the front rim of his hat. Surveying the area, the first thing he saw was the yellow circle Roger had staked out.

"I kept the crew moving back and forth along a straight line," the deputy said. "The area is pretty much the way we found it."

Jim nodded his head.

"Looks like some kind of animal killed him," Roger added. "Something big—a bear maybe. Poor Potter boy, he's still shook up about the whole thing. I had Nate go and take his statement. You know how Nate is with kids and all."

Jim stood silent for a moment, then asked, "Did you find the Bonn girl?"

"Not yet, Sheriff. We're not even sure they were together." Roger scratched his head. "Maybe, she—"

"They were dating, right?" Jim said.

"That's common knowledge."

"Then you can bet they'd be together. Not much more to do in this town for young people other than being together."

"They could've had a fight or something. You know, she got mad and went off by herself."

The sheriff gave him a cold glare. "Use the brains God gave you. We have two missing kids. One male, one female, who've been seeing each other for over a year and were last seen together. Add up the facts. I want this whole area searched. And I mean every stone turned."

"Yes, sir." The deputy paused. "I didn't mean anything by questioning...."

Jim gave up a half smile. "It's not you, Roger. I've just got too many things on my mind right now. It's turned me into a horse's ass."

Suddenly a voice cried out. "Sheriff! Sheriff—over here!"

Jim and Roger ran to the man in a flannel shirt. He stood on the road past the restricted section. "I figured you wouldn't want me to go down by myself," Harvey said very fast with excitement. "You know, disturbing evidence and all that. I watch the *Cops* show, so I know better. I watch every Saturday night."

"What is it Harvey?" Roger said impatiently.

"Look—look right down there. It's a car trunk sticking out behind those bushes."

"Tape off this area too," Jim ordered.

"I'll do it myself," Roger said.

Jim started down the hill. He immediately recognized the vehicle as Billy Clarksted's Dodge. The first thing he did was look inside. It might explain what happened to Nikki Bonn. Except for a large dent on the roof and a broken windshield, the car appeared all right. And empty. He returned to the road, noting the foot tracks in the dirt between the car and where the boy's body was found. The distance between each step was twice a normal stride. It told him that Billy had been running and running fast.

"Anything?" Roger said, spanning the tape along the tops of thin flat wooden stakes he had pounded into the ground.

"No." Jim looked at the men standing around, gawking down at the partially hidden car. He counted thirteen. There was a lot of land to cover with such a small group. He faced Roger. "Take the men and form three groups: three, three, and seven. Then meet back with me."

Roger didn't say another word and went off to follow Jim's orders.

Hiking further up the road, it wasn't long before Jim found the entry point the Dodge took into the field. He stooped down and touched the residue of tire rubber on the blacktop. The skid marks told him that the car had been forced into too sharp of a turn while the brakes were being applied. Normally, he would see such marks as a result of a blown tire. But that's one of the things he looked for when examining the vehicle. All tires were completely intact.

"Must have been run off the road by another car," Roger said, coming up from behind. "And at high speed." He had also seen the same kind of marks many times before. They were a common sight in this line of work.

The sheriff guided his finger along the black rubber streak. "There's only one set of skids here. Where are the other car tracks? And these are too straight. If he was being forced off the road there would be ripples in the line where the cars hit. Also add in the fact that there's not a flake of missing paint from either side of Billy's Dodge."

"Could have been a head-on. Billy saw the car coming, turned too sharp, and over he went. If the oncoming car didn't slow down, it wouldn't have left skid marks."

"Maybe." The sheriff stood up.

"You know," Roger said, looking up the road one way, then down the other, "this does have all the earmarks of a game of chicken."

"Until we know more, keep that to yourself. No sense starting stories with no proof. This is going to be hard enough on everyone concerned without them thinking the boy was playing asinine games."

Roger nodded and asked: "What are your orders?"

"First, the two smaller groups are to start at the Dodge. You'll see a trail of running footprints. Billy's I figure since the tracks lead from the car to where you found the body. Have one group on each side, five-foot distance between each man. Look for anything dropped by the boy or possibly thrown at him."

"That only covers a thirty foot area."

"It will be enough. At the speed he was running we shouldn't need to cover much more."

"And the third group?" Roger asked.

"Have them do a sweep, over and around the area Billy was found. Have them fan out for about a hundred yards past that point. Make sure they keep their eyes open for any more tracks."

Again, Roger nodded.

"As soon as the first two groups are done searching along Billy's trail have them meet up with the others. Form a straight line. Keep 'em going 'til the edge of town. If the girl was on foot she would have been moving the same direction as the boy. When Nate gets back—"

"He just pulled up," Roger said, pointing over Jim's shoulder.

"Have him canvass the site around the car and the path leading up to it. Get Ben Clemens out here with his tow truck. He's to bring the vehicle to impound. We'll check out the insides there."

"Right, Sheriff."

"Make sure the hill is inspected before the car is hauled up. Never know what might get squashed under during the tow. See to that yourself."

"Good as done," Roger said.

Both sheriff and deputy headed back to the group of waiting men. After a brief word, Jim continued to his squad car.

"Where you gonna be if we need you?" Roger asked.

"I'm heading over to the Clarksted's to tell 'em we found their son. I'd rather they hear it from me before someone at Doc Brown's office calls them." He took off his hat and wiped his forehead. It wasn't hot, but Jim was sweating. "Grew up with Martha's brother. It's not going to be easy telling her her oldest boy's dead."

"Never is, Sheriff," Nate said.

"True enough." He threw his hat down on the far side of the seat and got in. "I'll be back in a short time." He glanced at his watch. "We only got about two and a half hours of good light, maybe three. Get movin'."

Jim McNee pulled away from the hill as the small groups began carrying out his orders.

~·~

While waiting for the second ring to sound in the phone's earpiece, Jim stood in his kitchen pulling at the collar edge of his newly pressed shirt. He cursed to himself about too much starch. Finally, the other end picked up.

"Hello," JoLean said. Her crystal clear voice, for a brief moment, took on the same almost musical quality of her sister. It startled the man to hear what sounded like his dead wife.

He hesitated a second before saying: "Hi, it's me."

"Jim, where are you?"

"At home. I need you to keep Allie a while longer than planned. Maybe for the night. I'm not sure yet. I don't know how late I'll be."

"What's wrong?"

"I really can't go into it right now. Just stopped by to change into my uniform—and—" Jim took a short breath. "There's something I have to tend to. I'll call you when I know more."

"All right. Do what you have to. We'll be fine."

"Give Allie my love," Jim said, fighting back the remorse that he would be missing another night with his daughter. How long could he do this? One day he'd wake up and find he had run out of time. Allie would be all grown up and on her own. He can never get these moments back. They'd be lost—forever.

"You can count on it," she told Jim.

"JoLean…."

"Yes, Jim?"

"Thank you." He hung up the phone. Stepping over by the base of the sink, Jim stared out the small window that looked out over the side yard. He let out a deep breath, put on his hat, and left the house. The lawman marched across the yard to the Evans' residence.

He knocked once.

"Hi, Sheriff," Amy said, opening the door. "You need me to sit with Allie?" She glanced around. "Where is she?"

"Allie's at her Aunt JoLean's. I'm here to see you. May I come in?" Jim couldn't miss the sudden fright in the girl's eyes. The situation got just that much harder.

"Who's that at the door, Amy?" Barbara Evans, Amy's mother, asked coming down the small hallway. "Oh, hello Jim. Come on in."

"Evening, Barbara," Jim responded, removing his cap. "I need to speak with Amy. Maybe you and Kent should join us."

"Kent, could you come up here," the woman called out, a little tremble in her voice. She managed to smile at Jim. "He's building a bookshelf in the basement." Her words sounded strained. "Out of oak. Should be beautiful, when he's all done." She stepped back into the hallway and called down again. "Will you please come up, Sheriff McNee is here."

Moments later, Kent appeared, wiping his hands with a small towel. "Hi, Jim." A light dusting of sawdust covered his pants. "I thought Barb was kidding with all the 'sheriff' talk." He came over and shook his friend and neighbor's hand.

"Let's sit in the living room," Barbara said. "It will be more comfortable."

In silence they moved to the next room. All four sat.

"What's going on?" Benny said from the staircase railing.

Barbara stood up and rushed to her son. "Back upstairs. We'll talk later. Go to your room now. And I mean in your room. I better hear that door close, young man."

"Nobody tells me anything around here," Benny grumbled up the steps.

Barbara heard his door click shut, then returned to the group. "I'm sorry for the interruption."

Jim looked over to Amy.

"It's about Nikki, isn't it?" she blurted out.

"Let the man speak, dear," Kent said.

"She's right," Jim said. He had known the girl since Allie was a baby. Katie hired her to baby-sit one night. There was an immediate bond between the two of them. Katie trusted her. That was more than good enough for him. "It's about Nikki Bonn—and Billy Clarksted." He found it very hard to tell her what he had to. "This being a small town word travels fast. I got my information by a third party, so I need to ask you some questions. You were with both Nikki and Billy last night?"

"Yes, I was. I already talked to Principal Dalson about this."

"I know, but I need you to tell it to me now," the sheriff said.

"Is this about Nikki's disappearance?" Barbara asked. "Amy told us about her talk with Wright Dalson when she got home from school."

"Let the man get on with it Barbara," Kent snapped.

"Dad!"

"I'm sorry," Kent said, taking his wife's hand. "There's more to this, isn't there Jim?"

Jim nodded. "Amy, what time did you leave them?"

Amy's parents appeared surprised by the question, but neither said a word.

"About seven or so."

"Did you see them or talk with either of them later last night?"

"I didn't. I— What's wrong, Sheriff?"

Jim glanced down to the floor. "It pains me to tell you, but we found Billy's body off Route Twenty-five."

The tears Amy had forced back all day broke free and rolled down her cheeks.

"Oh my God," Barbara said, squeezing her husband's hand.

"I assume you've already talked with the Clarksted's, Jim," Kent said.

"I have. About thirty minutes ago. That's where I learned about the meeting at the school. The Clarksted's and the Bonn's have been in contact with each other. Amy, I would've come to talk with you on my own anyway—you being friends with Billy."

"Nikki?" Amy asked. Her tears hit the corner of her mouth when she spoke. "What about Nikki?"

"We haven't found any signs of her," Jim said, shaking his head.

"I've got to call Corin," Barbara said, holding back her own tears and rushing out of the room.

"Could be a good thing, honey," Kent said, trying to comfort his daughter. "She might be perfectly fine."

"Or not! Excuse me." Amy bolted up from her seat and ran toward the staircase.

The two men stood up as the weeping girl disappeared to the upper floor.

"I have to admit, Kent, when I first heard that Nikki and Billy were missing I worried about Amy. Don't get me wrong, this situation has my full attention, but your daughter is very special to my Allie. I'm not sure how Allie would react if something happened to her. She got Allie out of her shell when Katie...you know." He couldn't say the word.

"Amy feels the same about your little girl," Kent said. "Do you know how it happened? With the Clarksted boy, I mean."

"Maybe an animal. The body's at Doc Brown's. I'll be going over to his office in a couple hours. That'll give him a chance to do an examination. I'll see what he can tell me then."

"You said 'maybe.' Did you see the body?"

"Not yet. My deputy thinks it was a bear. But we've never had a bear attack in these parts. I'll wait for Doc's report."

"Will you keep us informed?"

"I can't promise anything. We have to keep things pretty tight during an investigation."

"Understood," Kent said, escorting the sheriff to the front door. "Only wish we could've been more help. You didn't get to ask Amy many questions."

"I got the one answer I needed," Jim acknowledged. "At seven o'clock last night, Billy Clarksted was still alive."

CHAPTER 20

An hour before dusk and outside of town, two cars secretly met on a secluded back road. Inside the black Cadillac, two men spoke. One was trying to convince the other that he had everything under control.

"I hope you're right," Jasper Fallon said, shaking a half burnt, but extinguished cigar at his hired lackey.

"I've already spoken with a few key members of the tribe's council," Bob Ryley said, "it should all go smooth." Ryley was a man of small stature with gray streaked hair and a completely gray mustache, who usually went unnoticed in a crowd.

"Talk is cheap," Jasper said, patting down his vest for a re-light. Finding none, he reached forward and pushed in the car's cigarette lighter. "Just get the job done. Have those papers signed and on my desk tomorrow. Am I clear on that point?"

"Yes, sir," Ryley replied, reaching into the inner pocket of his tweed jacket, reassuring himself that he had indeed remembered to bring the purchase agreement. Under normal circumstances, he wouldn't have such doubts, but this whole deal made him nervous somehow.

With nothing left to be said, Ryley jumped out of the Caddie. He heard the engine fire up behind him, but didn't bother to turn and acknowledge the departure. He despised that pompous fat man, though the money Jasper paid him bought a lot of tolerance.

Ryley returned to his rental car. After driving less than two miles, he pulled up to the Tribal Council Hall—a simple building with two exquisitely detailed carved totems on each side of the main entrance. As he approached, he spotted several men standing outside. The group seemed to be distracted.

"Evening gentlemen," Ryley said.

"Evening," most replied back in unison.

Eugene Skyhawk turned to a tall man with thick glasses. "Darrell, this is the man I was telling you about."

Ryley stuck out his hand, cutting Eugene off. "Robert Ryley, Mutual Land Development. But please, call me Bob. I hope all is ready."

"I'm not sure," Darrell Waters told him bluntly. "We are waiting on one of the council. Though, I suppose we can start without him."

"I see." There was a moment of awkward silence as the men stared blankly at each other. "I have a few things I need to set up. I will see you all inside." Ryley disappeared through the door between the totems.

Darrell turned to Eugene Skyhawk. "You were supposed to bring your Grandfather."

"I tried to find him. You know how he gets. He's like a ghost sometimes."

"Did you talk with Nate?"

"Not a chance. I wouldn't give him the time of day, why would I talk to him?" Eugene shook his head at the notion of speaking to his cousin. Better he should lose a finger. "I left word out for my Grandfather. If he's going to be here, he'll be here. If not, well, he's getting too old for making these kinds of decisions."

"Have more respect for our Shaman," one of the other men said. "He's always known what's best for our people. He's always put others before himself."

"Doesn't look that way tonight," Eugene said. "You decide Darrell."

"If he doesn't show up, we'll have no other choice but to proceed without him."

"That will not be necessary," Samuel Skyhawk said, walking up the small path. "Please forgive my tardiness." He stared at Eugene, who could not meet his grandfather's gaze.

"Give it no mind, Samuel," Darrell said. "We are pleased to have the benefit of your guidance."

"Even if I am getting too old?"

The men stood silent for a moment, then Eugene broke from the group.

"Forgive the folly of youth, Shaman. He is impatient."

"The impatience of youth is one thing, but the disloyalty of blood is quite another."

Several of the men mumbled their agreement.

"Let's get this meeting started," one man said. "Seems pretty cut and dry to me."

"All of you go in," Darrell told the others. "I wish to speak with Samuel a moment to bring him up to speed."

Samuel began his walk to the doors of the Council Hall. "I know all I need."

"But how could you?" someone said, "we just learned about it ourselves."

Samuel said nothing. The others didn't push the issue.

～～丶∣～

Jim McNee sat alone in the office of Doctor Horace Brown awaiting his report on the examination of Billy Clarksted's body. The room was large enough to hold several people and at that moment seemed particularly empty. It was comfortably furnished for an office—it even had a couch, which folded out into a bed, and next to it a small refrigerator. Having never been married, on late nights, Doc Brown didn't bother going home. With a spare suit in the closet and his food stash, the doctor often referred to this place as his apartment. A medical diploma hung on one wall alongside a license to practice medicine in the state of Nevada. On the opposite wall there was an eye chart with letters arranged in the familiar triangular shape that read, "I accept chickens in lieu of cash." Doc Brown had a weird sense of humor. Even with the lack of plants, photos, or knick-knacks, the office still had a homey feel.

The sound of the office door opening had Jim turning in his chair.

"Sorry for the delay, Jim," Doc Brown said. "The Collins boy got hit in the face with a baseball. Needed four stitches under his left eye." The older man, thin, distinguished white hair, and wire rim glasses, in his late fifties, early sixties—he never admitted to his true age—entered the office.

"Didn't mind," Jim said, "and it wasn't that much of a wait." If the truth be known his feelings were two fold—pulling him in different directions. On one hand, he wanted to get this over with, and on the other, he didn't feel much like talking about a dead high school boy. A kid who should be playing hooky, or necking with his girlfriend in the back row of the movie theater, instead of being the centerpiece on a morgue slab.

Doc Brown took his place behind his desk, adjusting his slightly arthritic body in the swivel chair of oak-trimmed, deep red, vinyl. The chair didn't match his nearly-two-month-old maple top, but it was broken in just the way Doc liked it. Jim couldn't ever imagine Doc parting with his old, worn friend.

The two men sat across from one another a lot like the chess games they'd played over the past twelve years. Though this was no game, and both knew it.

Doc tried to ease the tension a bit. "You missed all the fun," he said.

"Couldn't be helped."

Doc Brown pushed his glasses closer to his face as he opened the file. "Allow me to review my notes a moment. Don't want to leave anything out. Sometimes I get forgetful. Left my watch in a patient during an appendectomy last week. He didn't mind at first, but I had the alarm set. Thing kept going off in the middle of the night and waking him up." He smirked and glanced up at Jim.

Jim sat patiently.

"Please understand," Doc started out, "my findings are preliminary at best. There's a state examiner coming down from Carson City. A fellow by the name of Matt Blake. He's better equipped to deal with these kind of things. Worked with him last year. You remember when Luke Closer accidentally poisoned himself? Wouldn't have found the right cure without Matt's help. He's a real good man."

"That's fine, Doc," Jim said. "You did your best considering." Jim knew that old Doc Brown wouldn't be able to give him all he needed, but at least it would be a start—or so he hoped.

Doc read from his notes: "William Clarksted, age: eighteen years, height: six feet, two inches, weight: a hundred and seventy-nine pound, etc., etc., died between the hours of eleven and twelve last night. Cause of death was severe trauma to the circulatory system. Cause unknown."

"Unknown? It wasn't an animal attack?"

Doc Brown leaned back in his chair, removing his glasses. "Not any animal I've ever seen. The wound was too clean, indicating to me that there was only one blow. Sure there were some bruises and his wrist was broken. However, the killing strike was executed with one swift thrust and retraction."

"Still, maybe a bear or...."

"Whatever hit the boy's chest had four very sharp prongs going as wide as four centimeters in diameter and close to twelve centimeters in length. Does that sound like any bear you've ever seen?"

Jim just stared at the man.

"And there's another thing." He paused for a moment. "The area around his heart was completely and smoothly cut. No tearing of any kind. It appears as if the veins and arteries connected to the heart muscle were severed with great precision. Usually in this type of trauma there is damage due to the extraction, but not in this case—indicating great striking speed. The boy died instantly. He didn't suffer from the blow, if that's any comfort."

"It's not," Jim said.

"Keep in mind that my tests are incomplete—left the fancy stuff for the state examiner, but after taking X-rays of the wound, I did find some small particles."

"Particles? What kind of particles?"

"Not sure. They're almost like scales of some kind, but then again I'm not equipped to test them. Though under the microscope they look a lot like reptile scales. Lizard, maybe snake."

"Could they've gotten on the body while it was outside laying in the field? There's a lot of snakes where we found him."

"They were in the body, and embedded in the soft tissue."

"So what you're telling me is that Billy Clarksted was kill by a lizard with nearly five inch claws."

"No, I'm not saying anything like that. As I said, my findings are only preliminary. We will have to wait for the state examiner's report. I'm just not set up to make a better examination. He should be here around nine tomorrow morning. Until then the body's in the cold locker. It should keep all right. Anything that we would have lost, we've already lost with the boy's body being exposed in the field all night."

"I appreciate your time, Doc," Jim said. "Sorry if I was short with you. When I think about that dead eighteen year old boy…."

"Hell, I brought Billy into this world. Never thought I'd be seeing him out. But I have to detach myself—cut off my feelings for the boy. I couldn't do my job otherwise."

In his mind, Jim heard himself telling Nate those exact words.

"Have you heard anything about Nikki Bonn?" the doctor asked.

"Nothing yet. Had a crew out, but when night rolled in we had to call off the search. Didn't have enough men to search such a large area with only flashlights. We'll start again at first light. At least we've got the boy's car. We can give it a good going-over. Maybe it will give us a clue to what happened. And I hope so, we don't have much more to work with."

"Something will turn up, Jim. Things like this don't go on unanswered for long."

"Not a good bet, Doc. My gut's telling me something different."

CHAPTER 21

Nine-thirty-five, the next morning, in the basement level of Doc Brown's office building, he and his friend, Matt Blake, carefully examined the cold, lifeless body of Billy Clarksted. A white linen sheet covered the lower half of the corpse, while it rested on the stainless-steel slide-out rack of the center locker.

Accessed by a single staircase, the lowest floor of the building had been converted from a large furniture refuge to a scrub area and a small morgue moderately equipped with three, temperature controlled body lockers, leaving enough dry free space for a records storage room. The two men worked diligently to unlock the secrets of the boy's death.

"Look at this," Matt Blake told Doc Brown. Peeking out from the bottom of the man's long white lab coat were blue jeans and sneakers. At first glance, the young age of the state medical examiner deceived many, but after a few minutes of speaking, his knowledge and respect for his profession was obvious. Both Matt and Doc examined the large wound in the boy's chest. "Do you see it?"

"What am I looking for?" the older man asked.

"The angle," Matt responded. "See the way the skin was punctured. The angle is a downward thrust at about forty-five degrees." He pulled back the flesh with a thin metal probe. The tissue had settled forward, hiding the true shape of the damage. "With the smoothness of the wound, the action of the blow would have been natural, almost relaxed. One fluid motion."

Doc moved closer. "That was my finding too, but are you sure about the angle."

Matt continued his examination around the wound. "See? And there." He moved the probe again. "And there. See the angle? All conforming to the same general direction."

"You're right." Doc adjusted his glasses, pushing the lenses closer to his weathered face. "My old eyes missed something so obvious?"

"Your eyes aren't that bad, and it's not that obvious. I almost missed it myself. It's pretty strange to see something like this."

"That's somewhat of an understatement, I'd say. Whatever killed the boy had to be gigantic. Almost twice the boy's height." He heard his words, but had trouble believing what he had just said. Billy Clarksted stood over six feet tall.

"Or?"

Doc Brown cocked his head slightly to one side. "I'm not sure I understand. Or what?"

"Or—whatever attacked him did so from midair."

"Midair?"

"It came down on him like a hawk plucking a trout from the river."

"You can't be serious."

"You asked me my opinion—I'm telling you what it looks like. No matter how weird it sounds. And for the record it sounds weird to me too."

Doc Brown took a step back, scratching his head. "And the particles found in the wound? I've never heard of any giant birds with dark lizard-like scales. Unless, of course, you're counting myth and legend."

"Don't take my hawk analogy too literally. I'm not suggesting an actual giant bird. I only meant whatever killed the boy struck from above. But as for those scales, I can't say they are reptilian in nature. They don't match anything I've ever seen. I'm not even sure they're organic. I'll send a few back to my lab at Carson City. My people there should be able to tell us something more."

"Let's pray they do. I hoped a complete autopsy wouldn't be necessary. I'm not qualified and I know how the Clarksted's would feel about some stranger cutting up their boy." Doc immediately realized how that must have sounded. "Sorry, Matt, I didn't mean—"

"Forget it," Matt said, stopping the man's apology. "And who could fault them?"

"Let's get cleaned up," Doc Brown said, re-covering Billy Clarksted's body. "This whole thing disturbs me more and more by the minute. I could use a strong cup of Java. I'll buy."

"Sounds good," Matt said, looking down at the teen. He reached out for the sheet as if he was going to straighten it, then pulled back at the last moment. "Such a waste," he said.

"You should be the one to explain our findings to the town's sheriff," the doctor said, sliding the rack back into the cold locker. "I've already mentioned you were coming down to help me out."

The two men left the examining room. Doc Brown switched off the lights behind them. They made their way back to the small scrub area farther down the hallway. Their steps echoed throughout the empty corridor, neither men felt much like talking.

The footfall faded and a final cold darkness spread out across the lower level. For several minutes there was nothing, not an eyeful of light, nor an earful of sound—only a black void swallowing up everything. Then the dead silence gave way to a soft tapping that came from far within the examining room. Inside the frigid locker, Billy Clarksted's left hand twitched, and one eye slowly opened.

⌒⊱ | ⊰⌒

"Okay, Marylou...yes...I...yes," Nate White Moon said into the mouthpiece of the office telephone. "All right, we'll keep an eye open for him." The deputy grit his teeth in frustration. *How many times do I have to say it?* "We will. I'll see to it personally. Yes, someone will call you. I'm sure he's fine. This isn't the first...of course...as soon as we know something. All right, you take care now. Bye Marylou."

"What was that all about?" Jim McNee said, standing in front of the desk. "Anything on Nikki Bonn?"

Nate jumped in his chair at the man's sudden appearance. Busy taking the call, he didn't hear the door open or close, and without that warning he was unexpectedly face-to-face with his boss. "Nothing about the girl, Sheriff. Just Marylou Dunham. Seems Dwayne went on another one of his drinking binges last night and didn't come home. You know, the usual thing. He's probably sleeping it off somewhere."

"I've already thrown his butt in jail once this week. Damn fool, driving drunk again, I bet. He's going to kill somebody one of these days." Jim glanced at his deputy, then at the chair.

"Sorry," Nate said, and leaped up from the sheriff's seat.

Jim sat down. "This yours?" he asked, sliding the paper plate with a half-eaten hard salami sandwich to the other side of the desk. The meat had a heavy odor of garlic.

"You've got to be joking," Nate said, pushing the pungent sandwich away from himself.

"Would you two mind not pawing my breakfast?" Roger Anderson said, coming from the back room lockup, carrying a red toolbox.

Jim gave Roger a funny stare.

"It's homemade. What about it?"

"Your stomach," Jim replied.

Nate chuckled.

Roger put the steel box down on the small table next to the door, then walked to the desk. "How's things up at the search site?" the deputy asked, lifting the plate and sandwich. He took a bite.

"The group's starting on their second pass. If that doesn't turn up anything I'll call 'em all in." Jim glanced down at the open bottom drawer of the file cabinet behind the desk. He thumbed through the file labels. There were a few he hadn't seen yet. He hadn't had time lately to review all the new cases.

He pulled the first file and skimmed over the contents. "What's this report on Dora Lacwent?" The puzzlement clearly showing on his face.

"I filed that one," Roger said, swallowing his mouthful of sandwich. "Not much there really. She didn't show up for work last Monday, and I went to her house to investigate."

"I can read that much." Jim pulled the sheet so both his deputies had a good view. "It's this part that's not clear." He tapped the page hard with his index finger.

Roger leaned forward and read the piece that had piqued Jim's interest. "I wrote she must have left town."

"And this conclusion was based on an investigation?"

"It looked pretty routine. House was locked up. No sign of forced entry anywhere. Her car was gone. So, I figured she left town, maybe to visit relatives. Who knows?"

"That's right. You don't know. Think about it. A woman who has never left town in both our memories just picks up and goes. Doesn't that seem a little odd to you?"

"But old Dora has always been a little odd." Roger laughed.

"You want to laugh your way out of a job?" Jim said.

"Sorry, Sheriff."

Jim leaned back in his chair. "Think about it. Forgetting about Billy Clarksted being dead, what do we know?"

Roger shook his head.

"Nikki Bonn is missing," the sheriff continued. "So is Dora Lacwent. And not more than three minutes ago Marylou Dunham calls saying Dwayne didn't come home last night. And what about Simon West, Zeek Dyler, and the rest of that lot. Have you heard anything about them lately? Practically a night doesn't go by without hearing something regarding those trouble makers."

"Could be simple coincidence."

"Could be, but it doesn't seem likely." He looked over to the closed door that led to the holding cell area. "We got anyone locked up?"

"Not at the moment. Been sort of quiet in that respect."

Jim faced his deputies. "I want both of you to keep an eye open for Simon and his crew."

"You think maybe they're up to something?" Nate asked.

"Good question." Jim scratched his head. "Also, discreetly find out if anyone else is missing. And I mean real discreet. Don't start a panic."

"How do we do that?" Roger asked.

"You're law officers. Use all that specialized training of yours."

"All right, but you'd think people would report a disappearance."

"Some might, but there are elements of this town that wouldn't care one way or another."

"Every town has their share of rotten apples," Nate said. "No matter what the size. Big or small."

"But it's the others," Jim replied, "who make this job worth doing. Take Pamela Larson for example, or Tom Thatcher, or Doc Brown. There are some negative elements, but those fine people make up for the bad ones." *Wouldn't JoLean just love to rub it in, if she heard me lecturing these men on the worth of their job.*

"Speaking of Doc Brown," Nate said. "I hear he called in a medical expert from Carson City. Kinda thought the Clarksted family wanted Doc to handle things."

"They did. Doc Brown examined the body. He wants to have his facts double checked."

"But a stranger from Carson City?" Roger said. "We don't need some out-of-towner poking his nose in our business. That's nothing but trouble, if you ask me."

"No one did," Jim said. "Doc's acquainted with the man and he's not working in any official capacity. Just helping out Doc on this one. Seems there were some peculiar findings with the wound. There were some kind of lizard scales in the boy."

"Hell, I'd think Billy Clarksted would be smart enough not to be playing with rattlers," Roger said.

"I doubt Doc is thinking that small."

"I've seen a six-footer once. How big does he figure?"

"The way he described it, he wasn't talking just length."

"You know, Sheriff," Nate said. "I saw a snake at that carnival, in the freak show. It was huge. Ugliest thing I've ever seen."

"A python?"

"Not a python, exactly. To tell the truth, I don't really know what kind of snake it was. It may not have even been real."

"You just said—"

"I know what I said, but you've really got to see it for yourself. They called it a snake-man. It had blue eyes. Real weird. They fed it a live rat. One bite and a swallow, and bye bye rodent."

"Skip the details on its eating habits. The relative facts will do fine, please."

"As I recall, its body was long and scaly like a snake, but its head—its head was bigger, about the size of a grown man."

"Maybe that's why they call it snake-man," Roger laughed. " You're such a sap. Just a freak boa constrictor or something."

"With hair?"

"Where?" Jim asked.

"On its head. Thin hair, but it was hair. Brown."

"Sounds like another Jo-Jo the dog faced boy," Jim said, "but it wouldn't hurt to take a look. It's the only reptile around that would even come close to what Doc Brown described."

"You think that's such a good idea?" Roger asked. "Some people might not like it—you being the sheriff. Maybe I should go."

"People? What people?"

"Just people, that's all. You know how some tend to spew off at the mouth."

The sheriff ignored his deputy's concern and rose from his chair, heading to the door. "I'll be back in about an hour. Call me on the radio if you hear anything."

"Gotcha Sheriff." Nate snickered. "See if they'll feed the snake-man a rat while you're there. It's a sight."

"I'll pass, thanks." Jim walked out the door.

Nate chuckled to himself. "Took it all with one swallow."

Roger, still holding the salami sandwich, was about to take a bite, but stopped. He looked at it, then threw plate and all in the trash.

Nate burst out laughing.

~·~

Once driving on Juncture Road, it didn't take long for Sheriff McNee to spot the first of the large tents of Lilith's Carnival. He steered the cruiser into the empty portion of the field used for parking. Grabbing his hat from the seat, Jim got out of his squad car. Even with the hard dry earth, one could easily make out the variety of tire tracks from the past four nights.

Jim entered the main gate and approached a thick-armed man wearing a pair of oil stained overalls, standing in front of an open panel to the inner workings of the Tilt-o-whirl. He had a grease gun in his right hand and a rag in his left. A monkey wrench stuck out of the man's back pocket.

"I'd like to see the owner—Lilith," Jim called out as he drew closer.

The roustabout turned to face Jim and the color seemed to drain from his face. "Owner?" he replied. "Lilith?"

"That's what I said." At first Jim thought he simply caught the guy off guard, but his body language signaled a more than usual amount of nervousness. And he wasn't the only one reacting to Jim's presence. A couple of the other workers ducked to the back of their booths and out of his sight.

"I saw her down by the show tents," the carny said. "Try down there. I have a lot of work to do. Greasing gears. Tightening bolts. That kind of stuff." He began shooting black goo between several disks edged with metal teeth.

"I can see that," Jim said, staring at the steel monstrosity. He read somewhere that most of these amusement park rides were held together by only a few nuts and bolts. Having the chance to see one up close he realized that that was probably true.

Knowing he would get nothing more out of this man, Jim started down the midway. The carnival was scheduled to open at noon, and the workers were scurrying around finishing the final bits of preparation for the day's crowd. Taking the same path he took with the mayor the day they realized that a carnival had setup outside of town, he remembered Lilith telling them that she had decided to setup here after their group took a wrong road. That explanation didn't sit well with him then and it still doesn't now.

As Jim made his way through the carnival grounds, he casually kept his eyes moving, watching for anything unusual. To his right, one of the carnies was fixing a six-inch tear in the canvas wall of his booth. Large stitches closed the hole and now he was applying tar to the seam. To the left, a thin, wrinkled man sat in his chair with his feet up on the counter reading a copy of the local paper, *The Arkham Times*. Jim knew the old man was in fact watching him. Walking past, Jim heard the old man spit. By the heavy sound he must have been chewing tobacco. Roger made that same sound when he chewed during their fishing trips. A habit Jim had always found disgusting.

Reaching the farthest end of the midway, Jim came up to the first large tent. For a brief moment he smelled the stench of rotting eggs, but as quickly as the odor offended his nose, it vanished. Unlike the rest of the carnival, this corner was void of any activity, no workers, no open booths, not even as much as a tent flap rustling. Jim opened his mouth to speak, but before he could announce his presence, the big man, Lucas, popped out from between the tent slits, stepping squarely in front of the sheriff. The two men were almost toe-to-toe. A sudden feeling deep inside Jim McNee made him want to draw his gun. A purely instinctual reflex, one which he forced himself to resist.

"Can I help you—Sheriff?" Lucas said, towering over Jim. A fly buzzed around the bald man's head, followed immediately by a second. He made no attempt to shoo the pests away. "Is there something you need." The two flies landed on the man's face. One on his forehead, the other on his right cheek. The forehead fly crawled down and across his eyelid. Lucas didn't flinch, didn't budge, as the bug stopped to clean itself on the bridge of his nose, before continuing on to where the other fly seemed to be waiting.

Jim's eyes were fixed on the fly show, but he managed to say, "I'm here to see Lilith."

The two flies made small circles around Lucas's face and continued along and across his lips. "That is not possible," he said, the flies still clinging to his upper lip as he spoke.

"I'm here as the Sheriff of Arkham. It sure as hell better become possible."

"What is it Lucas?" Lilith said from inside the tent before stepping out into the light of day.

The flies jetted off. "The sheriff is here to see you, ma'am." His eyes did not meet hers when he spoke. He faced her, but he looked to the ground, almost as a bow.

"Welcome, Sheriff McNee," she said. "Lucas, please attend to your other duties."

He nodded and returned into the darkness of the tent.

"You have to excuse my servant. Sometimes he is overzealous in his dealings with people."

"Your servant?"

"Is that so surprising to you?"

"As a matter of fact, yes. A person in your…business having a servant seems rather ostentatious."

Her lips turned upward in a slight smile. "Lucas has been with me since it all began—the carnival, I mean. He's a helpful one to have around. Especially with some of the sideshows. When I get a new performer, sometimes they are unsure of the rules I impose here. Lucas keeps everything running smoothly. He handles problems before I have to become involved."

"Does that include handling your snakes?"

"Snakes? We have no snakes."

"I'm told you have one in the freak show."

"You mean the snake-man. Believe me when I say he is no simple serpent. I like to think of him as almost human. Just another creature of nature."

"I need to see him."

"My, my, Sheriff, are you asking for a free show?"

"No, ma'am. I'm conducting an investigation," Jim said in a stern voice with a hint of irritation.

"An investigation? Into what?"

"I'd rather not say at this time."

"Sheriff, if you want to see one of my freaks, it's only right that you tell me why. After all, my carnival is outside of town limits and your jurisdiction. I'm not required to answer any of your questions or give you access to any part of my carnival."

Jim felt himself becoming angry. "You're correct there ma'am, but I could restrict its access." He kept up his best poker face. "Declare this area off limits to the townspeople."

"I doubt such an action is within your authority. Besides, that would not help your investigation, now would it? It's your decision, Sheriff."

In a game of poker Jim would have tossed in his cards. He knew she had him and he knew she knew it too. With his bluff called there wasn't anything to be done without her cooperation. "A boy was killed a short distance from here," he reluctantly told the raven-haired woman.

"Are you saying there's some connection between this boy's death and my carnival?"

"At this point it's too early to say anything for certain. I'm following a lead. There were several strange scales in the body. Our local doctor thinks they might be snake scales."

"*Thinks* they might be?"

"He actually said they may be reptile scales, but he couldn't say for sure."

"And that is why you want to see my snake-man? I can assure you, Sheriff, he did not kill anyone, unless that anyone happens to be a rat—the rodent type, that is." She snickered.

Jim held back his frustration. Something really troubled him about this woman. Alarms were firing off up and down his insides.

"In the spirit of cooperation," Lilith said, "I will show you my snake-man. He is quite beautiful…and harmless."

"Your assistance is duly appreciated, ma'am."

"Anything to help, Sheriff. Please, this way."

Lilith guided Jim down two tents. Many small posters, all representing the freaks people would see inside, adorned the canvas. He studied each closely. "I don't see your snake-man depicted here," Jim said.

"The snake-man is one of my newer attractions. It joined us this stop. A fortunate set of circumstances allowed your little town the honor of his first viewing."

The sheriff remained silent and followed the woman into the tent where a platform had been set up.

"We open for business in an hour," Lilith added. "Lucas has moved the snake-man behind this stage."

She walked through the draped curtains off to the right behind which several small empty waiting areas had been constructed by other hanging curtains. From the corner of his eye, Jim saw something staring at him. When he turned to get a clearer view the strange thing retreated back into its own zone.

"You'll have to excuse some of the performers. They're not use to seeing outsiders when not on stage."

"Understandable," Jim said, turning his head just enough to finally see what was so interested in him. It was tall and thin with large protruding eyes. But the eyes were not human. More like the pictures he had seen of a magnified fly.

"Get back to your place," a gruff voice said from behind that curtain, followed by a loud slap. A short high whine filled the air.

"Lucas," Lilith said. "He's always so strict before a show. Everything and everyone has to be in proper order." Lilith pulled back another compartment's curtain. "This is what you wanted to see."

She led Jim to a large glass tank on wheels. The receptacle had four-foot by four-foot crystal clear walls with a similar hinged top except for the one inch holes which obviously provided fresh air. In the corner, wound in a tight coil, slept the so-called snake-man. Jim saw that Nate hadn't been exaggerating—the creature was ugly. Its large brown and green body had an enlarged, bloated head.

"Wake up my beauty," Lilith said, tapping the closed lid.

And the creature did just that. Its eyes flickered and its tongue shot out of its toothless slit of a mouth. It slowly uncoiled to the length of the container. When its head rose and the creature saw Jim, its human blue eyes shot open to their full measure. The freak began rolling around in the tank, beating its scaly tail hard against the glass. Jim took a step back, fearing the tank wall would shatter.

"He lacks good motor skills," Lilith said. "Those two small protrusions closest to his head. Those are all he has for arms—useless limbs. I considered having them removed but it does add to the man in 'snake-man.' Don't you agree?"

"I've never seen anything like this before," Jim said in wonderment and abhorrence.

"Are you sure?"

"I would remember if—"

At that moment, the snake-man leaped forward, striking its body against the glass. It rammed its head again, thrashing back and forth in the tank. The hisses that came from the creature's mouth almost began to take on the rhythm of words.

"He's easily agitated being so close to strangers," Lilith said. "And he must be hungry. He doesn't receive any food until he's on stage. We have a lovely morsel waiting for him."

"I've heard."

"Oh? I had no idea such a thing would interest you."

"Doesn't. All part of my investigation. Nothing more."

"As you can plainly see, my snake-man can barely control his movements in his tank. Outside of it he is totally helpless. So what do you think now?"

"The whole thing is cruel," Jim said bluntly, "bordering on sick. It's obvious the poor creature is suffering."

"What would you suggest? That I have him destroyed? All creatures, no matter how revolting, have a right to exist. And here he couldn't possibly harm himself—or others."

Jim held his tongue. Could there be anything more vulgar and at the same time so pitiful. The creature thrashed around the tank. It would stop every-so-often and look at him with those blue eyes. The eyes seemed to plead for help.

"I've seen enough," Jim said.

"Does that mean your suspicions have been relieved?"

They weren't, but he had nothing else. "That creature couldn't have caused the damage our town doctor described to me. I should get back to my office." *And not at all too soon.*

"As you wish." Lilith led Jim back the way they came. Outside the tent Lilith said, "You have a young daughter."

"Yes…yes, I do," Jim replied, surprised by this stranger knowing personal facts about his life.

"It must be difficult for a man to bring up a child on his own."

"It has its moments."

"I should say—all the uncertainty, frustration, and self-doubt. And it must be doubly hard being the sheriff, responsible for an entire town. The conflict of doing your job or raising your daughter. Which one to give your full attention to? Indeed, very trying."

"Like I said, it has its moments. But we get by."

"I have something for you, Sheriff." Lilith held out a red ticket in her long slender fingers. "Take this with my compliments. It's good for any show. We have some fine shows."

"Thanks all the same, but I can't."

"Please. It's my way of saying there's no hard feelings."

"Wouldn't be right to accept gifts," Jim said.

"A gift? You call a free ticket a gift? You must have very low standards. Please, come back when we are open. You'll have the adventure of your life, you make the choice. It is always your choice." She extended her hand a bit more.

Jim reached out and took the ticket from the mysterious woman. "Thank you," he said as he shoved the red slip in his shirt pocket.

"You can use it anytime. Anytime at all. It is your decision." Lilith grinned. "If that is all. I need to attend to other pressing matters. As I am sure, do you." She turned and disappeared back into the freak tent.

Jim retraced his steps through the carnival. Ignoring the many eyes following him, he got in his cruiser, and started back to town. He wasn't sure what he had accomplished by talking with Lilith. Indeed, she was a beautiful woman, but also bizarre. Her words echoed in his mind: "you make the choice. It is always your choice."

CHAPTER 22

Jasper Fallon won his bid for mayor with cold hard cash. His money bought the support that influenced others to vote his way. And other money bought the dark information that cast doubt on his opponents. All done, of course, through a middleman with no ties back to him. He always covered his tracks.

And he always got his way—

"I don't give a rat's ass what it takes, get it done," Jasper said from behind his desk, holding a cigar, which he rolled between his pudgy fingers under his nose while inhaling deeply. A hum of satisfaction escaped his lips. "It's a simple land purchase," he continued, reaching into his front vest pocket, pulling out a sterling silver lighter. Seconds later the tip of his cigar was a glowing red ember, releasing smoke into the expensively furnished office that included an extensive bookcase, an elaborate freshwater aquarium, and a delicate ivory statuette of a galloping horse.

"You know as well as I do," Bob Ryley said, "the land is on the fringes of the reservation. And any mining done will have to be approved by the tribe's council. But considering the events of last night, frankly, you can forget it."

"Are you deaf or just plain stupid? I'm not looking for any goddamn approval. You were to buy that strip of land outright. I couldn't have made myself any clearer." Heavy puffs expelled from his mouth with each word. "It's a piece of empty desert. There's no homes, no businesses. It's dirt. No one except the two of us know that there's a good sized copper deposit under that sand." Removing the cigar, he tapped the end into a nearby coffee mug, then like a pointer, he waggled it at Ryley. "I've already invested a good deal of capital, not to mention my valuable time in this project, and I demand results."

"Buying is out of the question," Ryley said. "I gave the council my best pitch. And at one point I even thought I had them. All that was left was fixing a price. But then some old man stood up and said something about the land being sacred ground." Ryley shook his head in utter disbelief. "Up to that point, the entire time that old man sat there, he didn't say a word, didn't as much as clear his throat. It was real weird— he spoke no more than two sentences and the rest of the council changed their tune. The deal flushed right down the toilet before my very eyes."

Jasper leaned forward in his chair. "That would be Samuel Skyhawk," he said, "the local witch doctor." Tapping his fingers on the desktop, he added: "Unfortunately, his people will follow him. Even his most stringent critics will not oppose his wishes."

"Something about him scared me," Ryley said outright.

The fat man began to chuckle, causing his cheeks to quiver. "What? That living fossil?" Then as quickly as it began, the laughter stopped. "I'm not paying you to be scared. You just do what you're told. I've worked everything out with nothing left to chance. All contingencies have been accounted for."

Ryley mumbled a few words under his breath.

"You got something to say," Jasper snapped, "then say it."

"It's just, well, was it a smart idea to call this meeting? People are bound to see me and later question the connection."

Jasper swept his hand through the air as if to brush away Ryley's concern. "Do you think I've gotten this far for this long by being careless? I have it covered. If anyone asks me, you're just another out-of-town land developer. You're simply paying me a courtesy call—seeing that I am the mayor of this fair town." He spun his chair around to face the window behind his desk. He stared down at Main Street and chuckled. "If you follow my instructions to the letter, things will go smoothly. Your credentials are impeccable. The company name I gave you to use is a legitimate development firm. You've been put on its payroll, at least on paper, so if anyone does bother to check all will appear in order."

"How did you manage that?"

"Never you mind. Let's just say it's part of my investment. It's a perfect setup, but more importantly, no one can trace anything back to me. As for the rest of it." Jasper Fallon got up from behind his desk and walked across the room while talking. "I wouldn't worry too much about what anyone sees."

He stopped in front of the twenty-five gallon fish tank, then picked up a small container of food, and sprinkled a tiny amount on the surface of the water. The fish immediately swam to the top to feed. "It's quite simple really. Arkham is like a fish bowl, a town in glass in a manner of speaking. I give out the goodies and people flock to me for what I have to offer."

Jasper pulled up his sleeve about four inches. "It's all under my control." He plunged his hand into the aquarium with an impressive speed. He grabbed one of the feeding fish and pulled it out in his closed fist. "Total control." He opened his hand and the fish fell back into the water. The tiny creature, apparently unharmed, swam back to the top of the water and continued his feeding with the others. "Of course, I'd never harm my fish," he said, lightly tapping on the glass, though not enough to disturb his watery pets. He grinned. "People—that's a different matter." He shook his hand dry. "Meeting with the council, you were introduced to one Darrell Waters."

"A tall slender man? Thick glasses?"

"That's him. Meet with Darrell again—personally. Convince him and he'll convince the others."

"But if what you said earlier is true, he'll still do whatever this Samuel Skyhawk decides."

"Then you have your answer," Jasper said. "Get rid of the problem." The fat man's forehead wrinkled as his eyes met Ryley's. "By whatever means possible."

The phone rang. Both men stood silent until the second ring. It was Jasper Fallon's private line, used only for very special projects. He walked back to the desk and picked up the handset.

He listened for a moment before saying simply: "When," then added: "I'll take care of it. Keep your ears open." He hung up the phone without any fanfare.

"Problems?" Ryley asked.

"Sheriff Jim McNee—again. He keeps sticking his nose where it doesn't belong." Jasper returned to his chair and pulled a handkerchief from his pocket. After mopping his forehead, "I have to get him out of my business once and for all."

Ryley appeared surprised by the man's reaction. "You're the mayor—just get rid of him."

"Life's not that simple. And I prefer a more subtle approach. It has to be done delicately—with finesse. Jim McNee has gotten in my way before. I control this town, it may be time to teach the sheriff that hard cold fact." He grinned, accentuating his double chin.

Deputy Roger Anderson hung up the phone as Doc Brown and Matt Blake entered the sheriff's office.

"Hi, Roger," Doc said, "Jim around?" In his hands was a folder with a page or two of loose-leaf paper sticking out along with the top of a color photograph.

"He stopped by for a minute, Doc," the deputy said from behind the desk, "then took off again." He gave the stranger with the doctor a quick appraisal. The man didn't look like such a big deal to him. "So you're that specialist," Roger said to the outsider. He didn't trust people from big cities. Felt they were always after something. Didn't matter who, men, women, doctors, police, he would rather do without visitors from Carson City or anywhere else. The people in Arkham were enough for him.

"Where's my etiquette?" Doc Brown said. "Roger Anderson, this is Matt Blake. Matt—Roger."

Roger stood up. The two men shook hands.

"Pleased to meet you," Matt said, ignoring Roger's tone. "And specialist is an exaggeration."

"Don't you believe it," Doc said, "Matt is one of the best. We were on our way to the Diner for a late lunch. Just wanted to drop our report off. I figured Jim could read it while Matt and I grab a bite, then we'd come back and talk the whole thing over."

"I can't say when he'll be back, but you can still leave the report if you want. I'll see he gets it."

Doc glanced at Matt. "We should really speak to Jim first. It's a little hard to follow."

"Suit yourself," Roger said, slightly annoyed.

Right then, the door opened. All three men turned thinking that Jim McNee had returned. Instead, Chester Nich entered with a heavy mail sack hanging over his shoulder. "Howdy Gents," he said with the usual smile. "Light load today, Roger." He pulled two pieces from his bag. "Something from the County Seat and a piece of junk mail. A seed catalog. How on Earth did you guys get on that mail list?"

"Couldn't tell ya," Roger said. "Another mystery of life, I suppose."

"When Jim gets back," Doc Brown said, "have him get hold of me. It's important."

"You lookin' for the sheriff?" Chester asked. "I saw him heading up to the mayor's office. And knowing Jasper Fallon, he's probably pissed off about something."

"Always is," Doc Brown said. "I've warned him about his high blood pressure. One of these days that man will most likely explode from an anger attack."

"That settles that," Roger said. "You know how the mayor hates to be disturbed with unimportant stuff. The offer's still good Doc, leave the file I'll see the sheriff reads it first thing when he gets back."

"The death of a youth should be considered important enough—even to a money-grubber like Jasper. I'll talk to Jim myself."

"Whatever you say, Doc," Roger said.

"You sure you saw him going up to the mayor's office?" Doc asked Chester.

"No more than five minutes ago. You could catch him if you hurry."

"My thought too," Doc Brown said. "Regardless of what I personally think of Jasper Fallon, the mayor should be informed as well. How's your hunger, Matt?"

"I could hold off on lunch for another hour or so."

"Hopefully, it won't be that long." Doc Brown looked thoughtfully at his friend. "In your business you must have to have a strong stomach."

"Why? Is the food that bad?"

"No, but the mayor is."

Chester laughed. "Good one, Doc."

"Is *his Honor* in?" Jim asked, the sarcasm dripping off his lips. The heat of the office space was eased slightly by a light breeze from an open window. The sky had been a perfect blue earlier that day, but now with the wind, heavy clouds were moving in from the southwest.

"One moment," Janet Cuvier said. "He's on a call."

When the small phone light finally went dark, Janet pushed the button on the intercom. "Mayor, Sheriff McNee has arrived."

"Get him in here," a staticky voice said through the small black plastic box.

"You heard," Janet said, pushing her blonde strands back behind her ears. She needed a good root job.

"Don't get up. I know the way." Jim glanced back at the woman, her short black skirt riding up on her perfectly sculptured thigh. She wasn't originally from Arkham. The mayor met her on one of his "trips" to see the Governor. That's what he says anyway. He was so impressed with her qualifications that he snatched her up right out from under the nose of another mayor, but he never said from which town. The qualifications that interested Jasper were most likely under her blouse.

"You can go in," she said.

Jim realized he was staring. "Just gathering my thoughts."

"Of course you were," she said, putting the end of her pencil in her mouth and biting down.

Feeling a bit embarrassed, Jim opened the inner door and hurried in. "I got your message," he said to the fat man behind the expensive oak desk. "You wanted to see me?" He hated his visits to this office. Meeting with Jasper Fallon was bad enough, but the room always stunk of cigars. Jasper never smoked tobacco in front of other people, so Jim wondered if Jasper really believed he was fooling anyone by lighting up behind closed doors.

"Sit down." The mayor didn't bother looking up as Jim walked to the desk, instead he kept scribbling numbers down on a yellow legal pad. When he finally raised his head, he was surprised to see Jim still on his feet.

"I'd rather stand."

"Have it your way." Jasper opened his top desk drawer and tossed the pad inside. "It has come to my attention that you went down to the carnival and had words with the owner Lilith."

"We talked. I wouldn't say we had words." Jim's face went stern. "How in the hell did you find out I went to the carnival? And what concern is it of yours?"

"I have my sources. I'm a busy man. I need others to keep me abreast of things."

"She's at her desk."

"I beg your pardon."

Jim held back his grin. "Never mind."

"As far as it being my concern—I *am* the mayor. I run this town. A fact that has never pleased you, but one you have to live with. If something happens in this town I want to know about it. Am I clear on this point."

"Crystal clear."

"As I was saying, you went down to the carnival this morning."

"What of it?"

"I'll make it real simple for you to comprehend. I'm ordering that stopped. Don't bother the owner—Lilith. I gave her my personal assurances that she could proceed with her carnival. I don't need you messing things up...for her."

"We have a boy lying dead over at Doc Brown's. I will do whatever I deem fit to find out who or what killed him."

"You're talking about the Clarksted's boy?"

"How many other dead boys do you think we have?"

"Don't use that tone with me—or you'll find yourself out of a job!"

"I may report to the Mayor's Office," Jim snapped, "but like you, I'm an elected official. You can't fire me. And that's one fact *you* have to live with." Jim had much more to say—things he had held back for far too long—but before getting the chance the intercom buzzed.

"Doctor Brown is here to see you and the sheriff," Janet announced.

"Can it wait?"

"It most certainly can't," a voice, definitely not Janet's, said over the black box. "And if you don't want me busting down your door...."

"Send him in," the mayor replied reluctantly, obviously recognizing the voice. "This day can't get any worse," he muttered. When not one but two men entered his office, Doc Brown and a stranger, Jasper added, "Apparently it can."

After brief introductions, the doctor opened his folder flat on the desktop. He took out the photograph of Billy Clarksted's bizarre wounds and handed it to the sheriff, who glanced at it, then handed the photo on to the mayor.

"Christ," Jasper said, "I haven't had my lunch yet. How do you expect me to look at food after seeing this."

Jim snickered, but the others didn't hear him.

"You should have seen Hank Thompson after he came out of the drug store's darkroom," the doctor said. "His face was two shades of green." He caught himself. "But this is really nothing to make light of."

"You find anything?" Jim asked.

"I'll let Matt explain. They were his findings."

Both mayor and sheriff listened while this stranger described something only real in a nightmare. Even with the facts to back him up, it all seemed so impossible.

"So, it wasn't a reptile," Jim said.

"No, I—"

"You see, Sheriff," the mayor said, drowning Matt out with his own, much louder, voice, "you bothered them for nothing."

"Them?" Doc Brown asked. "Bothered who?"

"The sheriff figured the carnival had something to do with the boy's death. But this proves him wrong."

"How?"

"If it wasn't a reptile, that includes snakes."

"All that means is that we don't know what killed Billy Clarksted. Nothing more, nothing less. If less is possible."

"What about the scales found in the wound?" the sheriff asked.

"Another mystery, I'm afraid," Matt said. "I couldn't identify them. I sent a few samples back to Carson City for further analysis. I'm not even sure they're organic."

"In plain English, please," Mayor Fallon said.

"All living things are based on carbon, which we call organic. Non-carbon, we call inorganic. And the scales appear inorganic."

"I still don't—"

"He means," Jim said, "the scales didn't come from anything alive."

"Very good, Jim," Doc Brown said.

"You think I don't pay attention during our chess games? You're always trying to cram that stuff in my head."

"Cram nothing. I was trying to distract you. How else do you suppose I win?"

Matt, Doc, and Jim laughed.

"Could we be serious?" the mayor said. "I'm very busy. I have no time for this jocularity."

"Relax, Jasper," Doc said. "I bet you left your blood pressure pills at home again. And as long as I'm at it, I told you to give up the stogies."

"Please! Can we get on with this and keep my medical history out of it?"

"You're an ornery cuss today," Doc said. "More than usual, I mean."

Jim fought to hold back his laughter. He noticed Matt Blake's face twitching as well. He took it on himself to get this impromptu meeting back on track. "Are you saying the scales came from a weapon of some kind."

"Finally, a sensible question," Jasper said.

"I can't say that. The scales aren't metallic either. They're closer to stone, but they're not stone."

"Are we back to the jokes again?" Jasper said in an irritated tone.

"It's no joke, Mayor. I can't tell you what the scales are made of. It's a mystery."

The discussion broke down quickly after that point. The mayor made clear his opinion that the whole thing was garbage and didn't want to hear anymore. Jim didn't know what to think, but he trusted Doc Brown. If his oldest friend says Billy Clarksted's death had some unexplainable peculiarities, then it did—plain and simple. His uppermost concern now was what to do next?

CHAPTER 23

As Jim sat in the cruiser outside the school, his chat with the mayor came flooding back to him. Jim didn't like being chewed out, especially from that fat bald man who lied, bribed, and cheated his way into the mayor's office. If Jim had any solid evidence on "his Honor's" other activities, he would throw him in jail so fast he'd lose his pants. Jim got close once, by accident—a fishy matter of redirected road construction funds—but the lead dried up as fast as it appeared and Jasper Fallon slithered away scot-free. Now this carnival thing. Jasper had his hand in it somehow. It had to do with money, Jim was sure. The mayor was never so passionate about anything except money. And the one other question that kept nagging at him: how did Jasper know about his visit to the carnival in the first place?

The bell rang inside the school, snapping Jim back to the present. Luckily, he had one window open or he would've missed the sound altogether. During hotter days, when the air conditioning was on and the windows were rolled up, he had to watch the onslaught of kids pouring through the doors signaling the school day's end.

"Base," Jim said into the car's radio mike. The children only now coming out of the building, some walking, some running.

"Yes, Sheriff?" a male voice responded.

"Roger?"

"Yes, Sheriff. Margy ran to the diner for a bite to eat. Something I can help you with? Any trouble?"

"Just wanted to let you know, I'm waiting to pick Allie up, then I'll be knocking off for the rest of the day."

"Sounds good, Sheriff. I'll pass the word."

"You can reach me at home if you need to. Out."

"All right. Base out."

Jim replaced the microphone on the dash as Allie came up to the half-opened window. "Hi, Daddy," she said, smiling.

"Hi, Angel. Jump in."

"I can't."

Jim stared at his daughter not understanding her response.

"The door's locked," she told him.

"Sorry." He reached over and yanked up on the small plastic knob releasing the lock, then continued to the door handle. The door popped open and Allie climbed in.

On the way home Allie told her father about the days' events, the "A" she received on her spelling test. The new story book her reading group had started. And most importantly the trip to the carnival tomorrow. "The whole class is excited," she said, "all except Kenny West. I bet he doesn't say bad words anymore."

The carnival. Those words started the flow of thoughts leading back to his job. Jim forced them away, forced them down deep—this was time to spend with his daughter, and of late time was a precious commodity. They pulled up in front of their home. The moment the engine stopped, Allie bolted out of the car and to the front door, where she waited for her father.

"What's the hurry?" he asked, putting the key in the dead bolt lock.

She shrugged.

Jim unlocked the door and held it open.

After entering, Allie took her shoes off, went into the living room, and stood in front of the TV. Taking the remote, she pushed the power-on button. The glow of the screen immediately bathed her in a white light.

"You hungry?" Jim asked, taking off his hat, putting it on the top of the couch. "You need a little something before supper or can you wait?"

"I can wait," she said, plopping down on the floor. She still had ten minutes until the Tom and Jerry cartoons came on. Jerry was her favorite. She didn't like real mice, but drawn mice were okay and she loved Jerry's big round ears. Besides, any mouse that can out smart a cat like Tom had to be pretty special. She had never seen Mickey Mouse hit a cat over the head with a frying pan.

"That makes one of us," Jim said, "I had to skip lunch." He went into the kitchen, opened the refrigerator and pulled out a package of Oscar Mayer smoked ham and a bottle of mustard. He reached for the bread on top of the fridge. Within moments he had his snack—it tasted good.

Jim returned to the living room. "Sure you don't want something small to eat? Maybe an apple?"

Allie began to snicker then pointed at his shirt. "You spilled."

Jim looked down at his chest. He had a large spot of mustard just above his badge. "Wouldn't you know." He glanced at his sandwich and saw where the yellow gob had slipped out. "Your father's a slob."

"Sometimes," she said with a giggle.

"I better get this in the washer." Jim jogged upstairs to the master bedroom and took off his uniform, figuring he may as well wash the slacks as long as he was at it. He removed the badge of office from his spotted shirt and placed the shield on the dresser. Then he firmly pulled the belt from the pant loops and emptied all four pockets. Putting on his street clothes, he carried the small bundle downstairs.

On his way through the living room he asked Allie, "Do you have anything that needs washing?"

"Maybe a couple things in my room."

"Go get them before your show comes on," Jim said.

Allie ran upstairs and gathered up her dirty laundry. From the second floor she heard the familiar ring. A sudden rush of excitement filled her as she hoped it was her Aunt JoLean calling. Arms full, she hurried down to the kitchen where she found her father already talking on the telephone.

"The file is in the bottom drawer of the cabinet next to the window," he said to whoever was on the other end, obviously not Aunt JoLean. "I put it there myself yesterday," he added. "Look again. I know it's there."

Allie made her way into the laundry room, hoping her father wouldn't have to go back to work. On top of the washing machine, she found her father's clothes waiting to be thrown in. She started going through the pockets of her own clothes. She remembered the time she left some tissues in a blouse. That entire load came out of the dryer covered with small white specks.

After being satisfied all her pockets were empty, Allie picked up her father's small pile. She heard him still speaking on the phone so she figured this would be a good time to help out. She went through his pants pockets like she did her own. She tossed them in the washer, then moved on to the mustard spotted shirt. It's a good thing she looked— there was something in the right-hand pocket. A piece of paper or something. She pulled it out. It was a red ticket.

"Admit one," she read aloud. Thinking it might be important, she decided to show her father what she had found. After putting the shirt in the washer, she ran to the kitchen.

"Look Daddy," she whispered, holding up the red ticket.

"Yeah, I'll hold on," Jim said to whoever it was on the other end of the line. He looked down at his daughter and smiled.

"Where'd you get it? What's it for?"

"A lady at the carnival gave it to me," he said, covering the mouthpiece with his hand.

"For free?"

"Yes, Angel. For free."

"Can you use it for rides?"

"She said it was good for anything." The voice came back filling Jim's ear. "I'm still here," he said. "Did you find the file?"

"Can I have it, Daddy?" Allie said. "Daddy?" She tugged on his sleeve.

He looked down at her, again, though not really hearing her words.

"Yes, Angel," he said.

"Oh, thank you, Daddy." Allie hugged her father and skipped back into the living room. She sat down in front of the TV still holding the red ticket as the Tom and Jerry show began.

CHAPTER 24

The next morning, Amy slowly answered the knock at her bedroom door. The drawn curtains cast the room in pale shadows that matched her grim mood. She had been crying and retreated upstairs for privacy, knowing she would miss her classes for a second day, though in her current state of mind she couldn't care less. Using a fresh tissue, she wiped away her tears, then opened the door for her mother who stood at the entrance with a half-smile of concern.

"Honey," she said, speaking in a soft tone, "there's someone here to see you."

"Tell whoever it is to go away—I don't want to see anyone."

"I thought you would feel that way and I told him so, but he's very insistent. He says it's important and that his name is Johnny."

Amy did her best to hide her surprise. "All right. Give me a minute. I need to straighten up."

"I'll tell him you'll be right down."

Amy ran a brush through her short brown hair and checked to see how red her eyes were. Nothing a few eye drops wouldn't fix.

At the front door she found Johnny waiting for her. "What are you doing here?" she asked, watching her mother disappear into the living room. Not giving her visitor time to answer, she grabbed him by the arm, pulling him outside onto the stoop, making sure the door closed firmly behind them. Unlike her brother, Benny, neither parent would ever eavesdrop on purpose, but the house wasn't that large and the echo of the front hall easily carried voices as far back as the kitchen.

"I need to talk to you. What I have to say can't wait."

"So I'm told," she snapped. Amy took a deep breath, then gave Johnny a sad smile. "I'm sorry, things have been real bad lately. I've got no reason to yell at you." She gently touched his arm. "Let's go somewhere and talk." Walking down to the street, there were no other cars except her own. "How did you get here?"

"I walked."

"Won't you be missed?"

"Can't be helped. This is the only time I could get away. Besides, no one will check up on me until it's time to open my booth. I'll be able to sneak back before then."

"Okay, you've convinced me. Let's go someplace. We'll take my car. I need a change of scenery."

The ride was a silent one—both driver and passenger not speaking as the road passed beneath them. Clearly Amy had been crying, but Johnny didn't feel he knew her well enough to ask why. He had learned in his short flight from authority, not to answer too many questions, nor ask too many as well.

Amy drove out of town about twenty miles to a small state park with a river running down its midpoint. The visitors' center, furnished with a small equipment shed, rented out canoes and inner tubes to tourists for drifting down the currents. The clear waters were very calm and had no rapids.

Along one riverbank, there were cement pits to build fires and a simple camping site. As Amy and Johnny drove past, three tents were already set up. A little further into the park a viewing area had been constructed for observing the river and the surrounding wildlife. She parked there.

"Nice place," Johnny said. "Quiet."

"I haven't been here for years. I used to love coming when I was a kid."

"I can see why."

"Now, what's so important you walked three miles to tell me?" Amy asked. Johnny going to all that trouble for her caused mixed feelings. On one hand, she was flattered—no guy had ever gone to these lengths to see her. On the other, guilt—for the same reason.

"This doesn't seem to be the right place, but I have to tell you. And you must listen to me and do exactly what I say. Promise me you will. Promise me."

"I will," she said, her guilt now giving way to fear—he sounded so serious. "I promise."

Johnny looked Amy square in the eyes. "Don't come to the carnival to see me anymore. Don't come to the carnival at all."

"Did I do something wrong?" Amy couldn't believe Johnny came all this way just to say he wanted to stop seeing her. It made no sense. It would have taken a lot less effort to simply give her the cold shoulder next time she came around—a lot meaner, but a lot easier.

"It's nothing you did. Please, just do what I say and keep your promise." The stress in his voice accented each word.

"Did you get in trouble for the other night? Are you worried about your job?"

"It's nothing like that. And it's not me I'm worried about. It's you. I'm worried about you. This is going to sound crazy, but people go into the carnival and don't come out. They disappear."

"That can't be right. I went and—My God, Nikki…Billy." She felt her tears beginning to well, but she fought them back. "My friends. No one knows what happened to Nikki, and Billy's dead. It all happened that night—the night we all went to the carnival."

"You didn't tell me you were with friends. I just assumed you came alone."

"I didn't want you to know. It was Nikki's idea for me to go and *accidentally* run into you."

"I should've warned you then," Johnny said. "How could I've been so stupid! So selfish!"

"You had no way of knowing." Amy took his hand between hers. "We have to tell the sheriff. He'll stop them. If they killed Billy—"

"We can't," Johnny said, not letting her finish. "I can't. If you talk to him, you'll have to do it without me."

"He won't believe me," she said, pulling back her hands. "You have to tell him what you know."

"I can't—I just can't."

"Why? Tell me why?"

"I broke out of jail up in Ely." He watched Amy's face for any signs of shock. Only none came. "I was engaged to a wonderful girl named Becka. Life with her was perfect. Except—except for her father. He was —is a judge with a lot of influence. He and I didn't see eye to eye on anything. In fact, it wouldn't be a lie to say he hated me. Becka and I continued to plan our wedding despite his constant objections." Johnny had to pause a moment. "Until the night, that is, we went to this small carnival that had just opened. We were having a terrific time, but then somehow got separated and I lost her. Days went by with no sign of her. She seemed to have vanished off the face of the Earth. The state police went over the carnival with a fine-tooth comb, but came up with zilch. Soon after, they focused their attention on me and finally charged me with her murder. Becka's father must have pulled in a few favors to make the charges stick. He blamed me for her disappearance and I would have to pay. I spent weeks in jail waiting for my trial—if you call what they roped me through a trial. It took only one day for a jury of my peers to find me guilty. But I'm not." Johnny didn't think it would be this hard to drudge all this stuff up again. "I loved Becka. There's no way I'd ever harm her."

"Didn't your lawyer believe you?"

"A public defender. 'Defender,' that's a joke. Sitting in my cell, it wasn't hard to reason out. He had to have been in the judge's pocket like the others. I didn't stand a snowball's chance. The judge wanted someone to punish and he hated me. And that was that."

"How did you get to Arkham?"

"Greyhound," Johnny said, not intending to be funny, but the accidental wit seemed to soften the edge a bit.

"No, I mean—you know—escape."

"On the way back to my cell, a couple of the officers were talking about a call they had received from farther up state, asking about the disappearance brought up at my trial. I couldn't hear everything, but one word stuck out: 'carnival.' I was being transferred to the state prison in the morning, and I knew I had to take a chance to get my life back. The cellblock I was in was empty except for a dead-to-the-world drunk. When the jailer brought me my supper I hit him over the head with one of the legs I broke off my bunk. I switched clothes with him, all the time thinking someone would walk in at any moment and I'd be shot trying to escape. I figured I didn't have anything more to lose, so I moved fast. I tore off two buttons getting the guard's shirt off. And with his keys I was gone. I didn't look back. I followed the carnival down here and landed a job. If I can get some proof about Becka then someone will have to listen to me." Johnny tried once again to read her expression. He assumed the worst. "You don't believe me either."

"I do believe you. I really do. Other people from town have disappeared too. One of my teachers—she's gone. And I've heard other stories, but they didn't seem to have any connection. Johnny you have to come with me and tell this to Sheriff McNee. You have to." Her eyes pleaded with him. "It will be better coming from you—he can help."

Johnny reluctantly shook his head. "I told you, I can't. You talk to him—tell him about the others." Though he knew the danger, Amy's words sparked something inside. Maybe she was right. If he ever hoped to prove himself innocent he would need help to get the evidence and someone to present it. His own credibility would fall short of believable.

After several seconds of numbing silence: "Where will you stay tonight?" Amy asked. "You can't go back to that carnival. What if someone there knows about you."

"I should be safe. It's been almost a week. If I were in any danger, it would've happened by now." Johnny wondered if he said that to convince himself as much as to convince Amy. "We should go."

"Johnny, I'm so scared for you. Please, come with me to see Sheriff McNee," she pleaded one last time.

His mind raced for an answer. Could this be a chance for freedom or a return to imprisonment? Something told him no matter what the choice his time was running out. He had to choose and choose now—for better or for worse. "Okay," Johnny finally agreed, "I'll come with you to see the sheriff."

"He'll be able to help you, I know he will." She kissed Johnny, but to her surprise he pulled away. "Something wrong?"

"It might be better for right now if we dial back the feelings."

"I thought—I thought you liked me," she said, leaning back.

"I do, but this isn't the right time."

"I'm sorry."

"There's nothing to be sorry about," Johnny said. "If things were different and all that crud."

"You're so poetic."

"Must be in my blood."

She smiled and said: "You're doing the right thing. Seeing the sheriff, I mean."

Johnny did his best to hide his apprehension from her. She had just asked him to take a chance that may lead to being locked up again. And all this coming from someone he didn't even know a week ago.

Amy turned the ignition key and started the engine.

"It will all work out," she told him, "you'll see."

They drove back toward town and talked the entire way. The conversation revolved mostly around Johnny's life before the carnival. How he and his older brother, Max, opened a garage, gambling it would lead them to something bigger. Or so Johnny hoped.

After being found guilty, Johnny told Max that even with him being in prison, he should still keep the garage open. He had the bank draw up papers putting all the accounts solely in his brother's name. Since the money had no connection with the crime, it wasn't a problem. "Besides," he told Max, "I'll need a place to work after I win my appeal." Though Johnny knew there would be no appeal. The judge had contrived a good case against him with the best circumstantial evidence at his disposal.

"How could he get away with it?" Amy asked in her small town naiveté way.

"You don't know the judge. If you did, you wouldn't ask."

Amy saw a car approaching from the other way. It passed them.

"That was the sheriff," Amy said, staring in her rear-view mirror as the cruiser made a U-turn. Its roof lights burst on. Johnny didn't bother to look—he knew what came next. The only thing out this way was the carnival. The squad car pulled up right behind the girl's car and let out a short siren blast.

"You better pull over, Amy."

She complied. Again staring in her mirror, she saw Jim McNee talking into his radio mic.

Amy got out of her car the same time the sheriff did. He drew his weapon. She gasped. Never having seen Jim in this light, it scared her.

"Hi, Sheriff." Her voice trembled. "We were just coming to see you."

"Amy," he said, his tone hard, "step away from the car."

"But—"

"Do it, Amy. For your own good."

"You better do what he says," Johnny told her through the door she had left open.

"I won't."

"Amy, he's not kidding."

"What will he do? Shoot me?"

"Goddamn it, Amy!" Johnny said. "Will you please do what he says. I don't want you getting hurt."

The girl looked over at Jim pointing his gun at the rear window of her car, then she looked back at Johnny.

"Please," Johnny whispered.

Amy finally moved aside—a heavy scowl covered her face.

"You, passenger, step out of the car," Sheriff McNee commanded in a loud and clear voice. "Real slow. Both hands in the air at all times. One false move and I will shoot. Understand?"

"I do," Johnny shouted. "There'll be no trouble."

"Please, Sheriff," Amy said, taking a step.

"Amy," Jim said, "stay right there!"

"I'm coming out," Johnny called to the sheriff. "Stay put," he told Amy, "it will be fine."

Johnny pulled the handle releasing the door. He pushed it open with his foot, while sticking his hands, right first, then left, into the air. He stood up slowly and faced the lawman.

"On the ground," the sheriff ordered, "arms and legs spread."

"You're making a terrible mistake," Amy cried out.

"Girl, I'm not telling you again."

At that moment Amy hated Jim McNee.

Johnny dropped to the side of the road. Several small sharp rocks poked through his clothing, but he made no moves that could be misinterpreted. Heavy footsteps came up fast behind him and a strong grip wrenched his right arm to the small of his back. A series of sharp clicks filled the air as handcuffs were locked in place. His left wrist was then yanked behind him and likewise secured.

"Stand," Sheriff McNee told Johnny, while helping him up by the elbow. Johnny saw the gun back in its holster, but it was not strapped down.

"No worries, Sheriff. I won't run."

"Against the car," Jim said, guiding the man's head gently to the hood.

Johnny remembered the bruised cheek from the last time in Ely and involuntarily winced right before his face touched metal.

"Spread your legs." The sheriff used his foot to force Johnny's legs apart and his feet back. The position made it next too impossible to move.

"Any weapons, needles, anything like that?" Jim asked Johnny, as he patted down his prisoner's legs.

"Needles?" Amy said, feeling so sorry for Johnny, but still hoping she would be able to help him.

"Lot of these guys are drug users. Can't be too careful." He slapped along Johnny's pocket. "You can get stuck with a dirty needle."

"Please, Sheriff," Amy said, "we were coming to talk with you."

"There'll be plenty of time to talk later on." After frisking Johnny, Sheriff McNee grabbed him by the arm again. "Stand straight." Jim helped him. "Face me."

Johnny did as he was told.

"Yeah," Sheriff McNee said, pulling a folded piece of paper from his front shirt pocket. He opened it and showed the wanted poster to Johnny. "That's you all right. Beard or no beard." He looked over at Amy. "You should be more careful young lady. I always figured you to have more sense."

"Sheriff—" Amy said.

"This man is an escaped murderer," Jim said over her protest. "Killed his girlfriend." He marched Johnny to the squad car and placed him in the rear seat, then stomped back to Amy.

"Sheriff," she pleaded, "will you let me explain."

Jim didn't hear her words. "I was so frightened for you. That man's face kept chewing on me since the first time I spotted him at the carnival. And again when you brought him home."

"Please, Sheriff."

"He's already killed one girl, you want to be next? It's lucky I saw the pile of wanted notices. Then I remembered. I'm just glad I was in time. Allie couldn't stand to lose you too." Jim McNee set out for his cruiser, then turned back to face the girl. "I couldn't stand it either."

Amy chased after him. "Will you please listen? He didn't do anything."

"You're late for school—get going."

"I won't," Amy shouted. "He didn't kill anybody. It was the carnival —Lilith's Carnival."

"Go to school. Now!" Jim walked around to the driver's side and got in.

"Fine," Amy said, "I'll just follow you back to town. I'll make you listen."

Jim pulled off his hat. He had seen that determined look in Amy's eyes only a couple of times, but he knew unless he was going to arrest and lock the girl away in a cell he would have to give into her demands. "All right. We'll meet back at the office. You can say whatever you want there." He started the engine. "But I don't see how it's going to change much. He's a murderer. Do you understand? A convicted killer."

"Just listen to what we have to say, Sheriff. Just listen."

"Fine, fine. You follow me back."

Amy hurried to her car.

"Whatever line you fed her," Sheriff McNee said without turning to Johnny sitting behind the metal screen barrier, "won't wash so easily with me."

Johnny remained silent in the back seat.

It seemed such a long, slow drive. Only seeing the back of Johnny's head, Amy wished he would turn around so at least she could wave to him. She wanted to blast her horn in frustration at the sheriff's slow driving. She wanted him to hurry. She wanted Sheriff McNee to believe Johnny's story. But most of all, she wanted Johnny to be free again.

Amy never realized how far they had to drive from the edge of town. She had driven down these roads so many times, but now, at this dreadful moment, they all seemed different somehow. After another long ten minutes, both cars pulled up to the front of the red brick building with "Office of Sheriff" spelled out with black arching letters across the front window.

Jim stepped out of the cruiser as Amy was pulling up to the curb. He helped Johnny from the back seat.

Amy put her car in park as the two men reached the front entrance.

Sheriff McNee opened the door to the office, leading his prisoner by the arm, directing him down the one small step inside.

Hearing the closing slam, Roger came from the cellblock. "See you got him," the deputy said. "Did he give you a hard time?"

"He cooperated all the way. Doesn't even deny who he is."

"Bring him on back. His room's a waitin'."

"You know the procedure, Deputy."

"I just thought."

"You thought wrong. He's going to be treated like any other prisoner. No more, no less."

"Yes, Sheriff." Roger took Johnny by the arm and led him to the chair next to the desk. "Sit," Roger ordered before sitting himself. He opened the top drawer, then the side drawer. "Damn. We got any more of those internment forms?"

"Sheriff, you're making a mistake!" Amy yelled, tearing through the door.

Her bursting in made Roger fly back in his chair.

"There are more forms in the file cabinet," Jim told Roger.

"Sheriff!" Amy said.

"Now calm down. We will talk after the prisoner is processed."

"He's not a prisoner," she said.

"Looks that way to me," Roger replied, walking to the metal gray cabinet.

"Get the forms," Jim said, "and after that take those cuffs off him. He won't try to run—"

"Thanks," Johnny said, it was the first word he spoke since being thrown into the squad car.

"—with the two of us standing here," Jim continued. "Amy, please sit over on that bench. Keep quiet and we will hear what you have to say in a bit."

"But Sheriff."

"Sit."

Amy sat with a huff, crossing her arms tightly against her chest. She watched Roger dig through the cabinet drawers. *How dumb do you have to be to have trouble finding a stupid form?* The waiting became almost unbearable.

"Here we go," Roger said, pulling the form from its folder.

Amy wondered if it takes him as long to find a pair of matching socks in the morning.

Roger made his way back to the desk.

"The handcuffs," Amy said. "Don't forget about the handcuffs."

Roger looked up at Jim.

Jim nodded.

"Wonderful," Roger grumbled, while getting up from his chair again. He trudged around the side of the desk, took a small key from his top right pocket, and removed the handcuffs. "Don't be getting any stupid ideas."

"He'll behave," Jim said, smiling at Amy. She didn't return the gesture, but he understood her anger.

Roger fed the form into the typewriter. He hit a few keys, then asked, "Name?"

"Johnny—Johnny Williams." He glanced at Amy to apologize for lying to her.

"Date of birth?"

It took Roger fifteen minutes to ask all his questions and type them up. Amy looked at her watch surprised how little time had passed. It seemed a lot longer. By then the morning was only a few hours old for her, but it felt as if it should be supper time.

"If you're finished, Deputy, " Jim said, "take him to the cell."

"You said we would talk," Amy protested.

"You're in enough trouble, girl," the deputy said, "harboring a fugitive."

"Quiet, Roger. She's not in any trouble. She didn't know."

"But I did."

"You're not making this any easier, Amy," the sheriff told her.

"That's what we have to talk about."

"We can talk with him in the cell. I can listen through iron bars as well as I can out here."

Roger took Johnny back to the holding cell. Jim took the opportunity to talk with Amy alone.

"We've known each other a lot of years young lady. I like to think you trust me."

Hesitantly, but coldly, she said, "I do."

"Amy, this individual is an escaped felon. He's been convicted of murder. You have to know how serious this is."

"I do, Sheriff, he told me—he told me about it all. He says he didn't do it."

"They all say that."

"I believe him."

"He'd say anything for you not to turn him in."

"You're not listening. He told me. He didn't have to, but he did."

"I can't explain the criminal mind. Maybe he gets some sick pleasure out of...."

Amy leaped up from her seat. "Talk to him! You'll see for yourself he's not lying."

Roger came back from the cellblock. "He's all locked up. Went in with no fuss, no muss. Wish all our visitors were as cooperative."

"Amy," Jim said, "you should get to school."

"Not until you talk to him."

"Did you ever think maybe he has something to do with Billy Clarksted's death?" Roger asked. "Or how about the other people in town disappearing?"

"You can't really think that," Amy said.

"It's all starting to make sense," Roger added. "The carnival comes to town. Funny things start to happen. An escaped murderer is working as a roustabout. There's your connection."

"It's not him," Amy said. "It's that carnival. He'll tell you."

"Let's not get ahead of ourselves," Jim told the girl. "I said I'd talk to the man, and now is the time."

"Sheriff," Roger said, "if you don't mind, I'll step out for a bit. I missed breakfast. Damn alarm clock didn't go off this morning, had to rush from the house. If it's okay with you, I'm goin' to run down to Harry's Diner and get some chow."

"Don't see why not. Things seem calm enough at the moment."

"You're all heart." Roger took his hat from the rack. "You have a quiet day, Amy. Your friend sure will." Roger snickered.

"Go get your food, Deputy," Jim said.

Roger left.

"Now, about school," Jim told Amy.

"Not until you promise you will talk with Johnny. There's something strange about that carnival." She crossed her arms and sat down again. "I'm not leaving until you give me your word."

"Fine. You win. You have my word. Now go to school."

She stood up. "I'm going. Just remember your promise."

Jim watched the door close behind the girl, then started back toward the holding cells. He hadn't gone three feet when the desk phone rang. He stopped to answer the call. "Sheriff's Office. Sheriff McNee speaking." He listened to the frantic voice on the other end. "It will be fine. Yes, yes. I'll send someone right over." Jim hung up the phone.

The sheriff glanced at the door to the lock up, then at the telephone. "Margy," Jim called out, "when Roger gets back from breakfast, tell him I'm out on a call." His promise to Amy would have to wait.

CHAPTER 25

A quarter block away from the sheriff's office, Roger turned slightly, glancing back over his shoulder to the front entrance, making sure no one had come out after him. Not that anyone had enough suspicion to follow him, still he found the urge to look too compelling.

Satisfied all was clear, Roger continued down the street, another two blocks to Harry's Diner. Along his way he passed a few of the townsfolk, who all wished him a "good morning." He would tip his hat to return the gesture. Outside the diner, the deputy found Old Joe Parker lighting up his favorite brand of filterless cigarettes.

"Those things are going to kill you, Joe," Roger told the old man.

"I know, my doctor told me that over fifty years ago. May he rest in peace." Old Joe let out a belly roar.

"It wasn't that funny," Roger said.

"Where's your sense of humor, boy?"

Ignoring the question and leaving Joe to his smoke, Roger entered the diner. The owner, Harry Gibbens, didn't do the cooking anymore. He had hired a couple of younger guys to take that on. Ones who could easily handle the lunch and dinner rush and put up with the heat and steam of the grill. Harry just tended the books and reordered the supplies.

Stepping through the door, Roger scanned the long serving area, both booths and counter. Nobody showed any signs of stirring at his arrival.

As with every other morning, knives and forks clanged against the heavy white diner plates as the regular crowd sat eating and chatting away. They all continued doing what they were doing and paid him no attention.

"Morning, Rog," Lizzy Mason said, while wiping down the counter in front of his favorite stool. She was the only person he would let call him "Rog." She had blonde hair tucked up in a bun under her diner cap. Her pink and white uniform always looked as if it was about to burst at the chest. Roger hoped he would be there the day it did. She regularly kept the top button undone which exposed a clear view whenever she reached under the counter for a clean cup.

Roger took his usual spot.

"What can I get you?" Lizzy asked with a beaming smile.

"For starters," he said, "a cup of coffee would make my day."

"You got it." She pulled a cup from under the counter.

It was Roger's turn to smile.

She filled the cup. "That it?"

"Who's cooking this morning? Glen or Jay?"

"Jay. Why?"

"In that case, I'll have three eggs. Over medium. Toast. Bacon. No, make that Sausage links. And juice."

"Orange or grape?"

"Grape sounds pretty good."

She wrote up Roger's order and put it on the spindle to the kitchen. "Order up," she called back to the cooking area.

"I don't like the way Glen fries up his eggs," Roger said as Lizzy turned back to face him. "I hate clear whites around the yoke. If Glen was cooking I would've ordered them scrambled. Jay, on the other hand, cooks all the white and still leaves the yolks nice and runny. The perfect egg in my book."

"You know," Lizzy said, "I've worked with those guys for over a year and I never really noticed."

"You don't eat the food here?"

"I prefer my own cooking, thank you very much."

"Call me when my order's ready," Roger said, jumping off the stool. He made his way to the pay phone hanging on the wall closest to the entrance. He reached into his left pocket, then his right. "Shoot," he said. "Hey Lizzy, sweetie, you got a quarter? I need to make a call and all I have are bills."

The waitress rolled her eyes and pushed the "No Sale" button on the cash register. She pulled out a coin and tossed it to the deputy.

He caught it clean. "Good throw. Make sure you add the twenty-five cents to my check."

"Was there ever any doubt, Rog?" she replied.

Roger shoved the quarter in the coin slot and punched out the number. After hitting the last digit, all he heard was a busy signal. He pushed down the phone lever and dialed again. No difference. After three failed attempts, he tried a different number.

That phone rang.

A woman answered.

"I need to speak with him," Roger said in a hushed tone, his back to the rest of the diner. "Tell him it's Roger Anderson."

After about a half-a-minute: "Where are you?"

"At the diner," Roger said.

"Are you that stupid? Calling me on this line. I won't tolerate slip ups."

"I had no choice. Your private line was busy and what I have to say is important, Mayor. It's real important."

"Then get on with it. Don't compound one stupidity with another."

"Seems the sheriff brought in one of those carny workers. He recognized his face from a wanted poster."

"I told him I didn't want him messing with the carnival. He's going to spoil things for me."

"I'm not sure he actually went to the carnival. He picked the guy up with Amy Evans."

"That doesn't change anything. It still endangers my setup. I'm meeting with that Lilith woman later today. If it's a problem, I can tell her I'll use my influence to have her worker released."

"The guy's an escaped murderer," Roger said. "Killed his girlfriend up in Ely. At least that's what the poster said. And the sheriff thinks he might be connected with Billy Clarksted's death. There's no way Jim will release him, for you or anyone else, being he's, like I said, an escaped murderer and all."

"I realize that—I'm not an idiot. What I tell her is one thing, doing it is a whole 'nother matter. When my business with her is over, well, that will be too bad. She'll find herself out one hired hand."

"I take it then," Roger said, "you're pleased with my call."

"In spite of your lack of judgment, you've done well."

"I want more money," Roger said abruptly. "If Sheriff McNee finds out I've been talking to you he'll kick my ass or shoot me. Maybe both."

"You'll get the usual amount this time. We can talk about a raise later. I have an important appointment to keep. And wouldn't you prefer someplace other than the diner to negotiate future affairs?"

"All right, but it better be soon."

"Tomorrow. Soon enough?"

"Fine. Tomorrow. I...." A loud click cut Roger off. "Asshole," he said, staring at the mouthpiece. His voice was accidentally loud enough for Lizzy to hear him.

"Problems?" she asked.

"No. Just talking to a jerk."

"Why are you calling from here when you have a phone back at the office?"

"Personal call," Roger said, shrugging his shoulders, and returning to his stool. "Sheriff doesn't like us making personal calls when we're on duty."

"I didn't realize he's that picky," she said, placing the large grape juice on the counter.

"He can be—about some things." Roger took a sip from the glass. "Office budgets and the like."

"Never would've thought that of Jim McNee. Well, I guess a person does have to watch the money. I know I have to. Quarter here, nickel there. It all adds up."

"I don't worry about money," Roger said, "once I get it, that is."

$$\sim \cdot \sim$$

"You must be doing quite well with our little community," Jasper Fallon said, "if your permit fee is any indication." He had gone to the carnival earlier than originally planned to collect his money, not knowing how Lilith would respond after learning of the sheriff's actions. She was a strange woman. Most people Jasper could easily read, but not her. At one point something deep inside told him he should forget about the final installment of cash and get out with what he had already collected. Invariably, his greed continued to spur him on.

"As I have told you before, your town does have its share of riches," Lilith replied in an almost emotionless tone. Her long raven hair draped forward on her shoulders, framing her face, intensifying those cold dark eyes.

Jasper picked up the stack of bills from the small table. He couldn't help notice that the three times he'd been in the trailer nothing ever changed. He didn't expect new carpeting or a rearrangement of the sparse furnishings, but a mislaid book, a discarded newspaper, even an empty beer can, something, anything to reflect the activities of day to day living.

"You have yet to enjoy the wonders of my carnival," Lilith said.

"I'm sure it's very nice." Jasper shoved the cash in the side pockets of his jacket. *To anyone dimwitted enough to fork out good money to see it.*

"Then, again, I offer you the chance. With my compliments," she said, holding out a red ticket.

"As I mentioned before, I really don't have the time."

"Time? What is five minutes out of the rest of your life? Please." She handed him the ticket. "It's good for any show. We have many fine shows."

For the first time since Jasper arrived did Lilith show any sign of enthusiasm.

"Simply choose one."

"Maybe on my way out." He took the ticket.

"Yes, on your way out."

Jasper started for the door and stopped just short of leaving. "By the way," he said, "our sheriff has taken one of your workers into custody. I hope that doesn't inconvenience you in any way." Jasper watched the woman closely, waiting for her to anger. But the anger didn't come.

"Oh, really," she said casually. "On what charge?"

"Murder and flight from the law. Seems he killed his girlfriend or wife, something like that. The sheriff is a stubborn one. He won't release your man anytime soon." Jasper didn't care if Lilith knew the truth now that he had his money.

"I've talked with your Sheriff McNee. He pestered me last afternoon with questions regarding my snake-man. He spoke something about a boy being killed near here. I assured him my freak had no possible way of being involved. Does he now believe there is a connection with my worker?"

"Your guess is as good as mine. I always have to pry information from him. If I could, I'd get rid of him."

"A strange revelation from one who controls an entire town."

"Well...I," Jasper said clearing his throat. "Well...yes—I do. But...I mean, well, I can't discharge him for simply doing his job. No matter how much the man bugs me." He did control the town, Jasper assured himself, it was just that some things were more difficult than others.

"Losing one roustabout does not concern me," Lilith said. "Workers are easy enough to come by. And we'll be gone by morning."

"Going far?"

"Just to the next town or so."

"Then I wish you a fine trip." Jasper opened the trailer door and took the first step.

"Don't forget about your ticket," Lilith reminded the mayor. "Good for any show—any show at all. The choice is yours. It is always your choice."

Jasper turned back to face the woman. "It was a true pleasure doing business with you," he said, but he found no one there to hear him.

～ ∙ ～

"Lucas, I have a task for you," Lilith said. "The Arkham sheriff is getting far too close and quickly becoming an irritant."

"He is easily dealt with," a voice called out from the darkness. "Just another lowly worm to be ground underfoot."

"Don't be so confident. This worm can't be handled as the others. He has his weaknesses, but he controls them, forces them down, back into the harboring recesses of his soul. All and all he displays an uncommon strength."

"Then what do you wish done?"

"We have a rare opportunity to deal with him on his own terms. He must not be allowed to interfere with my grand design."

"He is only one man."

"One man can spread the word," Lilith warned him.

"But your last attempt failed."

"Silence! Your kind are to serve, not question. You will obey my orders without hesitation."

"It is true that my siblings and I were created as slaves, but remember this, we turned on our creator and our former masters when they became arrogant."

"Humans are always arrogant," Lilith said. "What concern is that to me?"

CHAPTER 26

Mayor Fallon waddled down the midway, strangely at ease now that his business with Lilith had come to an end. And a profitable end indeed. He tapped his jacket pockets. The telltale bulges stretched a grin across his chubby cheeks.

Feeling content and a little smug, Jasper hurried on his way. Walking quickly, he barely noticed the small domed style tent with a woman, wearing a long multi-colored dress and a sash atop her head, standing out front.

"Would you like to know your future?" the gypsy asked him.

"I have no time for such things." Jasper rushed past the woman.

"Are you afraid of the things to come?"

Jasper stopped. "No one can predict the future. It's a waste of precious time."

"I can tell you of the riches and power so close at hand."

The mayor snorted. "You think me a rube? I'll tell you lady, I run my town. The whole town. People jump when I speak. What more can you tell me?"

"Much more, sir. Very much more. For only three dollars, all will be known to you."

"Three dollars? I wouldn't pay three cents." Jasper was about to continue on his way when he remembered the free ticket. He pulled it from his vest pocket. "The jokes on you," he said, showing the woman the red slip. "Now you have to tell me my fortune for free. I got this from Lilith herself. You can't scam me."

"Come," she said, entering the tent.

Jasper pushed the tent flap enough to enter. Inside, pillows covered the floor, encircling a small table topped with something covered by a blue piece of silk. Several charts hung on the tent walls—one of a large hand with all the palm lines labeled and inscribed, another had a circle divided like a pie into twelve sections, each centered with a strange symbol. Jasper had seen many things like this in the movies. He would have been disappointed if it would have looked any different.

"Sit," the woman said.

"Is this the part when I'm supposed to cross your palm with silver?"

"If you wish, but you have a ticket, that will suffice. May I have it please."

"And that's all you'll get from me," he assured her.

"It is all I need."

She pulled back the blue silk, revealing a perfect crystal globe.

"You have a lot to learn about business." Jasper gave the gypsy the red ticket as he sat on the biggest pillow. His large posterior eased into the cushion.

"Are you comfortable?" the robed woman asked.

"Very." Jasper let out a smug smile.

The globe in front of him began to glow.

The gypsy peered into the crystal. "I see you are a man of great proficiency—well practiced in what *you* call business. And you have honed your skill over many years." With a fine white mist, the globe began to cloud over, seemingly from the inside. "People call you thief, cheat, or swindler. You destroy others for your own avaricious gain."

"I'm as smart as the next man, but if the next man be a fool, it's his hard luck." He couldn't believe he said that. "I mean, business always has its chances. I am just careful to cut down on my own risks."

"You wish to possess all—to control all. In your world, you are supreme. No one questions you or your actions. You are all powerful."

"I've said as much outside," Jasper said, realizing that the woman was just changing his words around. "You're going to have to do better than that to impress me."

The mist inside the globe grew thicker. "You destroy anyone or anything that stands between you and what you want. You must control everything—you alone. You are alone!"

Jasper Fallon began to shake. "Stop," he cried out, jumping up from his office chair. "Stop saying those things." After a few moments to clear his head, Jasper said, "That's what I call a weird dream." He yawned once and rubbed a small piece of crud from the corner of his right eye. With each passing second the vivid dream faded more and more to a faint blur. Jasper snickered wondering what Janet must be thinking hearing him shouting at the top of his lungs. She'd be bursting into the office at any moment to investigate. When she didn't, Jasper began to doubt if he had really shouted out at all. There was no reason to believe he did—bad dreams had never bothered him before. He tried to remember the last thing he did before falling asleep.

Then it popped back into his head—the call he received from Roger Anderson informing him about Sheriff McNee's arrest of one of the carnival workers.

Jasper's anger flared up.

"Damn sheriff! He'll blow a real sweet deal for me. Gonna have to talk with the town council. It's finally time for a new sheriff. Roger's due for a promotion." Jasper grinned. He had enough dirt on three of the five council members, and with the unsolved murder of Billy Clarksted, they should be able to convince the other two of Jim McNee's incompetence. It should be enough to get an impeachment started. It's perfect—all the pieces are falling into place.

The mayor pushed down the button on his intercom. "Janet, get me Mitch Ferlow." After waiting impatiently for only one minute, he pushed the button again. "Janet, where's that call? Come in here." She gave no response. "Janet! Are you out there?"

Jasper hurried across the room as fast as his short legs would carry him. He tore opened the door. "When I call you," he started to say, but saw he was wasting his breath. "A fine time for a coffee break." Mayor Fallon trudged back to his desk. He picked up the receiver, the buzzing filled his ear. He punched in the number.

The phone rang on the other end, and so did the phone on the secretary's desk. "Janet," Jasper yelled, "will you get that other call?" The ringing in his ear and the ringing in the front office made him slam down the handset. He was about to push the button for the second line when it flashed off. "Isn't that just perfect."

Jasper tried the number for Mitch Ferlow a second time. The front office rang again. "Goddamn it!" He hung up his line. The office phone stopped ringing. "Sex or not, I'm going to have a talk with that girl."

For the third time Jasper called Mitch Ferlow, and for a third time the office phone rang. He was about to hang up, but stopped. He let it ring on the other end. "Three, four, five," he counted. "Six, seven." He pushed down the cradle button. The outer office phone stopped ringing in turn.

"Damn system must be on the blink." He dialed once more, but didn't listen for the ring on the other end. On cue, the receptionist's phone rang. When he slammed down the receiver, the outer ringing ended. "Terrific!"

Jasper stormed out of his office. Racing down the hall to the women's washroom, he hammered his fist against the door. "Janet, get your miserable ass out here," he yelled.

The mayor gave out a fake cough trying to choke back his harsh words, realizing he must look the part of a madman pounding on the bathroom door. Glancing around the hall, he was relieved to find it empty. He didn't need any witnesses to his outburst. This situation called for a more subtle approach—he cracked the door open a bit.

"Janet," he called out, his voice echoed against the tile walls and metal doors. After getting no answer, he peeked over his shoulder to make sure the hall had remained clear before poking his head in. He bent down, hoping to see his secretary's shoes, but all the stalls were empty.

Frustrated, Jasper started back to his office. Along the way he glanced out the window to the street below—the desolate street below. He saw no people, no moving cars, trucks or traffic of any kind. Several cars lined both curbs, yet not one person approached the abandoned vehicles.

Suddenly Jasper noticed the eerie quiet. The usual afternoon bureaucratical chatter had been replaced with nothing. He moved down the hall opening the door to each office. Like the street, all rooms were deserted. He hurried down the stairs to the main entrance. The offices on the first floor that he bothered to check were exactly like those of the second floor—empty.

After pushing his way through the large glass door onto the street, Jasper strained his neck both ways. He didn't see another living soul. A wave of panic engulfed him and he began trotting along the sidewalk shouting: "Hello! Hello! Can anybody hear me?" His pace quickened. "I'm your mayor—Mayor Fallon—Jasper Fallon!"

Jasper ran as far as Harry's Diner, sure that it would be the one place to find someone—anyone. There were always people at the diner from first open to the minute it closed.

"Where is everyone?" Jasper said, pressing his face up to the windowpane. His labored breath produced a white vapor across the glass. His eyes widened with the sight of empty booths and barren stools. He entered the deserted eatery.

"Harry? Lizzy? This isn't funny. Come on out. Joke's over." Jasper walked over to the counter. It looked recently wiped. Behind the counter a full pot of coffee sat on the warmer. He went around and gingerly touched the glass, then touched it again with less caution. The pot was cold. Dipping his finger into the black liquid, it had no hint of warmth. Without thinking Jasper stuck the coffee covered digit in his mouth. With a sharp cry he spit out the vile liquid.

As he wiped his mouth, Jasper heard a distant ringing—a phone ringing. He bolted from the diner and waited for the sound to repeat. A ring came from a payphone down the block and across the street. Jasper made a dash for it. Breathing hard, he hoped his labored pace would be quick enough. It wasn't.

Then the phone inside the drug store rang out. Another ring came from the bank. The next from the flower shop. Jasper stood in the middle of the street when all the phones rang out at once. Jasper spun one way, then another—his head began to swim in the ever increasing sound. The vibrations piercing his skull forced him to cover his ears. The mayor of Arkham, Nevada fell to his knees.

"Stop! Stop!" he shouted. The agonizing tones seemed to come from inside his head.

Finally, the many bells ceased, giving way to dead silence.

Jasper Fallon's eyes moved slowly from empty shop to empty shop. Where is everyone? Where did they go?

One lone payphone rang out.

Jasper felt himself rising to his feet.

The phone rang again.

He stumbled, uncontrollably, toward the ringing. His fast breath caused his lungs to ache. Jasper tried to resist moving closer, but he failed.

The phone rang.

Having no control of his hand, Jasper reached up, taking hold of the receiver. "Hell…lo," he stuttered into the mouthpiece.

"Jasper Fallon?" a woman's voice asked. "Mayor Jasper Fallon?"

"Yes," he said. He wanted to laugh. "Yes, this is Mayor Fallon."

"You have your town now. You can run it as you see fit."

"No!" he yelled, dropping the phone and letting it dangle.

Behind him, a heavy fog rolled in. As if being directed by some unseen force, he turned and moved toward the mist. He wanted to run away, but found that impossible. He continued forward—forward until his face hit an invisible barrier. He reached up and touched the surface— the smooth glass surface.

With both hands he pounded on the barrier.

"Help me! Someone help me!"

Through the glass he saw an enormous eye staring at him. As the mist cleared, he looked out at the pillows spread around the small round table. He recognized the far-off wall chart of a large hand with all the palm lines labeled and inscribed.

"You can't do this to me," Jasper cried, pounding on the glass. "I'm the mayor. Let me out."

His words went unheeded as the gypsy woman covered her crystal ball with the blue piece of silk.

CHAPTER 27

Cheers roared out when the school bus came to a stop in front of Lilith's Carnival. The low hovering dirt clouds encircling the tires quickly settled as the driver pulled back on the handle, opening the glass and steel doors with a grinding squeal. Pamela Larson, from the front seat, was the first person off. She stood by the door, counting each head as her students disembarked. She knew the count, but always made doubly sure—twenty-two children, she verified.

"Everyone stay with your partner," the teacher told her third grade class as they hopped off the bus. "Make two lines, side-by-side to each other."

Smiling and laughing with anticipation, the children hurried to do as instructed.

Mandy Hicks, a bookish looking senior, who volunteered to help out was the last off the bus, visually checking each seat for any item accidentally left behind. "All clear," she assured Mrs. Larson.

"You can join us, if you like, Jake," Mrs. Larson said to the bus driver.

"No, thanks," he said in a gruff voice. "Never liked carnivals—even as a kid. If it's all the same to you, I'll head back to town. Run a few errands, you know, that kind of stuff."

She hesitated, but then said, "If you're sure. Just be back by two-forty. We have to get the children back to the school by three o'clock."

Jake glanced at his watch. That gave him a good two and a half hours. "Two-forty it is. Won't be a minute later." He pulled the crank and shut the bus door. The engine roared up.

Mrs. Larson took a step back. "Let's all wave goodbye, children."

All the boys and girls waved, except for Brad Fisher. He didn't like Jake, who had just yesterday scolded him for sticking an arm out the window on the way home.

"He's dumb," Brad scoffed, kicking up a bit of dirt.

"You're dumber," Mary Taylor said.

"You're the dumbest," he shot back, "and I don't want you for my partner."

"Na-ah, you are! You're the dumbest in the whole wide world. I don't want you for my partner even more."

"Todd," Brad called out, "be my partner."

Todd shrugged. "I got a partner," he answered, pointing to Allie.

"I'll switch with her."

Todd shrugged again. "Brad wants me to be his partner," he told Allie. "Okay with you?"

"Don't ask her," Brad said, "just come over."

"I don't care," Allie said, knowing she really had no choice. "Who will be my partner then?"

"Mary," Brad said. "That's who."

Not Mary, she didn't like Mary. She's always so mean. Last week the ill-tempered girl stole Allie's pencil, then broke it in half after Allie saw it fall off her desk. Allie didn't really care about the pencil, but Mrs. Larson still made Mary stay after class. Mary blamed the punishment on her. "Mrs. Larson won't let us trade," Allie said, more hopeful than certain.

"Will to," Brad said matter-of-factly and pulled Todd to his side. "Mary's your partner now."

"You better not get me in any trouble," Mary told Allie.

"I won't."

"That dumb Brad Fisher."

"You're dumber," Brad shouted back.

"Stop the name-calling you two," Mandy said, examining the mixed up pairs. "Todd, shouldn't you be with Allie?"

Allie hoped Mandy would put them back the way they were. Todd liked to burp, but he was a lot nicer than Mary. He had never been mean to her.

"We traded," Brad said, "we all agreed. It's better this way."

"Yeah," Mary told the chaperon, "Brad's a big old creep."

"You're creepier."

"Maybe it is a good idea that the two of you traded partners," Mandy said, seeing the quenching of a potential problem.

Allie wanted to say something, but then quickly changed her mind. Mary may think she'd get in trouble. And Allie didn't want her new partner mad at her all day. She decided to do what her father had told her and ignore the girl.

The children finally re-formed two straight lines.

"Stay together," Mrs. Larson said, signaling Mandy to take up the rear. After passing through the carnival's main gate, Mrs. Larson asked the children what they wanted to do first. The kids shouted out several answers: roller coaster, Ferris wheel, merry-go-round. Brad yelled out the freak show. Mrs. Larson responded with an immediate and definite: "No." Maybe the performing dog show, or the hall of statues, but absolutely no freak show. It wasn't an appropriate attraction for children, she told him.

Over the next hour, the children spent the time going on rides as a group, sticking to the calmer ones that the entire class could enjoy. Of course, the wilder attractions caught the attention of many of the third graders. Mrs. Larson had noted that on the bottom of some permission slips the comments from parents with concerns about the faster rides. For each parent that left such a remark she gave a personal phone call. All parents consented to one wild ride for their children.

As a result, Mrs. Larson had promised her class that they would separate into two groups. One group for the roller coaster, the second group for the Ferris wheel, having each pair of students decide on which group to belong to and in turn decide on which ride.

Mrs. Larson designated her bunch for the roller coaster. The name threw her off somewhat: "The Mad Mouse." The sign over the entrance was of a large brown rodent running into a wall hole. A painted cat perspectively chasing it in the background. Even the cars were shaped and painted to resemble mice, right down to the ears and whiskers. She wasn't too excited about the high speed and whipping motions she had sentenced herself to, but she had a real problem with heights. And this roller coaster, unlike others she had seen, wasn't that far off the ground, maybe ten feet, twelve at the highest point. She'd be able to handle twelve feet a whole lot easier than forty or fifty. Luckily Mandy didn't mind taking the Ferris wheel and did so without question. The teacher didn't want to explain her fear in front of her students.

"Children," Mrs. Larson called out, "decide on your ride. Hurry please."

The boys and girls gleefully formed the two bunches. Mandy had only two extra with her, dividing the students well enough that both troops could be easily handled by a lone adult.

Mandy and the children set off for the Ferris wheel. "Wave to the others," she told her group. "Meet back here afterwards?" Mandy asked Mrs. Larson.

The teacher nodded.

They hadn't gone ten feet when Mary turned to Allie. "I change my mind," she said. "I want to go on the roller coaster instead." The girl broke away and ran toward the "Mad Mouse" line.

Allie chased after her. "We have to stay together," she said. "We're partners."

"I didn't want you as a partner," Mary said spitefully, "I just traded because Brad Fisher is really dumb, but so are you."

"I am not. I don't like roller coasters, that's all."

"You're a big scaredy-cat. Scaredy-cat, scaredy-cat."

"Stop calling me that. Besides the Ferris wheel is a lot scarier than some stupid old roller coaster."

"Is not! Roller coasters go real fast, Ferris wheels just go round and round, that's all."

"But it goes up real high."

"So what," Mary said. "Faster is better than higher. I'll go by myself. You can't stop me you scaredy-cat."

"We're supposed to be with a partner. Maybe we can trade again."

"I don't care what you do. I'm going on the roller coaster with the others. And you better not go crying to Mrs. Larson either."

Mary ran off and got in line. Allie looked back to where Mandy and the other kids had been—they were gone. She wanted to go back and punch Mary, but Mrs. Larson told her punching people was wrong. She watched as her classmates climbed into the painted mouse cars. Mrs. Larson was the last in line and took the rear rodent car.

Allie put her hand in her pocket and pulled out the red ticket she had found in her father's shirt. She'd have her own fun. She didn't need to be with Mary or the others. She didn't have to go on the roller coaster if she didn't want to. Her father told her the free ticket was good for anything. And she would find something better.

Allie wandered around the carnival, stopping for a minute to watch a bald man win a blue stuffed gorilla which was almost as big as her. She laughed as the man carried the huge toy on his shoulders.

Walking past all the gaming booths, Allie found several tents with people lining up in front. She heard screams coming from one of those tents and quickly stepped away from it. Then she spotted the sign with the painted animals depicting all sorts of beasts and creatures. Allie liked animals, so she moved closer.

Unlike the others, this tent had no line, only an old man sitting in a small booth. Allie cautiously approached him. He peered down at her through a metal grate and grinned. It was a long toothy grin, but only revealing his bottom teeth. She stopped, examining the sign. It had a tiger, and a zebra, a monkey, and a bear. She really liked animals.

"Hello little girl," the old man said. "Are you having fun here at Lilith's Carnival?"

Allie nodded.

"Would you like to go in?"

Again she nodded. "I have my ticket—see." Allie held out the red slip, showing it to the man.

"My, you must be a very special girl to have such a special ticket. Are you sure you want to use it? It's good for any show. We have many fine shows."

"Can I go in here?"

"If you choose to. It is always your choice."

"I like animals—I like them a lot."

"That's fine," the old man said. "Give me your ticket and you can go right in."

Allie stared at the animal sign once more as she surrendered the special red ticket through the slot in the booth.

"You can spend as much time inside as you like."

Allie moved up to the entrance, but stopped. She looked back to the grinning man.

"They're waiting for you inside," he told her. "All the different and wonderful animals. Go in and see."

Allie smiled and waved, then walked into the tent. The curtain closed behind her.

CHAPTER 28

The moment the two groups of third graders reunited, the children began swapping tales of a joyous escape from the brink of death defying danger. And still the debate of which, the Ferris wheel or the "Mad Mouse" roller coaster, was the most perilous continued—the argument not to be settled that day, but all agreed on the fun they had experienced.

Mrs. Larson gathered up the children. "Who wants popcorn?" she asked her class, already sure of the answer.

All recited a resounding "me—me—me."

"Then form two lines. All partners side by side."

As the children scrambled into position, Mrs. Larson asked Mandy, "Do you remember the location of the popcorn wagon?"

"Wasn't it down by the shooting booth?" Mandy replied. "If we can't find it, there are other things—ice cream maybe."

"Popcorn would be the safest. We can have each pair share a bag. That way we can be certain they won't eat too much."

The two lines of children were straight, except for one noticeable gap. Mary Taylor stood alone.

"Mary, where's Todd?" the teacher asked.

"I'm right here, Mrs. Larson," Todd said, standing next to Brad.

"Why aren't you with your partner?"

"I am. Me and Mary traded. Mandy said it was okay."

"Mary and Brad weren't getting along," Mandy explained, "so I let them change partners. I thought it would be all right."

Not wasting a second, Mrs. Larson asked, "Mary, where is Allie?"

"She's not with me," the girl said. "She didn't want to go on the roller coaster, so I went by myself."

"You know you're supposed to stay with your partner."

"She wasn't any fun. She didn't want to go on the roller coaster."

Mrs. Larson's eyes quickly scanned the area. "Allie," she called out.

Todd and a couple of the other boys snickered. They had never seen their teacher appear so worried.

"Mandy, make sure the children stay together. No sense having others getting lost."

"I'm sorry, Mrs. Larson. If I hadn't let them trade…."

"It's not your fault." The teacher had to stay calm for the sake of the other children. If she started to panic it would make the whole situation that much worse. She already saw concern on some of their small faces. Even though she wanted to scream Allie's name at the top of her lungs, she held back. "I'll look around. She couldn't have gone very far. If that fails, maybe the owner can put the word out to the workers to keep an eye out and start a search of the park if need be."

One of the girls started to cry.

"Everything will be all right," Mandy said, trying to comfort the child.

"Look," Brad said, "there's Allie."

Mrs. Larson turned, and to her relief, it was true. She rushed over to the little girl. "Are you all right, Allie?"

Allie had a blank stare at first, but then said, "I'm fine."

"Get in line," Mrs. Larson told her. When they get back to the school she'd have to give Allie a good talking to about leaving the group. She didn't want to do it here and spoil what had been an excellent day for her other students. Allie was a bright girl—she wouldn't have wandered off without a reason. And her partner being Mary Taylor, Mrs. Larson was sure she gave Allie a reason. She didn't blame Mandy for what had happened—she had no way of knowing the two girls didn't get along.

As the two lines of third graders marched off toward the popcorn wagon, Allie looked back at the animal tent. The curtain parted slightly and Lilith returned the small girl's stare, then smiled.

∼ ⋅ ∼

The Nevada desert road was full of dips and bumps, but that last one practically threw Bob Ryley out of the speeding jeep. Only by clutching the bottom edge of the bucket seat did he manage to save himself.

"You sure it's him?" Ryley asked the driver, Vic Gallo, a local who from time to time did special freelancing for Jasper Fallon. As he spoke, Ryley's right hand barely shielded both eyes from the blowing sands as the vehicle tore down the dusty byway. In his rush at hearing the news, he forgot his sunglasses.

"Positive," Vic replied with a hint of annoyance. "Old Samuel's been creaking around town as long as I can remember."

"How did you find him?"

"Dumb luck, plain and simple. I was out getting a final survey of the land and I saw some smoke. It led me right to him. Almost as if he was asking to be found. He was just sitting there by some real funny rock formations."

"Doesn't matter how it happened, I suppose," Ryley said. "Only matters that it did. I have my orders, and now you have yours." Ryley spit a piece of sand from his mouth. "That old man's not getting in my way again." Ryley stared out over the barren landscape. He didn't care much for the desert. It all appeared too much the same every place you looked—too easy to get lost. "How far to go?" he asked.

"Not long. Maybe three more minutes."

The ride seemed longer, but Ryley's watch confirmed the estimate. He felt the jeep brakes grab and he threw his palms against the dashboard to stop himself from bucking forward.

"He's just over that small ridge," Vic said, pointing to a mound of sand that matched every other mound of sand.

"You're stopping here?"

"Can't chance getting any closer. Don't want to let the old Indian know we're here—do we now?" Vic jumped out of the jeep, then reached under the front seat and pulled out a revolver. After making sure the weapon was loaded, he tucked it into the waistband at the small of his back and let his shirt drape over it. "You coming?"

"You were paid to do a job. I don't have to be a witness."

"Figures," Vic said, smirking and slightly shaking his head. "Chicken-shit." Vic marched away with a grin on his lips that he didn't bother hiding from Ryley.

The breeze blowing across the rocks and sand did nothing to relieve the desert heat. The sun beat down and tiny beads of sweat formed on Vic's forehead as he followed what was left of his previous footprints.

Luckily, he didn't have to hike far to the embankment where he first spotted Samuel Skyhawk. The old man was still sitting in front of the small fire. In all the time that had passed he didn't think the Indian had moved an inch.

Strange people with strange beliefs, he supposed.

Vic never had much use for the Indian population in and around Arkham. He'd be happy if they all stayed put on their government issued land. But, now staring at the old man, all he saw was a lot of cash—a whole lot. And besides what's one less Indian?

Slipping silently from his cover, he crept up behind the old man, carefully watching for any movement. The shaman seemed to be in a trance. His body so still that his breathing was barely visible.

Vic's hand moved to his back and he pulled his revolver. He looked at the gun, then at the silent, motionless elder. Vic returned the gun to his waistband. Instead, he picked up a nearby rock and with one swift blow to the back of Samuel's head, the old man gave out a gasp and fell forward toward his fire.

"Easy money," Vic said aloud. With all this desert it would be a simple matter to dispose of the body. He grinned, knowing he had no need to trouble himself with burying the old man. All he needed was to drop him in the middle of nowhere and let the desert scavengers pick and chew at the carcass until nothing remained. Nothing ever goes to waste in the wild. And if by chance someone did happen to stumble across the dead Indian, it would appear that he fell back and struck his head on a rock. Of course, he'd leave the instrument of death nearby to cinch the assumption.

As Vic drew closer, he noticed the amulet around Samuel's neck starting to glow. Or that's how it appeared—a trick of sunlight reflecting off the precious metal. It had to be made of pure silver.

Vic reached for the talisman. When he grabbed the metal, the light turned to heat. He screamed and pulled back a burnt hand. He gingerly examined his palm and fingers, which were now red and covered in blisters.

Suddenly from behind him came a loud roar. Vic turned to see an enormous cougar staring down at him from the same sand mound he himself used to spy on Samuel. Vic took a step back and tripped over the rock he used to strike the shaman. He fell to his side, then quickly rolled onto his belly and began crawling across the ground. His fingers dug deep into the sandy soil, hurriedly pulling himself away from the beast.

A second roar seemed closer than the first. Vic whimpered as he pulled himself along with greater speed. Without warning, he felt a tight grab on his shoulder.

He screamed.

"Jesus Christ," Bob Ryley said. "I send you out on a simple task and I find you crawling in the dirt like a baby."

Vic didn't seem to hear Ryley's words. "Where is it? Where is it?"

"Where's what?" Ryley saw the dark stain on the front of Vic's pants. "What the devil is going on," Ryley said, realizing that the man had wet himself.

"A cougar! A huge fucking cougar!"

"Pull yourself together. There's nothing here."

"There was! There was! You've got to believe me. It was going to kill me." Vic's eyes moved back and forth, turning his head trying to see past Ryley. "It might still be around here somewhere."

"I don't see anything. There's nothing here." Ryley turned his head and found himself staring straight into a strange pair of eyes. He let out a small yelp of surprise.

"Go! Leave this place," Samuel Skyhawk told the two men.

"Not so fast," Ryley said. "We have just as much right to be here as...."

"You will not have this land." Samuel extended his arm. An eagle swooped down, its talons poised to strike. Both men instinctually protected their faces in anticipation of the blow. Instead, they heard Samuel say, "this place is sacred."

Lowering their guard they saw Samuel standing alone. The eagle had vanished.

"Leave now," the old Indian ordered.

Without another word the men bolted, never looking back. The only noise was the sound of a jeep engine roaring to life.

Exhausted, Samuel leaned against a nearby boulder. These events had weakened him, but this was not a moment for rest. The time for the final battle was at hand. He could feel it. He must leave the protection of the stones and face his destiny.

"You're quiet," Jim said to his daughter, who hadn't spoken a word since getting into the cruiser. When he arrived at the school, he found her waiting alone on the curb. "How was your day at the carnival?" he asked while making a left turn. The steering wheel spun back in his hands. "Did you have fun?"

"It was okay," Allie said, staring out the side window of the squad car.

"Just okay? It must have been better than that."

"Not really."

"Allie, are you sick?"

"I'm all right."

"Let me feel your forehead." Jim extended his arm, but Allie pulled back and leaned against the car door. "I just want to check you for a fever." He tried again. Allie let him rest his hand on her forehead. "You feel normal."

"I told you so."

"Yes, you did. But it's a father's job to worry."

The remainder of the trip home was in silence. Jim glanced at Allie. He tried to tell himself that she must be tired. She'd tell him if anything had happened, having never kept secrets from him. That's what he told himself anyway, but deep down he knew something was wrong, something was bothering her.

The moment the car came to a stop in the driveway, Allie shoved open the door and rushed up to the house. Jim started to speak, but changed his mind. Instead, he got out of the car and cut across the lawn, the set of keys still in his hands. Allie stood by the front entrance, her tiny hands clasped together in a tight ball in the exact same manner he had found her waiting outside the school. With a single motion he extended the house key and inserted it into the lock.

The door was barely open when Allie pushed past her father and went to the living room. Jim started to enter the house when the two-way radio inside the cruiser crackled to life.

"Sheriff, this is base. Come in please."

Jim glanced through the doorway. Allie will be fine for a moment, he convinced himself.

At the squad car he grabbed the mike through the open window. "McNee here."

"Glad I got you," Nate said. "We have a slight situation here, Sheriff." The radio went silent.

After a few seconds of dead air, Jim said, "I'm not in the mood for guessing games. What's the problem?"

"It's Amy Evans. She's back and not at all happy." There was another pause. "You better get back here. Seems she wants to talk with you—and only you."

Jim could've smacked himself. With school out, of course Amy would charge right over to the jail. "I'm coming in now," Jim said. He returned the mike to its clip and looked at his watch out of frustration. He knew what time it was and he also knew JoLean's shift didn't end for another two hours. His only other baby sitter was right now down at his office causing a disturbance that he had to rush off and straighten out.

Having no other choice, he returned to the house and went to the living room. As expected he found Allie sitting in front of the TV set.

"Angel, we have to go down to daddy's office."

Allie stared blankly at the screen.

"Angel, did you hear me? Turn off the TV." The concern for his daughter intensified. The last time he had seen Allie act this way was when her mother died. She closed herself off for over a week. Jim watched his daughter stand and push the remote power button. The picture faded to black.

As silent as their trip home, the same was true for the ride to the sheriff's office. Jim parked in his reserved spot in front of the building and told Allie to wait a moment in the car. He hustled inside knowing exactly what he would find.

"Let him out now," Amy yelled at Nate, while hitting the deputy in the arm.

Without returning the blow, Nate held back the enraged girl. Jim noticed Roger sitting back in his chair, watching as if it were some glorious spectator sport.

"Everybody calm down," Jim shouted. The group froze for a moment.

Then Roger stood up. "We're handling it," he said.

"Right." The sheriff gave his deputy a cold stare. "Nate, I have Allie in the car. Bring her in for me, will you. I'll take care of this."

"Will do, Sheriff."

"And give me a minute."

Nate glanced at Amy on his way out. She stood in the middle of the floor, hands tightly against her hips. The door closed behind the deputy as Amy began to speak, but Jim raised his hand to stop her.

"Allie will be here any moment. I don't want her seeing you like this.

She already seems upset about something and seeing you having a tantrum will not help."

"Why did you bring Allie?" Amy said angrily.

"You didn't leave me any other option. I didn't have anyone to sit with her nor did I have the time to find someone."

"Is she sick?"

"I'm not sure." Giving it more thought, maybe Allie's strange behavior could be the start of the flu bug. "Something's wrong. Though dragging her around town can't be making the whole thing any better."

"See the kind of trouble you bring, missy," Roger said.

"Shut up, Deputy."

"Sheriff, she comes in here and—"

What part of 'shut up' didn't you understand? We can talk about this quietly and without accusations."

"Talk? That's all I wanted," Amy said.

That moment the door opened. Nate had Allie by the hand. "Here we go," he told the little girl.

"Quietly?" Jim said.

Amy nodded. She crouched down, as so many times before, meeting Allie face-to-face. "Hi, sweetie." She touched Allie's hand. "Your dad says you're not feeling well."

"I'm fine," Allie said, with a little more bubble in her tiny voice.

"I'm very glad to hear that," Amy said, hugging the child.

Jim put his hand on his daughter's shoulder as Amy stood up. He smiled. "Let's find something for you to do," he said. "There should be some crayons and a coloring book in the supply cabinet." This wasn't the first time Allie had to wait for her father in the office. They were rare occasions, but enough for Jim to buy her a small distraction.

On the third shelf of the metal cabinet was a rainbow box of Crayola's and a Tom and Jerry coloring book, which he placed on the small table next to the door leading to the lockup area. "Sit here, honey," Jim told Allie while pulling a chair out for her. "Daddy has to work. You enjoy your coloring."

⁓ ı ⁓

Allie watched the adults talking. It wasn't hard to see that they kept their voices in a forced hushed tone. At times the argument heated up, then with a glance over to her, the voices dropped. The little girl paid very close attention, waiting for the right moment. She sat quietly until she knew she was unobserved. Then she slipped off her chair and crept into the cellblock area. She walked over to the second cell. There Johnny laid on the bunk, his arm resting across his eyes. A moment later, realizing he was no longer alone, Johnny sat up.

"Hello," Johnny said, seeing the child watching him through the bars. "What's your name?"

Allie didn't respond. Instead she took a step closer, seemingly to study him.

"Should you be back here, little one?"

Still Allie remained silent.

"You're certainly quiet," Johnny said, springing to his feet. He walked over to the bars, getting a clearer look at his visitor. "Hey, you okay?"

Without warning the little girl's arm shot up, stretching well passed the limits of a small child. Her fingers elongated and wrapped around Johnny's throat. The strength of her grip was terrifying.

Johnny tore at the coils around his neck trying to break the strangle hold. Within moments, his head began to swim and he fell to his knees. A clatter sounded throughout the cell as his leg struck a discarded lunch tray, sending an empty soup bowl across the floor.

His one free hand groped along the floor until he found the metal tray. With the last of his strength he drove the edge down and into his attacker's exposed flesh. Allie screamed out as a silver goo dripped from the wound. The scream was nothing human.

The hellish grip not giving way, Johnny struck again with his makeshift weapon, smashing and bashing whatever he could. He missed several times, catching only the cell bars, producing a loud clang. The swirling continued as Johnny's blows weakened. The world started to darken and his arms fell to his side. A strange final thought skipped through Johnny's mind—his running was finally over.

CHAPTER 29

"Where's Allie?" Jim said, seeing the empty chair. An eerie scream immediately followed by wild banging from the lockup area halted any discussion or speculation. The sheriff, followed by the others, ran back to the cellblock. They found Johnny on the floor inside the cell coughing and gagging while defending himself with a metal tray.

With long distorted arms, the creature-child strangled Johnny, who barely managed to swing his weapon. With an animal-like veracity, it pulled and shook the helpless prisoner like a limp rag doll. His defenses failing, Johnny fell flat to the floor.

Not knowing what he was seeing, Jim drew his weapon. "Stop," he yelled.

The girl turned and snarled, exposing her sharp jagged teeth, saliva spilling from the sides of her mouth.

Jim's eyes widened. "Allie?" He rushed toward his daughter. Her hand became a brown scaly fist, which rose up, and struck the man in the middle of the chest. The blow sent him flying backwards to the wall. Jim let out a painful gasp as his breath was forced from his lungs when he hit the plaster. Somehow, he managed to hold onto his weapon.

"That is not your Allie," a voice said. Samuel Skyhawk suddenly appeared in the doorway, grasping at the doorframe for support. "It is a creature of evil. You must destroy it."

"I can't kill my daughter."

"It is not your daughter," the old man shouted. "You must trust me. Kill it now."

Jim couldn't believe that this thing was Allie, and yet he couldn't believe it wasn't. He looked at Nate, then at Samuel, then back at Allie.

He pulled the trigger.

All seemed in slow motion. The blast was like a crack of thunder far off at midnight. The pungent smell of the spent shell hung in the air like a heavy fog.

The creature howled as time seemed to return to normal. Jim's shooting eye was always sharp, and at this distance absolutely deadly. A single hole in the center of the creature's chest had its predicted results. The thing fell to the floor. All watched as Allie's twisted features shifted and transformed. First to a woman, then an old man, continuing through a multitude of faces, ages and shapes, finally becoming a form Jim knew: the man Lucas from the carnival. But with a shallow wheeze that form changed too. It became a thin creature covered with a thick hairless gray hide with large, round, silver eyes.

"Where's my daughter!" Jim yelled at the creature. "Where is Allie?"

Its wide, round eyes blinked once, then stilled and darkened, becoming coal black orbs. Then as if a final transformation, the body melted to a pool of silver slime, which in turn evaporated to nothing.

"What was it, Uncle?" Nate asked, his gaze focused on the small amount of silver powder—the only remnants of the creature.

"A shape-shifter," Samuel told them all, "a doppelgänger. But this creature is only a servant. Its kind has been serving evil for countless centuries."

Johnny moaned in the cell. He managed to roll on his side. The blood from the large claw marks on his neck stained his shirt red.

"We have to help him," Amy said. She pulled at the iron bar door.

"Get the cell keys," Jim told Roger.

"The key?"

"Are you having trouble hearing today? Get me the cell keys!" The deputy disappeared into the main office and returned with the large ring. He handed them to Jim, who opened the cell door. Amy didn't waste a moment. She rushed passed Jim to Johnny's side.

"He's hurt," Amy said. "Not bad, but he'll need some attention."

"I'll get the First-aid kit," Nate volunteered.

"Let's give them some privacy," Jim told the others. Samuel had already followed his nephew out, only Roger remained behind.

"You think that's smart?" the deputy asked. "He could be dangerous."

"We've seen no signs of that so far. Besides, he's in no condition."

"But Sheriff," Roger said.

"I said out."

Before leaving himself, the sheriff looked back at Amy. She was too busy with Johnny to notice. *All she wanted*, Jim thought, *was a chance to talk*.

Emerging from the lockup, Jim asked Samuel Skyhawk, "What do you know about that…that thing? And where is Allie?"

"I have told you all I know about the shape-shifter," Samuel said. "As for your daughter, I'm afraid she must be at that place of evil—that dark carnival."

"Then I'll get her back," Jim said, holding the crack in his voice at bay.

"Let's pray it's not too late," Nate said, returning after bringing Amy the First-aid kit and a bowl of cool water. "Count me in."

"In?" Roger said. "In for what?"

"This isn't your responsibility, Nate. Allie is my daughter. I'll get her back if I have to tear down each and every tent."

"You can't be serious," Roger said. "Mayor Fallon won't like that. He doesn't want you hassling those carnival people."

"What do you know about Mayor Fallon?"

"Nothing. I just…."

"You just what? I never told you or Nate about the mayor ordering me away from the carnival." Jim's face tightened. "You've been tipping him off—that's how that greedy bastard knew when to cover his ass." Jim swung his fist, hitting Roger square on the jaw. The man dropped like a stone. "All these years I've trusted you. If I had more time—" Jim shook his head while Roger shook off the blow. "Just get out," he said. "Get out now."

"What the fuck are you saying?" Roger yelled.

"It's simple enough, get the hell out. You're fired."

Roger's anger came to a quick boil. "We'll see what the mayor has to say about this."

"Not much, knowing Jasper Fallon. You're of no use to him now. Nate, help our *friend* here out."

Nate moved a step forward and took the ex-deputy by the arm. Roger pulled himself free from the man's grip.

"Don't touch me. This ain't over." Roger stormed to the front door, leaving it open as he left.

"I won't hold my breath," Jim said. He turned toward Nate. "I can't ask you...."

His friend motioned for him to stop speaking. "Let's go," Nate said.

"Not quite yet." Jim rushed back to the cell. Johnny sat on the edge of the bunk, Amy nursing his cuts and bruises. "Tell me what you know," Jim said abruptly, "but make it quick. I don't have a lot of time."

Johnny told his tale as best he could, as briefly as he could. He spoke of Becka, his escape from jail, the subsequent job at the carnival, and about his own investigation and observations. He made sure to include what he had heard from Thelma and Calvin, and, of course, Dean's strange disappearance. Summoning it all up this way, Johnny realized how little he really had.

"Come on," the sheriff told his prisoner.

Johnny stared at the man in disbelief.

"I said, come on. I need your help."

"My help?"

"The carnival—they have my daughter."

"How? Oh, my god," Amy said, her eyes instantly tearing up, "her class trip. I could have warned you. It's my fault."

"Nonsense. That rests solely on my shoulders," Jim said.

"You believe me then?" Johnny asked, a tone of relief swelled in his voice.

"It doesn't matter what I believe. I just know my daughter is trapped at that carnival."

"Sheriff," Johnny said softly, "there's a chance she's—"

"Don't even think that," Amy said.

"I agree," Jim said, stopping Johnny before he said the one word Jim was too scared to think about. "Just come on."

"Without my shoes?"

Jim looked down at the man's stocking feet. "We'll get them on the way out."

The two men headed for the door with Amy close behind. "I'm coming with you," she said.

"No," Jim said, turning around, pointing his finger directly at her. "No, you're not. I need you to stay here. I won't be able to watch out for you."

"Who said anything about me needing to be watched?"

"You will stay here."

"But—"

"No, buts. Just do it. Amy, I need you to do this. Please stay here."

She had never heard the man beg and thought this was about as close to the real thing that she would ever experience. It shamed her. "All right."

That being settled, Jim checked his weapon. "You coming, Nate?"

"Right behind you." Off to one corner, Nate stood with his Uncle Samuel.

The old man removed the amulet from around his neck. "Take this. It will protect you."

"Uncle, I can't—I wouldn't know how—"

"All you need is faith. To use its power you must pass it on."

"I don't understand. Come with us uncle. With your knowledge...."

"I am much too old," Samuel said, stopping him. "My place is here. I will stay and wait. Now go. Join the others."

Outside, the three men rushed to the squad car. Johnny took the back seat—the same seat he arrived in just hours ago. During the trip with lights flashing, the men sat in an uneasy silence. The five-minute drive seemed to take forever.

Nearing Lilith's Carnival, Jim switched off the lights. "Better not to announce our arrival too soon," he told the others.

Patchy clouds moved in front of the sun, filling the landscape with dull oranges and washed out yellows as the cruiser approached the main gate. From that vantage point it was obvious some of the larger rides had already been disassembled and moved. And one other thing seemed strangely clear, not a single soul remained at the carnival.

"They must have sent the workers on ahead," Nate said, gazing through the windshield.

"Not likely," Johnny replied.

"He's right," Jim said. "Something's very wrong here."

The men exited the vehicle—Jim being the last. He needed an edge. In the glove box, he found one and quickly joined his two companions. Nate had unsnapped his holster, and withdrew his revolver.

"Put the gun away, for now," Jim said. "No shooting unless it's absolutely necessary."

Nate followed the order and reholstered his weapon.

It gave Johnny a small sense of relief. He hoped very much to elude gunplay. Being unarmed himself, he stood at a distinct disadvantage.

Silently, the three worked their way down the midway, not seeing another living soul. The disassembling of some of the booths had begun —canvas walls brought down, frames pulled apart, tools haphazardly discarded—but there were no workers.

Then out of nowhere: "Johnny? Hey, Johnny, that you?"

"Who's there?" Johnny called out, his head turning, trying to find the voice.

"Me, Calvin," the gruff man said, stepping into view. He carefully looked one way down the midway, then the other. "I heard you were in jail." His voice dropped off seeing Nate and Jim in full uniform.

"I'm working it out," Johnny said. "Where is everyone?"

"Man, it got real crazy around here. Real crazy. Lilith went nuts. I mean real nuts."

"Where is everyone?" Johnny repeated.

"Then the screaming started," Calvin said, ignoring the question.

"We're looking for a little girl, Calvin. She's here somewhere. Help us find her."

"Thelma, she's gone. They're all gone."

"Do you see that man," Johnny said, pointing to the sheriff. "It's his daughter. She's missing."

Calvin's eyes dimly glanced over to Jim McNee. "Not me though. I hid."

"Calvin, listen to me. We need your help."

"Help? No. I been hidin' out. Waiting for it all to stop—waiting to get away. Man, the screaming, you should have heard the screaming. It was so loud." With a very shaky hand, Calvin put an unlit cigarette in his mouth and inhaled deeply. Calvin stared at his friend. "Johnny? That you? I heard you were in jail."

Jim touched Johnny on the shoulder and shook his head. "Seems he's gone too."

"The screaming...," Calvin mumbled.

"Calvin, help us."

"No, no," Calvin yelled. "I hid. I waited." Calvin slowly backed away from Johnny. "It's all clear now—all clear. I can get away." He turned. "The screams. I hid. I hid," he shouted as he ran off.

Nate started after the gruff man, but Jim stopped him.

"Let him go," the sheriff said. "Poor fool."

"What do you suppose he saw?" Nate asked.

"My guess is we'll find out soon enough," Johnny told him.

The three men continued their search. They hadn't gone much farther when Johnny noticed someone peeking at them through the slit opening in one of the remaining tents. He signaled Jim to go around back, while he and Nate went straight forward. Motioning to Nate his intentions, Johnny burst head first into the tent. The white shrouded figure tried to make a quick retreat, but instead ran squarely into the massive form of Jim McNee.

"Hold it right there," the sheriff commanded, grabbing his captive by the wrist. The flesh in his grasp felt more like sandpaper than skin. Jim glanced down at the hand coming out of the long flowing sleeve—the fingers were bent and fused together in a hook.

The strange creature pulled away hard and fell to the ground. Johnny made up the distance, trapping the hooded figure between himself and the sheriff.

"Where's my daughter?" Jim yelled.

From under the robe came only wheezes, coughing, and raspy gasps.

"I'm not sure it can speak. Must be from the freak show." Johnny knelt down, getting a closer look. As he figured, this person was the one who had been spying on him for the past few days. By its shape, Johnny realized the creature was female. "Can you understand me?"

She nodded.

"Where is Lilith?"

His question was answered with more gasps and what almost sounded like choking.

"She can't help us, Sheriff. We should leave her be."

Sharp, short groans came from under the cloak as if words were trying to form. None were understandable until, "Joh—ny."

"She knows you," Jim said.

Johnny gently pulled the hood back. The melted face underneath made him turn away.

"Joh-n-ny," she said again with much more effort.

The man looked back at the poor creature. Only her eyes were normal. A single tear ran down her cheek.

"Why is she crying?" Nate asked.

"She seems to be in great pain. But I don't think that's all." A shock raced through Johnny's body. "Sweet Jesus!" He pulled the twisted figure toward him. "I'm sorry—I'm so sorry." He wanted to embrace her, but that would only add to her suffering. "I didn't know. I didn't know it was you."

"You know this creature?"

"Becka," Johnny cried out. "This is Becka. She's the one I've been searching for."

"Hel—p me-e-e," she pleaded. The forced use of her mouth caused spit to run down its sides. Her eyes pleaded with him. He knew exactly what she wanted.

"I can't. Don't ask me."

"P-please—" She barely made out the word.

Johnny felt his heart pounding. "Stay here," he whispered to Becka. He walked over to the sheriff and deputy. "Can I have a moment alone with Jim?" he asked Nate.

Though puzzled, Nate said, "I'll wait outside." He left.

Johnny stood with a man he barely knew, contemplating what his reaction would be to his next request. "I can't leave her like this," he said.

"What you're thinking—I can't sanction it."

"Look at her. I can't let her keep suffering like this."

Jim unsnapped his holster and pulled out the revolver. He handed the weapon to Johnny. "Make it a clean shot." He, too, left the tent.

Johnny had the gun hidden behind his back, but when he looked into Becka's eyes again, he knew that wasn't necessary. He took careful aim and said a silent prayer. He was about to become that of which he was falsely accused. His finger began to tighten on the trigger, the steel cold against his flesh. He held the gun rock steady while Jim's words replayed in his mind: "Make it a clean shot." Johnny took a deep breath.

"I can't," he said. "Please forgive me, I can't do it."

Becka's eyes turned from pleads of mercy to terror. She slid back across the ground and raised her clubbed hand, pointing behind Johnny. She garbled out a warning, but it was too late. Something hit him hard from behind. He fell forward. The gun discharged, filling the air with a tremendous roar and the stench of burnt gunpowder.

CHAPTER 30

A shot rang out.

Outside the carnival tent, Nate White Moon instinctively ducked while reaching for his gun. Jim McNee stopped him before he could draw his weapon.

"You wanna tell me what just happened?" Nate said, seeing Jim's empty holster.

"Mercy. A small mercy."

As they stood in silence, a bodiless voice filled the air. The words seemed to surround them. "You are all fools—and quite predictable."

Jim recognized the woman's voice.

"You destroyed my servant," the words continued. "For that you shall pay."

A long shadow poured out from between two tents. With the late afternoon sun behind whatever approached, Jim and Nate had to shade their eyes to see. Coming into full view both men saw the blank expression and the emotionless stare on the blood-drained face.

"Billy?" Nate said. "You're supposed to be dead."

The boy's eyes filled with a blood lust as though both men were his most hated enemies. Nate had seen the body, the fatal wound in the boy's chest. Billy Clarksted was dead, but still he was coming toward them.

"Stay back. I don't want to hurt you." Nate extended his arm, palm up, to fend off Billy. With surprising speed and strength, the boy grabbed the deputy's arm. Nate tried to pull away, but within seconds a loud snap echoed out and Nate screamed as he fell to his knees—the broken bone protruding from his forearm.

Jim moved quickly and tackled the boy on his blind side, pulling him down by the waist. Even in pain, Nate assisted by throwing his full weight on the boy's body. Billy's arms and legs swung wildly, but being pinned on his stomach, the blows were ineffective.

The sheriff reached down to his belt and grabbed his handcuffs. Within seconds, he secured the boy's wrists.

"Throw me your cuffs," Jim yelled.

With his good hand, Nate pulled his handcuffs from their holder. The deputy winced when he tossed them. Jim made a one-handed catch and with one swift stroke he slapped the steel loop around one of Billy's ankles. Working quickly and by intertwining with the other set of cuffs, Jim had Billy neatly hog tied. The enraged boy grunted and snarled, but he could no longer hurt himself or others.

Nate rolled off, at the same time cradling his broken and bloodied arm. "You think that'll hold him?" He grimaced as his adrenaline slowed and his pain grew.

"Should," Jim said, kneeling down to his injured deputy. "We have to immobilize that arm."

Nate shook his head. "I'll be all right. Find Allie."

The sound of a woman's laughter seemed to swirl around the men—coming from all directions—taunting them, mocking them.

"Show yourself," Jim called out.

"Done." Her voice now came directly from behind. The men turned. Lilith stood there in her black robe, her arms crossed tightly across her body.

"Give me my daughter."

"In time, perhaps."

"I refuse to play your game. Where is Allie!"

"No game. I want you to join my carnival. I'm sure I can find something suitable for you. Maybe as a companion for my snake-man. You and he have developed quite a bond over the years. Is that not true?" She smirked.

"Don't give into her evil, Sheriff," Nate said

"Me, evil? All those who have joined my carnival are the true evil. I simply thrive on their essence. I gorge myself on their darkness—their sweet darkness. Now, give yourself to me or this innocent shall perish." The tent next to Lilith opened and there Allie stood, frozen in a trance.

With his one good arm, Nate had to hold Jim back. "She seems safe enough for the time being," the deputy said. "Don't do anything that could put her in danger."

Jim knew those would be the exact same words he would have used if he were in Nate's position.

"Come child," Lilith said. Allie walked toward the woman, her eyes blank and lifeless. Allie stopped and Lilith stroked her hair. "A precious little girl, indeed."

"Don't touch her!" Jim easily broke free from Nate.

"Take care," Lilith commanded with her hand around Allie's throat. "Such a pretty neck—so delicate, so fragile."

Jim slowly approached Lilith and his daughter. He stood in front of the raven-haired woman.

"I can feel your hatred," she said. "It's rather intoxicating."

"You want me to join you?"

"A simple exchange. Your body and soul become part of my carnival."

"First, release my daughter."

Lilith made a simple hand gesture. "Consider this a show of good faith." Allie took several steps back.

Jim felt relief as his daughter moved away. "You want me—here I come." With the speed his younger MP-self would have been proud of, he wound up and with all his might struck Lilith on the end of her chin.

Nothing happened.

"Useless human." Lilith's hand shot out, tightly grabbing the sheriff around the throat. Jim fought in vain to break the hold, but for such slender fingers, their strength was unbelievable. Then without warning, a sudden gunshot rang out. The side of Lilith's head exploded and Jim fell to the ground.

Gasping for air, the sheriff rolled on his back. He managed to look up. At the entrance of the tent where Jim had left him, Johnny stood with the gun still pointing at Lilith. Becka stood behind him—only her eyes peered out from under her veil.

Lilith screamed. But as the fresh air filled Jim's lungs, he heard they were screams of laughter. He watched as her skin pulsated and split, tearing and cracking. Large pieces of flesh peeled off the woman as her size swelled. The dark robe she wore burst open as large black wings tore through the delicate fabric. Her feet and hands sprouted sharp ebony talons. Her eyes turned a fire red and her teeth became sickly-yellow fangs. What was once a curvaceous body became a hellish nightmare of scales and black matted fur.

"Are you pleased with my true form, pitiful insect?" Her voice had become a low rasping growl with traces of a soft hiss. She grabbed Jim once more by the throat. Carefully and with purpose, she raked a pointed talon across Jim's neck. A trickle of blood ran down and pooled along his collar.

She laughed again.

⌁ ⌁

Nate dragged himself over to Allie and grabbed the little girl around the waist, pulling her clear of danger. He tried shaking her to consciousness, but she wouldn't come to.

"Allie, ya gotta help your Uncle Nate out here."

He shook her again.

"Please, Allie."

Finally the child's eyes blinked. Nate watched as she reached up and gently touched the amulet hanging out of his shirt. To his surprise, she spoke, but not to him.

"Yes," Allie said. "It's very pretty. I will." She took the chain and pulled it over Nate's head.

He was about to stop her, but then remembered Samuel's words: "you must pass it on." Nate let Allie remove the sacred relic.

Without a word, the small girl marched toward her father and the demon Lilith.

"Come back," Nate yelled, trying to stand, but the pain knocked him down.

⌁ ⌁

Ignoring the throbbing at the back of his head and taking careful aim, Johnny shot again, hitting the winged she-demon square in the back. A large hole appeared, but it sealed itself within seconds. At the same time, Jim reached behind to his waistband, pulling out Simon West's switchblade, which he had taken before leaving the squad car. He hit the small silver button, causing the razor sharp blade to lock in place. With every ounce of strength he plunged the knife forward, but the creature reacted faster than Jim expected, knocking the weapon from his hand.

"Leave my Daddy alone!" Allie shouted, raising the amulet high overhead. The silver metal began to pulsate with a white glow and two wispy phantoms, a cougar and an eagle, emerged from the charm.

Nate watched in disbelief as the animals changed from smoke to flesh and blood. The large cat roared and the majestic bird took flight. As a boy, he had heard stories of such powerful creatures—their images graced the totems outside the Tribal Council Hall.

The cougar gave out a low growl as it circled Lilith, slowly stocking her. But the eagle made a sudden frontal attack, swooping down and plucking out one of her red eyes. The demon screamed in pain, dropping Jim McNee to the ground.

Even while sliding across the ground, away from his captor, Jim's eyes never left the ensuing battle. The eagle and cougar were attacking simultaneously. The cat clawing and mauling, the eagle using its razor sharp beak to tear away pieces of demon flesh.

When Lilith knocked either totem animal back, it immediately recovered and continued the attack, hitting her hard. The demon tried to take flight, but the cougar leaped onto her shoulders, driving sharp claws into the scaled flesh, pinning down both wings. In shrills of agony the monster toppled. With a final killing bite, the cougar ripped out Lilith's throat.

In its death thralls, the she-demon began to crumble and rot. The animals circled, making sure they had finished their deed. All that was left of Lilith was a pile of bitter smelling ash.

Both cougar and eagle began to let off a soft yellow glow. The eagle gracefully circled its companion, landing gently on the large cat's shoulders. The radiance intensified like double suns. Jim had to divert his eyes for a moment.

Forming a glowing mass, the energy started to change, taking on the shape of a man—a strong young Indian in full ritual garb.

"Uncle?" Nate said, remembering images of Samuel in his youth from the old family photos he had seen all his life.

The Indian warrior raised his staff high, smiling a goodbye to Nate. The air became heavy as if charged. Another blast of light exploded silently, sending other small bursts to all parts of the carnival.

One burst hit Becka. She screamed and collapsed. Johnny ran to her side. He tried to touch her but the energy around her body held him back.

"Someone help her!" Johnny cried out.

After a moment the pulsating stopped and faded.

"Becka, can you hear me?" he said seeing her stir.

"Johnny," she whispered. A delicate hand reached up and touched his.

Johnny pulled back Becka's veil. Her face was as soft and beautiful as he remembered. The nightmare was over—finally over.

"Somebody want to unlock me," Billy Clarksted yelled, appearing fit and healthy.

Jim tossed the handcuff key to Nate, who made a one-handed catch—his broken arm completely healed.

As the sheriff got to his feet, he heard the sounds of people, of voices, of laughter. Over a hundred individuals emerged from the tents. Most of them were strangers, but others like Dora Lacwent, Dwayne Dunham, even a naked Snake West, Jim knew.

Nikki Bonn rushed to Billy's side just as Nate removed the last handcuff. Jim imagined the difficulty he would have in explaining the boy's resurrection to his parents. Indeed, the entire incident was going to be hard to explain. Though he did find some small comfort knowing that while some might call one man crazy for telling this story—and it was crazy—with these missing people recovered, the facts would have to be believed.

In the parking area a car drove up, sounding two short blasts from its horn. The vehicle stopped and the front passenger door opened. Amy Evans stepped out. JoLean Holt followed immediately from the driver's side. Both women stood looking out at the multitude of people.

"Oh my god," Amy said, seeing Nikki and Billy. She called out and ran to them. The three friends embraced. Amy and Nikki cried.

JoLean made her way to Jim. "I got your message. If you knew you were going to rush off, why was it so important I go to your office?"

"Message?" Jim said. "I didn't...."

"Daddy! Daddy!" Allie shouted, running up to her father. She hugged him hard around his waist.

"Don't I rate a hug too?" JoLean said, extending her arms.

The small child was more than happy to comply with her aunt's wishes.

"How did you know where we'd be?" Jim asked.

"I didn't. Samuel Skyhawk told me I should bring Amy out here. I can't tell you why, but I believed him. It's funny, when I asked him if he wanted to come along, he said 'when called.' I hope I did the right thing."

"You did fine—as always. Everything's all right now."

A passing man shook Jim's hand and a thin woman gave JoLean a hug.

"Jim, what's happening here?" JoLean asked.

"I'm not absolutely sure yet." He rubbed his neck where Lilith had clawed him. He found no signs of a wound. Jim reached down and gently stroked his daughter's hair.

"McNee," a voice shouted out. Jasper Fallon pushed his way through the crowd.

"Take Allie to the car, would you please. The other shoe's about to drop."

"I want them locked up," the fat man yelled. "All of them, locked up."

"Who, Mayor? Who should I lock up? Just point 'em out." The sheriff shook his head. "You warped little man."

Jasper stood speechless as Jim turned and walked away to rejoin JoLean and his daughter. He didn't get very far when he heard another voice. This one, however, pleased his ear.

"I'd like to thank you, Sheriff McNee," Johnny said, coming up to the lawman. "I have Becka back. Now I can go home and put my life back together." He handed Jim the revolver. "This is yours, I believe."

Jim returned the weapon to his holster. "There's still that matter of you being wanted for murder."

"Sheriff, I…."

Jim smiled. "I'll make sure you're exonerated of all charges. But by the looks of things that shouldn't be too difficult. Still, I will make it clear to all those concerned that you helped me and put your own life at risk in doing so. And when you get it all cleared up, there's a place for you in this town, if you like."

"Thanks again, Sheriff. Who knows, I might just take you up on that." The two men shook hands.

Jim watched Johnny and Becka walk over to Amy. He knew that there were still some things that weren't going to be so easy to fix. But with courage and a little faith all things are possible.

EPILOGUE

T hree weeks later.
Arkham Sheriff's Office Log: October 19.
Entry by Sheriff Jim McNee.

Nate should be back tomorrow. It will be good to see him. After the burial of his Uncle, Samuel Skyhawk, the tribe asked Nate to help pick his successor. I have to admit on hearing that, I was afraid Nate himself would take up the task. He assured me otherwise, saying something about years of renewed training. He is a fine deputy and a good friend.

My newest deputy is working out fine, even better than expected. A month ago, if anyone had told me I'd be firing Roger Anderson and replacing him with Simon "Snake" West, I would have locked them up for being drunk.

Dora Lacwent is tutoring Simon at night so he can earn his high school diploma. I saw Dora the other day. She said he was doing so well in his studies that she has encouraged him to sign up for a few classes over at the community college.

Other items: Had to break up a drag race between Billy Clarksted and Rodney Hill. Took no further action. Just two young men trying to have fun in a small town.

The rest of Arkham has been quiet, but there still seems to be a heaviness in the air. There are some things people don't talk about and just take what is for what is.

Personal note: I was asked today to run for mayor. The town council must be desperate to find a replacement since Jasper Fallon resigned. Told them thanks, but no thanks. Let them keep the job. I have the one I want.

ABOUT THE AUTHOR

Keith Ferrario enjoys horror movies, writing, and traveling. When it comes to writing, Keith's greatest influence for stories and writing style is the old black-and-white monster movies he still enjoys to this day. His love of horror goes back as far as he can remember. As a boy, watching *Shock Theater* and *Creature Features* on late Friday nights, he became a fan of Boris Karloff, Lon Chaney Jr, and Vincent Price. Shows like *Dark Shadows*, *The Outer Limits*, and *Kolchak: The Night Stalker* and comics like *Tales from the Crypt* and *The Vault of Horror* pushed him farther down this dark path.

Also by Keith Ferrario
Deadly Friend
Messiah
Monster

For more information:
www.keithferrario.com
keith@keithferrario.com
Twitter: @KeithFerrario

www.ingramcontent.com/pod-product-compliance
Lightning Source LLC
Chambersburg PA
CBHW050721180626
46814CB00002B/548